The
Gentleman
AND HIS
Vowsmith

The Gentleman

AND HIS

Vowsmith

REBECCA IDE

SAGA PRESS

LONDON **NEW YORK** TORONTO
AMSTERDAM/ANTWERP NEW DELHI SYDNEY/MELBOURNE

AN IMPRINT OF SIMON & SCHUSTER, LLC

1230 AVENUE OF THE AMERICAS, NEW YORK, NEW YORK 10020

This book is a work of fiction. Any references to historical events, real people, or real places are used fictitiously. Other names, characters, places, and events are products of the author's imagination, and any resemblance to actual events or places or persons, living or dead, is entirely coincidental.

First Saga Press trade paperback edition April 2025

SAGA PRESS and colophon are registered trademarks of Simon & Schuster, LLC

Simon & Schuster strongly believes in freedom of expression and stands against censorship in all its forms. For more information, visit BooksBelong.com.

For information about special discounts for bulk purchases, please contact Simon & Schuster Special Sales at 1-866-506-1949 or business@simonandschuster.com.

The Simon & Schuster Speakers Bureau can bring authors to your live event. For more information or to book an event, contact the Simon & Schuster Speakers Bureau at 1-866-248-3049 or visit our website at www.simonspeakers.com.

Interior design by Esther Paradelo

Manufactured in the United States of America

1 3 5 7 9 10 8 6 4 2

Library of Congress Control Number: 2025931202

ISBN 978-1-6680-7093-2
ISBN 978-1-6680-7094-9 (ebook)

For Sara, my very own Leaf.
Best friend and partner in crime.
May our conversations be forever unhinged.

Character List

HOUSE MONTERRIS

Valentine Monterris, His Grace the Duke of Vale
Georgiana Monterris, Her Grace the Duchess of Vale
Lord Francis Monterris, the duke's brother
Lord Nicholas Monterris, Earl Monterris, the duke's son
   and heir
Master Everel, the duke's cousin and vowsmith
Rowerre, valet of Lord Nicholas Monterris
Ambrose, valet of Lord Nicholas Monterris
Silla, the duchess's maid
Mrs. Podmarsh, housekeeper of Monterris Court
Castor, butler of Monterris Court
Avery, Lord Nicholas Monterris's echo

HOUSE SERRAL

Charles Serral, Marquess of Charborough
Lady Leaf Serral, the marquess's daughter
Lord Ricard Serral, the marquess's brother
Lady Theresa Serral, Lord Ricard's second wife
Lady Millie Radlay, Lord Ricard's daughter and companion
   to Lady Leaf Serral

OTHERS

Master Dashiell sa Vare, vowsmith
Lady Lisbeth Pomerin, companion to Lady Leaf Serral

Dr. Edwin Fanshaw, doctor employed for the lock-in

Rufus Gillingham, attending vowsmith in the employ of
Lord Ricard Serral

Lady Caroline Wivenwood, Lord Ricard Serral's first wife,
and Lady Millie Radlay's mother

Martin, Dashiell sa Vare's valet

The
Gentleman
AND HIS
Vowsmith

Chapter 1

Death is the only way to escape being a Monterris. Nic had been five when his father told him so, which was, if one thought about it, a bit messed up. When Nic was eight he'd said love was nothing but a bargaining tool. At eleven he'd clarified it was a bargaining tool should someone love *him*, a weakness should he deign to love another. And at fifteen that it was a weakness he could never indulge.

Wine, on the other hand, was encouraged.

Thank. God.

Nic downed his glass and returned it to the dresser with the rest of the antique glassware—a tarnished family, crowded around their decanter. "A decanter," he said, gesturing at the collection of charmblown glass inset with fine filigree feathers. "The best parent one could have."

"That's depressing."

He spun a grin upon the young man lying on the four-poster bed, his shirt open at the neck and his hair tousled. "Isn't it, though? But thankfully you're here to cheer me up."

"Is that even possible in this gloomy pile of a house? Every time I sneak in here it's like walking into a tomb."

"Except I am very far from dead."

The young man levered himself onto an elbow, his crisp shirt out of place against the fraying brocade bedcovers.

"Oh yes? Come here and prove it."

Nic pushed himself off the dresser, sending the glassware family tinkling. From her cage beside them, his long-tailed echo clicked her beak in protest and ruffled blue feathers edged in gold. "Hush, Avery." Nic pulled the embroidered cover over her cage. "Papa is busy."

"Papa. Papa is busy," she mimicked between trills.

"Avery?" the young man said. "A lovely name. Although not after Avery sa Barnet, I presume?"

"Then you presume wrong."

Brows rose. "I would have thought even a famous conjurer was beneath your touch, my lord."

"Beneath my father's, certainly, but you see I have more taste than snobbery." Nic made a mock little bow and dropped onto the edge of the bed. "That my father has never complained means he thinks me unimaginative enough that I named my bird Aviary."

His companion snorted and gripped Nic's arms, drawing him down. "That," he said, close enough for Nic to smell the wine on his breath, "is even more depressing."

"That's us. House Monterris, here to make you feel better about your life. Truly it is an honour to serve."

"You can serve me any time, my lord."

"No time like the present," Nic murmured back, and caught the young man's lower lip between his teeth.

A knock thumped on the outer door and Nic froze. "I told Rowerre I was busy," he said as footsteps crossed his sitting room, the floorboards creaking in protest.

"Then he is sure to tell whoever that is to go away."

Nic scowled at the closed bedchamber door, until an exploratory caress pulled his attention back to the young man lying in his bed. "I assure you, I'm far more interesting, my lord," he said, smiling an invitation beneath lowered lashes. A kiss teased Nic's lips, promising a blissful afternoon in which he could cease for a time to be Lord Nicholas Monterris, heir to a long, proud line he had better not fail. With a groan, Nic deepened the kiss, pressing his companion down into the pillows in a determined effort to ignore the approaching footsteps.

An apologetic knock tapped upon the door. "My lord?"

"I said I didn't want to be disturbed!"

"It's Master Everel, my lord." The words were muffled, but unfortunately unmistakable.

The young man pouted. "Who's Master Everel?"

"My father's cousin and indentured vowsmith." Nic sighed. "And secretary. And general doer of all the unpleasant things my father would rather not dirty his hands with."

"Ah, so the duke isn't one for letting men own themselves. Why am I not surprised?"

The knock stuttered out again. "My lord? His Grace has just arrived from town and wishes to see you. Now, I'm afraid."

Nic closed his eyes, allowing himself a moment as his heart sank through the floor—a moment just to breathe, such an easy skill of which his father seemed always able to deprive him.

Outside the door, Rowerre cleared his throat. "Shall I . . . tell him you're on your way, my lord?"

It wasn't a question. Not really.

"Yes, tell him I'm coming."

"You mean tell him you're *not* coming," his companion muttered as Rowerre's steps retreated. "So much for no time like the present."

Nic dragged himself off the bed. "Ah, but consider that absence makes the heart grow fonder. Or . . ." He reached into his breeches and adjusted himself. "The cock grow harder."

The young man gave him a look. "In your father's presence?"

"All right, maybe not," Nic said with a theatrical shudder. "But I will be back, so don't go anywhere."

"As my lord commands." His companion snuggled into the faded crimson bedclothes and shot Nic a look through his lashes, one hand sitting close to the bulge in his breeches. Nic groaned, but he knew all too well his father's dislike of being kept waiting. All he could do was hastily rebutton his shirt and pull on his coat, a glance thrown toward the mirror resigning him to complaints about his unruly hair.

"Wish me luck," Nic said, heading for the door.

Lifting a lazy hand, the young man trailed a few sigils through the air with the tip of one finger. Golden light spread through the room like a blooming lantern flame, only to fade away, leaving Nic's skin tingling.

"Needs more practice, but thank you. A fortunate garden party to you too."

"Do you know why he wants to see me?" Nic asked, glancing back at his valet.

"I'm afraid not, my lord." Rowerre grimaced. "He didn't send word ahead, but it must be important to bring him from London."

Nic returned the grimace, attempting to flatten his hair as he walked. "I was afraid you would say that." He halted at the top of the stairs, where threadbare carpet gave way to stone steps made smooth by the passage of centuries. His father kept his rooms in the oldest part of the house, claiming his personal suite was where King John had stayed six hundred years earlier, which, given how draughty they were, Nic could well believe. "I know it's probably too late, but you'd best see if I've left anything around the place. I don't need another lecture on the appropriate use of my time."

"I checked the front rooms when I saw the carriage, but I will look over the rest of the house now."

"Thank you. Whatever would I do without you?"

"It's nothing, my lord."

With a bow, Rowerre set off upon his mission, leaving Nic to descend the stairs alone. He'd always hated this part of the house, in part because it was his father's, but also because the old, central rooms smelled of decay—a smell that managed to be both damp and dusty. Monterris Court had once been a grand, stately manor, but a family history going back to William the Conqueror did not save buildings from collapse. Now it was a sprawling pile, a maze of faded rooms only one wing of which remained habitable. At least the windows here were intact, and no vines were growing in through the cracks in the walls—yet.

At the bottom of the stairs, Nic hid his reluctance with a sharp knock on his father's study door. Inside, a murmur became a footstep, and after a moment that dragged into eternity, the door opened upon Master Everel's scowl—a scowl etched upon his face like someone had scratched his features from shadow.

"Ah, you're here," he said, the word *finally* hovering unspoken. Turning, the old vowsmith added, "The young lord is here, Your Grace."

Young lord. He was sure the man only called him that because Nic hated it.

"Nicholas." The duke didn't look up from his papers. He sat at his desk, glaring at a line here, making a mark there—every single thing on the page more important than his son. Nic set a hand on the back of the silk-upholstered chair, unsure if this was the sort of meeting where he was expected to sit, or the sort where his father wanted him out of sight as fast as possible.

Despite the five-day carriage journey from London, the Duke of Vale looked as fresh and precise as ever. The long-sleeved black shirt that marked him as a Brilliant was both starched and fitted, the perfect canvas for a gleaming silk waistcoat in cream and gold, each button a delicately formed dragonfly. Nic had never owned anything so fine and could only soothe his envy with the knowledge that his father would soon return to his dull home attire.

"Thank you, Everel, you may go," the duke said at last, and Nic was grateful the ever-scowling vowsmith wasn't to be present. Small mercies, the true zest of life.

From a cage on the duke's lacquered side table, his echo groomed its black and gold feathers, watching Nic with disdain. "You too, eh, Revere?" he muttered.

His father pointed to the chair. "Sit."

Ah, a sit-down meeting. Nic wished he'd brought wine.

Once Nic had settled on the stiff chair, the duke finally deigned to look up. With no welcoming smile, he stared at Nic through a pair of smoked glasses—glasses in which Nic could see more of his own reflection than his father's eyes.

"This moment has always been coming," the duke said. "But I have now finally accepted an offer for your marriage."

Nic's stomach sank. Of course this moment had been coming, but with every passing year he had dared to hope a little more—hope his father's requirements for an acceptable offer were too high to ever be fulfilled.

"Did you hear me, Nicholas?" the duke snapped when Nic made no reply.

"Yes, sir."

"Good. The offer comes from Lord Charborough, negotiating for his eldest daughter, Lady Leaf Serral."

Nic's eyes widened. "The Serrals?"

His father's brows rose above his dark glasses. "You are surprised. You do not think the heir of House Monterris good enough for a daughter of House Serral?"

"I . . ." His father's brows rose higher and Nic decided honesty was, for once, the best course. "Frankly, I thought you hated the Serrals. Lord Charborough took your seat on the Council."

From behind those inscrutable glasses his father stared at him and Nic stared back, until the duke shifted in his chair, making its antique joints groan. "He did. And their being on the Royal Council of Magical Guilds makes them impeccable candidates. Lady Leaf also has an acceptable position on the Brilliance Register, and comes with a substantial dowry."

"Ah, that explains it."

"Sneer all you like, Nicholas, but as a ducal family, we must maintain our fortune above the king's financial threshold or risk losing everything." He gestured toward the letters patent hanging in pride of place beside the duke's favourite pair of pistols—pistols that shone like nothing else in the house. "It may be an old-fashioned practice from a time when dukes protected the empire's borders, but what is vowed into law cannot be unvowed. As a Monterris, *this* is your highest responsibility."

With a small grunt of effort, the duke rose to stare out the window, the paint on its thick ironwork crazed with age. "They want your high magical aptitude and we need their money," he admitted to the panes. "They have been informed of your preference for men, of course, and so an agreement on how best to ensure children shall form part of the negotiations."

"How lovely."

The duke turned from the window, the weak sunlight shimmering on his waistcoat's golden threads. "You think this is amusing?"

"No, sir."

"Good. It's time you grew up and took your responsibilities seriously."

Grew up. The duke always spoke like Nic was a child who had chosen to remain cooped up in a decaying mansion on the Northumberland moors. Pointing out the truth never helped, yet Nic said, "You could have presented me in town years ago."

"You know very well your mother could not have spared you,

and the estate could not have borne the expense. Now, had you made more of your remarkable magical talents and become a vowsmith, things might have been different. As it is, your choice to waste your time on less worthy pursuits has left us where we are."

An old complaint, often rehashed. Long before his birth, the Dukes of Vale had spent generations gambling away their grand fortune, and somehow it was Nic's fault for not becoming a vowsmith.

"Fortunately, being my heir counts for a lot even though you have achieved nothing that would allow me to leverage a greater price for you."

Price, like he was an animal to be sold at market.

"I did not send for you to argue, however," the duke went on, returning to his desk. "Rather to let you know that since the announcement has already been made, we now have three weeks to prepare for the lock-in. The old wings will be shut up and the central halls closed off for cleaning and repair. New furnishings will be brought in, and a tailor will be here next week to fit you for a new wardrobe. Master Everel will lead our side of the negotiations, though it is in our favour that they're to bring Master Vowsmith Dashiell sa Vare. I think—"

His father went on speaking, but Nic's heart stopped. He hadn't heard that name for years—a name that conjured a young man long faded from his thoughts, though some memories remained bright and unbreakable. Dashiell's dark, bronze eyes beneath finely arched brows. His ink-stained hands. The way his lips curved when Nic's humour drew from him an unwilling smile. He'd been good at making him smile.

"—can negotiate to our best advantage, you must embody your ancient and proud lineage. You must be my son, not your mother's, for the duration. Do you understand?"

His father looked over the rims of his reflective glasses, the scars around his eyes briefly visible and always disconcerting.

"Yes, sir," Nic said, glad he could manage as much. Because even had it been worth arguing with the man who owned his entire existence, he could not speak another word while his heart beat so fast. That name. So unexpected at this of all moments.

"Good." His father took up his quill—a man well satisfied. "Rowerre will prepare your wardrobe, and the servants will clear your rooms. We wouldn't want any of your . . . oddities being stumbled upon."

Oddities like his books on conjuring and far-off places, or the table crammed with mechanical trinkets and salvaged mechanisms, or the company currently awaiting Nic's return. He couldn't even manage a docile "Yes, sir" this time, not when his memory had betrayed him with a recollection of the all-too-brief occasion Dashiell had lain in that bed.

The duke dismissed him with nothing but a look, and having no desire to stay and no voice with which to object, Nic rose, chair scraping across the floor. His father winced—a small joy in an otherwise painful meeting. Even so, Nic hurried out with more haste than dignity, needing air, needing to think, to remember the young man who had so bewitched his youth without the feeling his father could see inside his head.

Out in the hallway, Nic leaned against the wall and just breathed. It was, for now, all he was capable of.

Dashiell sa Vare. Dashiell Bane-of-His-Existence sa Vare. Dashiell Perfect-in-Every-Way sa Vare. Youngest master vowsmith in three generations. And unless the intervening years had been very unkind to him, owner of the greatest hair ever. What had Nic done to warrant such punishment? Locked in with the Serrals while Dashiell sa Vare inscribed his bloody marriage contract.

Blissful oblivion waited upstairs in the arms of his latest pretty thing, yet no amount of oblivion would let Nic escape just how completely the last ten minutes had changed his world.

Chapter 2

Three weeks was forever until they had gone.

Nic had hoped to make them good weeks, but his father's presence made smuggling company into the house unwise and sneaking out even less so, while hours vanished into fittings and lectures and rehearsals preparing him for the last days of his life.

The only silver lining to the impending lock-in's dark cloud was Nic's new wardrobe, full of the latest fashions. Although much to his disgust, the duke had picked out what Nic was to wear for the Serral delegation's arrival. The coat was excellent, but the waistcoat . . .

He glared at it while Rowerre prepared his shaving water, glared at it while he buttoned up his crisp new black shirt, and was still glaring at it when a knock sounded on the outer door.

"Nicholas?"

Nic froze, neckcloth half-tied around his throat. The servants had been through his rooms days before, days during which his sitting room had returned to its usual state—untidy and full of things that may as well have been deliberately designed to annoy.

Unfreezing, Nic hurried out in his valet's wake, stepping in front of a pile of books as the opening door spilled the duke's heavy footfalls into the room.

"Father, I am almost ready to—"

"I was informed your rooms had been cleaned," the duke said, looking about with distaste.

"They were, sir. The maids went through twice alongside their usual—"

"They cannot have, or all this . . . *junk* would not still be here." He turned to Rowerre. "Fetch Mrs. Podmarsh."

With a quick, apologetic glance Nic's way, his valet hurried out. In the resulting silence, the duke strode to Nic's worktable, where boxes of mechanisms and gears and springs sat neatly stacked alongside tools and oil drippers, reels and cranks, and dozens of incomplete clockwork creations.

"How often have I told you not to waste your time on such non-sense?" the duke snapped, picking up a half-finished frog only to drop it with a metallic thunk, sending springs and screws scattering. Nic reached out as though to save it, aborting the gesture as his father turned a glare his way. "You are my heir and it's time you acted like it. All this goes."

As the duke stepped away from the table, Nic hurried over to gather up the frog's remains in shaking hands. "But, sir, it brings joy to—"

"*The Conjuror's Monthly*? Laurence Sterne?" Lanced through with horror, Nic spun as his father picked up books off the table before dropping them as though the bindings bit. "*Voyage d'Egypte et de Nubie*," he read, discarding that with as much disgust. "Ann Radcliffe! No one should touch anything written by that woman."

"It's an account of her travels, sir, along the Rhine and—"

Hurried footsteps brought Mrs. Podmarsh scurrying through the door, already bobbing a curtsy. "Your Grace sent for me?"

"Yes. The Serral delegation is all but here and these rooms have not been cleaned to my satisfaction. Have these books removed and that table cleared, along with anything else that is . . . out of place."

"Yes, Your Grace."

"No one is going to see the inside of my rooms except me!"

Nic cried, making a futile grab for the book the duke tucked under his arm.

"That," his father said, striding toward the door, "is not a risk we can afford. See it done, Mrs. Podmarsh. And as for you." He rounded on Nic. "Our guests are due within the hour and I want *Lord Monterris* there to meet them, so start at least acting like you are my son."

With that the duke strode out, leaving Nic's hands shaking with as much fury as grief.

"My lord." Rowerre touched his arm. "Shall we hide things?"

Out in the hallway, Mrs. Podmarsh was shouting for her maids. Soon they would descend upon him to clear away his joys, but Rowerre's pained expression was a timely reminder that not everyone thought such pursuits beneath him.

"Yes."

A smile lit his valet's face. "Bring what you can to the dressing room. Quickly."

So while the housekeeper shouted in the hallway, Nic grabbed his favourite travelogues and periodicals and all but threw them at Rowerre, before hurrying to his tinkering table. Most parts he could replace, but he piled the half-finished pieces into a box, followed by as many of the tools and spare reels as he could grab before footsteps approached the open door.

"Everything on the table and all the books," Mrs. Podmarsh said as Nic thrust the box into Rowerre's hands. "And anything else that looks . . . out of place." She didn't glance Nic's way, yet he felt her censure all the same.

"It won't be forever," Rowerre said, rejoining him as two maids carried clockwork parts clinking and clattering out the door.

"Won't it?" Nic sighed. "Marriage is quite definitely forever, especially with a vowsmithed contract. Did you know there are people who don't bother vowsmithing marriages? If I was French, or poor, I could do the thing and still run away afterward."

"I'm sure Lady Leaf Serral is a fine young woman, my lord, and your marriage may . . . settle His Grace somewhat."

"You mean her money will." Nic glanced at the mantelpiece clock—a heavy monstrosity of bronze and ormolu. "I had better finish dressing. All it will take is for the Serrals to be early and my father will have my head for being late."

By the time the maids had finished clearing his belongings, a deep, familiar anger had settled in Nic's gut. That the duke owned him was just the way Brilliance Law worked, but that he sought to control Nic's passions as well as his life always rankled.

"If you could just lift your chin, my lord," Rowerre said, holding the powder box. "I fear we are running out of time."

"No powder." Nic thrust the box away. "It's too old-fashioned."

"But, my lord, His Gra—"

"If he complains, tell him I insisted."

What could the duke do about it after all? Marry Nic off for the good of the family? Lock them all in the old, rambling house for the length of the negotiations? Oh, would you look at that. The worst was already happening.

"No, none of that either." Nic rose from the dressing table as his valet reached for rouge.

"But, my lord—"

"No buts, Rowerre. I'll be damned if I meet my future wife dressed like a puppet." His gaze fell upon the duke's chosen waistcoat. "And I'm not wearing *that*," he added, pointing at the gaudy garment, all pale green smothered in gold. "It's the most hideous thing I've ever seen, and I've been in the third duke's mausoleum."

Rowerre wrung his hands. "His Grace had that made specifically for the occasion."

"Then let him wear it." Alight with the freedom of knowing there was nothing more his father could do to him, Nic added, "I'll wear the understated cream with the red flowers. Since I'm walking to my execution, I may as well look good."

"Yes, my lord. The cream."

It was, in the grand scheme of things, a small act of rebellion, but it was rebellion all the same. Easier to do as he was told, yet his father's admonitions had never stopped Nic from conjuring and tinkering and dreaming of far-off places, had never fully quashed the rebellious spirit that allowed him to find life in the crevices of his dry existence, growing where it ought not have been able to grow.

"I hadn't a chance to mention before, my lord," Rowerre said, returning with Nic's chosen waistcoat hooked on one finger. "My cousin sent over your sales for the last batch. I left the envelope on the mantelpiece in your bedchamber."

"Oh, thank you." Nic felt suddenly much smaller—a hopeful child again. "Do they . . . want more?"

"His letter says they continue to be well received, as such curiosities make excellent gifts. It seems the shopkeeper is requesting another dozen small automata and a couple of larger ones for special occasions."

"Oh." A smile tugged at Nic's lips. "I'll look through what I have, but I think without taking from Mama's collection I'll have to make most from scratch. Something to keep me busy during the lock-in."

Rowerre held his waistcoat ready. "Yes, although getting into the old grotto for parts may prove difficult. His Grace has had the old wings locked up."

"Of course he has." Nic sighed. "A problem for another time unfortunately, or I'll be late."

Time was short, yet once dressed, Nic couldn't help stealing a look at the envelope on his mantelpiece. Inside, a small collection of bank drafts added up to more than he'd received for the last batch, meaning Nic now had more money hidden away than he'd ever seen before. Although that wasn't saying much.

Rowerre appeared in the doorway. "His Grace is waiting, my lord. I feel the most pressing need is your hair."

"My hair?" Nic turned to the mirror and found his sandy hair sprouting from his broad brow in a look he liked to think of as romantically dishevelled. An unruly haystack, his father called it. "I like it like this; it makes me look dashing. Roguish."

"Roguish, my lord?"

"Yes, like a highwayman."

Worry lines creased Rowerre's face, cutting his wrinkles deeper. "I might lose my job if you meet the Serral delegation looking like a highwayman."

"Father would never let you go, but you may tidy it. Just a little."

"Somewhere between highwayman and the heir of House Monterris?"

"Something like that, yes."

With his valet's skilled hands and a generous amount of oil, it was the work of mere moments. "All ready, my lord," Rowerre said, stepping back with something of a proud smile. The oil added burnish to Nic's wavy hair and the cream waistcoat looked elegant beneath his perfectly cut coat. Now he needed only to slip his stockinged feet into his shoes and he would be ready. Ish. Could one ever be truly ready for such a thing?

"All right, Rowerre, wish me luck," Nic said, striding back into the sitting room. "Likely I will need—" He froze. On the dressing room door hung the waistcoat his father had ordered for the occasion. Or rather, half of it. Only the left breast remained, cut from hem to neckline, leaving torn cording to sag like loose strands of skin, while on the floor golden buttons shone.

A step scuffed beside him and Rowerre drew a sharp breath. "I . . . How? I don't understand, my lord. We were only out of sight a few moments."

The room lacked shadowy places where someone could hide,

meaning the culprit had come and gone while they'd been in the bedchamber. Behind him, Nic's echo, Avery, let out a relaxed coo and fluttered her dark wings, untroubled by any disturbance.

"Whoever did this worked very fast." Nic ran his fingers down the cut fabric. "Quick, check if anyone's in the hallway."

Rowerre hurried out as Nic bent, examining the cloth. The cut had a perfect edge, so straight and fine it was as though the other half had never existed, while the air around it had the slightly sticky feel of fresh magic. Nic closed his eyes, listening for sigils yet hearing only Rowerre's returning steps.

"No sign of anyone, my lord," he said.

"No." Nic pulled his thoughts back to the room, where the last of the afternoon sunlight crept its fingers across the faded carpet. "Cut by magic—a very fine splitting charm." He drew a golden loop with his finger, then pinched and pulled sharply upward, ripping the air. "Much better than anything I could do."

"But then who?" Rowerre drew close, peering at the cut. "His Grace has never hired servants with the Brilliance."

Nic slowly shook his head. "I know. I couldn't feel any sigils, though, so perhaps the charm was made by the tailor and lay dormant somehow."

"Is that possible?"

"No, but I don't like the other answers."

On the mantelpiece, the ugly ormolu clock chimed the half hour and Nic grimaced. "Also I have to go or my father might try something like that on me. Will you clean it up?"

"Of course, my lord," Rowerre said, his gaze sliding away along the wall as though he were deep in thought. "You go. I'll take care of it."

"And don't tell my father."

Without looking around from contemplation of the fading paintwork, Rowerre shook his head. "No, my lord. I wouldn't dream of it."

———

For three weeks, the central rooms had been locked up for refurbishment, and as Nic entered the great hall he couldn't but stare at the result. The whole room shone. Moss had been scraped from the corners; the tall, stained-glass windows had been cleaned, the parquetry polished, and the walls repainted. Fine brocade had replaced threadbare drapes and the frames of every portrait gleamed. Even the central pillars, which had once been chipped and choked and blackened, were now smoothly polished with hundreds of perfectly wrought enamel vines climbing to the vast ceiling, from which a pair of shimmering chandeliers lit the whole.

Where the money had come from for such a transformation, Nic dared not ask.

"You are late," the duke said in greeting. "They are already outside, and that is not the waistcoat I ordered for the occasion."

Trying not to think about someone doing slicing charms in his rooms, Nic waved a dismissive hand. "We found it didn't quite fit. Is Mama not joining us?"

"Your mother is unwell and has chosen to remain in her rooms for the evening." The duke's words were clipped and precise and every one of them was a lie. "How, exactly, can it have not fit? The tailor finished it mere days ago."

"I couldn't tell you, sir. Perhaps the stiffer fabric sits differently."

"*Sits differently* isn't—"

Voices echoed in the entry hall, and never had Nic been so grateful for the approaching hell. There was no time to change, only to turn and receive their guests.

For the last three weeks, Nic had been trying not to think about this moment. Trying not to wonder what Lady Leaf would be like, nor what changes time had wrought on Dashiell. Had success altered him? Turned him into just another vowsmith? Or would something of the young man he had once called friend still remain? Now the moment of truth had arrived and it was too late to run. Although as a Monterris, it had been too late since the day he'd been born.

With a groan of old hinges, the entry doors swung open, spilling a tide of murmuring guests into the room. Castor, Monterris Court's aging butler, stepped forward. "The Most Honourable Marquess of Charborough, and his daughter, the Lady Leaf Serral," he intoned as the first two guests approached.

A brief glance at Lord Charborough gave Nic the impression of a large, broad-shouldered man with an easy smile and gold glinting in his neckcloth, but of more interest was the young woman at his side. Lady Leaf had a pleasant countenance, every feature well proportioned, yet where her father smiled, she looked utterly bored. Even the pale yellow gown she wore did nothing to enliven her appearance, though it was ruched and ribboned along the hem like it had been edged in daffodils.

Two women followed behind his bride-to-be, both in gathered gowns that dropped soft fabric from high waists. Though they were young, one wore a grey lace widow's cap over her curls.

"The Right Honourable Lady Radlay and the Lady Lisbeth Pomerin."

Lock-in parties could include any number of extra guests invited for the occasion, but as Lady Leaf's companions approached, Nic had the feeling of being socially underdressed without any of his own. At least years of having to learn the peerage stood him in good stead. Lady Lisbeth Pomerin had to be one of the Earl of Withington's daughters, while Lady Radlay was surely Baron Radlay's widow. He had a suspicion, too, that she was related to the Serrals. A daughter of Lord Charborough's brother perhaps?

As though Nic had summoned the man by thought alone, Castor announced, "Lord Ricard Serral and Lady Theresa Serral."

Nic had spent some time reading about the Serrals in the old society journals. He had gleaned the impression that Lord Ricard was the family businessman, while Lord Charborough gave talks on classical literature—what the duke might have called an unfortunate ordering of birth.

Not as striking as the marquess and his daughter, Lord Ricard and his wife were still an elegant pair, attired in muted blues and greys and with silver gleaming around the lady's throat.

"Dr. Fanshaw," Castor announced as a square-jawed young man with spectacles followed in their wake, looking rather out of place in the white shirt of a non-Brilliant.

A doctor was a sensible addition to a lock-in, yet Nic couldn't but glance his father's way and wonder whether the duke had expected quite so many guests.

"The Serral negotiation team," Castor said, and as a group of vowsmiths, negotiators, and scribes all entered together, Nic hunted the crowd, as afraid of finding Dashiell as of not finding him at all.

"Master Vowsmith Dashiell sa Vare," the butler intoned, and Nic's breath caught as the vowsmith stepped forward, attired in the formal black of his craft. It made him look older than Nic knew him to be, and for a brief moment he allowed himself to stare—at his gleaming dark tresses, at the gold epaulettes that marked his guild rank, at features grown even more handsome with time. And when their eyes met, it was, for a fleeting moment, sixteen-year-old Dashiell sa Vare who stared back.

Nic's heart lurched into his throat and he looked away, anywhere but at the way the vowsmith's lips twitched as he sought to suppress a smile.

The Marquess of Charborough appeared, eclipsing Nic's vision. He had an intense presence, seeming overlarge for the space despite his broad smile.

"Nicholas, this is Lord Charborough," his father said, performing a proper introduction. "Charles, my son, Lord Monterris."

"Delighted to meet you, Monterris," the marquess said, his piercing gaze raking over Nic. "When last I saw you, you were a bulge in your mother's stomach. A pity we haven't yet seen you in town. Allow me to introduce my daughter, Lady Leaf Serral."

As the lady drew close, Nic's initial good impression solidified. Pretty of countenance, she had a pair of dark eyes and a direct gaze that met his without a hint of shyness. "Lord Monterris." She curtsied. "What a relief to find you do not have a tail after all."

Nic, about to bow, found himself swallowing a shocked laugh. "A tail?"

"Leaf," Lord Charborough hissed, the apologetic look he threw Nic owning a hint of long-suffering.

"You must also be pleased that Lord Monterris has no tail, Papa," she said, seeming to enjoy her father's discomfort. "Since none of our acquaintance was able to assure us otherwise."

The red-faced marquess led his daughter hastily away, leaving Lord Ricard Serral and his wife standing before them. "Vale," Lord Ricard said, the duke's name a snap. "I think you have not been introduced to my wife, Lady Theresa Serral, and my daughter, Lady Radlay."

While the duke murmured his delight, Nic watched Lady Leaf walk away, as much bemused by her statement as her lack of chagrin.

"My son, Lord Monterris," the duke said, claiming Nic's attention. "Nicholas, Lord Ricard Serral."

Nic smiled and bowed, greeting first Lord Ricard and then his wife, before being introduced to Lady Radlay and Lady Lisbeth Pomerin. None of them noted aloud his lack of tail, and Nic would have glanced after Lady Leaf again had Lord Ricard not gestured Dashiell forward.

"I think I need not introduce Master sa Vare to you, Vale," the man said, his smile not reaching his eyes.

"Indeed no." The duke bowed. "Master sa Vare."

"Your Grace," Dashiell said, his voice twanging deep into Nic's memories. "It is an honour to be back here again."

"The honour is all ours," Nic's father said. "It is a pleasure to have such a celebrated vowsmith in our midst, especially one we can claim as our own."

There was more respect in that welcome than Nic had ever received from his father, and he had to swallow a sudden urge to explain under what circumstances Dashiell had left so abruptly all those years ago.

"You remember my son, Lord Monterris?"

"I do," Dashiell said, and Nic envied the quiet ease with which he renewed the acquaintance, when surely everyone could hear Nic's heart pounding. "It's a pleasure to see you again, Lord Monterris."

Determined not to appear like the cloistered provincial he was, nor to betray any sign that Dashiell had once meant the world to him, Nic conjured a bland social smile. "And you, Master sa Vare."

Having invited no further conversation, Dashiell was forced to move on, and Nic had the doubtful satisfaction of watching him walk away.

If only that could have been the end, rather than just the beginning. Soon the doors would be locked and there would be no way out, though in truth there had been no way out for a long time.

Death was the only way to escape being a Monterris.

Chapter 3

The doors were locked. Charms were set to detect any Brilliant attempting to leave the house. And within the hour, Nic stood to one side of the negotiation chamber wishing he were anywhere else.

The chamber *had* been a dilapidated dining room with torn and mouldering wallpaper, but like the great hall, three weeks had made a dramatic difference. Now fresh paper adorned the walls, the floor had been polished and the carpets replaced—even the ironwork pillars of the upper balcony gleamed.

In the centre of the grand space, a row of negotiators, scribes, and clerks sat on either side of the long table, the head vowsmiths facing off over a hideous epergne. On the Monterris side, Master Everel, on the Serral side, Master sa Vare—or rather at present, Lord Ricard Serral, who seemed to have taken over.

"Time to begin?" he said once they were all settled.

"Indeed." Master Everel gestured across the table. "If Master sa Vare would take his seat."

Lord Ricard had been leaning on it, but flinched away. "Yes, of course. The table is yours, Master sa Vare."

"Thank you, my lord," Dashiell murmured, taking the seat, though if he hoped to be free of Lord Ricard, he was to be disappointed. The man hovered, looking over his shoulder at the spread of papers. "For our part," the young vowsmith said. "We're happy to keep this first meeting brief, a mere statement of terms and the initial formalities with the principals."

"That is satisfactory to us." Master Everel's gaze flitted from the vowsmith across the table to the lord at his back. "Will Lord Ricard Serral be present at future meetings? If so, I must amend the register, as he's not listed."

"No, oh no." Lord Ricard laughed heartily. "I may stick my nose in every now and then, but I trust Master sa Vare to keep us abreast of progress."

Master Everel made a note. "Then when you are ready, Master sa Vare," he said, starting the dullest half hour Nic had ever suffered.

The delegations began by each reading and repeating names and details. Lord Nicholas Francis Monterris, Earl Monterris, born fourth of April, 1791. Lady Leaf Clementia Serral, born eleventh of July, 1796. Contract negotiated between House Monterris, headed by Valentine Nicholas Edmund Monterris, His Grace the Duke of Vale, and House Serral, headed by Charles William Algernon Serral, the Most Honourable Marquess of Charborough. From there, they listed points of discussion.

Financial settlements, land agreements, and Brilliance standing were all to be expected, but Nic hadn't expected terms like *personal aggregate worth* or *stud agreement*—words that sounded dull and innocuous on Dashiell's lips but made Nic squirm. Across the room, Lady Leaf Serral smiled faintly, with the distant look of one whose thoughts had wandered somewhere more pleasant.

While the vowsmiths discussed a negotiation framework, two men brought in a pair of letters patent, each a long parchment document set with a heavy seal. The one by which Charles II had raised the Monterris family to their dukedom, Nic had seen any number of times, but side by side with its Serral counterpart, it looked more tatty and faded than he remembered. The letters patent granting the Serrals their rank still possessed a golden tinge, with colour lingering in the portrait of William III. Despite their grandeur, they looked a little ridiculous hanging on easels at the head of the table, as though they were art rather than old documents inked by dead kings, which somehow still possessed the power to control their lives.

Eventually a negotiation framework was agreed upon, but just as Nic thought he might finally be able to escape in search of wine, Lord Ricard Serral cleared his throat. "We also request a full audit of the Monterris family holdings."

Before he'd even finished speaking, Lord Charborough hissed, "Ricard!"

"I told you I wouldn't agree to this without one, Charles, and I meant it."

"Unfortunately," Master Everel said, looking over his spectacles in a way surely meant to cow the blustering lord, "as the head of the family, only Lord Charborough can make such a request."

Across the room, the brothers stared at one another, a look containing so many unspoken words that it sucked all air from the room. Was it possible the Serrals didn't know how debt-ridden the Dukes of Vale had become? Nic glanced at his father. Having royal accountants rummaging around for an audit would be a nightmare, yet the duke eyed Lord Ricard with sardonic amusement rather than annoyance.

After several long seconds, Lord Charborough turned from his brother's fierce gaze with a helpless flail of his hand. "Oh, very well. I request the audit, but it must remain confidential."

"Don't want anyone hearing of such unseemly behaviour, Charles?" the duke murmured, a low sound somehow more horrible than his shouting.

Lord Charborough certainly seemed to think so, his expression sliding into a grimace as the delegations made notes. "Are we done now?" he demanded. "I'm hungry and all this nonsense is . . ." He waved a hand, trying to find the right word. *Demeaning*, Nic would have chosen. Or perhaps *nauseating*.

Master Everel pushed back his chair. "Done, my lord, but for the initial binding of the principals, which will take only a moment. If Lady Leaf and Lord Monterris would join us. Master sa Vare?"

Determined to exude a carefree ease, Nic followed Lady Leaf to the centre of the room.

"Hands," Master Everel said, holding up a contract page that was already covered in inked sigils. Nic lifted a hand over one side of the paper, just as the duke had shown him in their many, many rehearsals. Lady Leaf mirrored the gesture.

"If you would repeat after me, my lady," Dashiell said at her shoulder. "I make myself known as the Lady Leaf Clementia Serral."

"I make myself known as the Lady Leaf Clementia Serral," she repeated, the words turning the network of sigils beneath her hand from ink to gold.

"To this agreement I pledge my word," Dashiell went on, and this time when the lady repeated, he formed a few sigils with both hands—*arme bruss cor ma tevore.* He worked with quick ease, but there was something of an accent to the way he shaped them that was uniquely his, the feel of his magic against Nic's mind achingly familiar. Too late Nic realised he was staring, their eyes meeting over the lady's shoulder as Dashiell said, "And to this union I pledge myself."

Nic's heart thudded loudly in his chest, but the moment the words were out of his mouth, Dashiell looked away, leaving Nic feeling exposed, flayed open by words not even meant for him.

"And to this union I pledge myself," Lady Leaf said.

With her half complete, Dashiell took the paper from Master Everel, though it trembled ever so slightly in the young vowsmith's hand.

"After me, if you will, Lord Monterris," Master Everel said.

Nic cleared his throat. "I know it, Master Everel, thank you," he said, though a more accurate reply would have been "His Grace made me practice it last week until I knew it better than my own name."

"I make myself known as Lord Nicholas Francis Monterris, Earl Monterris," he began, sigils flaring gold beneath his hand. "To this agreement I pledge my word, and to this union I pledge myself." He looked up and, meeting Lady Leaf's gaze, murmured, "Since I have now proven I do not possess a tail."

The lady laughed, and as they grinned at one another over the contract, Nic dared to hope that perhaps the lock-in wouldn't be so bad.

Dashiell lowered the paper. "Now we are finished, Lord Charborough."

For the second time that day, Nic stood in his dressing room contemplating his new wardrobe, only this time he was on to his third glass of wine and there was no sign of Rowerre.

Just as Nic was thinking he needed a fourth glass before he could decide on a coat, the sitting room door opened only to slam shut. A few blinks and Rowerre stood in the doorway, profuse apologies pouring from his lips. "I didn't mean to keep you waiting, my lord. Lord Charborough brought so much luggage that every hand was needed, and then I had to wait upon Lord Ricard Serral, for it seems he did not bring his own valet."

Before he'd finished, he was across the small room, riffling through Nic's new waistcoats, barely pausing long enough to take each in.

"Surely one of the footmen could do that?" Nic said. "I can tell my father I am already far too much work for you."

"Oh no!" Rowerre spun, face paling. "Please don't tell him I mentioned it. I should not have spoken. Will you wear the new blue, perhaps? Or the red? No, not the red, too strong. Baffling that the tailor thought it suited you."

Rowerre's hands shook as he unfolded an exquisite blue waistcoat. "With the cream neckcloth, my lord?"

"Are you all right? Lord Ricard wasn't a brute to you, was he?"

"A brute? Oh no, not at all, my lord. He was perfectly gentlemanly. Now, you need new stockings. And a fresh shirt. And I shall fetch the oil for your hair, as it will not remain tidy without it no matter what I do."

Nic smiled at such fussing. Ever since Nic had been a boy, Rowerre had strived to make the best of a poor wardrobe and no money, shielding his young charge from the disappointments of his situation. And its loneliness. Now he had the latest fashions to play with, Rowerre went to work with gusto, and helping Nic dress seemed to calm his nerves at having been so late.

"I saw Master sa Vare making his way to the drawing room as I was coming up," Rowerre said as he was fixing Nic's hair. "He's grown into a very handsome young man."

"Yes, he has," Nic agreed distantly. His valet's hands paused in his hair, causing Nic to look up, meeting the man's gaze in the mirror. "What?"

"Nothing, my lord," Rowerre said, a smile flickering at the corner of his lips as he returned to taming Nic's golden mop.

"Nothing?"

Rowerre couldn't contain his spreading smile, though he tried. "Nothing, my lord."

"Nothing, huh? Well, I can assure you that whatever you're thinking isn't going to happen, because that ended years ago."

"Of course, my lord."

"You're still smiling."

"Wouldn't dream of it, my lord."

"You know I can tell when you're up to something because you say *my lord* constantly."

"Merely showing the necessary respect to your rank, my lord. There, that will have to do. If I wrestle with your hair any longer, you will be late."

Nic rose from his dressing table. "You're still smiling."

"For no other reason than because I'm proud of you, my lord. Of the man you've become despite . . ." He waved a hand, the gesture seeming to encompass both everything and nothing, and Nic pressed his lips tight against the urge to cry.

"Oh, stop it, or I'll be going down there with hideous red eyes," he said, and set his hands on Rowerre's shoulders. "Likely I'm too drunk to do this justice, but thank you."

Rowerre acknowledged the words with a fleeting squeeze of Nic's arm, before turning away to fetch his shoes. "You are very welcome, my lord."

The ceremonial drawing room at Monterris Court was in the oldest part of the house. The grand space, with its high vaulted ceiling, ran alongside the great hall and was even more impressive. Though it was rarely used, tonight half a dozen chandeliers created a starry sky that twinkled above a sea of guests—every humble negotiator, lawyer, and scribe from both sides of the table having been invited to the first night's evening party.

Dashiell was, of course, present. He had changed from the plain coat and epaulettes of a working vowsmith into an evening coat with broad lapels. It was cinched well in at the waist too, which Nic decided was a crime against him personally. Like the bright bronze buttons that exactly matched the colour of his eyes. Nic assured himself he only stared because it would be impossible for anyone not to.

It fell to Nic's lot to escort Lady Theresa Serral into dinner, and given the length of the table and the enormity of the old centrepiece—a golden statue of songbirds taking flight that was too heavy for a single man to lift—she was also the only one he could converse with. The long, ancient wooden table could seat more than a hundred people, but they only used it once a year, when the three remaining members of House Monterris sat in state to celebrate the date in 1683 when King Charles II had elevated them to their dukedom—a silent celebration due to the necessity of shouting the length of the table.

"This is quite the dining room, Lord Monterris," Lady Theresa called to him, her voice joining the general noise of other guests raising their voices and craning their necks. "Do you eat in here every day?"

"Thankfully not," Nic returned, leaning toward her so he needn't shout. "We usually dine in one of the parlours, but when we do eat here conversation is, as you can imagine, impossible. His Grace sits up that end, Mama down that end, and I sit perfectly between them and stare at the birds." He gestured to the centrepiece. "They make excellent conversation."

Her laugh sounded discordant amid the noise. "Where is Her Grace? I admit I was surprised not to see her this afternoon."

"I'm afraid Mama is rarely well enough for large gatherings, though I hope she will join us often once the party is smaller."

More lies, but Lady Theresa bought them with a solicitous smile as everyone always did. "Well, it is too bad Lord Francis is no longer with you to make a fourth at dinner. Then at least you would have someone to shout to over the birds."

At mention of his uncle, Nic reached for his wineglass.

"Though of course it's not merely a pity you lost him because now you lack dinner conversation," Lady Theresa went on, reaching a sympathetic hand in his direction. "How crass of me to make it sound so."

"I thank you for your sympathy, Lady Theresa," Nic said, hoping to turn the conversation. "But while I'm sure my parents miss him greatly, I was only a squalling annoyance swaddled in blankets when he died."

"Blankets and attendants, I'm sure. As Vale's heir, you must have been quite protected. Smothered, even. Little wonder he never brings you to town, though I must say your absence has elicited much conjecture over the years."

She spoke lightly, but Nic caught the sharp way she watched him. He was used to being stared at in the nearby towns, yet such scrutiny coming within the court's walls made him uncomfortable.

"I recall how relieved I was when my Edmund was born," the lady went on, showing no interest in the grand spread before her. "With only dear Millie from Lord Ricard's first marriage, it was such a comfort to give him two heirs, and *I* am not providing for a duke." Her laugh was sunny yet lacked all warmth. "Dear Leaf has quite the task ahead of her, poor thing. People said the same of your mother too, although Lord Francis was alive then and might still have had children. Poor man. We heard almost nothing about what happened, you know, which caused quite the stir. People made up all sorts of stories to be interesting. Everything from him drowning in the lake to being murdered!"

She laughed at what seemed to her a good joke, but Nic just pressed out a flat smile. There were some things only a Monterris ought to know. "I'm afraid I know no more than you, Lady Theresa, having been so young at the time."

"A pity! But perhaps I can find out more while I'm here, since there will be nothing else to do."

Nic's appetite for food deserted him, but his appetite for wine tripled and he spent the rest of the seemingly interminable dinner listening to Lady Theresa Serral's endless descriptions of her own house and gardens, numerous repetitions of just how fortunate he was to have ended up with her niece—whom she looked at so often along the table that Lady Leaf turned her chair away—and broad hints that said niece was too good for him. "I just don't know what can have come over Lord Charborough that he agreed to negotiations at all!"

How shocked she would have been to learn Lord Charborough had instigated them—a fact Nic heroically kept to himself.

Back in the drawing room after dinner, Nic found that their guests had become little more than a swirl of colour, yet still he made straight for the table where an army of wineglasses stood filled and ready to battle his troubles.

Having downed the first in a single gulp, he reached for another, only to find Lady Leaf watching him from a nearby sofa. His bride had changed into a white silk evening gown adorned with knots of ribbon. A pearl necklace encircled her throat and her maid had pinned flowers through her hair—white flowers that stood out against her dark curls. It was a charming look, Nic had to admit, earning her covert glances from more than a few young men in the room. Dr. Fanshaw in particular seemed unable to drag his gaze away, nodding almost at random to the lawyer attempting to make conversation with him.

Nic made his way over. "Good evening, my lady. How are you enjoying the party?"

"I'm finding it devilish boring," Lady Leaf replied with a sweet smile. "But it's so kind of you to ask."

Lady Lisbeth rapped her friend's hand with her fan. "Pay no heed to her, Lord Monterris. Leaf says the same of all social gatherings. I, myself, am having a delightful evening."

"Which *you* say of all social gatherings be they never so dull," Lady Leaf said.

"I do not! Besides, how could this one be dull when we have finally met the invisible heir!"

Nic blinked at them. "Invisible heir? Is this perhaps related to the tail observation?" The feeling he hadn't had enough wine for this made him glance, longingly, in the direction of the refreshment table.

Amusement danced in Lady Leaf's eyes, but it was Lady Lisbeth who said, "Well, your father comes to town but you do not. I know Her Grace cannot spare you, but you can't blame people for wondering if perhaps there is some other reason you have never been presented at court."

"Such as my having a tail."

"Oh, that is just my favourite," Lady Leaf said. "There are many others. That you are hideous, or mad, or that you died in infancy and His Grace just doesn't want anyone to know. Or that your magical affinity is so high you've turned invisible. Or that you did something monstrous and so your father keeps you locked away like in some gothic novel."

"Yes!" Lady Lisbeth gripped her friend's arm. "Like Emily St. Aubert in *The Mysteries of Udolpho*. You really must read it, Leaf."

As understandable as it was, the discovery that he had been the subject of ton gossip for years annoyed Nic. "Well, I have read it," he said. "And I can assure you that as remote as Monterris Court is, it boasts no wicked Italian counts and no black veils, and the only time I have ever been locked away is thanks to this contract. Now if you will excuse me, I think I need more wine."

With a nod Nic left them for the refreshment table, gnawing over the sour taste left in his mouth. Already he'd had enough of the lock-in and they'd hardly begun.

Lock-ins were a ridiculous custom. Long abandoned in every other situation, they'd been retained for marriage contracts due to their importance. In such contracts, families were not only negotiating the terms of the marriage settlement but also bargaining magic rites, trading responsibilities to the crown, and jostling to increase their lineages on the Brilliance Register. For those without magic, marriage could be straightforward, but magic had turned marriages between noble families into serious business.

"Lord Monterris. You look to be deep in thought."

Drawn from his abstraction, Nic turned to find Dashiell at his side—a shock no amount of wine could have prepared him for.

"Oh." Nic downed a mouthful, hoping it would help. "I was merely wondering how different life would be in a world without magic."

"Without magic? I . . . am not sure I can even imagine how such a world would function. That's like wondering about a world without gravity."

"Is it? Yet there are more people without the Brilliance than with it, and they seem to live just fine. Better, perhaps, for not having to lock themselves in to negotiate marriage contracts."

Dashiell's lips twitched as he suppressed a smile—a familiar sight that pulled old memories across nine years of absence. "The only thing magic has *ever* wrought," the vowsmith murmured. The low sound sent a frisson through Nic's skin, and the humour in those bronze eyes invited something of their former intimacy as though those nine years could just disappear.

Nine years of silence.

"Not the only thing it has wrought, Master sa Vare," Nic said coolly. "Merely the most annoying at present."

He made to move away, only for a young man to appear at Dashiell's side, joining them with a self-assurance many would have killed for. "Master sa Vare," he said, his gaze fixed on Nic. "I have not yet been formally introduced, if you would do me the honour."

"Of course." Dashiell's tone chilled. "Lord Monterris, allow me to introduce Attending Vowsmith Rufus Gillingham. Mr. Gillingham, Lord Monterris."

The attending vowsmith wasn't dressed in the height of fashion yet he wore his modest attire well, more than making up for it with a handsome face and a winning smile. And eyes that slid down Nic's body in a quietly suggestive manner that was, for Nic at least, far more familiar ground.

"A pleasure to meet you, Mr. Gillingham," he said, wondering if the lock-in might yet be enjoyable after all. "I hope you did not find the journey too taxing."

"Not at all, my lord," Gillingham said. "I travel a lot with Lord Ricard. He is never still, you know, always darting here and there about some business or other. You get quite used to sleeping on the road and meeting new people."

"I envy you that. I have spent most of my life in this house, though it does mean I know it very well."

The young man's smile broadened. "Well, then perhaps you would care to give me a tour later on?"

Plenty of young men had used that line over the years, and glad of the opportunity to show Dashiell that his presence mattered as little as his absence had, Nic acquiesced with an ironic bow. And tipped what remained of his wine onto his feet.

"Ah," Nic said, the room spinning as he set his empty glass down. "I think perhaps I need some air. If you will excuse me, Mr. Gillingham. Master sa Vare."

"Until later then, my lord," Gillingham said with a wink, and before Dashiell could speak, Nic escaped.

Rather than making for the terrace where he could be followed, Nic stepped into the nearby service passage. There, he wobbled unsteadily along in his wine-splattered shoes, humming as he left the muffled chatter behind. Glad to escape all the curiosity and noise, he began forming sigils to complement his song, conjuring first a deep, midnight-blue light, followed by stars, silver trees, and a flock of echoes gathered in a forest clearing. Soon, his humming became words and he sang about a man seeking to befriend the wild birds.

Nic added the man and walked on, throwing the scene before him with outstretched arms and upraised voice.

A second figure appeared in the passage, its face a pale oval like the old, broken-up automata he often pilfered for parts. Unlike the rest of Nic's scene, it didn't move, and in the haze of drink, it took him all too long to realise he hadn't conjured it.

The pictures faded as Nic dropped his hands and peered through the draining colours. The pale oval turned away, a ghost amid conjured ruins.

"Wait, who're you?" he called as it walked away. "You shouldn't be in here. I'm Lord Nicholas Monterris and I command you to stop."

Nic's insides shrivelled at how much he sounded like his father, but although he suddenly felt a lot more sober, the figure disappeared into the deep shadows ahead as though he had imagined it.

"Hey!" Nic walked on. "Come back!"

A truly eager man might have run, but Nic owned enough wariness to keep to a quick walk, eyes darting at the dark shapes of unlit lanterns and closed doors. No sounds came to him now, not even the distant tinkle of glass and laughter from the abandoned party—just his breath and his hurried heartbeat, and the scuff of his shoes on the dusty floor.

A door creaked open, spilling moonlight into the passage ahead. For a moment a shadowy figure stood silhouetted against the pale light.

"Hey! If you're with the delegation, you're not meant to be in here."

Nic hurried to the open door, stepping out into an old gallery that had been all but abandoned to the garden beyond, ivy left to creep in through cracks around the windows. There was no sign of the figure, although the door out to the walled garden stood ajar and Nic strode toward it.

Chill, damp air hit him as he pulled the door wider. Mist had descended like a thick blanket and a sheen of moisture already covered the ground. It would be a thin crust of ice by morning the way the temperature was dropping.

"Well, enjoy being locked out there all night," Nic muttered, and was about to close the door and bolt it when he caught sight of the figure again. It had stopped to watch him, perhaps thinking itself invisible in the thickening mist. It might have been but for the sharp edges of its white face.

This time Nic didn't shout, just stepped out after it. The figure turned away and Nic sped his pace, cutting toward it across the garden bed, eyes for nothing else. Puffs of condensed breath appeared before him, but he wasn't cold, not with the lingering wine and sudden purpose. In the passage he'd seen a face like an automaton, but that shouldn't be possible. Every single one had been broken apart and left in the old grotto to rot.

Probably not smart to follow it, really, the sober part of Nic's mind told him, but he kept on, pushing through bushes and kicking tufts of furled winter flowers. He had to know who it was. Or what. And if it was a fully functional automaton, he had to know how.

Nic's next step squelched. Cold ran up his leg and soaked into his wine-splattered shoes. Then something grabbed his ankle, and unable to save himself, he toppled face-first into water. It rushed into his mouth and his nose, tasting of dirt and fish and the green gunk of stagnant ponds.

Fingers closed around his arm, and though he tried to fight, he was hauled up in a flurry of spray and swearing. And there, splattered in mud and bathed in cold silver moonlight, stood Dashiell, ankle-deep in the water.

"What do you think you're doing running about in the mist

while drunk?" he snapped, and for a moment of mingled hurt and joy he sounded just like Nic's old friend. "Are you trying to drown yourself? That would be dramatic."

"Trying to—? I was following someone. Was it you? Did you grip my ankle too?"

"Grip your ankle? You tripped on the reeds."

Dashiell pointed at their feet. The pair of them stood at the edge of the pond where dark green reeds swirled like ribbon. Nic's cheeks reddened, each heavy breath producing a cloud that tangled with Dashiell's in the cold air. He ought to thank him, but though he tried to swallow his anger, he found that it stuck painfully in his throat.

"Come on." Dashiell took Nic's icy hand in his. "You need to get inside and change before you freeze to death."

"Oh, but that would be so dramatic," Nic snapped, pulling free and almost tumbling back into the water. "And apparently I like being dramatic."

Dashiell rolled his eyes and Nic had a strong urge to punch that all-too-handsome face. Instead, he shouldered him out of the way and climbed out of the pond, water streaming off him.

"Thank you ever so much for your assistance, Master sa Vare," Nic threw back as he made for the gallery's golden glow, his shoes squelching in a way that would make Rowerre weep. "Truly I would have died without you."

"You were certainly drunk enough."

"Let me be the judge of that."

Nic glanced over his shoulder as he spoke to find Dashiell following, but in letting his gaze linger a moment on the way the vowsmith's wet clothes now clung to his body, Nic tripped on the edge of a flower bed. He saved himself from falling face-first into mud and dormant flowers, but it was a close thing, and there was Dashiell again, gripping his elbow to steady him.

"Maybe you should drink less next time," the vowsmith said, the words close by Nic's ear.

"And maybe you should mind your own damn business instead of following me around."

"I only followed you because I wanted to talk to you. And . . . to warn you about Gillingham."

Nic had almost reached the open door, but he spun back at that, finding golden light illuminating Dashiell's troubled expression. It owned only concern, yet Nic couldn't have stayed his flirtatious tongue even had he tried. He lifted a brow. "Oh, is that what this is about?"

"Yes, look, he—"

Nic stepped close, anger spurring him to glare his challenge right into Dashiell's face. "Jealous?"

"What?" For a breathless moment Dashiell stared back, lips parted, before he looked away. "That's ridiculous."

"You're ridiculous." Nic strode on into the house, carrying a twisted sort of triumph he knew he hadn't earned. "I don't need your help."

"Nic, he's a dishonest rake," Dashiell hissed, hurrying after him. "And he's already been hauled up in front of the guild chair twice on charges of misbegotten information, so if he's not trying to get secrets out of you for Lord Ricard, I'll eat my damn hat."

"Then go eat it. I can take care of myself."

Dashiell stopped with a scuff of damp shoes, leaving Nic to stride on, grimly satisfied at finally silencing him. Hoping Rowerre had a fire burning in his rooms, he headed for the old style-wing stairs with all the pride he possessed, still shivering and trailing reeds.

"Wait, Nic." Footsteps hurried after him as he mounted the stairs. "Nic!"

"Surely you mean 'Lord Monterris,' as I gave you no permission to be informal," Nic threw over his shoulder.

And tripped over Rowerre.

Foot snagged, Nic landed hard, wrists jarring as he caught his weight. Yet Rowerre made no complaint, no attempt to move or apologise, not even a groan.

With a pained hiss, Nic rolled over. "Rowerre, what on earth are you—?"

Breath hitched in his chest. Rowerre's neck was bent and his limbs pointed in all the wrong directions, like he was nothing but a collection of parts waiting to be assembled. His glassy eyes stared at nothing and his mouth hung open, blood pooling around a piece of paper crushed in one hand.

"No. No!" Nic gripped his valet's broken arms as though a shake could wake him. But Rowerre did not wake, and as an all-too-final realisation crashed through the shock, it left a hollow gouged in Nic's stomach. "Please, no," he whispered, lowering his head to the man's lifeless shoulder. "Don't leave me."

"Nic." Dashiell knelt beside him, a hand gently pressed to his arm. "I'm so sorry."

A few moments before, Nic would have snapped and shrugged him off. Now he could only be grateful he wasn't alone as tears slid down his cheeks. Through the haze of wine and shock, he couldn't even make sense of what had happened.

Overhead, a step scuffed on the upper landing. Before Nic could make sense of that either, Dashiell had leapt up and was taking the stairs two at a time, disappearing from view.

"Dash!" Panic sheered through Nic's chest and he ran after him, brushing away tears. "Dash, wait!"

At the top of the stairs, he ran into a breathless Dashiell, who caught his arms to steady him. "I lost them. They were too far ahead of me."

"You think someone saw what happened?"

Dashiell shook his head in disbelief. "They must have, but . . ."

He trailed off, and dropped his hands from Nic's arms, sliding back into the form of Master sa Vare, professional vowsmith. "I ought to fetch the doctor and inform His Grace. I'll . . . I'll be back soon, all right?"

And without waiting even for a nod, Dashiell strode away, leaving Nic reeling.

Chapter 4

Within five minutes, guests blocked the stairs, craning their necks to see the body. Despite the interest, only the doctor had drawn close, running expert hands over Rowerre as though to be sure he was truly dead.

In Dashiell's absence, Nic had returned to the step beside his valet and there he remained, knees to his chest, as conversation passed over his head.

"Explain more precisely, Master sa Vare," the duke said. "You came in from the garden, but did you find him like this or see him fall?"

"Unfortunately, we found him so, Your Grace." Dashiell stood facing the gathered party, tall and assured. "Although perhaps this conversation could be had without so many people gawking at the poor man."

"Yes, indeed," Lord Charborough said, stepping forward to claim a commanding role. "We ought to allow the man some dignity." Employing a scowl and an imperious wave of his hands, he shepherded the crowd of negotiators away. Mutters trailed in their wake.

Paying her father no heed, Lady Leaf moved into the unspoken space left around Rowerre, bending to get a closer look.

"Leaf," her father snapped. "Curiosity is inappropriate. Do consider what Lord Monterris will think of you."

"That I am rightfully troubled by the death of his servant?"

"Leaf!"

Nic thought he caught a roll of her eyes as she straightened. "It's important to consider the evidence in cases of foul play. What do you say, Doctor?"

"Oh, uh, certainly, my lady." Dr. Fanshaw reddened under her direct stare. "I, uh—"

"Foul play indeed." Lord Charborough frowned at his daughter. "The poor man merely fell down the stairs."

"Just as Lord Ellis's son merely fell down the stairs during his apprenticeship," Lord Ricard Serral said with a nasty laugh. "Truly, you were fortunate to depart this place in one piece, Master sa Vare."

They'd found Louis sa Ellis the same way, lying twisted and broken at the bottom of the stairs.

"Are you calling me a murderer, Ricard?" the duke asked, a hint of bite behind the cool words. "Or claiming my house is cursed?"

"I don't yet know enough to say, but I would deny neither."

"Ricard!" Lord Charborough hissed. "There is no need for this. An accident, no more. Very unfortunate timing, of course, since we have already locked the doors, but your servants aren't Brilliants, are they, Val? One can leave and take a message to his family."

"As he had no family," Nic's father said, "I am less concerned about funerary arrangements than the cause of his fall. Rowerre was well used to the house. If this was an accident, it's as extraordinary as the timing."

The duke's words sent a chill through Nic's skin, but Lord Ricard only laughed. "Very dramatic, Vale, but we don't need the added entertainment of a murder mystery to keep us occupied. Or to distract us from the negotiations. I, for one, will sleep soundly tonight."

"There was a torn page," Nic said, hardly aware at first that the words were coming from his mouth. "He had a torn page in his hand, but now it's gone."

The duke looked to Dashiell. "Master sa Vare?"

"I didn't see it, but Lord Monterris was in a much better position to observe the details."

Nic was grateful for the vote of confidence, yet doubt coloured the watching faces.

"Shock," Lord Charborough said with a pitying shake of his head. "Dr. Fanshaw is an excellent physician, you know. He can give the boy something to ease his nerves."

"Indeed" was the duke's cold reply. "Regardless, we ought to put an end to festivities for tonight."

And that was it. His father's imperious finality ended all conversation, and the remaining members of the house party turned their backs on a man's death. Rowerre had been a servant, unknown to the Serrals, but he had meant everything to Nic. And so he didn't move, to leave now an abandonment Rowerre would never have committed.

"Lord Monterris," Dr. Fanshaw said, clearing his throat when only he and the duke remained. "Allow me to help you to your room. I can fetch a seda—"

"He doesn't need help," the duke said. "I will thank you to take care of the body and leave my son to me."

"Of—of course, Your Grace, my apologies."

The duke approached down the stairs, glaring at Nic. "Get up," he said. "This is no way for a Monterris to behave."

When Nic didn't move, his father gripped his shoulders and hauled him to his feet, fingers biting in hard.

"Stop!" Nic cried, as he was dragged up the stairs and onto the upper landing. "You're hurting—"

A fierce slap struck his cheek, momentarily stealing both voice and thought.

"Pull yourself together," the duke said. "I will not have my heir snivelling on the floor in front of our guests. He was just a valet."

Just a valet. The words stung more than the slap.

"Go, and do not humiliate me like that again."

Nic dared no words, dared not even a glance back, just started toward his rooms under his father's watchful eye. As he walked, he tried to think, to work through what needed to be done next, but a thick wool suffocated every thought beyond the need to change his sodden clothes. Falling into the pond seemed a whole lifetime ago.

"Nic." Dashiell's gentle voice met him in the shadows of the long hallway. "Are you all right?"

"Of course I'm all right," Nic said, distantly impressed by how steady his voice sounded.

He didn't slow, leaving Dashiell to fall in beside him.

"I can—"

"I said I'm fine. And if you're hoping to gain favour with my father, you're better off leaving me alone."

"I'm not hoping to gain favour with His Grace. That's not why I'm here."

Nic spun on his heel. "Then why are you here? You could have refused this job when the Serrals came to you—probably should have, given how long you were with us. Yet here you are."

"Do you wish I had?"

The question owned a breathless quality, seeking to steal truths as though they were much needed air. Nothing existed beyond their shadows, but though a dozen answers knotted like tangled wire in Nic's throat, he uttered none of them, leaving the silence to stretch and grow cold.

"What does it matter to me?" he said eventually. Dismissive. Cold. "I don't care what you do so long as you don't talk to me like we're still good friends. Now, if you'll excuse me, I can get to my door without your help."

Dashiell hesitated, a man holding himself still while he weathered a different urge. Finally he nodded, the movement almost perfunctory. "I understand. Just . . . tell me you're all right. I know how much Rowerre meant to you."

"No, you don't. But I assure you that I am *excellent*, Master sa Vare. Good night."

Nic continued in the direction of his rooms, needing to be alone, yet when Dashiell didn't follow, his relief was not unmixed with a twisted, foolish sorrow.

Nic took forever to get to sleep that night and even longer to wake, his body unwilling to move. And when the sun rose, Rowerre didn't wake him—couldn't—his ongoing absence destroying all hope it had been just a terrible dream.

When at last Nic's body accepted wakefulness, it was nearing noon. For as many years as he could remember, Rowerre had greeted him with a soft good morning and a piece of interesting news. Today there was only silence. Someone had left a small breakfast tray on the side table.

Dragging his heaviness with him, Nic pulled himself out of bed. Between bites of bread that tasted of nothing, he dug his own clothes out of the perfectly ordered dressing room and slowly drew them on, life returning to his limbs bit by bit—only to leave him standing in the middle of his bedchamber unsure what he was supposed to do. Down in the negotiation chamber the delegations would be hard at work deciding his future, while elsewhere guests would be being entertained as though nothing had changed.

Not ready to force smiles, Nic instead made his way back toward the stairs down which Rowerre had fallen in the hope that being there again might help and the sure knowledge that it wouldn't. Perhaps if he could make sense of what had happened, of the missing paper and the footsteps and the suspicious timing, it might ease the gnawing fear it had been no accident, might give meaning and closure to Rowerre's death and somehow make it easier to bear.

Despite being full of guests, Monterris Court was blissfully quiet as Nic returned along the hallway, but as he reached the top of the stairs, rustling sounded on the landing below.

"Who's there this time?" he said.

"Who what time?"

Nic descended to the second landing. There Lady Leaf Serral crouched, examining the topmost step of the next flight, the figured muslin of her morning dress gathered at her feet.

"What are *you* doing here?"

"The same thing as you, I imagine," she said, still staring at the floor.

"You don't think it was an accident."

Lady Leaf gave him a look that ought, by law, to have been reserved only for irritating small children, not one's intended. "An accident that just happened to take place the first night of our lock-in? After which Master sa Vare heard running footsteps? And these are long stairs, so if your valet just slipped, he probably wouldn't have tumbled so far or hit the landing so hard. So yes, he may have been pushed."

The same thought had occurred to Nic, yet he voiced the objection he kept butting up against. "But why?"

"Perhaps someone is trying to scare us because they don't want this contract to go ahead. I can't say I'm that keen on it myself, though I wouldn't kill someone to stop it." She looked up from her examination of the steps. "You don't seem *that* bad."

"Thank you?"

"Look, you can't say you want to marry me. Bad blood between our families aside, we've only just met. And besides, I snuck a look at the preliminary documents and know for a fact you're as gay as a spoon."

Nic stared at her. "A spoon? Are spoons particularly gay then?"

Lady Leaf rolled her eyes. "It was just the first thing that came to mind."

"You can't know much about men then. Or spoons."

"Can you just let me get on with this?"

"Sure."

"I can't see any scuffing on this step, but—"

"What comparison would even end with 'as a spoon'?" he asked. "Is a spoon really the epitome of anything except spoonishness? There would be better comparisons for shiny, and round, and—"

"Really? This is the conversation we're going to have?"

Nic shrugged. "You started it."

"A man has been murdered here."

"Yes, my man. It's more awful than I can express, so I don't really want to talk about it."

She straightened, grimacing. "Were you two . . . ?"

"What? No! Dear God, woman. He's been with me since I was a child. He was my uncle's valet first and was more like a father to me than my actual father."

"I'm sorry! I just thought . . . after the previous conversation . . ."

"About homosexual cutlery."

She opened her mouth, closed it again, and waved her hand like she was shooing an annoying fly. Or an annoying husband. It didn't work, and ultimately, she settled for folding her arms and glaring. "Can we forget about that and start this conversation again?"

"But then I would miss out on having such an excellent thing to tease you about. Forever." For the second time she rolled her eyes, and Nic found himself laughing despite everything. "Look on the bright side," he said. "You could be marrying someone far less amusing."

"Oh no, a serious young man? What a *tragedy*." With another expressive roll of her eyes, Lady Leaf started down the stairs, look-ing at each step as she went. "There's no sign of a struggle anywhere."

"Sign of a struggle? Like what?"

"Torn-out hair, scratches, scuffs, blood drops, that sort of thing. Although I suspect the maids have already cleaned." She looked up at him. "You don't recall seeing anything out of the ordinary, I sup-pose?"

"Apart from Rowerre lying dead on a set of stairs he rarely uses?"

Step by step, Lady Leaf descended backward toward the lower landing, seeming to own no fear she would trip and become the stair's next victim despite the swishing length of her gown. "That's a good point. You have servants' stairs?"

"Yes, but even so, this part of the house isn't on his way to any-where he would usually go. There's no way belowstairs from here and the only nearby rooms are in the style wing."

"And your rooms are in the east wing, with ours?"

"The hook wing, yes."

For a moment she stared at him, head cocked. "Oh, right, you name your wings after echo anatomy. My father calls it pretentious, but I think it's just confusing myself."

"No more confusing than sailors using *port* and *starboard*."

"I suppose not." She stepped down a few more stairs, sighing at the nothing she found. "So you don't think your man—what was his name again?"

"Rowerre."

"So you don't think Rowerre could have been heading to the west—sorry, the whatever-you-call-it wing on the west side of the house?"

"No, there's nothing in the style wing. Or the lesser style."

Lady Leaf lifted a curious brow. "Nothing?"

"Nothing worth the walk. It's been unused for years and is cur-rently locked for safety."

"How many years? Five or five hundred?"

Nic shrugged. "I don't know. Lots. It's falling apart, not that I should tell you so."

"Why?"

"Because it doesn't exactly look good on our part to have a whole wing of the house we've never bothered to fix, but there are so few of us, what would we even do with a whole other wing?" Surprise flickered across her face and Nic folded his arms. "It's not that weird."

"No, of course not. Not weird at all."

The lady kept edging down the stairs until she reached the bottom, where she crouched in a sweep of her gown to first examine the floor, then the walls.

"What are you looking for?"

"Blood."

"What? That's sick."

She fixed him with that look again, the one that could have withered entire plants—no, whole forests. "Not because I like blood, rather because a splat would suggest a forceful impact. There's no sign of anything, though, not even scuff marks, so perhaps he was in the air rather than rolling."

"How do you know this stuff?"

For the first time her expression grew sheepish, and she glanced around to be sure they were alone. "Have you heard of Mary Mallowan?"

"No, ought I have?"

She shook her head, disappointed. "Probably not. She writes wonderful books where her heroes have to solve murders and some of them are very tricky. Sometimes the smallest clues are the most important, like a drop of blood in an unexpected place, or a door locked from the inside." A wicked glint flickered in her eyes and she lowered her voice to a whisper. "My maid smuggles them into the house in her drawers because Papa forbids books that aren't *serious and improving*. He thinks they are worse even than that ridiculous *Mysteries of Udolpho*."

When Nic didn't immediately answer, Lady Leaf pointed an imperious finger at him. "And if you try to forbid me reading them once we're married, I warn you I know plenty of ways to get away with murder." She smiled a sunny smile. "But I'm starting to think maybe we'll get along fine after all."

"Are you?" Nic asked, bemused.

Quick steps came along the passage, heralding the arrival of Lady Leaf's companions in a swirl of charmspun lace and curls. The pair were opposites in every way, Lady Lisbeth Pomerin fair and buxom with wide eyes and a soft voice, while Lady Radlay was dark, her beauty in her expressions and her intelligent stare.

"Oh, Lord Monterris." Lady Lisbeth dropped into a quick, breathless curtsy. "We were just looking for—"

"Cousin! There you are." Lady Radlay joined Leaf at the bottom of the stairs with an indulgent little huff. "I should have known we would find you here. Uncle Charborough would be furious to know you're poking around."

Leaf waved this off. "Then it's just as well Papa is busy with his books, as always. Is something amiss? Or were you looking for me out of boredom?"

"Not so much boredom as because Lady Theresa found us stitching in one of the sitting rooms, and no sooner had she joined us than she ripped up all unpleasant saying—"

Lady Lisbeth cleared her throat. "Perhaps not in front of Lord Monterris, Millie?"

Millie Radlay rolled her eyes, looking like an older version of Leaf as she did so. "It's not like I'll manage more than a few days cooped up with her before we get into an argument, Lizzy, so he'll find out sooner or later." Catching Nic's confused expression, she

leaned forward conspiratorially. "I don't get along with Lady Theresa. She's been my father's wife for twenty years now, yet somehow things still manage to get more acrimonious between us every
year."

"Really, Millie, you shouldn't say such things to him."

"Oh, he's all right," Leaf said, dismissing Lady Lisbeth's concern. "He hasn't heard of Mary Mallowan, but he has no tail, is not
hideous, doesn't seem to be mad, and is also not a complete dunce
like I feared."

"Leaf!" her companions both cried in unison, causing a glim-
mer of amusement to brighten Lady Leaf's eyes.

It still irked him to have been the subject of town gossip, yet Nic
was determined to prove them wrong all the same. And so, with a
fine court bow, he murmured, "I am most humbled to be deemed
not a dunce."

"Not *a complete* dunce," Leaf said. "But likely still a dunce."

"Leaf!" Lady Lisbeth cried again, while Millie just shook her
head, laughing. "You really ought not say such things to the man
you are to marry. Only think what your father would say."

"I would rather not."

Nic found himself so much in agreement with this sentiment
that he played into her joke by kneeling at her feet. "I pledge to you,
my lady, that I will do all I can to improve upon my dunce status.
Ask of me what you will."

Enjoying the amused stares of her companions, Nic waited
while Lady Leaf considered this, tapping her chin with one finger.
"Take me to see the . . . whatever it was called. The wing that's all
locked up."

"The style wing. Why?"

"Because you are trying to lessen your dunce status. Besides,
what else is there to do? We may even find some answers, if for
some reason your man was heading that direction."

"Why would he . . . ?" Nic trailed off, remembering the torn page in Rowerre's hand and the strange, automaton-like figure he had followed into the garden.

He looked up at Lady Leaf, this bright young woman he ought to be impressing with the greatness of House Monterris, not taking adventuring into the abandoned style wing. His father would hate it. Forbid it. Kill him if he found out. Yet as that knowledge hit Nic's defiant core, it became reason enough for going. And if Rowerre had been heading there, Nic owed it to him to find out why.

"All right." He rose to his feet. "But no one else can know or I'll never hear the end of it."

Leaf's eyes sparkled and she glanced at her companions. "Make sure no one comes looking for me, won't you."

Millie Radlay sighed the sigh of the long-suffering, but Lady Lisbeth twisted her hands together. "You shouldn't be going off alone with Lord Monterris, Leaf."

"Why not? I'm already stuck marrying him. And you promise not to start kissing me, don't you?"

This she threw at Nic, who stepped back, holding up his hands in defence. "Gay as a spoon, remember?"

Lady Leaf grinned. "Let's go then."

"The door on the second floor is less exposed than this one. Along the upper gallery and turn right. I'll meet you there in ten minutes."

"Why, where are you going?"

"To steal a lantern and some of the housekeeper's keys, of course."

Chapter 5

The door creaked. Nic froze, holding it half-open as he breathed the dusty scent of long-forgotten rooms.

"What is it?" Leaf whispered.

"Someone might hear us."

She looked around, all too pointedly, from the empty passage to the empty gallery to the equally empty garden beyond the window. "Who? It's the first negotiation day, Millie and Lizzy will keep Aunt Theresa away, your father has an audit to prepare for, and mine brought almost his entire collection of ancient Greek texts. Everyone else is quite busy."

Taking her point, he pushed the door the rest of the way.

The room that emerged into the light of Nic's lantern was a small antechamber of sorts. It owned dusty chairs and peeling wallpaper, while the paintings had long since been moved elsewhere, leaving squares of less-discoloured wall. In one corner, mould climbed the rotten wainscotting in a delicate pattern like it had been painted on.

Nic closed the door behind them, leaving his lantern all that cut the velvet darkness. "Well. This place hasn't gotten less spooky."

"You don't come here often?" Leaf ran a finger across the fragile old silk on a fraying chair. "If this was my house, I would be in here every day."

All his life the decay of Monterris Court had been a shame his father was desperate to hide. Nic found he preferred the idea that it had value, even just as something to stare at.

"I go down to the grotto often," he said, deciding it was worth confiding in her. "But I haven't been up here since Dashiell and I went on an adventure to an Egyptian tomb."

Leaf looked up from her examination of a broken table. "You mean Master sa Vare? You know each other?"

"You didn't read that in those preliminary papers you snuck a look at?" When she didn't answer, Nic shrugged and added, "It's no secret that he was my father's apprentice for years. We used to sneak away when we could and go on boyish adventures. This room was the cabin of our ship on the Nile, I believe."

They'd even tried sleeping in there once, dragging bedding and cushions from all over the house. With a pair of lanterns on the floor, they'd snuggled into the heavy blankets, only to lie awake listening to every tiny sound before giving up in the early hours and trundling back to their own beds.

And then one day he'd left without even saying goodbye.

"That's cute," Leaf said. "Though it doesn't look much like a cabin."

"And the rest of the wing doesn't look much like an Egyptian tomb. It's called having an imagination."

He strode to the next door—which had once led down a gangplank and onto the banks of the Nile—and leaned against the frame while she finished her survey of the room, ghostly in her pale dress. As he watched her, a prickling crept across his scalp and crawled down his spine, like a whisper made visceral, and he glared at the door. "Someone has smithed here recently."

Leaf glanced over. "How do you know?"

"I can feel the sigils, like . . . a whisper scratching at the back of my mind."

"You can feel magic?"

Nic realised she was staring at him and stopped his search along the doorframe. "Is that strange?"

"I don't know. Perhaps not for people as high on the Brilliance Register as you. I've never heard of it, although my magical education has been limited to charmspinning, conjuring flippancies, and poetry. Enough to prove capacity for breeding purposes rather than to make use of said capacity."

Catching the bitter note, Nic tilted his head. "If you could do anything with it, what would you do?"

Her brows rose into surprised arches. "Personally? Nothing. I find everything about the Brilliance boring. But I hate that women aren't able to do whatever they like with it, so my greatest wish is to open a school for Brilliant young ladies. I've been trying to convince Papa to fund it, so far to no avail. He says people would laugh."

"I don't think people would laugh, but that's what my father would say too."

"Something we have in common. What about you? If you were free to do anything at all, what would you do?"

"Conjure. Sing. I also like making little automata." Despite how easy he found confiding in her, the admission felt shameful, spoken over the ever-present echo of his father's disdain. "And I would love to travel," he added, hoping this might raise him in her estimation. "I'm slowly collecting travelogues when I can affo—when I can."

"None of that was in the notes either."

Nic snorted a humourless laugh. "Well, no, it wouldn't be. My father deems none of my pursuits worthy of my name."

"Oh, but these were the notes Gillingham rummaged up. He's one of Uncle Ricard's men, you know, and he's frighteningly good at finding out things no one else knows. Aunt Theresa hates him. Papa too. Thinks he's bad for our reputation, having gotten so many warnings from the guild."

"I guess it's hard to find out anything about the invisible heir."

Leaf shot him a theatrical grimace. "I think I ought to apologise for that; you were very unhappy with me last night."

"Not with you, just . . . with the idea of being scrutinised, of being a novelty. I assure you I am disappointingly dull. I don't even have an interesting name like Leaf."

"For which you ought to be thankful! My mother's whim, you know, and an eternal burden to me."

She headed for the door as she spoke, but Nic held out his hand. "Wait, let me find this smithing first."

With a mock little curtsy, she waited while he examined the doorframe, his fingers eventually finding what his eyes had not—tiny sigils inscribed into the wood.

"Someone has smithed into the frame."

"What does it say?"

Nic drew the lantern up. "It's too small to read, but it doesn't feel nice. Rather like my skin is trying to peel itself off so it doesn't have to walk through with me."

Lady Leaf shuddered. "What a delightfully macabre image. Is someone trying to keep people out?"

"Most likely my father. He was well known for his tiny sigil-work as a vowsmith—before he inherited and had to stop working. And his magic always feels faint like this, because it's so like mine, I think. Master Everel's too, as though the family resemblance makes it harder to sense. Still, best to be safe."

Nic pulled the pin from his neckcloth as he spoke and set its tip to the tiny sigils. Dragging it along, he scratched a line through them all, disrupting their shapes and the feeling of fresh magic.

"Isn't hidden smithing illegal?" Leaf asked when he stepped back.

"In general," Nic said, replacing the pin. "Although on a duke's private property, I think anything goes." He pushed the door and it swung silently open—a yawning invitation.

Leaf strode through, eyes darting to see the next room all at once, just as though it was a marvel. It might have been in its day, back when the long mirrors weren't cracked and tarnished, when the wooden floor had shone and the chandeliers hadn't been pulling away from the plasterwork. Now it looked as though the long gallery had crashed into something, leaving even the wainscotting dropping to a seasick angle.

"It's beautiful," Leaf breathed, turning slowly.

"I think you mean it *was* beautiful."

"No, it still is. Perhaps even more than when it was first made. Look at the way the cracks run up the glass like silk webs. In the plaster too. The bits that have fallen away make a pattern of decay that speaks of . . . of *life*. Rich, true life, like damp earth."

"And people think I'm weird," Nic muttered, following her through the long room, lantern aloft. "Is there anything in particular you're actually hoping to find?"

Leaf slowed as she ambled into the next room—a small dining hall where broken windows let in not only the weather but vines that curled around an old charmspun aviary. "I don't know," she said, moving to admire a patch of moss spreading from the damp, split wood beneath the window. "You said those stairs don't get used because no one comes here, so it makes sense to see if there's any reason—" She stopped abruptly. "Wait, why were *you* on those stairs last night?"

"Oh." He ran a mental catalogue over the evening's events and decided honesty was best. "Because I took a walk out into the walled garden to escape the party and fell into the pond. And since that garden is at this end of the house, it was the quickest route back to my rooms."

All right, partial honesty.

"That explains why you were dripping wet. You shouldn't have drunk so much, I imagine."

"So I have been informed."

She moved on to admire a large table that had been left to rot, the legs at one end having sunk through the floor, leaving it sloping. "Oh, I didn't think about the possibility the floor was dangerous," she said, the first inklings of doubt creeping into her words. "Hopefully it's just because the windows are open here."

She walked on, and with the lantern held high Nic followed, amused by her fascination. Each room begat another, all full of cracking paint and faded furnishings. With every step, the floor creaked and groaned, while damp crawled up walls in patterns of lichen and moss. As they went, Leaf grilled him about Rowerre's usual habits, and where else he might have been going.

"Perhaps your father ordered him to check these doors were locked," Leaf suggested, stepping into a gallery with more broken windows open to the weather. Here, too, moss grew across the floor and mildew graced the walls like finely patterned paper.

"Master Everel does jobs like that for him."

"But he's your head negotiator. Surely he's too important for such menial tasks."

"Oh no, he's a very good vowsmith, but my father owns him like he owns me, so he's stuck here being my father's secretary rather than working for the guild."

Leaf's brows rose. "He's a Monterris?"

"An Everel, but he's Father's cousin. If it were up to me, I would give him to himself, although he's been here so long now that he might not even want to be sasined. Master sa Everel does sound very odd."

"Leaf sa Serral has a nice ring, though," Leaf said. "I had sasinage papers drawn up for myself when I was eight, you know. I have so far presented them to my father twenty-three times to no avail, though he did almost give in once, before this whole contract thing."

Nic's experience of high society was limited to books and gossip pages, yet he doubted that a desire to be sasined from one's family was common, especially for a woman. No doubt she had been told all her life that her duty was to marry for the family, yet Leaf wanted freedom, and he couldn't but admire her for it.

"Twenty-three times?" he said. "Nicholas sa Monterris sounds good too, though as my father's only heir I could have asked four thousand times and gotten nowhere."

Leaf paused to look around the old gallery, broken windows opening it to the elements along one side. "That is the joy of having two sisters and three brothers, I admit. I intended to keep asking until he gave in, as it's all I've ever wanted, but this marriage has somewhat ruined—oh! What in all the world are those?"

She pointed at a pile of chipped automata parts, faces and arms and legs all jumbled in with moth-eaten fabric and scattered gears.

"They're automata. They were originally part of the old grotto display, before they were all broken up. I forgot there were some up here."

"They're so creepy."

Nic stared at the blank white faces. "I guess."

"You don't think they're creepy?"

"Not really. They don't work unless you wind them and they need a smithed reel to do anything interesting. These are just scrap. I often dig through the piles in the grotto for working pieces to make my own automata."

"What sort? Not like this, I hope."

"No, more like frogs that can hop about or mechanical echoes that move their wings. And clocks. Lots of clocks that tell the time in different ways. It's important to visualise life passing you by in as many ways as possible."

"See, these are the sorts of things that ought to go in the preliminary notes. 'Has morose sense of humour. Likes to conjure. House has an army of creepy broken automata. Doesn't appreciate being likened to silverware.'"

"Spoons just aren't very gay."

She snorted a laugh he could only describe as unladylike, and he liked her the better for it. "We should probably get back," she said. "But perhaps we could come here again tomorrow?"

"For fun, or because you actually think we'll find answers?"

"Both? The only other lead we have is that torn page you said Rowerre was holding, but it could have been anything."

"Something someone didn't want found on his body."

She tilted her head, fixing him with her curious stare. "Did Lord Ellis's son really die here, falling down the stairs?"

"Yes, about five, maybe six years ago. Father hasn't had an apprentice since."

Receiving only a frown, Nic turned back the way they had come, but Leaf's gaze lingered on the pile of broken automata. "Why were they broken up? You said it like it was done deliberately."

"Because they were thought to be dangerous." For the first time that afternoon, Nic found himself loath to explain, and couldn't but think of her aunt's far more pointed questions at dinner the night before.

"Dangerous? Well, perhaps we should go, and maybe explore somewhere else next time."

"As you wish." He gestured toward the door. "Shall we?"

"After you, my darling husband."

Nic wasn't sure if the epithet was nice or he was just tired. It had been an odd afternoon, but he was glad he had happened upon Lady Leaf on the stairs. He'd been dreading everything to do with her, but he wouldn't actually be sorry to spend the entire lock-in in just such bouts of exploration. After they had finished with the house, they could go through the garden and the crypt and out to the old magic-scarred tower where the locals saw ghosts at night.

"You know," he said, stepping back into the previous room. "If you want creepy, the tower—"

He stopped, feet sticking to the floor. Leaf bumped into him, yet he stood his ground, even when she peered around to see what had frozen him midstride.

"What is it?"

Nic nodded at the corner, where a figure stood perfectly still in the shadows. "Hello?" he hazarded, earning not so much as a twitch. A sense of inevitability crawled over him as he stepped closer, edging forward like a hunter creeping upon prey. Or a frightened young man trying to look brave. He knew which he wanted to be.

"Nic," Leaf hissed. "Who is it?"

Nic lifted his lantern, and its light shone off metal gears and a pale angular face. And the gold cording of half an ostentatious green-and-gold waistcoat.

"It's—"

With the click-click-click of old clockwork, the head turned until the empty sockets stared right at him. And all at once Nic wanted to take back everything he had said about the automata not being creepy.

A clank of gears resounded within the automaton's casing, and with a squeak of something turning unwillingly, a metallic voice emerged from the lipless mouth. "I am here for you."

Another clank like a typewriter hitting the end of its row sent vibrations shuddering through the casing. "I am here for you," it ground out.

Clank.

"I am here for you. Nicholas."

It stepped forward, arm lifting upon a fast ticker of tiny gears. The lantern slipped from Nic's hand and hit the floor. Glass cracked, tinkling loose as the light died in a hiss of hot oil, plunging them into velvet gloom.

"I am here for you. Nicholas."

Chapter 6

Leaf's fingers closed around Nic's wrist—a tight band of panic in the dark. "It's . . . talking to you."

He shook his head. It ought not to be able to, ought not to know his name. Ought not to be standing there at all when every other automaton had been broken down, yet it creaked and shuffled a step closer in the darkness. "Nicholas," it said again in its tinny tone. "I am here for you." And as it stepped forward, a deeper darkness spread from it, smothering even the faint light coming from the broken windows behind them. Colour flickered on the automaton's face—not just colour but features, an expression there and gone as the reel within the thing spun on.

Nic stepped back, pushing Leaf with him. "We need to get out of here."

"I am here for you. Nicholas," the soulless voice creaked. It was less voice than musical grinding, but Nic couldn't appreciate the difference while it was his name the thing crunched between its metal teeth.

"It knows you," Leaf said, still holding his arm. "Is it supposed to do that?"

"What do you think?" He took another step back.

"I don't know! We don't have automata at Charborough House. Maybe—"

"Maybe now is not a good time!"

The automaton clunked closer, and a real face appeared on the pale circle for the space of a heartbeat, lips smiling as it spoke his name. "Nicholas."

"You said they were all destroyed because they were dangerous." Leaf's words were breathless. "Dangerous how, exactly?"

"I said not a good time."

"Then when would be a good time?" Her voice rose a full octave. "I'm already imagining the worst, so the truth could hardly be more terrible!"

The automaton clanked and vibrated another step closer. Its gears were desperately in need of oiling, yet it moved with an inevitability that filled Nic with dread. "I am here for you," it said, splaying darkness toward them like thick oil.

Lady Leaf punched his arm. "Nic? Answer me!"

"Fine. One of them killed my uncle."

"What?" The word was so shrill only animals ought to have heard it. "We have to get out of here. Now!"

They were almost at the door, where all-too-cheerful daylight crept across the floor toward their feet. "Is there anything behind us?" Nic asked.

"No, but this is the only door in or out. We're stuck."

"Windows?"

"We're on the second floor!"

"Do you have a better idea?"

Her footsteps scurried about behind him as Nic watched the automaton emerge from its darkness, a sketch slowly taking form from shadows. "Nicholas," it whirred, and lifted its other arm, stepping again and again, faster now. Nic darted back, almost stumbling over his own feet, and slammed the door in the thing's face.

For a moment there was no sound but Leaf's steps and the hasty pull of Nic's breath, then a bump as the whirring mechanism brought the automaton up against the door—a door that shook as the thing kept trying to walk into it. One of the hinges had already fallen out of the rotting woodwork and the others were more rust than metal. Nic retreated, watching the remaining hinges wiggle.

"Quick, over here," Leaf said. "We can reach that balcony from this window. I don't know what room it leads to, but there's no other way. Look"—she hooked Nic's arm and dragged him over, pointing—"we should be able to reach it if we take turns standing on that gargoyle."

Nic eyed the crumbling gargoyle dubiously as Lady Leaf hoisted her skirt and stepped onto the windowsill. "Give me your hand."

A heavy thud echoed as one of the remaining hinges snapped, dropping the door onto its corner like it was leaning to catch its breath. The automaton peered through the gap, its face flickering.

"Hand!" Leaf cried.

Nic took her hand and she lunged for the neighbouring balcony. It was no easy manoeuvre, yet his attention kept slipping to the automaton, to the click-clank and whirr of its joints as it pushed the door slowly before it.

"Almost," Leaf said, straining. "Remind me not to wear satin slippers next time. I've got it!"

She pulled her hand from his and hauled herself over the railing like a woman who had spent her childhood climbing trees. And with her feet firmly planted on the other side, she reached back, proffering her hands.

Nic didn't take them. His gaze was caught on the automaton, which had the door half open now. Its full form made a mockery of the pile of broken pieces in the corner, from which sightless eyes stared through blank faces at this walking, talking reminder of life.

"Nicholas. I am here for you," it grated, the words reaching down into Nic's gut like icy fingers. He kept telling himself it couldn't really be talking, couldn't really still exist at all, yet having pushed the door wide, it clanked into the room, the rectangular slits of its eyes fixed upon him. "I am here for you."

"Nic, come on!"

He took Leaf's hands, heartbeat thundering in his chest. At any other time he would have been as terrified of the distance to the ground, but with the automaton at his back it seemed the lesser of two evils, and Leaf's strong grip refused to let him fall. He took a lunging step, trusting his full weight to the gargoyle for a stomach-dropping moment, before he was over the railing on the other side.

Having regained solid stone beneath his feet, Nic turned back, only for Leaf to yank him away into the adjoining room. "Come on! I'm not hanging around to get murdered, thank you."

It seemed unlikely the thing could follow them, but a hint of panic edged Leaf's voice so Nic let himself be pulled away. He ought not to have brought her into the style wing in the first place and couldn't make her stay now, could only hope the experience wouldn't leave her afraid of the house that would soon be her home.

In silence they hurried back through the abandoned rooms, only slowing once they'd put some distance between them and the automaton. "So how exactly was your uncle murdered?" Leaf said, her eyes still darting at every shadow.

"I don't know the details, only that it was an automaton. I would appreciate you keeping that piece of family history to yourself, though. It's not common knowledge."

"Who would believe me if I told them? I won't tell anyone about this adventure either, lest they cart me off to an asylum! It really did just happen, though, didn't it?"

"Pretty sure, yes."

Nic met her worried look, resolving to keep their explorations to the main part of the house in future, at least until he worked out why a fully functional automaton still existed and how it knew his name.

After returning Leaf to her companions, Nic scoured the library for books on the grotto display. It had been famous in its day, bringing people from miles around to see the mechanical marvels much beloved of the third duke, before his descendants had let it fall into disrepair. A few books on England's grand houses mentioned it, but beyond calling it a wondrous sight, none explained exactly what the automata had actually *done*.

After two hours, he had gotten nowhere, and the longer he sat in the dusty old library, the more unreal the whole scene began to feel. He could almost believe he had imagined it. Almost. The grinding of his name and the flicker of a face in the dark remained visceral, both mysteries that demanded answers. And so in a hollow, troubled mood, Nic went to see his mother.

Monterris Court had four wings, numerous galleries and conservatories, chapels and rotundas, and a crypt like a sprawling underground library of bones, yet the duchess's only use for its enormity was to ensure her apartments were as far away from the duke's as possible. Visiting her was like walking into a whole different world, her taste in decoration as far removed from her husband's as her rooms were. Nic doubted his mother had ever been able to buy anything new, but things had a way of ending up in her part of the house if she liked them. Everything from vases of silk flowers and delicately wrought candelabras to paintings of bright, sunny days and curtains in mismatched colours.

As Nic entered the long gallery of the lesser hook wing, his mother's echoes started chirping in their grand aviary—a magically wrought, curved metal cage shaped like golden clouds. The duchess's echoes were far from the prettiest their breeders had produced, but she collected them like she collected furnishings—the only requirement that they make her smile.

"Yes, yes, hello to you too," Nic said to the singing birds. "Thank you for announcing me so eloquently."

"Hello. Hello," one sang back as the others lost interest in him, trilling to one another instead.

As Nic approached his mother's door, he caught the sound of her humming. It merged discordantly with the echoes' gentle coos—the duchess's complete lack of musicality equalled only by her persistent joy in singing. Nic smiled as he knocked, grateful for a sound that carved a familiar welcome from the day's strangeness.

After a few moments, the Duchess of Vale's maid opened the door, a hawkish glare easing at sight of him. "Master Nicholas."

"Afternoon, Silla. She sounds happy."

"Yes, Her Grace has been calm and well today. She's dressing for a grand ball and you know how that cheers her up. Shall I ask if she'll see you?"

"Please."

Silla pressed a wry smile between thin lips and went back inside, leaving Nic to the familiar experience of staring at an inlaid wooden door while he awaited permission to see one of his parents.

When Silla returned, she held open the door. "Her Grace will see you, but says she cannot be kept long. She doesn't wish to be late, you know." They shared a look of deep understanding as Nic stepped inside.

Nic found his mother in her dressing room, a soft, scented space with a view of the overgrown rose garden through numerous narrow windows, each tipped with wrought-iron flowers. Despite Silla's warning, the duchess appeared to be in no hurry. A dozen little boxes of perfumed powder sat open before her, while she hummed and plucked the petals off a flower in a gold-painted vase.

"Oh, Nicholas," she said, far more musically than she ever managed to hum. "How nice of you to come." Though she often seemed to look right through him, her smile held genuine pleasure as she turned to face him. Soft curls danced across her brow and the fabric of her dressing robe hushed as she moved. Ethereal, he had heard her beauty described, and though Nic had been told he looked like her, his mirror reflected none of her sweetness.

"You make it sound like I never come to see you," he said, dropping into a chair. "When in truth I am here so often you must surely want rid of me."

A shadow flitted across her face and Nic wished he had spoken more carefully. One never knew what might set off one of her moods.

"What party are you dressing for, Mama?" he said to retrieve her smile.

It returned with a tremble. "The Haywards are giving a ball. I did tell you, dear. You were included on their invitation, as always."

"That is very kind of them. Do give my apologies. Unfortunately, I have work I must tend to."

"Oh!" She swatted his leg. "You remind me. Silla? Silla. Fetch that sweet little timepiece Nicholas made that stopped working." Turning back to Nic, she added, "I'm not sure what happened to the poor thing, but I'm afraid it needs some love."

She liked his creations, each one receiving pride of place on one of the many tables throughout her rooms—her aesthetic half bright florals and half clockwork trinkets.

The one Silla returned with was a small frog with a clock set into its belly, its inner reel making it croak the time. Nic took the metal creature from her hands. One of its legs was all but detached. "I'll see what I can do," he said. "Although it might not be worth the effort. Probably none of it is, but it's good to keep busy."

"And I like having them about me, each a little friend." The duchess spoke brightly, her cheer so fragile he didn't want to shatter it with his own troubles, yet the frog in his hand was made from all the same parts as the automaton he and Leaf had run from in the style wing.

"You're good at what you do, Nicholas."

Nic looked up, catching a hint of lucidity in his mother's gaze. It unnerved him as much as her encouraging words, and he fiddled with the loose trim on his chair. "How nice it would be if my father ever thought so."

"You are not enough his son." She reached out, her hand a trembling butterfly unsure it could make the distance. "He doesn't understand you."

Nic wished he hadn't spoken the thought that so often filled his mind. Better to drown in it than risk cutting his hurts deeper. Or hers.

He squeezed her hand in gratitude, searching for a more cheerful subject, but her eyes were already glazing over as she escaped somewhere he could not follow.

"What do you know about the automata in the style wing?" he said, before he lost her completely.

"Automata," she said vaguely, and turned to pat her dressing table, searching for the diary that was never far from her hands. She pulled it close, and its spine cracked as she opened it to the most recent page. "No. No, I need you here for me," she said, shaking her head as she dipped her quill and began writing.

Nic tensed. He had sent her into the darkness and now had to tread carefully. Or escape. He knew which was easier.

With a creak of stiff padding, Nic rose from the chair, broken frog in hand. "I should let you get ready for your party, Mama." He planted a kiss upon her cheek and, disgusted at how relieved he felt to be able to escape, headed for the door. Only to stop and turn back, an unasked question burning on his lips. "Did one really kill Uncle Francis? An automaton?"

She flinched and stopped writing, leaving ink bleeding into the paper.

"Mama?"

"You said something, my love?"

"I asked about Uncle Francis."

Dropping the quill, she returned to plucking petals from her flower, letting each fall onto the diary's ink-covered pages. "The house hated him. It hates all of us."

"Did it hate Rowerre, too?"

Silla cleared her throat as a flicker of confusion stilled the duchess's hand. Of course no one had told her.

"Time to go, Master Nicholas," Silla said, opening the door.

Nic hesitated, but as his mother snatched up her diary once more, he wished her farewell and fled, prey to the fervent wish he hadn't come at all. What had he expected? A detailed explanation of a family history both his parents avoided? A sensible conversation about his worries and the grief that twisted inside him? To be able to rant about Dashiell trying to slide back into his life like he had never left? No. Her ability to help him had disappeared a long time ago.

With their party having shrunk to just the two families and their head negotiators, dinner that night was a far smaller affair. In the lesser dining room, Nic found himself seated with Lady Leaf on his left and Lady Radlay on his right—a position far enough from his father that he might have celebrated, had Dashiell not been seated opposite. The young man did his duty by his own dinner companions, but once or twice Nic caught the vowsmith throwing a concerned glance his way.

Dinner itself was sumptuous—far finer than anything Nic had ever eaten in his own home. The soup was replaced with a first course consisting of a glazed ham, a fricassee of chicken and mushroom, crimped cod with oyster sauce, a roast sirloin of beef, two pies of some kind, any number of vegetable dishes, and a whole army of sauce boats. Nic wished he felt hungrier, but his mind was too busy chewing over problems—the automaton that had known his name, the strange figure from the garden, and why someone might have pushed Rowerre down the stairs.

During the first course, both Leaf and Lady Radlay were occupied with other conversations, leaving Nic to his thoughts and Dashiell's increasingly frequent glances. They were all solicitude—enraging after nine years of silence had made them strangers. Nic ignored them—ignored everyone—until with the arrival of the second course, Lady Radlay turned her attention his way.

"I hear you had quite the entertaining afternoon, my lord," she said, spiking fear that Leaf had told her friends more than she ought. "Almost I wish I had joined you," she added in a lowered voice, throwing a meaningful glance Lady Theresa's way.

"I think perhaps the enjoyment has been overstated," Nic replied. "Though it was nice to get to know your cousin a little better."

"How true. I had only met Lord Radlay once before we married, and never had a private conversation. It takes some getting used to—suddenly living with someone you don't know. And then to living all by oneself within a few years."

"I am very sorry for your loss."

Lady Radlay waved this off with a dismissive fork. "Given he was far more interested in his horses than me, I hardly knew him, so it was not so great a loss. Ah! But I hope you will not tell my stepmother I said so."

"I shall certainly do no such thing. I didn't know him either—Lord Radlay. But then I don't know anyone except by their name in the peerage."

"I cannot decide if that is a blessing or a curse, and so instead I will say how lucky for you that now you know me." Her eyes danced with amusement, and they spent the next ten minutes flirting delightfully over the syllabubs.

As the second course was removed, Castor came by, topping up their wineglasses.

"I think I might do some exploring of my own tomorrow," Lady Radlay said. "I noticed a pavilion in the middle of your lawn earlier and had quite the urge to see it. What a strange location for a pavilion, I thought. Was it built for something in particular?"

"Not that I'm aware of," Nic said, swallowing memory of what he and Dashiell had used it for one sultry afternoon in high summer. Stripped to their shirtsleeves, flicking water from the stagnant fountain at one another had become wrestling, which had become inexpert but enthusiastic kisses that left them raw and breathless. And an awkward walk back to the house full of subtle touches and lingering smiles.

"Well, perhaps you could take me out there tomorrow if the weather turns fine," Lady Radlay said. "Though I suspect we will be cursed with rain."

"I like rain," Nic said, thoughts still elsewhere.

"But good heavens, my lord, why?"

"It makes music."

He hadn't thought before speaking, but in the aftermath of his words, Nic found his gaze drawn across the table to Dashiell. Their eyes met.

"Listen, can you hear that?"

"Hear what?"

"The music." Dashiell had pressed his nose to the cold glass as they watched rain fall upon the gardens. *"Rain is like music falling from the sky."*

"That's beautiful," Lady Radlay said.

And although Nic didn't answer, he couldn't but think of that young man with his nose pressed to the glass and recall he had said exactly the same thing, when what he'd really wanted to say was *"You're beautiful."*

For a beat longer than felt proper, their gazes held, before Dashiell looked away.

"Oh? Well, I would like very much to see a ghost," Leaf said, drawing attention from all along the table. "Do tell me what you have seen."

Master Everel, seated to her other side, smiled rather paternally upon her. "Well, my lady, there have been many sightings of a young boy who walks the upper gallery at night in his bed shirt. Many servants have even spoken to him over the years. He asks for water, but whenever it's brought to him, he's gone."

"Oh, that's chilling, Master Everel." Leaf gave an eloquent shudder, spoon frozen midair. "Do you know who he is?"

At the head of the table, the duke cleared his throat. "Believed to be young Lord Edmund Monterris, who died of fever in 1676, though I have not seen him myself."

"Have you, Master Everel?"

"No, my lady, though I have seen the Pale Lady." By now the whole table had stopped their conversations to listen, and with so attentive an audience, Master Everel drew himself up. "She walks the front courtyard, you know. A ghostly woman in a white dress who paces back and forth, awaiting a husband who will never return."

"I think I would rather meet the little boy than the Pale Lady," Leaf said.

The duke, far less entertained than his entranced guests, gave his longtime vowsmith a warning look before saying, "Believed to be Lady Elizabeth Reed, waiting for the second duke. He died in battle between signing their marriage contract and the wedding ceremony."

"How very romantic it is to have ghosts," Lady Theresa said. "Do you not think so, my lord?"

Her look along the table caught her husband paying more attention to his plate than the conversation. "Only if you find such stories entertaining, my lady," Lord Ricard said. "Perhaps Vale will let you borrow one."

"Are there any others, Master Everel?" Millie Radlay asked despite her father's disinterest. "I'm glad we don't have any, but I would very much like to see one while we're here."

"Many, my lady," the old vowsmith said. "Although if you wish to see one, it's best to ask the servants where to look, since they walk the house at all hours." He turned as Castor passed behind his chair. "Castor, have there been any sightings of late?"

The butler's eyes bulged at suddenly finding every pair of eyes fixed on him. "Uh, only the Faceless Man, though I do not think it an edifying—"

"The Faceless Man?" Millie and Leaf exclaimed together, each turning in their chairs. "Who is he?" Leaf added.

Castor rolled his gaze toward the duke as he said, "A dark figure with no face who walks the house and grounds at all hours, but I really don't feel—"

"I think we have entertained ourselves quite enough," the duke said, nodding for his butler to escape. "Some history is best left untouched."

"Oh!" Across the table, Lady Theresa sat bolt upright, eyes bright. "Is it the ghost of Lord Francis?"

"Theresa!" Lord Charborough snapped. "That is quite uncalled for."

Lord Ricard huffed a laugh. "Is it, Brother? Perhaps we could ask how he died and finally put all the rumours to rest."

"There are other ghosts," Master Everel said quickly. "Like the two young men the townsfolk see at the old tower. They're thought to be the sons of the second Earl Monterris, clinging to the last remnants of the old castle. And we've lost no small number of serving staff over the years to the Mad Friar. He can only ever be seen in the corner of your eye, but anyone hearing his cries is instantly overcome with a dreadful malaise that makes them want to take their own lives."

Even Lord Ricard looked horrified by this, a moment of silence holding the table spellbound.

"That is quite enough, Everel," the duke said, tone bored. "There is no such thing as a Mad Friar. We have just been very unlucky in our serving staff."

Leaf turned to Nic. "How do you go on with so many ghosts in the house?"

"I don't know, I've never seen one," he said as all eyes turned his way. "It really isn't like living in a gothic novel, I assure you."

Upon which utterance, the duke was finally able to turn the subject.

It stayed turned until the gentlemen, rejoining the ladies in the drawing room, found Leaf and Millie planning to search the house for ghosts. Nic was tempted to amuse them with more stories, until Rufus Gillingham rose from a chair to smile at his arrival.

"Lord Monterris. A very good evening to you."

"And to you, Mr. Gill—"

"Gillingham," Lord Ricard interrupted, entering in Nic's wake. "Finished with the letters already?"

"Unfortunately, the evening mail has not yet come, sir."

Lord Ricard glowered. "Damned rural fastness. May as well call it the midnight mail at this rate. Ah well, you had better join us for a drink while we wait."

A nod of thanks to his patron and Gillingham turned back to Nic with a suggestive lilt to his smile. "Not that I am at all sorry it is late. I was hoping for a chance to remind you that you owe me a tour. Tonight, perhaps? Once I am done with Lord Ricard's letters."

With all that had happened since Gillingham first proposed their tour, Nic's interest in the man had waned, yet the combination of Dashiell's presence and Dashiell's very sensible warning left Nic with the contrary desire to encourage the young vowsmith's advances. He told himself it was just that he could do with the distraction, and that it would be interesting to see how far the man would go for information, but it was with a sidelong glance in Dashiell's direction that Nic said, "I look forward to it."

Dashiell had taken a nearby chair and was reaching for the newspaper when Gillingham, grinning at Nic, said, "And I'll make sure you look back upon it with equal fondness. After all, my company can be enjoyed forward or backward as you please."

Dashiell smothered a sudden cough, and wearing something of a mischievous smile, Gillingham turned his way. "Master sa Vare, that was very fine work in the chamber today. Particularly as regards—"

"Need I remind you, Mr. Gillingham, that we do not discuss a contract with its principals," Dashiell interrupted, all cold civility.

This only deepened the attending vowsmith's smile. "Ah, of course, how could I forget the guild tendency to be dull and straitlaced? Perhaps I, too, should have been taught by such a high stickler as His Grace." He rolled his gaze back Nic's way. "Your father is quite renowned in guild circles, my lord. Not only for having produced the youngest master vowsmith in three generations"—a gesture at Dashiell—"and for being the greatest loss to the profession when he had to give it up, but for being such a stickler for the rules that people would go to him with their questions rather than check the charter themselves."

Nic glanced at his father, who was standing by the fireplace with Lord Charborough, the two deep in quiet conversation. "I can well believe it."

"Both His Grace and Master Everel were excellent teachers," Dashiell said. "No young vowsmith could have had more esteemed masters."

"How true." Gillingham turned again to Nic. "Given such fine examples, I'm surprised you didn't continue the family tradition, my lord. Your affinity for the Brilliance would surely have made you a remarkable student."

Nic had no desire to defend his choices to Lord Ricard's hatchet man, so instead he threw the question Dashiell's way with a challenging smile. "Oh, I began study. You would have to ask Master sa Vare whether or not I was a remarkable student."

Gillingham spun on the vowsmith. "Master sa Vare, you must tell me, though I will not hear anything but praise."

"Then why bother asking?"

"Ah, Lord Monterris, he disparages you!"

"That is not what I said." Dashiell scowled at the man's grin. "Ni—*Lord Monterris* was an excellent student. He just did not always wish to apply himself to what was put before him."

"So, he was distracting," Gillingham said. "Now that I can well believe. I find him immensely distracting."

Nic hadn't thought it possible for Dashiell's scowl to darken further. "No," the vowsmith said. "He was a helpful and encouraging study partner, and I'm sure I am where I am today only thanks to his assistance."

Nic doubted the sincerity of words spoken to cow the impertinent Gillingham, but all at once he remembered studying with Dashiell as though it had been yesterday. The way his fingers pinched his quill, his little frown of concentration, and his shy smile whenever he noticed Nic watching him. Until the day his best friend had just walked away.

"Ah yes, assistance," Nic said. "Like when I snuck that bottle of brandy into the hayloft."

A flicker of a reminiscent smile broke through Dashiell's severity. "Master Everel never looked more sour than when he realised he had to deal with two drunk ten-year-olds."

"You vomited into the old horse trough," Nic said.

"Well, you fell out of the loft!"

"I merely misjudged the distance to the edge."

"And had a bruise the size of a hand for weeks."

They grinned at one another, the reminiscence returning the old Dashiell for a moment in which Nic's heart yearned toward him. To have his friend back was like drawing suddenly near a crackling fire, without having realised how cold the room had truly become. He wanted never to step away, wanted to reach out and hold the flames no matter how much it would hurt—how Dashiell would inevitably disappear again as though it had all meant nothing.

Rather than thaw Nic's anger, the realisation of just how easy it would be to fall in love with Dashiell again only bit his rage deeper.

"Sounds like you were left to run wild," Gillingham said, and Nic found he didn't like the shrewd look the man threw them. "I admit I did not realise you were here for as long as you were, Master sa Vare."

Stern Dashiell returned upon crashing brows. "It is much easier to learn when you don't have to move every year or two. I was very fortunate that His Grace was kind enough to keep me as long as he did."

Kind. Whether or not Dashiell knew it to be a lie, it was a nicer fiction than the truth—that the duke had kept his star pupil as long as possible because his own son was proving an endless disappointment.

The drawing room door opened, spilling a pair of maids into the room carrying tea trays. Castor followed, a sheaf of letters in his hand.

"The evening mail has arrived, Your Grace," he said. "I have left your correspondence on your desk, but these are for Lord Ricard Serral."

Gillingham rose, his winning smile in place and his hand outstretched. "I'll take them."

Receiving no complaint from Lord Ricard, the butler let Gillingham take the stack before holding out a separate envelope with a large black seal. "And this one is addressed to you directly, Mr. Gillingham."

The young attending vowsmith stared at the envelope as a tense hush spread through the room. His jaw tightened, then he snatched the envelope abruptly. "Thank you." And with a hint of anger behind his forced smile, he glanced at Nic. "Unfortunately, it seems I have rather pressing business this evening, my lord. Our tour will have to wait until tomorrow night."

"Of course."

With a broad smile for the gathered company, Gillingham wished them all a good evening and was gone before the maids had finished setting out the tea trays.

"What was that?" Nic asked, turning to Dashiell as talk resumed around them.

"The black seal every vowsmith dreads," he said, grim satisfaction in the lines of his face. "Guild excommunication letter."

"He's been kicked out?"

Dashiell risked a glance up as Lord Ricard followed Gillingham out in a sweep of irritation. "So it would seem. In truth, I'm surprised it took this long. He—"

Whether because he thought better of confiding his opinion or because Lady Theresa was watching them, Dashiell swallowed his words and rose. "Can I fetch you a cup of tea, my lord?"

My lord. He had brought that on himself, snapping at Dashiell's use of his nickname the night before—a timely reminder that however good it had felt to fall back into their friendly banter, he was a stranger now, a vowsmith there only to do his job before returning to his real life.

Between Dashiell's proper demeanour and the ongoing weight of Rowerre's loss, Nic found he couldn't face any more conversation and shook his head. "No, thank you. I am quite worn out and shall bid you good night."

Nic glanced at the gathered company, and the thought of having to take his leave and suffer his father's glares only added to his exhaustion. "I'll just slip out, though," he added. "If you would kindly indulge me with your silence."

"Of course, but are you—?"

"Good night, Master sa Vare."

With no desire to catch his father's attention, Nic slipped out into the hallway without pausing to light a candle. A guest would never dare, but Nic had lived his entire life within these walls and made his way toward the hook-wing stairs with no need of light. With every step, the house darkened around him, slowly smothering all but the scuff of his shoes—a scuff that became a creak as he mounted the stairs.

Nic remained alone in the unbroken darkness until he reached the third-floor landing, when a light glimmering below suggested someone else had decided on an early night too. As it started up the stairs in his wake, Nic turned away.

The hallway leading to his rooms ran the length of the hook wing—a threadbare tract of carpet along which he was the only occupant. The guests were all on the floor below, making the sound of movement ahead enough to stop Nic in his tracks. It couldn't be Rowerre, and surely any other servant would be carrying a candle, yet as he listened, the movement seemed to draw closer.

"Hello?"

The darkness shifted, sending a frisson of terror sliding through his skin. A white oval hung in the hallway's empty dark, featureless but for the slits at mouth and eyes. It owned no real eyes, yet for the space of half a dozen heartbeats, it stared at Nic and Nic stared back, a caught breath tightening his chest.

It stepped forward, the movement slow but unstoppable like

the automaton in the style wing, and Nic's heart slammed into his throat. He could not tear his gaze away, could not move, until a bloom of candlelight behind him fell upon a figure made of shadow.

Nic turned and ran, a dozen desperate strides sending him crashing into someone at the top of the stairs. He fell back with a cry as faltering candlelight flickered upon Dashiell's features.

"Nic?"

The vowsmith's warm scent. His worried tone. Nic's name upon his lips. It all spoke of safety, and with fear thrumming in his veins, Nic gripped Dashiell's hand without thinking.

He spun to stare back along the passage, but it was empty. No automaton or shadowy spectre, just the darkness of the house stretching away beyond their golden sphere.

Nic let go Dashiell's hand, his cheeks heating. "Did you see it?"

Silence pooled, and Nic dared not look around to catch the vowsmith's expression.

"See what?"

"The ghost."

More silence, and when Nic finally turned he found Dashiell staring at him—a stare that made Nic all too aware of the lingering sensation of skin against skin tingling upon his palm.

"A ghost?" Dashiell said at last. "You're sure?"

Nic had been, yet as Dashiell raised his brows, doubt crept in. He forced a laugh. "No doubt I am just tired and was thinking of Master Everel's stories."

The vowsmith didn't look entirely convinced, but as Nic's heart rate slowed from its rapid tattoo, he realised Dashiell must have followed him. "Is there something I can do for you, Master sa Vare? You seem to be on the wrong floor."

"It's . . . I wanted to talk to you about Gillingham."

"Again? You have already warned me, and—"

"And you are quite capable of looking after yourself, I know."

Dashiell held up a placating hand. "But please, I need you to under-stand that excommunication won't stop him; it just means he'll have no boundaries anymore, no reason to stop short of . . . of *any-thing* to get what he wants."

A thoughtful warning spoken with a genuine note of care, and Nic found himself once more drawn to the vowsmith like a man reaching cold hands to that comforting fire. How much easier to hate him for the years of friendship lost, but all Nic could hate was the complicated mess of emotions Dashiell's very existence left in his breast—a mix of hurt and anger and joy and desire and a des-perate need to show him just how insignificant he was. It all came together in a sneer.

"Oh, I see," Nic said, stepping close. "You really are jealous, aren't you?"

The vowsmith's breath hitched. "No, I—"

"Is this what you want?"

Nic gripped Dashiell's face and kissed him—a fierce, furious kiss sure to be pushed away, an insult to be spurned. For a heart-beat Nic revelled in the cruelty of it, until Dashiell kissed him back. Hard. Desperate. Sure.

The candle fell to the floor, dropping them into darkness as Dashiell shunted Nic toward the wall. He hit it with a gasp, only to be pressed against it with the full length of Dashiell's body, the sen-sation eliciting a guttural groan he could not have suppressed even had he tried. Pinned and wanting, he grasped at the vowsmith's coat, hands running over shoulders that felt different yet familiar.

Alone in the dark, their tongues slid against one another, their kiss growing hot with need. Every part of Nic was aflame and he could feel hardness swelling in Dashiell's breeches like a promise he wanted kept, the thought of it enough to drive all remaining sense from his mind. The vowsmith seemed similarly afflicted, de-vouring Nic with a fervour bordering on madness—a madness Nic shared when fingers closed upon a handful of his hair and tugged, hard enough that he was forced to bare his throat with a moan that emanated straight from his groin.

This was not the old Dashiell, the years stripped away. This was a whole new Dashiell, the past but a fuel—a fuel that burned hot enough to sear them both. And Nic wanted to be seared, to be consumed, to give in to the wildest desires nine years had wrought.

Until as abruptly as they had begun, Dashiell pulled back. He stood drawing heavy breaths in the dark, before he turned away, becoming nothing but footsteps retreating toward the stairs. Nic blinked, body hot, lips raw, his mind ablaze with need, with memories and heat and a desperate urge to call the man back. But the words lodged in his throat. As though history had repeated itself, Dashiell had been right there, solid and tangible and present and his, and now he was gone.

Chapter 7

Nic lay awake well into the small hours, unable to stop reliving that kiss. Eventually he fell into a doze, only for Dashiell to follow him into his dreams. There, he berated Nic for falling out of the hayloft and missing his vowsmithing exams, complaints that began to emerge in the grating voice of an automaton—an automaton that chased him clanking through the night. Nic woke in a sweat when the automaton became Dashiell and pushed him down the stairs.

Nic glanced at the clock beside Avery's covered cage—a mechanical echo capable of trilling the time when wound up. It was not yet seven, but preferring not to return to his dreams, Nic pulled himself out of bed. Wine would help. Or perhaps seeking some answers about the automaton in the style wing followed by wine.

"Good morning, lovely," he said as he pulled the cover off Avery's cage.

"Morning," she chirped back, bending her head to nip at her feathers. "Good morning."

Not that it was a good morning. Every inch of Nic's skin felt too tight, traced through with the ghosts of touches he couldn't stop thinking about. Yet to start thinking about them would take him right back to that wall, Dashiell's weight against him, hot and hungry.

God, he needed a strong drink. Or two, he decided, as he stepped into his dressing room to be assailed with the increasingly familiar weight of loss. Ringing for Rowerre would bring only a random assortment of footmen to his aid—men who could help him dress and even organise his wardrobe, but who were not Rowerre. As Nic dressed, he wished he'd had the chance to tell the man just how much his care had meant.

Carrying that weight with him, Nic let himself out of his rooms. A glance along the passage to where he'd seen the ghost revealed only threadbare carpet and empty air, but as he made his way toward the style wing, he couldn't shake the feeling that something was watching him all the same.

"Oh! Lord Monterris!"

Nic jumped as Lady Radlay appeared, straightening up from where she'd been leaning near the style-wing stairs.

"Lady Radlay," he said, his heartbeat a rapid drumming in his chest. "What are you doing here?"

"She's my lookout," Leaf said, stepping around the corner. "I've been trying to pick the lock but it's harder than I expected."

"Pick the lock?" Nic looked from Leaf's innocent expression to Millie Radlay's profile as she turned away, trying not to laugh. "It's not a little early for exploring run-down rooms?"

"Oh, Serrals are accursedly early risers, I'm afraid. Besides, I could ask you the same thing. Or do you just happen to be strolling this way with something heavy and key-like in your pocket?"

"I need to see that automaton again," Nic said. "I need to find out where it came from and how it works."

Leaf's eyes widened. "You want to see that thing again?"

"That thing was wearing the ruined waistcoat I asked Rowerre to get rid of." Nic glanced at Lady Radlay, whose intent gaze had fixed on the side of his face. "That's a long story, but yes. I'm going to find the automaton."

"Potentially murderous automaton," Leaf corrected. "I had better come with you."

"Leaf!" Lady Radlay cried, before glancing along the passage and lowering her voice to add, "You said you just found dilapidated rooms yesterday."

Leaf took her cousin's hand. "And so we did. I am merely teasing. We won't be long, and no one is likely to come looking for us, but if they do—"

"You are going to owe me for this." Lady Radlay pouted. "Playing watch while you go off adventuring with Lord Monterris is going to get very dull very fast."

"You're an angel, truly." Leaf kissed her cheek and spun away as Millie glared. "And I promise I'll make it up to you. Like next time you need me to cover for a visit to Mr. Tem—"

"Leaf!"

Millie's cheeks reddened and she looked meaningfully Nic's way, but Leaf just waved a hand. "Oh, don't mind him, he's practically family already," she said, hooking her arm through Nic's and pulling him toward the style-wing door.

"I'm also really quite hard of hearing, I promise," he threw over his shoulder to a still furiously blushing Lady Radlay. Once Leaf had dragged him around the corner, he added, "Your poor cousin, my lady, you quite mortified her."

"Oh no," Leaf said, holding out her hand for the key. "It is impossible to mortify Millie. She will tell me off later for risking secrets in front of you, though. Here." Having unlocked the door, she handed back the key and bent to pick up the lantern and candelabra she'd left on the floor. "But you won't tell Aunt Theresa, so Millie needn't worry."

"She said yesterday they don't get along," Nic said as they once again stepped into air that managed to be both damp and dusty at the same time, leaving a chalky taste on the tongue. He wasn't sure bringing Leaf along was wise considering what answers he'd come to find, but doubted he could change her mind.

"Oh, they hate each other," Leaf said, far more cheerfully than the words ought to have allowed. "It's a long story, but the short version is that Millie is Uncle Ricard's daughter with his first wife, Caroline Wivenwood. Have you heard of the Wivenwoods?"

Nic shook his head as they made their way through the shabby antechamber.

"No? Well, Sir Bertram Wivenwood—Millie's grandfather, you know—fell into such disgrace that his knighthood was revoked by the king. Uncle Ricard was lucky the marriage contract had been so carefully smithed that he wasn't drawn into it. You see, once Lady Caroline was no longer the daughter of *Sir* Bertram Wivenwood, it was automatically annulled. Millie was only a baby, but Aunt Theresa has always disliked her, saying she brings shame to the family through her mother, and other such nonsense. Really, I think my aunt is just jealous because Uncle Ricard adores her, but I dare not say so."

"Poor Millie. And to have been widowed so young too."

"Exactly so! You'd think my aunt could show more compassion, but no." Leaf sniffed. "Don't tell anyone I told you, though. They all hate when it gets brought up. Here, take the lantern; my arms are getting tired carrying these."

He took the lantern but gave the candelabra a stern look. "Why do you even have that?"

"In case I need to whack anything."

Clearly seeing nothing amiss with this statement, Leaf strode on ahead, eyes darting from shadow to shadow. Nothing had changed since the day before. Dust still blanketed every surface, turning already faded furniture a ghostly grey in the morning light, and the tang of mildew hung in the air. While the rest of the Court had possessed the silence of a house not yet awake, here the silence befitted a slowly decaying tomb.

They made straight for their destination, yet even with her heavy candelabra in hand, Leaf slowed as she approached the room where they'd first found the automaton.

It was empty.

The door it had chased them through lay flat on the floor, and Nic stepped over it as they retraced their escape route. There the open window from which they'd leapt, there the pile of broken-up automata parts in the corner, but of the walking, talking automaton there was no sign.

"I'm not sure if I'm more relieved or terrified," Leaf said.

A shiver ran through Nic's skin. He'd hoped they would find it, hoped to find it had walked into the wall and run itself down so he could prove to himself it was just a machine.

"Nic?" She touched his arm.

"I told you I walked out into the garden the other night," he said. "But I didn't tell you why. I wasn't just escaping the party; I thought I saw an automaton of sorts, so I followed it. I saw it again last night. A white, featureless face and a body of shadows—shadows like the ones that spilled from the automaton yesterday. Heavy and oily."

This time Leaf shivered. "Well, that's extremely creepy. You think it was the same automaton?"

"I don't know. It didn't speak either time."

"Oh, do you think it could be that Faceless Man that Master Everel told us about?"

"I suppose it could have been. Since I've never seen a ghost, I don't really know what one is meant to look like."

"Ghostly, I should think."

Nic gave her a look. "That doesn't help as much as you think it does. Come on, let's check the other rooms just in case."

A thorough search of the upper style wing achieved nothing beyond giving Nic a fine covering of dust and an appetite for his breakfast.

Thankfully, they were late enough to the breakfast parlour that Nic was spared the torment of having to sit down and politely drink tea with Dashiell, but the very knowledge that he remained in the house made him yearn for something stronger to drink. The absent automaton wasn't helping either, nor the possibility that Rowerre had been deliberately pushed down the stairs.

All in all it had been a very inauspicious start to a lock-in.

Unfortunately for Nic's desire to drink, the duke had planned some entertainments for his guests. That day it was to be a tour of the house and grounds, or rather a tour of the parts of it His Grace deemed worth showing. Unable to cry off, Nic could only hope to glean some answers about ghosts and automata as they went. Failing that, walking around the Court might at least distract him from endlessly reliving the moment Dashiell had pushed him against the wall.

All hope of answers, or even entertainment, was soon dashed. In every room his father bored on at length about Monterris family history, slowing the pace of the tour to a crawl. Every king to have stayed at the Court was mentioned a dozen times along with every ancestor to have commanded royal soldiers—the duke's pride in his name taking on a visceral dimension that crushed his audience even as it enlivened him. Only Lord Charborough seemed to enjoy himself. While Nic and Leaf hung back, Leaf's father walked at the duke's side deep in conversation between stops on a tour that, by the end, felt interminable.

When Nic finally escaped to dress for dinner, he was even more in need of wine than ever—a feeling that didn't dissipate upon finding a young man rustling around in his dressing room. "Uh, hello?" he said, causing the man to flinch and drop Nic's shirts.

"Lord Monterris! I'm sorry, His Grace sent me. I'm not a valet, strictly speaking, but Rowerre was teaching me before . . . well . . ."

Rowerre's replacement.

"Ah, I see. It's Ambrose, isn't it? You're one of our footmen?"

"Yes, my lord, but I've been learning and I've always wanted to be a gentleman's gentleman."

Nic had been ready to hate the man, but found that he couldn't. He sighed, a little knot of grief loosening slightly. "I'm sure you'll be excellent, Ambrose. So long as you can keep the fire tended and my wardrobe in something approaching good order."

"I can do that, my lord."

"Oh, and do your best to make sure I'm not late for things. Rowerre sometimes joked I could replace him with a nagging clock."

Nic smiled wryly at the memory, but Ambrose's eyes widened and he turned in search of something, anything, that would tell him the time. He discovered the mantelpiece clock and his lips moved as he did mental calculations.

"Uh, my lord, I think perhaps you ought to dress for dinner."

"Surely it can't be later than six."

"It's half past, my lord."

"Shit. You see? This is why I need a valet. I can dress myself but I cannot keep track of time worth a damn."

Thankfully, Ambrose worked quickly and soon had Nic in a fresh shirt and breeches. While he prepared a neckcloth, Nic said, "You've worked here for a few years, haven't you, Ambrose?"

"Yes, my lord. About four now."

"Have you ever seen a ghost?"

Ambrose paused about his task. "Not myself, no, but there are plenty of stories belowstairs."

"About faceless men and mad friars?"

"Yes, and one of the chambermaids used to go on about a dark sense of doom that filled the abandoned rooms. If you would lift your chin, my lord."

Nic lifted his chin. "I suppose the house *is* very old. Did you know there was a castle here before the manor? Lots of battles came right up to the gates. Malcolm III. William the Lion. The civil wars. The first duke was even executed in the courtyard. That's a lot of magic and hate and blood that has spilled into these grounds. Perhaps the house really does hate us."

The young man seemed to have nothing to say to that, just as he had nothing to say when Nic's hair gave him trouble and Nic said, "It's my highwayman look, you know." It turned out Ambrose was not Rowerre, and though he'd known Rowerre could never be replaced, it was disappointing all the same.

Nic arrived in the drawing room that evening to find every other guest already present. Including, to his surprise, his mother. She sat on a large sofa near the fire, gazing upon the room like a woman holding court. Silla stood behind her, and though Nic was used to his mother's maid always being close at hand, her presence drew curious glances.

Leaf was sitting with Lady Lisbeth, who was smiling admiringly upon Dashiell as he recounted some tale or other for their entertainment. Dashiell, whom he had kissed in the dark. Dashiell, who had kissed him back with a heat that still burned beneath Nic's skin. As though it had only just happened, the man's hair was beautifully dishevelled to a degree that caused Nic physical pain, and he made for the comparative safety of his mother's conversation.

"Good evening, Mama," he said, taking a seat beside her.

"Oh, my darling, I was wondering where you were." She met his gaze and he was glad to find her more lucid than usual. "Isn't this a delightful party?"

"It is, Mama; you are to be congratulated."

She leaned close, smile mischievous. "You know I am not one to brag, but to have brought the Havellens out of seclusion *is* quite the achievement."

Nic risked a glance at Lady Theresa seated nearby.

"Lord Monterris," this lady said with a sardonic smile. "How very much I learned about your family today. Of course it was just like dear Millie not to join us, choosing instead to monopolise her father's time." She clicked her tongue and glanced at the duchess. "Millie is my stepdaughter, Your Grace. The only child of my husband's first and very unfortunate marriage to Caroline Wivenwood." She sniffed. "It's been almost thirty years but people still pry about it. No doubt you are well used to the same vulgar curiosity about Lord Francis."

The duchess flinched. Her smile turned glassy and Silla took half a step forward, only halting when Nic said, "We usually find people considerate enough not to bring him up in general conversation, Lady Theresa, but I am glad you enjoyed the tour."

The lady looked like she would retort uncharitably, until the dinner bell rang over her scowl. Grateful for its timing, Nic rose to offer his mother his arm. "Shall I take you into dinner, Mama?"

"That would be lovely, dear one." She set her hand on his arm, but as they reached the dining room, her fingers dug hard into his coat sleeve.

"The house hated him," she whispered, grip tightening. "It hates me. Hates all of us." Her eyes glazed as she slipped away from him, into one of her dark places. "Shall I make you one, Georgie? You wouldn't have to be so alone."

"Your Grace?" Silla took her hand, gently prising her grip from Nic's arm. Conversation bubbled around them as the others took their seats at the table. "Your Grace?"

His mother flinched and looked at the footman holding out her chair. "Oh, is it time to eat? How delicious this all looks." And with a rustle of skirts, she sat, a brittle smile for anyone who stared.

Nic moved to his place, still able to feel his mother's fingertips biting into his arm. *Shall I make you one, Georgie?*

"Are you all right?" Lady Leaf slid her chair closer amid the hub-bub. "You look worried."

Whatever else he might share with her, his mother's strange utterances weren't among them, so he said, "Just hungry. I should rather ask how you are, after such a dull day."

"Oh, it wasn't so bad to learn about the family I'm marrying into. And my father seemed to enjoy himself, which doesn't hap-pen often, I can tell you."

"A thrilling afternoon, in fact?"

"*Thrilling* is taking it too far."

Across the table, Dashiell was lifting his spoon to his lips—lips that had sought to devour Nic the night before. Yet for all the signs Dashiell showed of recalling the incident, Nic might have imagined the whole. Between spoonfuls of soup, the vowsmith was attempt-ing to make conversation with Dr. Fanshaw, but nothing he said seemed to hold the other man's attention. His gaze kept slipping toward Leaf. When one question went entirely unacknowledged, Dashiell's brows rose, and Nic found himself staring at their elegant arch, the curve of those soft, dark hairs the most expressive part of Dashiell's face.

"Hmm, you're right, he is very handsome," Leaf said. She'd leaned close to see what he was looking at, and Nic turned so fast that his neck twinged.

"Do you . . . ?"

"Do I what?" Lady Leaf stared back, her soup spoon hovering. "Oh, do I love him?"

"Shh," Nic hissed.

"I was just trying to understand your question," she hissed back. "And to answer it, no. Not that it's any of your business. I've never been in love. I don't think I know how to be."

The noise around the table sounded extra loud in the wake of her admission, and when he didn't answer, she said, "Well?"

"Well what?"

"Do *you* love him?"

"This really isn't the best place for this conversation."

"You started it. Besides, no one is listening."

That at least was true, the room full of cheerful conversation. "I—we have . . . a history," Nic said, keeping his voice low all the same. "I told you he lived here as an apprentice and, well . . ." He let the words fade, unsure how to explain. It had begun as friendship. Then longing had sparked as they grew from boys to men, a longing it had been impossible to contain. For a time, they'd stolen only kisses, but an ever-increasing awareness of each other's bodies had led to more. To illicit touches beneath the table while they worked. To the pair of them pressing against each with an unskilled, breathless need neither knew how to use, everything about their time together a delicious torture until one morning Dashiell had crept into his room. Into his bed. Then had been gone.

"Oh, do you have a sexual history?"

"Shh! What? No! And what sort of question is that for—"

"My, my, lovers' quarrels already." Lord Charborough directed one of his broad smiles at them, an amused twitch lifting the corners of his lips. "What can you two be whispering about so fiercely?"

Nic hadn't realised how quiet the rest of the table had become. Everyone was staring at them.

"Singing, Papa," Lady Leaf said, taking the scrutiny in her stride with a bored inflection Nic could only admire. "Since we are to have music this evening and Lord Monterris enjoys conjuring, I requested he grace us with a song. Unfortunately, he is being stubborn and I will require all your entreaties if I am to hear him sing."

It was nicely done, but Nic had to master the urge to kick her beneath the table. His father was already scowling.

"My son has long given up performing, I'm afraid, Lady Leaf," the duke said. "Further study in such an art would hardly have been fulfilling."

"Oh, let him entertain us, Val," Lord Ricard drawled, throwing something of a challenging look toward the duke. "You once said all study can be made fulfilling if it's desired, did you not? Besides, we wouldn't want the evenings getting dull, eh, Charles?"

Thus applied to, Lord Charborough rumbled agreement without looking up. "It *is* a private party."

Nic's unshakable love of the art warred with his father's disapproval, and as the other guests added their voices, he had the odd feeling he was walking into a trap. Yet all he could do was smile and agree, stomach churning all the while.

Dinner seemed interminable after that, but eventually the duchess rose from her seat, signalling it was time for the ladies to retire to the drawing room. Leaf followed with her aunt and companions, and in their absence Nic fully intended to devote himself only to his wineglass.

"It'll be nice to hear you sing again."

Nic startled, almost knocking his glass over. "What?"

"I recall you were quite talented," Dashiell said, no sign in his bearing that the night before had happened at all. "At conjuring, I mean."

"*Talented* is an overstatement, but I used to enjoy it."

"Used to? You conjured fireflies on the roof while we were locking the doors the other day. They were very good," Dashiell added when Nic said nothing, shocked to discover the vowsmith had been watching him. "The use of *ka* instead of *hemet* was particularly inspired. Although I admit I'm guessing and will be embarrassed when you tell me you used totally different sigils."

Despite everything, Nic found himself smiling back. "It was *ka*. It makes a nicer curve, though it can be hard to connect onto *shem* in the progression." Holding up his hands, he mimed the movement. As he went from *ka* to *shem*, he paused. "See? Easy to tangle yourself up there."

"I wouldn't dare try, truthfully," Dashiell said. "My hands are far too used to holding a quill. I'm getting scribe's hand. It's very distressing."

"Scribe's hand." Nic snorted a laugh. "That's not a real thing."

"Oh? You malign my suffering? Cruel, my lord, cruel. I'm too young to die."

Forgetting where they were, Nic balled up his napkin and threw it across the table, both of them grinning as Dashiell took the ball of linen in the face.

"That might be considered proper behaviour in the scullery, but not at my table, Nicholas," his father said, breaking off his conversation to glare. "My apologies, Master sa Vare, it appears my son has not yet left the nursery."

"I'm afraid I greatly provoked him, Your Grace, and utterly deserved it." Dashiell nodded an apology in the duke's direction while Nic tried to sink through the floor.

When the duke went back to ignoring them, Dashiell said, "Did you ever get that conjuring tutor you wanted?"

"No."

With anyone else, Nic would have shrugged and said he had changed his mind, but Dashiell would know it for a lie.

"I'm sorry."

"Sorry?" Nic huffed a humourless laugh, their friendly moment fracturing upon too many hurts. "Of all the things you have to be sorry for, that's not one of them."

The words were out before he could retrieve them and Nic wished he could shove the balled-up napkin into his own mouth. Across the table, Dashiell's lips parted and for a moment it seemed he might answer, before he looked away—the vowsmith as intent on ignoring the past as he was on leaving that furious kiss unacknowledged. Nic told himself he didn't care. Whatever they might once have had was long gone. He'd gotten on with his life. He'd had his share of lovers—*nameless, forgettable, not Dashiell*—and now he was getting married. Best to leave Dashiell in the past where he belonged.

With a scrape of his chair, Lord Ricard stood. "Well, if you'll all excuse me, gentlemen," he said, an empty smile sweeping across the table. "I am expecting important correspondence via the evening post."

"Come," Lord Charborough said, lifting his glass. "Let Gillingham take care of it. You are a guest and ought to act like one."

"Spoken like a man for whom business is something that happens to other people, Brother. As well I tell you to give up your dusty books. No. You stay and enjoy your wine while I have a care to our fortune."

Lord Ricard strode out on the words, leaving the duke to murmur, "I hope Gillingham is a very good scribe, since he is no longer a vowsmith."

"Wasn't that a shock?" Charborough said. "Although I can't say I like the man much myself, and greater men than he have been kicked out of the guild. Do you remember when Lord Everington was excommunicated, Val?"

"For smithing contracts under a false name, no less." The duke laughed—so rare a sound that Nic stared. "And not being good enough to pull it off."

From there, the duke and Lord Charborough fell into reminiscences about old times, bringing more smiles to the duke's face than Nic had ever seen. Side by side, they sat talking like no one else existed, the familiarity that of old friends, whatever he'd heard about the dislike between their families. It seemed they could have gone on so for hours, leaving the rest of the company to desultory talk, but after ten minutes the duke's scowl returned and he rose abruptly, suggesting they join the ladies.

Nic was more than happy to do so, but as he made for the door, his father's hand dropped onto his shoulder. "A moment, Nicholas."

The rest of the gentlemen filed out, leaving the duke fixing Nic with one of his heavy stares—a look made worse by the dark glasses behind which he had tucked away all emotion. "You will not sing tonight, Nicholas. I will make your excuses, and in future I suggest you make no such promises."

"But, sir—"

"No," the duke snapped, grip tightening on Nic's shoulder. "We don't need another useless conjuror in this family. That is my final word."

He let go and strode out, leaving Nic standing alone, breath caught in the wake of such coiled fury. It was nothing he hadn't heard before, yet it was some minutes before he could pull himself together enough to return to the drawing room.

There he found Lady Lisbeth already sitting at the pianoforte, while Millie searched through a stack of old music. By the fire, Lady Theresa and the duchess sat in what could have been called a conversation had it been going both ways, while Leaf admired the echoes that called the drawing room aviary their home. Dr. Fanshaw stood at her side, and Nic would have left the man to his attempted flirtations had Leaf not caught sight of him and beckoned him over.

"Nic. You must settle a disagreement."

"Hardly a disagreement, my lady," the doctor murmured. "I merely made the observation—"

"I thought these birds were bred as companions," Leaf interrupted. "But Dr. Fanshaw has pointed out they have quite large claws. Are they hunting birds?"

With an apologetic glance at the doctor, Nic said, "They were originally bred for hunting and we still keep hunting stock, but not in the house. These are gentle." With a flick he unlatched the cage door and reached inside. At a whistle, the largest male hopped toward Nic's hand and curled its long, scaly claws around his fingers.

"This is Lord Featherington," Nic said, bringing the bird up to his face.

"Love Nicholas," the regal echo trilled, nuzzling first one side of Nic's jaw and then the other.

Leaf laughed, and at the applause behind him, Nic discovered the whole room was watching. Including Dashiell, perched on the arm of a nearby sofa. Embarrassed, Nic gave a half shrug. "They're really very sweet."

"That they are," his father agreed with something of a snap. "Now if you'll all excuse me. Her Grace is tired. I must escort her to her rooms before we begin our evening festivities."

The duchess sat staring at nothing, hands clasped in the soft folds of her pale blue gown. Nic was glad she had come to dinner, but was equally glad for the duke's rare display of care as he offered her his arm amid cheerful good nights.

"He's very attentive," Leaf said, watching Nic's parents leave arm in arm.

"Only because guests are watching. Do you want to hold Lord Featherington?"

Leaf hesitated, caught between desires. Courage won. "All right, what do I do?"

"Hold out your hand like this—that's right, and now just relax." She nodded, and Nic gave the regal echo a small nudge. With a flap of glorious gold-spotted wings, Lord Featherington hopped onto Leaf's hand.

She flinched, but the bird was too old and well trained to be troubled, settling tall and proud with its claws curled around her wrist. "He'll nuzzle you if you put your face close to his," Nic said.

"Are you sure?"

"Don't worry, they don't eat people."

With a nervous smile, Leaf leaned in. Once she was close enough, the echo nuzzled first one of her cheeks, then the other, before sitting back and trilling, "Love Nicholas."

Chuckles spread through the room and Leaf looked around at their audience. "Well, not yet, but he's very bearable."

Nic couldn't help glancing at the doctor over Leaf's shoulder and never had he seen a more miserable expression. The man was clearly smitten, and Nic's heart twisted in sympathy. Too well did he know the feeling of love where no love ought to live.

As though summoned by the thought, Dashiell approached as Nic put the echo back into the aviary.

"He's a beautiful specimen," he said, eyes on the bird as Nic locked the cage door. "One of yours?"

"If you mean did I train him, yes. You know nothing is really mine."

When Dashiell didn't answer, the urge to demand what had happened the previous night almost overwhelmed Nic. It tasted bitter as he swallowed it, and he turned to watch Dr. Fanshaw squire Leaf toward the pianoforte.

"The doctor seems to have quite a liking for Lady Leaf," he said instead.

"Yes, he does, doesn't he," Dashiell agreed. "Of long standing, I believe. Unfortunately for him. He's Lady Charborough's physician, you know."

Nic risked a sidelong glance the vowsmith's way. "Unfortunate because his position precludes him being able to marry her?"

"No." Dashiell met his gaze. "Because she doesn't seem to have noticed he exists."

Nic's heart gave a heavy thump at so intent a stare, but before he could question any underlying meaning, a distant scream tore at his attention. The low chatter around them stuttered to a halt, heads turning toward the door. Lord Charborough got to his feet. "What in God's name was—?"

The scream came again, high-pitched and wild.

The duchess.

Leaving frightened questions milling in his wake, Nic tore open the door and sped into the hallway. There he paused only to listen, before following the high-pitched wail at a run, a fearful pulse thrumming in his ears. The scream wasn't coming from his mother's rooms but from the upper gallery of the negotiation chamber, where an open door led from the hallway to its interior balcony. Charging through, Nic found the duchess backed up against the wall, her eyes fixed upon the centre of the room.

"Mama?" Nic gripped her arms before turning to look for what troubled her. "What is—?"

The rest of the question remained unspoken, swallowed along with Nic's breath as the other guests piled in behind him on a chorus of queries and cries.

"By God," someone whispered, but if God had ever watched over Monterris Court, he had surely abandoned them now, for there, hanging from the central chandelier, was Rufus Gillingham. The young man dangled like a lifeless doll, his weight tilting the chandelier such that half of its candles had fallen from their sconces onto the table below, where a tall ladder sat at a drunken angle.

"The house," the duchess wailed, shaking in Nic's arms. "It's coming for us. It's coming for us all!"

"Nonsense," the duke said. "Silla? Silla! Take Her Grace to her rooms. She is naturally quite overset by such an unpleasant sight."

The duchess spun upon her husband. "It hates you most of all," she spat. "None of us are safe!"

Nic squeezed her arms. "Mama, it's all right. Here, look at me." His words drew her gaze with the effort of one swimming against a strong current. "I'm sure it was just a terrible accident," he said, not believing his own words. "And Silla is here now, see?"

"Yes, Your Grace, come now," Silla said, pressing out a flat smile for Nic alone as she took over. "Let us get you to bed."

As Silla led the duchess away sobbing, Nic became aware of the silence along the balcony and turned to find half the guests watching him, as though his mother was more frightening than the hanging body. Lady Theresa looked disgusted, but when he glared at her she looked away with a theatrical shudder. "How horrible," she said. "Leaf, Lizzy, do look away. This is no sight for delicate eyes. Where is Ricard? Someone ought to—"

But before she could finish her words, a rush of late footsteps heralded the arrival of Lord Ricard. The man pushed through the collected guests in the doorway only to halt abruptly, eyes caught to the dangling figure. "Gillingham! What—?" His gaze flitted about the room, taking in the terrible details, before he gripped the duke's shoulder, pulling him roughly around. "Explain this, Val."

"I cannot." The duke straightened his dark glasses and brushed the creases from his coat. "It was you who left to meet with him, not I."

"And did not find him awaiting me as expected!"

"Poor man," Lady Theresa wailed, lifting the corner of her shawl to her eyes. "To climb all the way up there and do such a thing, when he was always so cheerful." She turned dawning horror toward Master Everel. "You don't think it was that malaise, Master Everel? Perhaps he heard the Mad Friar and—"

The duke heaved a put-upon sigh. "Mere stories, Lady Theresa. It is more likely he took his own life due to his excommunication."

A sensible suggestion, but Nic thought of Dashiell's warning the night before—the man had been sure to go on working, might even have revelled in the lack of boundaries left to him. Gillingham had seemed the sort of man who slid easily through life upon a suggestive smile, and after Rowerre and the automaton and the ghosts, it was hard to believe the answer was so simple—thoughts Nic kept to himself because the implications were too terrible to consider.

Perhaps having something of the same thought, Dr. Fanshaw cleared his throat. "We ought to send for the magistrate."

"Edwin!" Lady Theresa cried. "You cannot mean it. And have some puffed-up nobody asking questions? I shudder to think."

"And what then of the contract?" Lord Charborough asked.

Nic caught a flicker of disgust on Dashiell's face before the vowsmith tucked it away. "Unfortunately, you are correct in your concern, Lord Charborough. Whatever I might personally feel about the situation, breaking the lock-in by bringing in a third party would void the contract, requiring one of you to retract and pay both the compensation payment and the guild breakage fees. Unless you wish to invoke the Requisite Care Clause, of course, though I warn you there is no way the contract could be finished in the few days it would take the king's men to arrive from London."

"No! Gosh no." Lord Charborough let out a tight laugh. "No need to do that, making ourselves the talk of the town in the process? No. It's plain the man killed himself. Nothing more to be said."

There was nothing plain about it, and the ease with which a young man's death could be dismissed the moment it got in the way chilled Nic to the bone.

"Well said, Charles," the duke agreed. "Perhaps we ought to stop staring at the poor man and leave the servants to the unenviable task of getting him down. In the circumstances, however, it would be ill-considered to continue with our evening entertainments. Best we adjourn; we've all had quite the shock and the ladies are clearly distressed."

All eyes turned to Lord Ricard, still frozen at the railing. For a long, tense moment, he did not move, did not speak, just stared out at the dangling body of his man. Before, with a disgusted huff, he spun away and strode out without a word.

Chapter 8

Nic dressed early the following morning and hurried down to the breakfast parlour. He preferred to breakfast in his rooms, but today he needed to find Leaf, and as she was an early-rising Serral, the breakfast parlour seemed the wisest place to begin. Unfortunately, at the parlour door he all but ran into his father—another famously early riser.

"Ah, Nicholas, a moment." The duke gestured toward the adjacent sitting room. Foreboding swelled, but Nic could hardly refuse and so he followed in silence, his anxiety deepening when his father closed the door behind them.

"We need this contract to go ahead," the duke said, leaning on the arm of one patterned silk armchair. "Nothing can get in the way. We cannot afford to pay either compensation to the Serrals or the guild breakage fees—we can barely afford to be hosting this event at all."

The question of what this had to do with Nic almost slipped from his lips, only to be caught on the memory of having endangered the contract by kissing the Serral family's head vowsmith.

"You have been cold to Master sa Vare since he arrived," his father went on. "And insulted him last night with your childish behaviour."

"Do you mean when I threw the—?"

"I will hear no excuses, Nicholas. As Master sa Vare is the head vowsmith of the Serral delegation, earning his ire will serve us ill.

After last night's unfortunate happenings, we must tread carefully. Some of the non-Brilliant members of the Serral negotiation team left this morning, and while I do not think Charles wants the infamy of invoking the Requisite Care Clause and forcing the king to come running to his rescue, let's try to keep it that way. So for the sake of your name, if not common courtesy, it is time to put aside your foolish jealousy and be civil to Master sa Vare. Your previous friendship ought to have been an unforeseen boon for us."

When Nic could find no words, his father looked over his glasses, brows raised. "Is it so shocking an expectation, Nicholas? You seem to be winning over Lady Leaf; just extend that charm to her head vowsmith." With an imperious finger, the duke gestured to the closed door. "I left Master sa Vare breakfasting, so go in there and be charming. Do you understand?"

"Yes, sir."

The duke pushed his glasses back up his nose, like a bird settling ruffled feathers. "Good." He pulled open the door but, before Nic could escape, added, "I know sometimes I might seem harsh, but as a Monterris you have one responsibility and that is the preservation of your family. You bear one of the oldest, proudest names in England and it is your duty to uphold it as your ancestors did before you. Whatever it takes."

"Yes, sir."

The automatic reply seemed to satisfy the duke, who strode out, his imperious footsteps echoing away along the passage.

After a moment to gather himself, Nic made his way to the breakfast parlour. The door sat open, and as he approached, the scratch of quill on paper mingled with the whisper of sigils, their accent distinctly familiar. Nine years may have changed much, but they had not changed the feel of Dashiell's magic, and no amount of anger could displace the comfort such familiarity bestowed.

The vowsmith sat alone at the breakfast table, meal forgotten.

As he worked, tiny swirls of shadow spiralled from the paper, and without conscious thought, Nic felt the sigils in his skin. It took less than a line to realise Dashiell was inscribing a poem, smithing raw emotion onto the page. But he was working too fast, not paying attention to the fine details needed for such a task, and first one sigil twanged wrongly, followed by another, and Nic winced. "I think you meant to use *el* there. And *miir* on the line before."

Dashiell dropped the quill and, glancing up, crumpled his page into a ball. "I didn't see you there." He threw it into the grate, where it caught fire and burned brightly into ash.

"I'm sorry, I shouldn't have corrected you. Given the speed you were working—"

"It's fine; it was nothing important. You know, I've never met anyone else who could feel sigils like you do."

"That's probably for the best," Nic said, taking a seat at the table. "I wouldn't wish it on anyone."

Having pushed his ink and quill away, Dashiell reapplied himself to his neglected breakfast. "Do you still get those awful headaches because of it? You used to curl up in the den and not move for hours."

Dashiell's words were light, but his grim expression proved he hadn't forgotten how bad it had been whenever Nic's manifesting affinity had run ahead of his ability to hold it, whenever the noise of a world filled with magic had seemed to press upon his skull like lead plates, whenever the doctors had dosed him with Brilliance-suppressing elixirs and still his father had demanded he study and study and never stop.

Here sat the only man who knew those parts of him, yet Nic dared not let him in again. Charm, his father had demanded, not openness.

"Only rarely," he said, the words dismissive. "Do negotiations continue today? After what happened last night?"

"They do. Your father suggested pausing a day out of respect, but the Serrals wouldn't hear of it. We're moving to a new room, though, thankfully."

"I'm surprised it wasn't Lord Ricard who wanted to pause proceedings. It's more my father's style to press ahead with a complete lack of empathy."

A notch appeared between Dashiell's brows. "Perhaps empathy is something generally lacking among peers rather than it being a quirk of your father's—though I realise I shouldn't say so to you."

"Because he's my father or because I'm a peer?"

"Both?"

"Well, since I said it first, you are absolved. And I do wonder if it's not so much something inherent in the titled class as it is an outcome of running a family like a business. The guild-and-contract system controls who does and does not have access to the Brilliance, which means we are all owned by the head of our family like chattel. We're assets, not people."

"That's just the way we have forged contracts since the Family Register Act of 1541."

"Ah, but have you ever considered it could be done differently?"

Dashiell's brows rose. "It is hardly my place to debate King Henry's wisdom no matter how long dead he is, although you make a good point." A small, reminiscent smile turned his lips. "I don't recall any of our tutors being so philosophical."

"No, they were all prosy bores."

"Prosy bores who would never have brooked a challenge to the contract system, nor have questioned the necessity of magic like you did the other night."

Nic grinned. "Shocked you, that did."

"Only because I'd never thought about it before!"

"Oh, so not because you've become a prosy bore?"

Dashiell smiled, a true one with a hint of affection that sent

Nic's heart racing. It was all too easy to fall into such conversations, too natural, like the longer they sat together, the less the intervening years mattered.

"Unfortunately, becoming a prosy bore is something of a job hazard for vowsmiths," Dashiell said, his smile turning wry. "Though I like to think I'm not so far gone yet."

Nic made no reply, needing to break the flow of easy conversation no matter how many witty retorts came to mind. He feigned interest in his breakfast.

After a long, somewhat awkward silence, Dashiell cleared his throat. "And your plans for the day? I . . . noticed you're getting along well with Lady Leaf Serral."

It sounded like jealousy. It looked like jealousy. And in any other circumstances Nic would have revelled in the jealousy. Instead, he forced himself to ignore it and preserve what remained of his sanity.

"Yes," he said lightly. "We get along well. She's not what I expected and it will never be a love match, but how many peers can boast one of those? I hope you're negotiating her a good stud to bear our children."

Dashiell had been about to take a bite of bread, and had Nic waited a few moments, he might have choked on it. As it was, he coughed and gave Nic a look of such censure that he couldn't help but grin.

"Well?" he said, triumphant. "That's what you call it, isn't it? A stud and a mare? I imagine they are awkward discussions."

"Not my favourite part of negotiations," the vowsmith admitted, "but I understand the need for families to ensure progeny."

"You do?"

Dashiell frowned. "You don't?"

"Well, if you're negotiating for someone else to provide the . . . raw material for a child, let's say, then you're already creating something that is—in this case—not really a Monterris. And if you're already signing into vow law an heir that is zero percent Monterris, why not have another heir who is zero percent Monterris? You could just . . . choose one. Anyone would do. Or at least anyone of an acceptable Brilliance level."

This speech earned a silent stare from across the table, Nic unable to tell from the slight frown and parted lips what Dashiell thought of it, only that he found it impossible to answer.

"You really are remarkable, Nic," he said eventually. "Lady Leaf is an extremely fortunate young woman."

A desperate yearning cut through the armour he'd held tight since Dashiell's arrival, and Nic dared not speak. He needed to push away the warmth and joy of such conversations, along with any treacherous inklings of hope that they could ever be more than strangers again. It had seemed so easy at the outset, but every moment spent alone with him only made the next harder to bear.

And then as though the words had been weighing on him, Dashiell went on, "About . . . about the other night. When I followed you. I shouldn't have . . ."

Having begun, the vowsmith seemed incapable of finishing, leaving annoyance to flare in Nic's breast. "Have what?" he said. "Have run away? Have kissed me back? Have pushed me against the wall? Have pulled—"

"All of it!" Dashiell cried.

A beat of silence fell, followed by a second. Then more calmly, he added, "It was . . . extremely unprofessional of me, and I'm sorry."

"Sorry. Yes, of course you are." Nic stared down at his hands. He ought to escape before he said something he would regret, but it was too late. They had already said too much to allow him to fold his hurts away, so instead he looked up, meeting the gaze of the man who had once meant everything to him. "What did I do? You didn't even say goodbye."

Dashiell closed his eyes. "Nic . . ."

"If you didn't want the same thing I did, you could have just said so."

"That's not—" The vowsmith shook his head. Glanced to the open door. "This isn't a good time for this conversation."

"And when is? Never?" Nic rose from the table. "Good luck with the negotiations today, Master sa Vare."

As he reached the door, Dashiell's chair scraped back. "Nic, wait."

The desire to walk out warred with a yearning to remain, and giving in to a sliver of hope he couldn't escape, Nic turned.

His expression a plea, Dashiell stood with his fingertips to the table, something hesitant in the way he seemed to both lean forward and hold back. "It was nothing you did," he said when Nic lifted haughty brows. "Nothing *we* did. I . . . cannot explain, but I need you to know that."

For the space of a heartbeat, a breath, a whole lifetime, Nic met the vowsmith's gaze unspeaking, the urge to throw disbelief in his face withering beneath such open sincerity. And because despite all the hurt, Nic wanted to believe him—wanted it to be true.

Not willing to dare further words, Nic nodded.

"Ah, Lord Monterris, good morning to you!"

Nic flinched at the jovial greeting, the sudden arrival of Lord Charborough sending his heart hammering harder than had Dashiell's admission. The man showed no sign of noticing anything amiss, however, nodding to a rather red-cheeked Dashiell. "Master sa Vare."

"Good morning, sir," Nic said, and would have continued past him into the hall had Lord Charborough not touched his arm to stay his progress.

"If the day warms up, you might take Leaf out into the gardens," the man said. "She was much overset last night, and some sunshine and exercise will do her good. Can get caught in her head a bit too much, that one. I would do it myself, but I am close to finishing a very important translation. Ancient Greek, you know."

Nic didn't know, but readily agreed, assuring the marquess that he would happily take Leaf anywhere she wished.

"Capital!"

With his daughter apparently dealt with, Lord Charborough continued into the breakfast parlour, allowing Nic to escape without glancing back.

Chapter 9

A search of the house eventually discovered Leaf in the great hall talking with Lady Lisbeth. Despite his desire to discuss Gillingham's death, Nic would have left them to it had Leaf not beckoned to him, a hint of relief in her expression.

"But, Leaf, you must help me," Lady Lisbeth was saying as Nic approached. "I don't wish to ask Lord Charborough; it would look too particular."

"As though Papa would even notice, Lizzy," Leaf said, adding, "Good morning, Lord Monterris."

"Lord Monterris," Lady Lisbeth echoed, but her thoughts were clearly elsewhere, for she went on, "I just need to find out whether he is of good family or not. Leaf, perhaps you could—?"

"Oh, just ask Nic, Lizzy; he will know."

Nic tensed at finding Lady Lisbeth's penetrating gaze suddenly upon him. "What will I know?"

"Lizzy wishes to be assured that Master sa Vare comes of good family. A beautiful face offsets only so many ills, after all."

"Leaf!" Lady Lisbeth cried. "Gosh, my lord, what you must think of me. My apologies, it was merely idle curiosity and I will not trouble—"

"It's no trouble," Nic said, though the smile he forced felt like a rictus. "Master sa Vare is the third son of Sir Jasper Vare, a baronet from Sussex. He kept his eldest two sons but sasined Dashiell at birth so he could take on a profession. I've never met Sir Jasper, but from all I've heard, he is a superior man and the family is well respected."

Lady Lisbeth's pretty round face took on a thoughtful look. "A baronet? And Master sa Vare is very highly regarded in the guild, isn't he?"

"As the youngest master vowsmith in three generations, I should think great things are expected of his career, yes."

The lady smiled. "Thank you, Lord Monterris, though I don't doubt you think me very odd for asking."

"Not at all."

Lady Lisbeth seemed on the brink of asking more questions, but Leaf tucked her hand into Nic's arm and said, "Lord Monterris and I are going for a walk, Lizzy. I'll be back for luncheon. Probably."

Not giving Lady Lisbeth a chance to protest, Leaf steered Nic away across the hall. "I'm sorry," she said as they reached the safety of the gallery. "I shouldn't have thrown her question at you like that, given . . . you know, you and Master sa Vare."

"Despite what I said last night, Dash—*Master sa Vare* and I are nothing to one another."

Leaf fixed her gaze on him. "You don't have to pretend with me, you know. If I change my mind and decide I'm madly in love with you, I'll let you know. Until then, feel free to pine over whoever you like."

"I don't pine."

Leaf lifted one arm horizontally like a tabletop and set her other elbow on it, pretending to prop up her chin while gazing at him in the most pathetic manner. "Oh, don't you?"

"I do *not* look like that."

She raised a brow and strode on, triumphant.

"Leaf! I don't, do I?"

The laugh she threw over her shoulder was full of mischief,

but she relented, saying, "All right, maybe not quite that bad, but clearly he's the one you should be marrying, not me. He looks at you almost as pathetically."

"Now *that* I don't believe. I might not be able to see my own face, but I can see his and it doesn't pine."

"Hmmm, no, not pine, I suppose. He has more of a stare, that one."

"Which, true or not, does not change whom I'm being contracted to."

Leaf stopped, laugh fading from her eyes. With a wry grimace, she touched his arm. "I know. I'm sorry."

The sudden softening of her manner pierced his defences as her teasing had not, and Nic found himself unable to immediately reply for the lump in his throat. "It's fine," he said, trying to believe it wasn't a lie. "But I didn't come find you to talk about this. Tell me, what would your Mary Mallowan think about what happened last night?"

Leaf gripped his arm. "You don't think he killed himself either."

"I don't know yet, but it doesn't feel right. He wasn't exactly a morose young man, and your uncle showed no sign of letting him go. Besides, even if he wanted to kill himself, why go to all the trouble of doing so there of all places?"

"I hadn't thought of that. It was a very showy place. Although if he was murdered, we could ask the same question—why go to the trouble of doing it there? It would have been a lot more work than just murdering him in his room, for example."

"Or pushing him down the stairs."

"Yes. And so we're left with the same problem. Your valet *could* have tripped down the stairs, but he might also have been murdered. And Gillingham *could* have killed himself, or he was murdered and hung from a chandelier. I suppose it looks less like murder if you hang someone from a chandelier."

Nic winced. "Can you stop saying that?"

"Saying what? *Chandelier*? I think they call it a lustre in France, but—"

"No, that's what the dangly bits are called."

"Really? I didn't know that."

"What did you think they were called? Dangly bits?"

Leaf shrugged. "I'd honestly never thought about it, but I don't see why you want me to stop saying *chan*—the *c* word."

Laughing, he gripped her shoulders. "Leaf, stop talking and take a deep breath. I wasn't trying to stop you saying *chandelier*. Look, see? I said it. *Chandelier*. We have a lot of them in this house; I'd be in trouble if I didn't like the word. *Chan-de-lier*." With a flick of his fingers, he conjured a small ring of light that hovered in the air beside them, its minuscule candles flickering.

"Oh, that's so pretty. You're really good at that."

"Mere showiness, I assure you."

Leaf stared at his conjured chandelier as it twinkled and faded into the dust motes. "Yes, but that doesn't change the fact that we need to know for sure whether Gillingham was murdered. Else every other question is pointless."

"You see, that was the word I wanted you to stop saying."

Leaf looked entirely baffled. "Which word?"

"*Murder*. And *murdered*. And *murderer*. And—"

"What would you rather I called it? Premeditated life extinguishing?"

"You know what? Forget I said anything."

"I can do that, but will it give me my five minutes back?"

On those words, she set off along the hallway, leaving Nic to follow.

"Cruel, my lady, very cruel. I may or may not get . . . get *murdered* during this lock-in, but I certainly shall never survive more than a week of your barbed tongue once we're married."

"There, see? It wasn't so hard to say, was it?"

"No, it wasn't." He caught up as she mounted the stairs. "Where are we going?"

"To find Dr. Fanshaw and ask him about Gillingham's body."

Falling in beside her, he said, "And to think your father suggested I take you walking in the gardens."

"That is just the sort of thing he would say. I cried on him last night and begged him to call it all off because I was afraid, but it didn't work. He told me I was being a silly little puss and promised me five thousand pounds."

"Five thou—!" Nic snapped his mouth shut, glancing around the empty stairway. "Is he buying your cooperation?"

Leaf beamed. "Oh, *always*. Papa hates confrontation, or even deep conversation—especially if emotions are involved. He would rather throw money at things until they go away. Anything a jovial laugh cannot fix, money surely can."

"That's quite sad."

"Isn't it, though. Don't worry, I have zero illusions about him. I've been saving all the little bits he gives me so I can fund that school I want to open, but he's never given me quite so much in one go. I'd be pleased, but likely it means he's far more worried than he's letting on."

"You're serious about this school."

"Oh yes. It's still at the early planning stage, but I'm determined. I thought I would open it in London, but lately I've been thinking Bath might be better. There's something soberly dull about Bath that might lend it an edge of respectability in case people kick up a fuss."

"There are plenty of schools for young women though, surely."

"Yes, but they only teach sigil poetry and charmspinning and maybe a few old household magicks if they're lucky. I want to teach women how to be vowsmiths. How to be artificers. Fascinators. Apothecaries. Whatever aspect of the Brilliance they want to learn."

It sounded sensible to Nic, but he could imagine his father's scowl.

"And what will you call it?"

"I don't know, maybe Lady Leaf's Brilliant School for Young Ladies. What do you think?"

"It would sound fancier in French. Lady Leaf's l'École extraordinaire pour jeunes femmes."

"You know, I've always liked the way *Brilliance* sounds in French. *Extraordinaire* sounds so much more like they could take on the world."

They found Dr. Fanshaw on the terrace enjoying the weak morning sunshine, a copy of the *London Gazette* across his knees.

"Dr. Fanshaw." Leaf strode out with purpose, the triple flounce of her muslin dress bouncing with her quick steps.

"Lady Leaf!" The doctor almost threw the newspaper down, so quickly did he rise. "Good after—I mean, good morning." He bowed. "Lord Monterris. I was just enjoying some sunshine, as I am told it never lasts in Northumberland."

"That is very true," Nic agreed. "If the sun is out, it's best to grab your umbrella."

Dr. Fanshaw adjusted his spectacles and smiled at Leaf. "As well that you interrupted me then, my lady. Was there . . . is there something I can do for you? You are perhaps not feeling quite the thing?"

"Oh, you know me, unlike my mama, I'm always well." Leaf waved a dismissive hand. "No, we want to ask you about Mr. Gillingham."

The doctor's eyes widened and his gaze shied in Nic's direction. "Mr. Gillingham? I am not sure I follow—"

"Were you there when he was taken down from the chandelier?"

"Uh, yes? But it is hardly an edifying topic for—"

Leaf sighed and turned to Nic. "Then Lord Monterris will ask about it. Nic, why don't you ask the good doctor his opinion on the state of the body since I am too delicate."

The sharp barbs in Leaf's cheerful tone weren't lost on the doctor, who shook his head. "I assure you, my lady, that my reticence has nothing to do with any presumption of your delicacy. I am merely aware my noble patron would be displeased if he found out."

"My father will only hear of this if you tell him, sir," she said. "Nic won't do so, and for all anyone who might be watching knows, we are still discussing the weather. What we are not doing is talking about whether you examined the body."

Wry amusement crinkled the corners of the doctor's eyes. "Then I am not telling you that I did, although only briefly. To ascertain for the death certificate that he was indeed dead."

He was rewarded with a broad smile. "Thank you, Doctor. I do not suppose in the act of performing that brief examination you noted anything odd?"

"Odd, my lady? In truth, I cannot say I looked closely enough to notice anything. The man took his own life and there, I'm afraid, my duty as a doctor ended."

"And how sure are you of that? It was a very strange and difficult place to choose such an act, don't you think?"

Dr. Fanshaw's jaw slackened, and for a moment he looked far more youthful than Nic had assumed. "Are you suggesting his life was ended by another's hand?"

"No, not yet," Nic said. "Let us say we are concerned it might be the case and would like you to tell us we're wrong."

"Another, rather more thorough examination of the body ought to help, don't you think?" Leaf added.

The doctor licked his dry lips. "I . . . I suppose I could go and have another look. The servants carried him down into the crypt—to keep the body cool, you know, while his family is notified."

"Excellent, then shall we go?"

"Of cou—wait, *we*?"

The Monterris family crypt was a broad, sprawling collection of underground rooms, many long collapsed or bricked up. Built under the original castle to protect it from desecration in more turbulent times, it now acted as an eternal reminder of the sheer weight of Nic's ancestors. He didn't often venture in there, the shiver that rippled through his skin as they descended the stairs not all due to the drop in temperature.

Leaf, walking before him, tightened her shawl around her shoulders. "I'm a little disappointed," she said, looking around at the simple stonework. "I was expecting more skulls set into the walls and skeletons lying about."

"You use your ancestors as decoration at Charborough House, do you?" Nic said.

"Sadly, we don't have a crypt, but I consider this very poor form and can assure you I will be making changes once I'm mistress here."

"Just tell me which duke's bones you'd like to start with."

Nic caught amusement flicker across the doctor's face. "The problem with bones, of course, is that they all look alike," the man murmured. And upon receiving a grin from Leaf, he reddened and gestured with his lantern toward a side room. "It's, uh . . . he's through there."

Leaf led the way, only to halt abruptly beneath the arch.

"Oh. Nic, perhaps you shouldn't—"

Her warning came too late to save him from the shock of finding not one but two bodies laid out on the heavy stone slabs. On the nearest, the pale, lifeless form of Rufus Gillingham, on the farthest, Rowerre's much beloved features.

"Oh."

He ought to have known his valet would be there, Nic's heavy grief tinged now with shame that he hadn't thought to come sooner. Someone else had laid Rowerre's body out neatly, had straightened his clothing and tidied his hair, only the discolouration on his face proof he wasn't just sleeping. Nic swallowed a lump in his throat.

Leaf slid her hand into his and squeezed. "If you want to leave, you can. We—"

"No, that's all right." He squeezed back. "I'm . . . glad to see him. It was just unexpected."

"Well, you take all the time you need; we can look at Gillingham." Lifting her lantern, she stepped over to Gillingham's body and leaned in. "He looks remarkably unchanged."

"You've seen a lot of dead bodies?" Nic asked, finding he didn't want to get any closer to the lifeless young man who had smiled at him so suggestively.

"None," Leaf said. "But that's why the doctor is here. Shall we, Doctor?"

"If you wish, my lady, though I admit this is starting to feel more like one of Mary Mallowan's novels than I like."

Leaf's eyes brightened. "Oh, how famous! I didn't realise you read them too. Most people I meet have never heard of her, and here you were all along. How do you find them?"

"I find them both extremely enjoyable and very informative, my lady. *The Scarlet Widow* in particular. I had never before thought about how much information could be found in a blood pattern."

"Yes! That book was remarkable. And *To Stage a Murder*. I have never looked at a stagecoach quite the same again."

For a few minutes they shared their love of Mary Mallowan books back and forth over Gillingham's corpse, until Nic cleared his throat. "Perhaps this conversation could be continued after you've looked at the body?"

"Oh, of course!" Leaf gave a start. "I do love to find a fellow reader, but perhaps we should focus on this first, Doctor."

"My apologies, yes. I suppose I will start with his hands and—"

But Leaf had already bent a closer look upon Gillingham's face, and with a gentle touch to the dead man's temple, she even turned his head. "What do you make of this?"

Joining them, Nic peered at what she had uncovered, only to pull away, unsettled by the sight of dark bruising on Gillingham's scalp and the belated realisation he was staring at a corpse. The doctor didn't have such squeamishness and brought his own lantern close.

"Blood does have a tendency to pool in the lower parts of the body after death, and he has been lying here since last night."

"This isn't the lowest point, though, and there is a gash here, look."

The doctor did look, shifting his head close to hers. "Perhaps he hit his head while on the ladder."

"Yes, but if it occurred right before death, it shouldn't bruise, is that not right?"

Dr. Fanshaw looked uneasy. "That is indeed a current theory, but it hasn't been definitively determined by—"

"And what do you make of his neck, Doctor? Is this more or less bruising than you would usually see on someone who has been hung?"

"You must know I do not often see victims of hangings in my line of work—a lot more nervous complaints and bouts of gout!— but the damage does seem mild."

They went on talking so, slowly walking the length of the body, but Nic found his attention slipping. Leaving them to it, he moved to Rowerre's side and let the talk of bruising and undamaged fingernails become so much noise behind him. After all, this was where it had started—someone pushing his valet down the stairs. Of course it could have been an accident, yet as Nic stood there beside him, he realised he didn't want that to be true. He wanted Rowerre's death to make sense. Wanted someone to blame.

His father had called Rowerre just a valet, but to Nic he'd never been *just* anything. It had always been Rowerre who had comforted, Rowerre who had helped, Rowerre who had mitigated the loneliness of growing up in an emotional desert. And now Nic could never thank him.

Some time later, Leaf laid a gentle hand on his arm, bringing him back into the present. "Nic?"

"Yes? Sorry, my thoughts wandered." He touched the corner of his eye, dabbing away a tear. "Have you come to any conclusions?"

"No definitive conclusions, my lord," the doctor said. "Though Lady Leaf has a very good eye for details and an impressive knowledge."

Nic knew avoidance when he heard it and folded his arms. "Did he kill himself or not, Doctor?"

"I . . ." The man huffed out a heavy sigh. "It is impossible to prove for sure, but no. In my professional opinion, Mr. Gillingham was hung while unconscious or, perhaps, while already dead."

The man's words slowly seeped into Nic's understanding, turning his stomach. "Hung while dead?"

"You can as easily hang a corpse as a man, my lord. I wish I had better news, but I'm afraid we may indeed be locked in with a murderer."

Chapter 10

The negotiation chamber was empty, and although the chandeliers remained lit, it had a sombre air. Leaf stopped at the top of the stairs and stared out at where the body of Rufus Gillingham had hung, seeming almost to float in place like a macabre lustre.

"Someone wanted to make a point," she said. "Or a warning, perhaps. The choice of room feels significant."

"It does," Nic agreed. "Though I can't say I like the idea this might have something to do with the contract. The man had a lot of enemies?"

"I believe so." Leaf started down the stairs. "Although how many of them are in this house?"

Nic followed. "A fair point, though if we're considering motives, Rowerre never left the house for long enough to make enemies, and any he made here could have pushed him down the stairs at any time."

"That suggests it was one of my party who killed him, though I cannot imagine why. Unless he was murdered for a different reason, like perhaps he saw something he shouldn't have. Or it was over that piece of paper you saw in his hand."

"Or, as much as I hate the idea, he could have just tripped. He was late dressing me for dinner that night because he'd had to wait on Lord Ricard first, so perhaps he was tired and careless. I didn't get the chance to ask how many other—"

Having reached the bottom of the stairs, Leaf spun around.

"Wait on Uncle Ricard? But why? He brought his valet with him. As did Papa."

Nic stared at her, unable to fit this information into his mind without knocking other things out of place. If Lord Ricard had brought his own valet, why had Rowerre gone to wait on him? His hands had been shaking when he'd returned.

"Perhaps that was just a lie then," Nic said, though the possibility rankled. "I suppose he could have just been late."

"Maybe." Leaf turned a slow circle, taking in the negotiation chamber from the bottom of the stairs. "Let's see. If Gillingham was murdered and then hung, he must still have been killed in here because someone would have seen a body being dragged around. But once he was dead, all the murderer would have needed to do was let the chandelier mechanism down, tie him up, and lift it again."

"And bring the ladder in afterward."

"Exactly. Now where is the mechan—oh, is this it?" She headed toward where a hinged section of wall stood outlined against the new wallpaper. "It's not hard to find."

Like every other large house, Monterris Court was full of interconnected service passages—narrow, unfinished spaces for accessing things like chandelier mechanisms and dumbwaiters. They were, naturally, the parts of the house that were cleaned the least.

"That," Leaf said, having pulled open the door, "is a dead mouse."

Nic made a show of examining it closely. "Are you sure? Perhaps it's a bird in disguise. And if it is a mouse, shouldn't we find out who killed it? If we don't, they might come for us next."

He was beginning to enjoy her withering looks.

"Why did I bring you with me?" she asked.

"Because you're scared of dead mice? I can assure you, Charborough House will have dead mice, too, if you look in the right places."

"Wrong places." She stepped resolutely over it and turned to where the mechanism sat in a small alcove. There, the chandelier chains entered through what passed for the ceiling in these passages, down into the alcove where a pulley-and-wheel system made it easy to wind them up and down.

"It all looks normal to me," Leaf said, looking at the handle and wheel. "Not that I have any idea what they're supposed to look like."

Nic soon came to the same conclusion. "All looks fine," he said, but Leaf had already moved on to examining the floor. He frowned at her. "What are you doing?"

"Looking for clues, obviously. Why don't you make yourself useful and help."

She was already staring at the floor, so Nic peered along the service passage instead. It led away toward the drawing room and the great hall, darkness deepening as it went. Out of sight, something rustled.

"Did you hear that?" he asked.

"Sounds like a less-dead mouse," Leaf said, not looking up from the dusty boards. "You had better go question it about its very dead friend."

It did sound like skittering claws, yet it seemed not to move, rather to stick in place like the creature was trapped. It kept scratching, the distant sound possessing a silky edge.

With a sigh, Nic fetched a candle from the chamber.

Back in the narrow space, he followed the sound deeper into the mazelike passage made up of mechanisms and hatchways, dumbwaiters and doors—every breath full of dust and smells he didn't want to investigate too closely. The scratching grew louder, and as he reached a corner, Nic slowed.

He let the candle lead the way, thrusting it out before stepping into its light. The new passage it illuminated was much like the last, except there, just beyond the candle's reach, the suggestion of a white face hung in the air.

"Shit," Nic breathed, only for the face to vanish as though blinked away, a mere flicker of imagination in the dark. He started after it, two steps all he managed before a faint hint of magic tingled along his scalp. No sigils, no accent, just an uneasy prickling that stuttered his steps to a halt.

"Hello?" How to talk to ghosts had not been part of his education, but with his heart thumping hard, he took another step. "Is someone there?"

Shadows shifted at the edge of his candlelight, reaching out like moths drawn to the flame. The thin fingers thickened, twisting into coils like the inky night that had spilled from the automaton, and Nic stepped back—one step, two, his grip tightening on the candle. And like an animal sensing weakness, the darkness lunged. Nic gasped as it surged toward him, filling the air and pouring into his open mouth like so much ice.

Nic screamed, but no sound came out. He stumbled against the wall, but there was no wall, as there was no passage—only the darkness that had swallowed him as he had swallowed it, leaving him stranded in nothing.

"Nic?"

Leaf's voice chimed like a song echoing through water, and Nic spun toward it, the air thick and sticky with magic that trickled cold down his spine. He tried to call back, to beg help, but the words seemed to wad in his mouth, not even a muffled plea escaping the smothering dark.

"Nic!"

Her hand closed around his, and he grasped it like a lifeline. As though a spell had been broken by her touch, the darkness fell away, shedding its chill onto the floor. And there stood Leaf, eyes wide, holding as tightly to him as he held to her.

"What in the world was that?"

"I . . . I don't know." He dared not move, caught to the floor as though even to breathe too heavily might bring it all back. "I thought I saw that automaton and then there was just . . . darkness and—"

Leaf took the candle out of his hand and walked a short way along the passage. It was all Nic could do not to grip her sleeve and pull her back. "Well, if it was here, then it's gone," she said, "but that darkness was strange, so thick I couldn't see you. Was that magic? I've never seen anything like it."

Nic's heart still pounded, yet each breath that didn't bring back the solid night calmed the most pressing of his fears. "It had the feel of magic, but there were no sigils—no signature."

"Maybe it really is a ghost. Or it was that automaton. You said it did something similar in the style wing. Oh, what's this? Could this have something to do with it?"

Leaf pointed to the wall a little farther on, and unsticking his feet from the floor, Nic joined her. The candlelight illuminated a mass of silvery strands bunched up and spilling from a timber wall brace. A hint of gold sparkled in the light.

"It's sigil tape," he said, untangling the slippery ribbon from the rough wood where it had been caught. "This must be what I heard rustling. It has a few uses, but around here it mostly makes automata go."

"I thought clockwork made them go."

"Clockwork powers all the gears and rods, but how do they know where they should move to? What they should do? What hour to chirp or croak?" He gestured to the tape. "It's like . . . in-structions, I guess. Although I use a much narrower gauge than this for my small creations."

"Not yours then."

"No."

She indicated the tape he had gathered in his hands. "Can you read that? I have to admit my sigil knowledge is confined to what makes nice poetry, but you could read it, couldn't you?"

Nic grimaced. "Maybe? It's not the same as reading a book, though. Smithing work is worse than sigil poetry because it works backward and forward and up and down depending on the sigils. One halfway along the reel could change the meaning of the very first, so it's . . . complicated. And some are for movement and some are for speech, and honestly I've never been good at reading them because being able to feel them makes it harder, like reading while everyone in a room is talking at once. But," he added, seeing her disappointment, "I could try. And even just translating a small amount might tell us what it does."

"Well, that's your next job."

"Anything as long as I don't have to come back in here again."

It was a short walk out of the narrow passage, but Nic had to fight the feeling the walls were closing upon him all the way. Even when he escaped into the chamber, he found it haunted, with not only the ghost of Gillingham's hanging body, but also the threat of living darkness now filling every corner.

"I . . . I think I need some air," he said, blowing out the candle.

Leaf squeezed his arm. "All right, well, you take all the time you need, and when you're feeling up to it—" She pointed at the sigil tape bundled in the crook of his arm like a strange, slithery baby. "And maybe you could talk to your servants and find out whether anyone came in to clean after the session concluded, or whether the room was empty the whole time. And where that ladder came from too. The more we know, the easier it will be to narrow down possible suspects."

"And what are you going to do?"

"I'm going to search Gillingham's room and see if I can find anything that might tell us why. It's probably a long shot, but in Mary Mallowan's books the strangest, smallest detail is often the key to the whole mystery."

Nic agreed to the plan readily enough, yet couldn't but wonder

whether Mary Mallowan had ever had to worry about cold darkness sliding down her throat.

Despite Leaf's plan, Nic found himself standing outside the new
negotiation chamber as the Court's many clocks sounded the
lunch hour. Inside, a babble of voices rose as chairs were pushed
back, and upon a tide of approaching steps the door swung open.

Two scribes emerged first, both starting at the sight of their
principal. With awkward bows they quickly walked on, throwing
back curious glances. He should have waited elsewhere, he knew,
but the morning had left him on edge and he needed to talk to
Master Everel now.

Once the lesser members of the negotiation teams had walked
past with murmurs of "my lord," Nic strode in. The new negotiation room was much smaller than the previous one had been, but
what it lacked in grandeur it made up for in cosiness. The teams
had used every available surface to pile their papers upon, pushing
aside vases and ornaments, and their chairs sat clustered around
the shorter table in a companionable fashion. At the far end stood
the two easels with their letters patent, and two master vowsmiths,
who both turned as Nic approached. Master Everel's brows rose.
Dashiell just watched him, something in his expression reminding
Nic of how they had last parted.

"Master Everel," Nic said, determined to show no such con-
sciousness. "A word, if I may?"

The older man's brows rose still further. "As you wish, my
lord."

Dashiell, all black clad and smart with his gold epaulettes,
nodded in a businesslike manner and started gathering his things.
"I'll leave you to it."

Determined not to watch him leave, Nic turned to look at the letters patent instead. Beside him, Master Everel said, "What can I do for you?"

Not wanting to explain until Dashiell departed, Nic said, "I'm always impressed by how well-preserved this document is, given it was written over a hundred years ago."

"One hundred and thirty-three years to be precise, but vellum is quite a remarkable material. And your father looks after it well."

With a last swish of papers behind them, Dashiell's steps started for the door.

"It must be difficult to store," Nic said, listening to the departing footsteps. "Especially since ours seems to be twice as long. The merry monarch must have been a wordy man."

"Doubtful. It is merely that a marquess is just a peer, while a duke is expected—nay, required—to protect the realm against all dangers. Thus, a ducal letters patent contains many extra lines of sigils stipulating requisite holdings, finances, and Brilliance. But I do not think you came here to ask me about our letters patent."

"No." A glance around the room assured Nic that Dashiell was gone, yet for all his earlier impatience, his question stuck on his tongue. "The automata, from the grotto, what exactly did they do?"

Master Everel's thick grey brows rose, wrinkling his forehead. "Do? Very little. In the old days, I believe they performed a play in the grotto, with conjured backdrops and other such fripperies. Lord Francis made them do more interesting things. Conjured on them. Made them reels." The old vowsmith gave a derisive little snort. "Although much good it did him."

"Conjured on them?"

"On them. With them. I don't understand the specifics, only that he should have left them well alone."

Not in all his years had Nic heard anyone speak of his uncle without immediately changing the subject, and emboldened, he said, "How did he die?"

"That, you do not wish to know."

"I am not a child, Everel. I'm asking because I do wish to know."

The old vowsmith sighed, settling his weight on the edge of the long table. "I don't know the details, only the outcome. It was after one of Lord Francis and Her Grace's nasty fights."

"Mama and Lord Francis?"

"Yes, they fought a lot—two different temperaments, you know, made for quite a fractious house. Well, this time he had gone and made one of those wretched automata for her, smithed its reel to speak to her and conjure faces, things like that."

Shall I make you one, Georgie? You wouldn't have to be so alone.

"It was quite impressive what it was capable of," Master Everel went on. "Though I don't imagine he expected your mother to turn it on him."

"Are you saying my mother killed Uncle Francis?"

"No, I am saying it was her automaton and he is the one who smithed its reel. God only knows what was on it. They were all broken up after that, as you know, and that is the end of the story."

Except that it wasn't, because in the style wing they'd found a walking, talking, totally complete automaton and it had called to him. Almost Nic said so, but this honesty from the vowsmith who had always been his father's right hand was new and strange, and he wasn't ready to return the gesture.

Instead, he turned back to the letters patent—the smithed law of a long-dead king far safer. "You have to make the contract connect to all of that?" He gestured at the seemingly endless lines of sigil-inscribed law.

"And to all that," Master Everel replied, pointing to the far shorter letters patent of House Serral. "And every other even vaguely related document that exists, because you are the heir to a dukedom. There can be no holes. No mistakes. The net must hold."

The net must hold. Nic had always found the old vowsmith saying painfully apt. For them the net was how they referred to the interlaced and connected strings of magic that held contract to contract, maintaining order and rank and magical control, but for Nic it was more literal—the net that kept him trapped within his life.

"Well, you have my sympathies," Nic said. "That cannot be easy with my father breathing down your neck."

"Indeed. Was there anything else you needed?"

Plenty, but Nic shook his head. What he needed was to escape, to think, to clear his head of the troubled thoughts digging deep roots into his mind. Because with two dead bodies, the lock-in that had started as an annoyance had become a threat. And all too easily could he imagine an automaton reel containing instructions to murder.

Nic spent the afternoon talking to the servants—not to Castor or Mrs. Podmarsh, who were the duke's creatures, but to the housemaids going about their work, to the footman who had let down the chandelier, and to the group of new laundry maids hired for the lock-in. Once he'd finished with the house staff, he headed out into the gardens to speak to the groundskeeper. He learned a lot about what it took to keep so large a house running, but no momentous details about either death.

As the sun set, Nic returned to the house through the old forecourt near his father's rooms—the forecourt where King John's carriage would once have stood, the duke had informed them all during his tedious tour. Unfortunately, being the oldest part of the house also made it the coldest, and Nic shivered as he paused on the threshold to check his boots.

Away along the hallway, the door to the duke's rooms was closed, but voices murmured within. No doubt his father was dressing for dinner, or receiving an update on the negotiations from Master

Everel, and not wanting to have to account for his absence from that day's entertainments, Nic crept silently forward.

Barely had he made it half a dozen steps before the duke's door clicked open. Instinctively, Nic flinched back into the shadows by the forecourt door as Lord Charborough stepped out, adjusting his coat.

Nic's brows rose. What could be so important as to bring a guest to his host's private rooms at such an hour? Especially when the duke had likely spent the day in his study or entertaining his guests, providing Lord Charborough plenty of opportunities to make requests.

Having closed the door behind him, the marquess headed up the worn stone stairs to the second-floor passage and, all too curious now, Nic followed, keeping his distance. The man seemed to be making for the guest rooms—no doubt his own to dress for dinner—and Nic was beginning to feel foolish tailing him when Lord Ricard emerged from one of the sitting rooms. Arms folded tight, he blocked his brother's way.

"Charles."

"Ah, Ricard."

"Don't 'ah, Ricard' me. I've been looking for you all afternoon."

Nic pulled back out of sight and strained his ears.

"Have you?" Lord Charborough said with a light laugh. "Whatever for?"

"I want you to invoke the Requisite Care Clause."

"What?"

"I said—"

"I heard what you said. Here, step inside before someone else does."

Swift steps. The click of a door. And Nic's heartbeat had sped to an anxious flurry. The Requisite Care Clause—the one the duke had said only that morning that he did not want them to invoke. It was an old law, put in place after a memorable case in 1606 when a lock-in host had threatened guests with starvation if they did not agree to terms. Triggering it would bring a collection of royal vowsmiths and guards charging up from London, and Dashiell had warned there would not be enough time to complete the contract were it invoked so early. Thus it was with a sick swirl is his stomach that Nic hurried to the sitting room door and leaned his head close, desperately hoping no one would come by and see him eavesdropping.

"—that's a failure of their duty of care."

"But Gillingham took his own life, unless there is something you're not telling me, Ricard."

Nic held his breath.

"What I'm telling you is that you need to invoke the damn clause."

"No. Imagine the talk!"

"It wouldn't be us they would be talking about." A beat of silence, followed by another, then Lord Ricard snorted. "Oh you're back at that again, are you? I thought that might be what this was all about. How pathetic. But you know what? I don't care. You gave me your word. You said—"

"Lower your voice! Someone might hear you."

"It makes no difference to me," came Lord Ricard's drawling reply. "I would as happily tell even the scullery maids that you aren't a man of your word."

"Is that a threat?"

"Don't be so dramatic; it doesn't suit you. I am merely reminding you that you made a promise not to make decisions without me, yet here we are."

A footstep and the shifting of cloth sounded beyond the door, and in a low voice, the marquess snarled, "And I have kept that promise again and again even when I did not want to, because I meant it, but this one is for me. Whatever you may wish, I am still the head of this family. My word is final and I am saying no. I did not come all this way to invoke the damn care clause and embarrass us all. And if you use the threat of public spectacle to cow me into following your orders again, like with that damn audit, I'll wash my hands of you."

"Like you could manage without me." Lord Ricard scoffed. "Even here, you sit surrounded by your dusty old manuscripts rather than taking care of this family."

A flutter of paper sent Nic's heart thudding hard against his ribs.

"Stop this," Lord Charborough said. "I know what I am doing, Brother."

"Oh, we all know what, or should I say *who*, you're doing."

"Keep your mouth shut."

"Why should I? You knew I didn't want this contract, yet you went ahead with it anyway."

"And if you had less damned spite, I wouldn't have had to!"

The silence grew taut. Nic knew he ought to move away before one of them made for the door, but shock kept his feet rooted to the floor.

"Just let it go, Ricard," Lord Charborough said after a time, his voice softened. "He has already suffered enough for the mistake."

The answer was a bitter laugh. "If I could believe it *was* a mistake."

"Perhaps if you tried."

On those words, footsteps approached, and with his heart in his throat, Nic darted away along the passage. At the sound of the door opening, he forced himself to slow to a leisurely pace—just a man walking about his own home—and not glance back.

All the way to his own rooms, the conversation churned through Nic's thoughts. And he realised that there was, of course, one very good reason to spend time in someone else's private apartments—a realisation soon followed by another: that Nic didn't really know his father at all.

Chapter 11

Nic was caught in his own thoughts as he made his way down to dinner that evening. Frightening thoughts, from the doctor's pronouncement to the figure in the passage with its living darkness, not to mention Everel's tale and the knowledge that the automaton in the style wing had been the last Lord Francis had made—the one that ended his life. Yet somehow the conversation he'd overheard kept edging its way in, scratching at him with its unanswerable questions and uncomfortable conclusions—uncomfortable to the point that when Nic all but ran into Lord Charborough on the way to the drawing room, he found himself reddening.

"Ah, Monterris," the man said, falling in beside Nic on the landing. "You have my thanks for taking care of Leaf today; she is in vastly improved spirits."

It was a shock to realise that Lord Charborough had asked him to take Leaf out for a walk only that morning, as he himself had work to attend to—a thought that set Nic's imagination wondering what such *work* looked like, only to immediately wish he could scour the result from his mind.

"No thanks required, sir," he said. "I enjoy her company and am glad to be of assistance."

"Yes, I had a feeling you two would get along. The silly little puss was quite set against coming, you know, but I knew all would be well."

Having reached the bottom of the stairs, they turned together toward the drawing room only to be brought up short. A footman stood before the closed door, his expression apologetic.

"The party is meeting in the second drawing room this evening, my lords," the man said, gesturing along the hallway.

"Oh, what is this?" Lord Charborough said. "Change of room? Whatever for?"

"I couldn't say, my lord. You will find His Grace in the second drawing room."

Unable to satisfy the marquess's curiosity, Nic just led the way, leaving Lord Charborough wondering aloud at the inconvenience. He strode in at their arrival, cheerful question already on his lips. "Ah, Val. What's the meaning of changing rooms on us?"

"It seems one of the servants spilled hot coals while tending the fire," the duke said, rising to greet his guest. "We are fortunate to have avoided greater damage, but the floor is heavily singed."

"Ah, rotten luck, that. Was a very fine space."

The same, Nic had to admit, could not be said of the second drawing room, a far smaller space that would not be large enough to set out the card tables after dinner.

"Oh, do you mean like this?"

Sigils whispered against Nic's mind as Lady Lisbeth demonstrated some charmwork to Dashiell, the accent of her Brilliance altogether strange. Through the glimmering air, the vowsmith glanced his way, perhaps thinking of their conversation that morning, or wondering what of the magic Nic felt. It would have been so easy for Nic to stroll over and reassure him, to retrieve something of their old friendship, but it was also far too dangerous.

Nic was saved from the urge by Leaf's arrival, her evening gown a gossamer cascade of pale green layers. "Oh good, you're already here." She took his arm and resolutely led him to a sofa as far from the others as they could get.

"All right, me first," she said, straightening her skirts as she sat.

"Gillingham's room is a mess. It is, of course, entirely possible he was just untidy, although I think it's more likely someone searched it before I got there and didn't bother straightening up after themselves."

"Searched it? Any idea what they might have been looking for?"

"No. His portmanteau and all his valises were open, clothing and personal items strewn around along with papers and even a few books. Some of it was quite interesting, but not worth killing him for. How did you fare? Any luck with that tape?"

Nic had almost forgotten about the tape, having done nothing more than drop it on his worktable before seeing Master Everel. He wasn't quite ready to share the contents of that conversation with her, however, so he said, "Nothing yet, though I spoke to a number of the servants. None of them saw or heard anything suspicious, and none of them saw Gillingham at any point in the afternoon. I asked one of the maids about when the room was cleaned, and she said the central rooms aren't being properly cleaned at all, but the glassware was cleared away at the end of the session."

"Not being cleaned? Surely they must be."

"That was my thought too, but she was very definite that Mrs. Podmarsh—that's our housekeeper—had given orders that other than tending fires, the only thing to be done in the central rooms is clearing tables."

"Perhaps she just meant during daylight hours," Leaf said. "My grandmother is like that, you know, hates having servants scurrying in and out and insists they work only when she's not around. What about the ladder?"

"The groundskeeper brought it in yesterday because one of the portraits in the hall needed rehanging."

Leaf gave something of a defeated shrug. "So it would have just been lying around for anyone to take."

"So it seems."

"Then neither of us found anything useful."

"There is something else."

She raised her dark brows in hopeful anticipation. The rest of the party remained gathered around the fireplace in a bubble of bright chatter, yet Nic lowered his voice all the same.

"I overheard your uncle and your father arguing," he said. "After I saw your father come out of my father's rooms."

"Out of your father's rooms? Do you mean his study?"

"No."

With barely a pause for breath, Nic proceeded to tell her everything he had seen and heard on his way in from the grounds, from Lord Ricard's demand to have the Requisite Care Clause invoked to her father's plea for him to let his anger go. While he spoke, Leaf's expression shifted rapidly from shock to confusion to a pensive little frown, her hands clasped tightly in her lap.

"That makes it sound like our fathers have . . ."

"Yes," Nic said when she didn't finish. "That's what I thought too."

A crease cut between her brows. "And you're saying it was my father who initiated this contract?"

"He didn't tell you so?"

"No! He said your father made the offer. That is just like him, though, to lie if it meant avoiding an argument. Not that it stopped me putting my sasinage contract in front of him for the twenty-third time."

"You keep count?"

"Yes, I find it helps cushion the refusal somehow."

For a few long seconds, she stared across the room at her father standing by the fire, his broad shoulders squared and his gaze resting upon the duke with a faint smile.

"And Uncle Ricard didn't want him to make the offer at all," she said after a time, as though she was slowly working through the implications of his words. "And wants to browbeat him into giving it up by invoking the Requisite Care Clause. I think my uncle dislikes your father very much."

"While your father likes him very much."

"Yes," she agreed. "That might be so, although it doesn't help us with who killed Mr. Gillingham."

"No," Nic said. "And it—"

Leaf gasped, gripping his arm. "Unless Uncle Ricard wanted a reason to invoke the clause! A valet dying wouldn't be enough, I shouldn't think, but one of the negotiation party would be."

"But why Gillingham? He could have chosen one of the others rather than his own man."

Nic tried his best not to think about Dashiell's lifeless body hanging from the chandelier and failed.

"Perhaps because it was easiest. They spent a lot of time together, and though Uncle Ricard would likely have kept Gillingham on despite his excommunication, without his ties to the guild his usefulness would have been greatly diminished."

She wasn't wrong, and Nic found himself watching Lord Ricard across the room. The man sat with a newspaper open before him, ignoring everyone gathered in preparation for dinner. "He did leave to meet Gillingham not long before the man was found. For all we know he asked Gillingham to meet him in the negotiation chamber."

"It fits horribly well," Leaf said. "Although if he did kill Gillingham to make my father invoke the care clause, does Papa's refusal mean he will have to try again?"

The horrifying possibility that Gillingham's death might not be the last shivered through Nic's skin. "We had better keep an eye on him this evening."

"Agreed," she said. "Although that might be difficult if he leaves early again."

On her words, the dinner bell sounded. One by one the gathered company got to their feet, their movement dragging the evening inexorably on.

"We could be wrong," Nic said, all too aware of how much wishful thinking rang in his words.

"We could be," Leaf agreed, rising. "But it wouldn't change the fact that unless it was one of the servants, Gillingham was murdered by someone in this room."

That evening's entertainment was to be cards, so after dinner the whole party—Lord Ricard included—made their way to the conservatory. The conservatory had always been Nic's favourite room. It owned less grandeur for grandeur's sake and, with its long bank of windows, was often the lightest, warmest room in the Court. Indoor plants flourished in a collection of ornamental pots and containers, filling the space with greenery, while a large cage of echoes helped Nic feel less alone whenever isolation became a visceral ache inside his flesh.

Card tables had already been set up, yet as the guests filed in, Lord Ricard said, "I'm all for cards, but I seem to recall Lord Monterris promised us a song."

It was a private party and Lord Ricard was a guest, but to make such a demand seemed poor form. Lord Charborough must have thought so, for he said, "It hardly seems appropriate after last night, Ricard."

"Then he can sing something sad."

It was almost a snap, and as Lord Ricard threw a sneering glance the duke's way, Nic realised the request had nothing to do with him.

All eyes turned to the duke and Nic could imagine the war taking place inside his father's breast. Which was the lesser evil?

Satisfying Lord Ricard's gleeful prodding by refusing permission, or letting his son sing?

We don't need another useless conjuror in this family.

The hissed words had cut deep, and in that moment Nic decided he didn't want his father to choose for him. Nic had never been a good enough son and never would be, but with Leaf and Dashiell and his mother smiling his way, he could choose to fly.

"Something sad?" Nic said, making a bow. "I think I can manage that."

"Well, well," Lord Charborough said, flicking a glance the duke's way. "So long as you're sure, Monterris, let's pull over some chairs."

A flurry of activity filled the room, all scraping chair legs and rustling skirts as their guests made a makeshift arc. At its focal point, Nic stood stretching his fingers, his excitement fast mingling with dread as every eye settled upon him. The duke's were indiscernible behind his glasses, but Nic knew the blank stare of a man holding in fury when he saw it. Sitting close next to him, Lord Charborough had one leg stretched out before the echo cage, while at the back of the group, Dashiell stood with his hands loosely grasping an empty chair. Of all those present, the duchess had seen Nic perform the most, but still she sat close, wearing a broad, eager smile.

His chosen song told the story of a maid who fell in love with a lord, a tragic tale for which Nic conjured no pale canvas, no golden garden, just a single, detailed tree made from dozens of curling scrolls. He traced them slowly, much as a beginner might when learning a sigil's shape, and knew the joy of having his audience's rapt attention.

Like the tree, the song had a deceptively simple beginning, only to grow in range with its characters' sorrows—characters he formed as silhouettes, each with a heart coloured for their mood. He'd always loved the way it looked and, full of pride, his voice rose and his fingers danced.

As he sang, Nic found himself looking at his mother. She often slipped into dark moods and seemed rarely to live in the same reality, yet she alone had always encouraged him, always listened. She listened now as his song swelled and Nic didn't care what anyone else thought. Let them see who he was, consequences be damned—let his father see what Nic could have accomplished had his skills been encouraged, not condemned.

The fury that burned inside him at everything he had been denied cracked out into the fury of the song's penultimate verse, the hurt of his characters bleeding out as though Nic had cut himself open. It carried him to the end without making a single egregious error, and upon the last notes, he lowered his hands and let both the song and the conjured lights fade away. His fingers ached, but his heart sang.

His small audience applauded, seemingly as much in surprise as pleasure.

"Excellent work," Lord Charborough said, though beside him the duke kept his arms folded. "Very nice."

Lady Lisbeth dabbed her eyes. "That was so moving."

"Quite a performance indeed," Lady Theresa agreed.

Rising from her chair, Leaf came forward, all smiles beneath an attempt at formality. "Lord Monterris, that was *truly* a joy. Thank you."

Nic bowed. "I am glad to have entertained you, my lady."

"I did not think you were so well practiced," she added in a lower voice. "And now I must apologise for doubting you."

"When one's father hates what you love, you don't stop doing it. You just stop doing it where he can see."

He had meant the words humorously, but her smile turned sad as she glanced toward the unmoving duke.

"The perfect appetiser to cards, don't you think, Val?" Lord Charborough said, rising from his chair.

"Indeed." Nic's father did not so much as glance at his son as he rose. "Everel, have the footmen reset the chairs."

As the hubbub of movement once more rose around him, Nic found Dashiell had not moved. He was still holding the back of a chair, still watching him.

"My darling," the duchess said, coming to clasp Nic's hands. "You are always so remarkable. And so brave."

"Thank you, Mama." He squeezed her hands. "I could not do it without you."

"All I've ever wanted was to save you."

Her gaze slid out of focus as she spoke, leaving disquiet squirming in Nic's stomach. "Save me?"

"From the house."

Leaf had disappeared as the chairs were reset, but in a flurry of emerald skirts she returned to grip his arm. "Nic, we are making up tables. Come be my partner for Battara."

"Oh. Right. Of course. Will you be playing, Mama?"

She blinked, a hint of confusion behind her eyes as she shook her head. "No, my love, you go. Enjoy yourself."

Leaf had hurried off again, and by the time Nic joined her at the table she had already collected Dashiell as well, the smile she shot Nic as he sat beside the vowsmith one of mingled mischief and triumph. It was all Nic could do not to glare back.

"Oh, may I join you?" Lady Lisbeth said, letting go of Millie's arm and sailing over, eyes on Dashiell. "Do you need a partner, Master sa Vare?"

"I do indeed, my lady," Dashiell said, gesturing to the empty seat across from him. Lady Lisbeth hastily settled into it, leaving Millie to pull a face at her and turn away to join her father and stepmother at the other table. The doctor made up their fourth, while the duke and Lord Charborough pulled out chairs at the third table.

"Your Grace," Master Everel said, with a light touch upon the duchess's arm to get her attention. "Shall we make up a team?"

It was cordially asked, but Nic cringed inwardly before the question had fully passed the man's lips. His hope that his mother's quiet mood might hold shattered as she spun a scowl on the old vowsmith.

"Do not touch me! As well I should partner with a snake!"

Lady Theresa gasped, gripping her husband's arm as the room stuttered into silence. Nic's stomach dropped, and he couldn't but think of how their guests had stared at his mother the night before, seeming to find her wild cries more upsetting than Mr. Gillingham's hanging body. It mattered not that she was distressed while her oddities were so distressing to them.

Nic made to rise, but stopped when Silla broke away from her place near the door—she the only one who dared move amid the frozen tableau. "Your Grace," she said, taking her mistress's arm. "It has been a long day. How about we get you settled in for a rest?"

The duchess flinched and looked down at her maid's hand, confusion fading in and out upon her face. For a moment Nic thought she might argue, but the anger that had flared at Master Everel's touch shrank away and she nodded.

Nic let out a slow breath as Silla led the duchess toward the door, hating the taste of relief his mother's docility left in its wake. Despite her calm demeanour, stares followed her all the way, only turning to the duke once the door had closed behind her. But whatever surprise others might have felt, Nic felt none when his father just looked away.

"Shall we dice instead, Charles?" the duke drawled, the words an end to the incident as far as he was concerned.

Lord Charborough hesitated, glancing at the door, but as there seemed nothing to say, he soon assented. Master Everel was sent for dice and the evening spun on, leaving Nic with the feeling every curious eye was now on him. "They have never gotten along," he said loud enough for the other table to hear. It wasn't a lie so much as an omission, the statement papering over years during which Master Everel had been the bearer of the duke's commands, refusing her requests and calling in doctors.

"Like Millie and Lady Theresa," Lady Lisbeth whispered with a theatrical grimace, causing Leaf to laugh.

"Oh no, Lizzy, that is far worse."

As the party settled back into easy talk, Nic glanced toward the door, wondering if he ought to go after his mother. It would look particular and Silla was better at settling her, yet a creeping sense of guilt remained as the evening continued without her.

Leaf slid a pack of shimmering cards across the table to Dashiell. "Master sa Vare, I assume you number shuffling among your many talents."

"I wouldn't call it a talent, my lady," he said, picking them up, "but I'm certainly capable."

He began shuffling, the easy movement of his fingers drawing Lady Lisbeth's rapt attention. "That is what you call merely capable, Master sa Vare?" she asked as he dealt. "I am sure I could not work so swiftly without the cards going all over the floor."

"It is a lucky side effect of smithing that one becomes good with their hands. Although my skill is nothing to what Lord Monterris can do, of course."

It was lightly said, but Nic suddenly felt he was sitting all too close. Safest to excuse himself, to go after his mother and stop recalling just how skilled Dashiell's fingers could be and where on his body they had traced. Still, he did not move.

"It must be very interesting, being a vowsmith," Lady Lisbeth said, taking a cake from a proffered refreshment tray. "Do you enjoy it?"

"For the most part." Dashiell dropped a last card in front of himself before setting the remaining stack in the centre of the table. "Like everything, there are times it's tedious, but I enjoy travelling, and the Brilliance itself continues to fascinate me."

"Where have you travelled?"

"Well, I have been to many places around England—Devonshire, Cheshire, Yorkshire, Cornwall—but have also been to Paris, Amsterdam, and Naples, among others."

While Nic had been nowhere, his knowledge of the world gleaned from pictures and travelogues.

"So many places," Lady Lisbeth said. "Do you have a favourite?"

"If I had to choose, I would say Cornwall," Dashiell said. "It's quiet and beautiful, with moorlands that stretch for miles, although in truth I get fidgety if I stay in any one place too long. A side effect perhaps of never having thought of anywhere as home."

Nic felt rather than saw Dashiell's gaze shy his way, and didn't meet it. He had felt elated after the song, but now his hands sat as heavily on the table as his heart sat in his chest. Never had he considered—truly considered—just how different their lives had become. All those years ago they had just been two boys learning the same craft, each the only company the other had. While Nic's horizon had not broadened in the intervening years, Dashiell had travelled widely, plied his craft on his own terms, and been free in a way Nic had never known. Nine years had done nothing for Nic, but it had made a charming man of the world out of Dashiell.

Little wonder the vowsmith had been sorry for his moment of unprofessionalism in the dark hallway outside Nic's room. He had long since left poor, provincial Nic behind.

Never had Nic felt so shrivelled up with shame, thus it seemed fitting that his evening entertainment was to be watching Lady Lisbeth flirt with Dashiell as they played. She seemed to have decided that a promising career and a beautiful face could indeed offset the ill that was his lack of title, and Nic couldn't blame her. He really was beautiful, with his even features and his perfect hair and a pair of lips that curved just so. Yet only part of Dashiell's beauty could ever be captured in a portrait, most of it stemming rather from the movement of those expressive brows, from the way his lips pressed tight to smother an inappropriate laugh, and the quiet way he observed the world, his bronze eyes seeming to genuinely see where others merely looked. Nic watched him between points, wondering what he thought of the lady's interest.

"Oh no, I fear I have quite let you down, Master sa Vare," Lady Lisbeth said, setting her final card on a losing point with a carelessly formed sigil. "We shall have to improve our game to beat these two. They're very in tune with one another."

"Beginner's luck." Dashiell flicked a laughing glance Nic's way.

Nic's brows shot up. "Watch who you're calling a beginner."

The words were out before he could think better of them, before he could consider the meaning he had both intended and not in equal measure, before he could look away from Dashiell's intent gaze, stealing his breath with its calm, unblinking confidence.

Nic looked at the door again, wondering if he could slip away unnoticed. In the end, he settled for taking a gulp of wine and leaning back in his chair, attempting bored indifference.

Leaf called for another cake and Dashiell for more wine, while Lady Lisbeth watched the vowsmith take up the cards and shuffle again. He did have very nice hands. Long fingers, neatly kept nails, and the strength of one who has honed his ability to form accurate sigils over and over again without error for hours on end. He had calluses where he held his quill, but Nic hadn't noticed the other night, his touch having been all thrill.

"I am determined we shall win this round," Lady Lisbeth said as a celebratory crow rose at the other table, someone having dropped a final sigil onto a winning point. "Leaf and Lord Monterris cannot have all the luck."

Dashiell finished dealing as Leaf, having licked icing off her fingers, surreptitiously wiped them on her dress. Nic lifted his brows at her, grinning—a grin that froze as Dashiell shifted in his chair, his knee coming to rest against Nic's. It was just a knee, just a touch, but Dashiell did not move it away. He picked up his cards as though nothing had happened, leaving Nic's heart thumping.

Play resumed, but Dashiell's knee didn't move, and if not for Leaf's skill at the game, they would have lost every point from then on to Nic's abstraction. Rounds went by, each sigil and card nothing but a beat in a song of ever-increasing torture. He could have moved his own damn knee but didn't, and by the fourth glass of wine was wondering if they'd both gotten caught in a strange game where they refused to be the first to move, since to move would be to admit they had touched at all.

Two hours passed—three—before Nic realised only the two tables at play remained. The duke and Lord Charborough had gone, as had the servants, leaving only the gently smouldering fire and a collection of candles fighting back the night.

At the other table, Lady Theresa yawned and declared she didn't know when it had gotten so late. Spits of rain were beginning to slash the windowpanes as Dashiell dealt another round. He showed no sign of fatigue. Nic couldn't decide if the time had sped or dragged, couldn't even recall how many rounds he and Leaf had won. There had just been the touch of Dashiell's knee and the steady intake of his breath, his ever-present scent and a curl of hair that kept falling onto his brow that Nic longed to brush back.

Feeling more drunk than the amount of wine he'd imbibed ought to allow, Nic stared at that curl as he took up his cards. As he splayed them out, he wondered if Dashiell could feel it there, tickling his brow. And didn't realise until too late that Dashiell was watching him. Nic should have looked away, yet something in the vowsmith's expression held him there like a gripped hand.

"Ah, another loss," Lady Theresa sighed at the other table. "We played well, Doctor, but I fear we are undone and I am for my bed."

With scrapes of chairs, the other table was breaking up. Lady Theresa strode over, stifling a yawn, and set her hand on Leaf's shoulder. "How are you faring, my dear?"

"We are up by one, Aunt, but as I fear this will be our last, it may yet end in a draw," Leaf said. "But in case we decide to play a tiebreaker, don't wait up for me. I have Lizzy to bear me company."

"Well, don't stay up too late, or you'll be abed until noon."

After a murmur of good nights, only Millie remained from the other table, having leaned on the back of Lady Lisbeth's chair to observe the play. She was soon stifling yawns, her eyelids drooping.

"Oh, poor Millie," Leaf said. "Perhaps we should call it a night after all."

"One more hand will not take long," Lady Lisbeth said. "You must watch Master sa Vare shuffle, Millie; his hands are so quick you can hardly see the cards."

"She will see nothing at all with her eyes half-closed. Here." Leaf slid her remaining cards across the table to Nic. "You can play for us both. Lizzy, give your cards to Master sa Vare. We can safely leave this round and the decider to them."

A little reluctantly, Lisbeth handed her cards to Dashiell, holding them so he would have to touch her fingers. He did so without any awkwardness, and both he and Nic rose to wish the ladies a polite good night.

"Are you sure you don't wish to stay and watch them wage battle, Leaf?" Lady Lisbeth said. "It's sure to be entertaining."

"Oh no, maybe tomorrow night. I daresay Lord Monterris and Master sa Vare will not be far behind us."

The look she threw Nic was so arch that he almost announced his intention of retiring as well, his cheeks heating as she steered her two companions out of the room and firmly closed the door. In their wake, distant thunder rumbled.

Dashiell settled back into his chair. "Shall we?"

Nic's heart thumped against his breastbone. Dashiell had only indicated the cards, yet when Nic tried to speak a nonchalant "Why not?" it came out a strangled cough. It was Nic's turn, so he played a card, and by some miracle it must have been the right sort of card, because Dashiell followed it with one of his own.

Card after card they emptied their hands with hasty sigils, not speaking even when Dashiell won a particularly surprising point, his hand sweeping in to take the cards without a smile. He looked bored. Ready to be finished. He played at random, discarded at random, a little notch between his brows growing deeper and deeper.

Eventually the last point was played and Dashiell sat back, leaving the messy pile of cards strewn in the centre of the table. Nic had won in the end—at least he thought he had. It hardly seemed to matter.

Bit by bit the room had grown dark around them as the fire died, their pool of candlelight all that remained. Outside, light drops of rain struck the windowpanes, and thinking of another time they had sat in this very room on a gloomy day, Nic murmured, "Can you hear the music?"

Dashiell didn't smile.

Assailed by the sudden need to escape before he broke, Nic rose. "I'm for my bed."

"Yes." Dashiell pushed back his chair. Abandoning the cards and the wineglasses, he walked around the table putting out the candles. A lick to his fingers and each one hissed into darkness, leaving a curl of smoke rising to the ceiling.

Soon only a single candle remained. Gesturing to it, Nic said, "You can take that one. I know my way." And feeling like a ghost, he made for the door, shadows slowly swallowing him.

"Nic."

Nic halted yet did not immediately turn, something in the tenor of his name part question, part plea. He ought to say good night and leave rather than risk more beautiful regrets Dashiell would have to apologise for, but knew he wouldn't.

He turned slowly, not hiding his wariness, nor the hard swallow he forced down upon finding Dashiell standing close in the half-light. For a few long seconds, the vowsmith didn't speak, didn't move, before he lifted his hand to the hair at Nic's temple. Gentle as a breeze, that soft touch ghosted down his cheek, fingers coming to rest upon his chin. Yet for all its lightness, Nic felt the trail like it had been seared into his skin, and it was all he could do not to hold his breath.

There was little difference in their heights, yet Dashiell tilted Nic's face up to better catch the meagre light—a man seeking to look his fill, gaze hungry.

"You're beautiful," he murmured, and still holding Nic's chin, he leaned close. For a moment he held their lips a breath apart, before he brushed the tip of his nose against Nic's—a forgotten gesture recollected upon a rush of memories, each of a time they had stood so while Dashiell asked his silent permission.

Chest tight, Nic returned the gesture, knowing what it meant and wanting its every consequence.

The kiss that followed began softly, pressed to Nic's lips with the caution of one expecting him to disappear, to push away—a reasonable fear after their last kiss had ended in apology and anger over the breakfast table. Likely it would again, but Dashiell's overt desire was as intoxicating as the wine, suspending every impulse toward self-preservation.

Nic leaned in, deepening the kiss, knowing he might never again have the opportunity to do so. Every touch and taste and tiny moan could be the last and he wanted them all, lifting his hands to Dashiell's face like this time he could truly hold him present forever.

As though Nic's fervour had been the true permission, Dashiell's hesitance evaporated upon a guttural, needy groan. His hands slid down Nic's back to his hips and gripped tight, pulling their bodies hard against one another, the layers of fabric a cruelty.

With his thoughts whirling into a tangle, Nic gave ground until he hit the covered aviary, and they were back where they had left off in the hallway outside Nic's rooms, gasping and hungry. Only this time when Dashiell pulled away, it was to shed his coat, his fingers plucking at stubborn buttons.

Coats and waistcoats abandoned, Dashiell once more pushed Nic up against the aviary, hard enough to shake the curving metal bars. Nic might have protested against frightening the birds, but Dashiell slid his knee between his legs, stealing what little remained of his sanity. So instead he tore at the buttons of Dashiell's shirt and pulled it up over his head.

The man who emerged, naked to the waist, was magnificent, his hair tousled from its former neatness and his eyes ablaze. Their long-buried ember had been fanned to an inferno now, as much by their incomplete history as the illicit moment they were stealing, by a night spent wanting and wanting and unable to have.

Nic ought to have felt cold when he pulled off his own shirt, but the warmth of Dashiell's chest pressed to his allowed no chill as they backed toward the moonlight. No words, just a shared need, just Dashiell's hands and his heat and the breathless huff of his desire. It turned into a short laugh as Nic's heels hit the window seat and he overbalanced, dropping onto its worn cushions—the perfect symmetry of such a moment bringing them back to where it had all begun.

Nic remembered that first kiss for his own stunned joy, and for the way Dashiell had looked at him afterward, awestruck and shy.

But the years had changed much, for as they sank into the space their prior selves had occupied, there was nothing shy in the way Dashiell sat astride him, pinning Nic possessively in place. Nic had never seen such fire in him. He had always been polite, mild, soft-spoken Dashiell, not this glorious creature, groaning against Nic's open mouth as he ground their hips together.

God knew he had dreamed of this moment, but even in his wildest imaginings, it hadn't been quite like this.

Able to reach nowhere else, Nic ran his hands up the smooth expanse of Dashiell's back, causing him to arch and pull from their kiss with a gasp. With another lover, he might have chuckled at such sensitivity, but all he wanted was to make Dashiell do it again, make him bare his throat so Nic could slide his tongue down its ridges.

All of a sudden, Dashiell pulled away, stumbling to his feet. Nic endured a flare of panic that once again it was over before it had begun, but Dashiell was pulling off his breeches, working with a speed that made Nic recollect all that had ever been said about a vowsmith's skilled hands.

Following suit, Nic discarded the last of his own clothing, throwing aside his breeches to find Dashiell standing naked in the shreds of storm-mottled moonlight. Nic almost swallowed his tongue. The years had filled him out, replacing a slim youth with a man so perfectly proportioned that a sculptor might have wept—he had a pair of muscular thighs and broad well-defined shoulders, yet there was a delicacy to the bones of his wrists and ankles that drew the eye just as hungrily.

For whole heartbeats, Nic found himself able to do nothing but stare. Dashiell stared back, tension growing every second they did not touch.

The vowsmith broke first. One step, two, and with the groan of a man goaded beyond bearing he pulled Nic close until they stood skin to skin, their kiss a fight for mastery. But despite the anger he'd been carrying, here and now Nic realised he wanted nothing more than to lose, such that when Dashiell spoke his breathless question against Nic's lips, he was ready for it.

"May I—?"

"Yes."

The speed with which Nic answered seemed to act as a final goad, and gripping his shoulder, Dashiell turned him to the window. Nose inches from the glass, Nic had a moment to breathe, to anticipate, the thrill of expected touch making his skin tingle.

Before he could ask the next question, Dashiell's hands were on him, already slick with oil. But Nic's surprise that he was so prepared lasted only a moment, because everything Dashiell had said and done all night had been leading to this. Now his gentle but expert ministrations were enough to spark a flare of jealousy toward everyone else the man had ever touched—a foolish thought soon chased away by the glorious sensation of Dashiell easing into him.

Nic wished he didn't have to stifle the cry that tore up his throat, wished he could give voice to the mingling pleasure and pain as Dashiell pushed deeper, but some small part of him was just aware enough to remember they weren't alone in the house. To remember how dangerous it would be if they were caught.

And so he pressed his open mouth against his forearm and cried out against his own skin, letting the world shrink to the rain outside and the rhythmic huff of Dashiell's breath. Revelling in every thrust, Nic dropped a hand to his own straining cock and gave himself over entirely to the sensations, the pair of them moving together as though they had melted into a single gasping body.

Nic lasted longer than he thought he would in such circumstances, but it could never be long enough and all too soon he spent onto his own hand as Dashiell's final cry was bitten back into his throat. And there they collapsed together against the window, a sweaty pair of bodies shuddering the last of their passion against the cold glass.

Dashiell groaned, and levered himself off Nic's back. "God, I needed that."

"*You* needed that?"

The groan became a laugh. "All right, *we* needed that. Needed to get that out so we could stop thinking about it every waking second. Although I think we both would have been happier if we'd had this closure years ago."

Nic ought to be glad that Dashiell's mind had been veering toward this as much as his, but something about the word *closure* chilled his skin faster than the cold glass against which he leaned.

They had not begun with a promise of more, yet nor were they strangers, able to fuck and escape because it all meant nothing.

Nic turned to find Dashiell drawing on his breeches in the pale, stormy moonlight. And as he pulled on his own, he watched for any sign of discomposure, any sign he wasn't the only one whose heart ached in the aftermath. But Dashiell just gathered his clothes as though nothing momentous had happened.

With his shirt back in place, he turned to use the dark window over Nic's head as a poor mirror, those fingers that had touched every part of Nic's body now perfecting the folds of his neckcloth. Perhaps he sensed he was being watched, for once he had finished, he glanced down.

"Your song was amazing, Nic," he said, meeting Nic's gaze with a guarded look. "I knew you were talented, but . . ." His smile became a wry, lopsided thing. And with the incomplete compliment hanging between them, Dashiell bent to press a soft kiss to Nic's lips. It lasted only a heartbeat before the vowsmith pulled away, his smile there and gone as fast—everything about him so achingly tender yet restrained like he feared to let go of something held tight beneath his skin.

Nic couldn't but think of a younger Dashiell, creeping into Nic's room the day before he'd left. They'd kissed until their lips were raw, and half-clothed had ground out inexpert pleasure against one another in the failing candlelight. Yet in the aftermath something had been wrong. It was the same now, Dashiell moving to escape with equal speed, pulling on his coat and folding himself back in behind a faint impersonal smile.

"I'm glad we got our closure," he added once he looked again like the professional vowsmith he'd come there to be. "Even if we had to wait nine years for it."

There was something final about the words *what happens next*, not a conversation but a conclusion Dashiell had already decided upon—a conclusion so obvious it merited no discussion.

When Nic didn't answer, a wary light crept into Dashiell's gaze, yet he didn't linger. He made for the last candle they'd left burning, still awaiting him on the table.

"Would you like me to light another for you?" he said, picking it up.

"No."

"Right. Well. Then I guess I shall bid you good night, Lord Monterris."

"Good night, Master sa Vare."

Nic wasn't sure what he'd expected, but it hadn't been this easy stride toward the door, all hint of hesitance left behind. Dashiell didn't even glance back. He just stepped out into the dark hallway carrying his candle, his departure slamming shut a door they had only just opened. Because whatever Dashiell wanted to call it, after nine years such a moment was no closure. It was a resurrection.

Chapter 12

Nic avoided breakfast the following morning, refusing to leave his rooms until negotiations had begun for the day. He told himself he was too tired to make small talk. That he hadn't slept well. That he was just lying in for his health. It had nothing—all right, *everything*—to do with Dashiell.

Eventually the promise of wine lured him out of bed, and he sat at his workbench drinking while Ambrose watched on warily. He'd brought up a breakfast tray that Nic was ignoring, and seemed unwilling to click his tongue in fond disapproval the way Rowerre would have—a fact that made Nic empty the last of the decanter into his glass.

"You had better fetch more," he said, holding it out to his new valet.

"Of course, my lord." Ambrose took it, but hesitated. "Perhaps you would also like some tea? I brought up—"

"Tea is for men who didn't wake feeling like they've been trampled all over. Enough wine and I will soon feel much better, I assure you."

Ambrose went out, leaving Nic to drink and stare at the tumble of sigil tape he'd left on his workbench the day before. Perhaps if he stared at it long enough the solid darkness would leap out and swallow him. Then he needn't keep reliving Dashiell's . . . everything.

At the thought of Dashiell's everything, Nic tipped the remaining dregs of wine into his mouth, only for someone to knock on the door. Nic leaned his head back with a sigh. "What?"

"What?" Leaf repeated, opening the door without invitation. "*What?* Is that how I can expect to be greeted as your wife?"

"Leaf. What are you doing here?"

"Checking on you of course," she said, closing the door. "Also, Millie and Lisbeth are embroidering and talking about romances and I just don't see the appeal in a book where no one gets murdered."

Quick steps brought her across the sitting room, and plucking at the pale cambric of her morning dress, she sat next to him at the table.

"Leaf?"

"Yes, darling?"

"You can't be here."

"Yes, but everywhere else is boring and we have to discuss our investigation somewhere safe. Besides, no one will know."

With perfect timing, Ambrose backed in carrying a fresh decanter. After bumping the door closed with his foot, the new valet froze. "Lady Leaf, my apologies, I—"

"Don't worry, Ambrose," Nic said. "She was just leaving."

"No, I'm not. Ambrose can be our chaperone if you insist on being so stuffy."

The young man set the decanter on the small dining table, a wary look shot from Nic to Leaf and back. "I . . . I could tidy his lordship's wardrobe?"

"Perfect," Leaf said. "I'll shout if he's being ungentlemanly."

"Very good, my lady."

Ambrose waited a moment as though for a contrary order before turning stiffly and striding into Nic's dressing room. Overloud sounds of activity soon emanated through the open door.

"Oh, are those your creations?" Leaf said, jumping up as she caught sight of the automata on the mantelpiece.

"Some of them. Mama has a lot more in her rooms."

Leaf examined a mechanical echo and stroked a small cat that purred at her touch. "They're amazing, Nic." Moving along, she picked up one of the many frogs and wound the key. As it started to hop, she set it on the floor, where its throat bulged with a scrape of fine metal plates. "I can almost smell the pond."

"You can," Nic said, rubbing his eyes as though hoping to clear the wine from his hazy thoughts. "That's *tah eb bett mora nur bat nur bat haam*." He formed the sigils and the scent of pond bloomed and faded, leaving Leaf's eyes wide.

"You put scent onto its reel? I didn't even know smells could be conjured."

"Really?"

"Really. How did you do it?"

Nic shrugged. "I worked from the basic format used to make sound and speech. The interesting failures kept me entertained for months, but then . . ." He gestured at the frog. "Swamp stink. And nicer smells of course, but I'm amused that the first I made was swamp stink."

Leaf wound up the frog a second time and set her nose so close that the metal creature almost hopped into her face. "That really is amazing. And no, I've never heard of smells being conjured, but you should ask your Master sa Vare; he'll know."

"He's not mine and I will absolutely not be doing that."

She gave him a long stare that he entirely failed to hold, recollections ruining his focus as much as the wine. Leaf narrowed her eyes. "Have you been drinking?"

"Before breakfast? What a terrible idea."

"But you have been, haven't you?" She looked to the empty wineglass and the decanter Ambrose had left on the table. "Are you all right, Nic? Did something happ—?"

"No. I merely have rotten habits. Now, you said you wanted to talk about our investigation, so talk."

A worried frown darkened her brow, and for a moment Nic feared she would take his hand or make some other show of sympathy calculated to induce tears. Thankfully she refrained, instead returning to her chair with a sigh.

"We ought to go over what we know," she said. "To begin with, I watched Uncle Ricard last night."

Nic winced. He had utterly forgotten to watch the man, so caught up he had been on Dashiell. Two men had died and all he had thought about was the vowsmith's knee against his beneath the table.

"He looked to be in decent spirits," she went on, "although nothing out of the ordinary. Spending time with Millie always cheers him up. Our fathers just diced for a while and then bid the company good night. That they left together and early does, I suppose, lend some weight to your suspicion, however."

For the second time, Nic found his imagination taking him too far toward what might happen beyond the duke's closed door, although this time when he pulled his thoughts back, it was a naked Dashiell that waited.

Nic's breath hitched.

We both would have been happier if we'd had this closure years ago.

Leaf nudged him. "Nic?" She gasped and lowered her voice to an excited whisper. "I thought there was something you weren't telling me. Is that what's wrong? Did you and Master sa Vare—"

"No! Shh!"

Nic looked around to be sure Ambrose was still in the dressing room. "All right, yes, but you can't tell anyone."

"What was it like?"

He thought of Dashiell's hot chest pressed against him. Of the hunger with which the vowsmith had gripped his hips. Of his cock filling Nic up completely.

"Fine."

Leaf had that look again.

"All right, it was great, but it's not like it was my first time. And you don't have to look so smug."

"Great? That's all I'm going to get? After everything I did to get you two time alone."

"What . . . what more do you want?" Nic met her curiosity with a mixture of amusement, horror, and all too strong an urge to share every detail.

"I don't know. Millie tells us all sorts of things from her trysts. It sounds very exciting, but also a little . . ." Leaf made a face. "Is it so worth it?"

"Yes."

"You answered that fast."

How could he put into words how it felt? He had wanted Dashiell for years, only to have to tuck that desire away deep down where it could no longer hurt. And then when he'd been sure he was over it, the man had walked back into his life and slammed him into a wall with a need that bordered on desperation, before taking him by the very window seat where they'd first kissed.

Nic shrugged. It was easier not to think about why he had already downed three glasses of wine on an empty stomach that morning. Except that said stomach was starting to rebel.

"All right, well, we should probably decide what to do next," Leaf said, letting the subject drop. "I feel certain that Uncle Ricard killed Gillingham, but we'll need to prove it. Unfortunately, we have no witnesses, no definitive evidence, and I cannot convince myself that if making Papa invoke the clause was his motive that he would have murdered your valet first. Unless—"

She broke off on a gasp and gripped Nic's arm. "The paper," she said. "You said he had a piece of paper. And he claimed he had to wait on my uncle."

"Yes, but we know he didn't."

"No, although if you wanted to get into a guest's room, that would be a good excuse, wouldn't it? Uncle Ricard has all his papers with him and even some archival material that we brought for the contract. Could His Grace have sent Rowerre to steal something from my uncle?"

Though the question of what and why hovered on Nic's lips, the possibility made a terrible sort of sense. "You think Rowerre might have been killed because your uncle wanted back what was stolen?"

"If it was important enough to steal, it's important enough to want returned." She jumped up. "We need to search my uncle's rooms."

Lord Ricard's guest suite was near Leaf's on the second floor. She had wanted to go at once, but Nic had needed food. And water. And half an hour sitting still. And even then he was only moderately confident he wasn't going to be sick.

"You really shouldn't have drunk anything so early," she said for the fifth time as they made their way to the man's door.

"Probably not, but it worked."

"How so?"

"Well, I feel awful about something different now, don't I?"

Leaf's eyes narrowed. "I thought you said it was great. With . . . you know . . . I mean."

"It was, yes." Nic winced, trying not to think about Dashiell's muscular thighs and failing. "Can we just focus on this?"

For a moment it seemed like she would ask more, but their arrival at Lord Ricard's rooms stayed her tongue. Instead, she shot him a warning look, and pushed the door open.

Hello?" she called, poking her head into the room. "Uncle Ricard?"

No answer, no sounds. Leaf stepped inside, beckoning Nic to follow.

"Let's be quick. There aren't too many places to look, so with both of us we should be done in a few minutes. I'll check the archival boxes," she added, heading for the dressing room. "You look around the writing desk and in all the drawers out here."

"Yes, ma'am."

She didn't rise to the bait, just disappeared through the door with a swish of pale cambric.

Heaving a sigh, Nic took in the main room and the enormous number of papers Lord Ricard had brought with him. The writing desk was covered in half-finished correspondence and stacks of received letters, while piles of ledgers sat lined up along the sideboard. Rowerre's page had been torn from something, so Nic riffled through each ledger in turn, taking care not to mess up Lord Ricard's seemingly meticulous system. None were missing pages, so he moved to the drawers.

"So did you lie on the floor?" came Leaf's voice from the adjoining room. "You and Master sa Vare."

"Leaf!" Nic pulled open a drawer harder than intended, sending the contents rolling around. "Not really the time for this conversation."

"You say that a lot."

"It comes up a lot."

"Well, when is a good time?"

"When is a good time to ask for details about your not-quite-husband's illicit sex life?"

"Yes."

Nic closed the drawer. "Never?"

"Oh."

He moved to the sideboard and yanked each drawer open in turn to find them all empty. No more questions emerged from the dressing room, leaving a silence that had weight.

Nic sighed. "Leaf."

Paper rustled.

"Leaf, I'm sorry I snapped. It's just hard to talk about him."

No answer. Nic touched his forehead and let go of a second, heavier sigh.

"Against the window," he said. "It's poetic really, since that window seat is where I first kissed him."

"Nic."

"It won't happen again, though. I'm sure he is quite done with me now."

I'm glad we got our closure. Even if we had to wait nine years for it.

"Nic."

"So I'd really rather not talk about it."

"Nic!"

"What?"

"I think . . . I think you need to see this."

He found her kneeling on the floor before a row of flat boxes lined up against the dressing room wall. Each had been labelled with a year, 1770 to 1790, but Leaf had a smaller box open on her lap, one crammed full of neatly stacked papers. The topmost page at which she stared looked like the contract being negotiated downstairs. It even had both the Serral and Monterris crests traced upon it.

"What is this?" Nic took the page. "What is it doing—?"

The question died on his lips.

Contained herein is the as-yet unvowed
marriage contract between
Valentine Nicholas Edmund Monterris,
His Grace the Duke of Vale
and
Charles William Algernon Serral,
the Most Honourable Marquess of Charborough

To be negotiated autumn 1788 by
Master Vowsmith Nicholas Everel and

A second vowsmith hadn't been listed. Nic couldn't lift his gaze from the paper. He kept reading the names as though with scrutiny they might change.

"I guess you were right about them," Leaf said, a note of sadness in her tone.

"But . . . then why did he marry my mother?"

Nic looked up to find Leaf slowly shaking her head. "And why did Papa marry mine?"

"You didn't know about this?"

The question was more accusatory than he had meant. So much his father had never said. So many secrets even his heir wasn't to know.

"No, I had *no* idea." Leaf couldn't stop shaking her head, her eyes glazed. "No one ever told me."

Staring at the contract, Nic couldn't but recall how calmly his father had informed him of his future, yet it must have been in his mind that this was not the first time a Monterris and a Serral had been contracted to wed.

Chapter 13

They found Lady Theresa sitting with Millie and Lady Lisbeth in the saloon. She had her embroidery in her lap but was setting no stitches.

"I know I should not say so, but I cannot be sorry," she was saying. "The number of times I begged Ricard to be rid of the man are beyond counting, and—"

She broke off as Leaf strode in, Nic following in her wake.

"Good afternoon, Aunt," Leaf said brightly. "How glad I am to have found you."

"Oh, good afternoon, dear. Lord Monterris." The lady cleared her throat and lifted her chin, defiant at having been overheard. "You have need of me?"

Leaf sat next to her aunt, leaving Nic to sink into one of the chairs opposite. From the other sofa, Millie gave him a questioning look, while Lady Lisbeth went on setting tiny stitches on a handkerchief.

"Yes, Aunt, I have something to ask you," Leaf said. "About Papa. And His Grace."

"What . . . what about them, dear?"

The lady's determined smile looked so painful Nic could almost feel her stomach sinking.

"They had a contract to marry, did they not?" Leaf took her aunt's hand, trapping her. "Do tell me what happened. You can well imagine how curious we are to discover we're the *second* Monterris-Serral contract in two generations."

"What?" Millie cried, reaching for Lady Lisbeth's arm. "Did I hear that right? Uncle Charborough and His Grace?"

Lady Theresa turned a frown upon her stepdaughter. "You need not crow so, Millie. Such interest doesn't become you."

"But, Lady Theresa, if it is true, then it is a very great surprise," Lady Lisbeth pointed out while Millie flushed. "Is it really so?"

Lady Theresa squirmed beneath their collective gazes. "Yes," she said at last. "It is true, but it did not go ahead and so is not spoken about. In truth, I had completely forgotten until you mentioned it."

Unconvincing words, her smile overbright. Leaf pressed on. "I assume Mama knows," she said, pinning the lady with her sharp gaze. "But why have I never heard anything about it before now? Was the contract not made public?"

At Leaf's question, Lady Theresa glanced at Nic. "Not outside of the families, no. There were whispers, of course, because they were very close, but it all faded when it came to nothing and they've barely seen each other these twenty years. I pray you will not ask me more questions; I know very little. I was only newly contracted then myself and hardly a member of the family."

"But, Aunt, everyone says our families hate each other. Is this why?"

"I am sure I don't know." Lady Theresa sniffed and took up her embroidery, sticking the needle in hard. "I myself have always been very kindly disposed to His Grace. It was he who vowsmithed your uncle's first marriage contract, you know, and so carefully that dear Ricard was saved from disgrace when the Wivenwoods ruined themselves. To think he might otherwise have gotten stuck married to that woman."

Millie leapt to her feet, red-faced, and shot a disgusted glance at her stepmother as she strode out. In her wake, Lady Theresa sniffed and stabbed her embroidery again. "She is always so touchy, though anyone in their right mind would agree the family is better off without the Wivenwood connection."

"Aunt, I still don't understand," Leaf said, ignoring this. "Why didn't Papa and His Grace marry in the end? What happened?"

"Oh, I don't know. People used to say they were in love, you know, but I've never seen a more hot-and-cold pair. Obsessed with each other, yes, but it was impossible to tell one day to the next whether they loved or hated each other. It looked about the same." With a smile at Leaf, she added, "Your papa has mellowed a lot since he married dear Cynthia and well has it been for him."

"But why didn't it go ahead?"

Nic did his best to look like part of the furniture as Lady Theresa's gaze once again edged his way. "We really shouldn't talk about it. Your father would very much dislike it if he knew."

Leaf grasped her aunt's hand again, her gaze beseeching. "Oh, Aunt, you cannot be so cruel as to leave us guessing. I will have to ask him myself."

"Oh no, don't do that. He can get so very unpleasant about it." For a moment the lady looked genuinely fearful. "As long as you don't tell anyone that we've been speaking of it, I will tell you what I know—but mind! It isn't much more than I have already said." Finding three pairs of eyes fixed intently upon her, Lady Theresa wriggled uncomfortably. "I believe there were disagreements as to who would step down, that being the only way the heads of families can marry, you know. Either my dear Ricard would be the Marquess of Charborough or Lord Francis would be Duke of Vale, and I understand it wasn't a pleasant time. That is all I know." She held up her hands in surrender. "So ask me no more questions, I pray. And none of you—you too, Lizzy—can say *anything*."

All three gave their assurances and the lady relaxed back into the sofa. "My, what a strange day this is shaping up to be. Although we seem to be having a lot of them and I can't say I'm enjoying it."

"Master sa Vare told me that strange moods are common in lock-ins," Lady Lisbeth said, smiling over her own stitchery. "Though he also says he's never been in one quite like this before, and that for all the grief, he's enjoying it very much."

"Oh, he said that, did he?" Lady Theresa smiled roguishly upon her. "A feather in your cap to be sure, my dear."

Lady Lisbeth flushed and threw a wary glance Nic's way. "Oh no, ma'am, I am not so vain as to take credit for such a statement, but he is a very charming companion. So considerate, you know, and attentive. Don't you think?"

"Sadly, what I think is of little moment, since it is your father you must convince, but yes. I admit I find Master sa Vare altogether charming. He would make an excellent husband."

Nic had never been more in agreement with her. Unfortunately, the smug knowledge that he was himself the likely cause of Dashiell's recent enjoyment was soon shattered. What did it matter when the vowsmith was far more likely to marry Lady Lisbeth?

Nic stood abruptly. "Well, thank you for enlightening us, Lady Theresa. Now I'm afraid I have things I must attend to."

Upon murmurs of "my lord," Nic escaped into the hallway, but no sooner had he drawn a deep breath than Millie was upon him.

"Lord Monterris," she hissed, gripping his arm. "Where is Leaf?"

"She's still—"

He broke off as Leaf followed him out.

"Leaf." Millie let Nic go and grabbed Leaf's arm instead. "Quick, let us find somewhere safe to talk."

Having bundled them into a nearby sitting room, Millie closed the door and began pacing the rug, her cheeks flushed. Nic watched her, anxiety swirling in with the wine dregs in his stomach.

"Millie, whatever is the matter?" Leaf glanced at Nic. "Aunt Theresa was monstrous, but no more than usual."

"Oh, she is always beastly, I know," Millie said. "But this time she has gone too far because she knows she is lying."

"Lying? What about?"

Millie spun to face them. "About Papa being grateful for the contract His Grace smithed. The one that *saved* him from my mama. You think my father travels all the time just for business?" She spat an angry laugh. "That is what Lady Theresa would like to think, when in truth he has never stopped seeing Mama, never stopped loving her. He told me years ago that he tried to have the contract changed, but that the duke had reason to hate him and so would not do it." She looked to Nic then, and her expression softened. "I do not blame your father, though, not really. It would have been a great risk to his reputation to make changes to a contract years after the fact. If only he had been less precise in his initial wording, instead of naming her particularly as the daughter of *Sir* Bertram Wivenwood."

If I could believe it was *a mistake,* Lord Ricard had hissed. Nic found a fist gripped his heart. "He loved her and had to give her up?"

"There was no choice. Once her name reverted to Miss Caroline Wivenwood throughout the net, she shared in her father's disgrace and was cast out by society. Uncle Charborough put his foot down and insisted Papa marry again to hush up the talk and . . . he did."

"Oh, Millie." Leaf wrapped her arms around her cousin, pulling her close. "I am so sorry. What an awful story. Poor Uncle Ricard too. I never knew."

"No, of course you wouldn't. He only told me when I married Lord Radlay. Marriage seems to make one immediately adult enough to be told things one was too childish to know the day before. It's very odd. Even Mama never mentioned it in any of her letters, nor during the few times I've seen her."

Nic's thoughts kept sliding back to the argument he'd overheard, to Lord Ricard's anger. "So that is why your father hates mine."

"I'm afraid so, my lord, yes," Millie said.

"You don't need to 'my lord' him, Millie," Leaf said. "He's one of us now."

Millie managed a laugh at this. "Certainly more than Lizzy has been of late, mooning over Master sa Vare at every moment."

Nic dared not glance Leaf's way. "I am certainly not doing that."

"Exactly so, but yes. I don't know whether that is the entirety of the reason—I'd never before heard of this contract between Uncle Charborough and His Grace, for instance, but I would say what happened with Mama is at least some part of why he didn't want your contract to go ahead. He even told me that he was so angry after he lost her that he tried ruining some of your father's business dealings for a while."

Nic bit his lip. Had his father just been heartless, or deliberately cruel? And had that been the reason his contract to wed Lord Charborough fell through?

"What year was your mother's contract nullified, Millie?"

"Seventeen eighty-seven," Millie said. "I wasn't yet one year old."

His heart ached to imagine the young family's pain, being forced apart because of what some pieces of vow-lawed paper said. It was the sort of pain that could twist someone up and fill them with hate—could produce a man as sour at the world as Lord Ricard Serral.

"That's the year before their contract, Nic," Leaf said. "I wonder if that means anything."

"I don't know," he said, thoughts drifting to another person whom time had twisted up and destroyed. "But I have to go."

"Go? Where?"

He met Leaf's curious gaze with a sad smile. "To see my mother."

Nic stood fidgeting outside the door, the footsteps beyond seeming to take an eternity to reach him. Eventually, it opened and Silla peered out. "Ah, Master Nicholas. I'm afraid Her Grace isn't in a good—"

"I must see her. I'll . . . I'll do my best not to upset her, Silla, but this is important. I'm sorry."

He slid past her mid-objection only to be brought up short in his mother's sitting room. The duchess's rooms were always bright and airy, but today Nic squinted into darkness. The heavy curtains had been drawn with only the faintest cracks of light sneaking in around them, leaving his mother nothing but a collection of shadows sketched in her favourite chair.

"Mama?"

He had the feeling she turned her head, but it was hard to be sure while his eyes adjusted to the lack of light.

"Mama? It's Nic. I've come to sit with you."

Thanks to a long acquaintance with the space, he made it to the opposite chair without tripping or walking into the corner of the table. The aged cushions creaked as they sank beneath him, drawing her attention, yet she just watched. Or at least stared in his direction. It wasn't always the same thing.

For a few moments, Silla bustled about, drawing a blanket across the duchess's knees, refilling her water glass, and tidying the fading flowers in the vase at her elbow.

"Silla, could you leave us, please?" Nic said. "I'll call if she needs you."

The look he got said *She always needs me*, but she went, closing the door and leaving Nic alone with his mother. She hadn't moved, only the fingers twisting her blanket's tassels showing she lived at all.

Nic leaned forward, setting a hand on hers. It didn't still its writhing task. "Mama? There is something I want to ask you."

No answer, yet her eyes flickered in a way that was far from absent.

"It's about . . . my father and . . . Lord Charborough."

He watched for a reaction and wasn't disappointed. She flinched as though he had flicked something toward her face, but didn't speak.

"I found a copy of their marriage contract."

Beneath his hand hers clenched into a tight ball.

"Can you . . . can you tell me what happened? Did you know?"

"Yes." It was barely a whisper. "No. Not at first."

"You found out after you wed?"

Her nod could have been a twitch, so infinitesimal it was.

"What happened?"

She shook her head, a gentle quiver like she was trying to dissipate a smothering cloud.

"Mama?"

"Duty is all there is. All there can be now."

Nic's brow crinkled. It sounded like something his father would say, though he couldn't tell if she was quoting, only that she clenched her hands until they shook. Her nails cut into her palms, but Nic's need to understand flared hot and he pushed on. "Surely a marriage between our families would have been as useful then as now. Did they just disagree about who would step down or was there more to it?"

Had she been holding anything, it would have snapped. Instead, it was her skin that broke, sending a slow dribble of blood trickling down one palm.

With a hiss, Nic grabbed his handkerchief and pressed it to her hands, trying to gently prise her fingers loose. "Hush, Mama, it's all right," he said, guilt weighing heavy. "We'll get you cleaned up and ready for that party in no time."

"What party?" she laughed, each word edged in fury. "I am but a prisoner. When you own me, will you set me free?"

It was Nic's turn to flinch, so fierce were her words.

"We are the possessed," she went on, throwing wide her arms

only to let them fall. "Luck is all that can bless our existence with meaning. How fortunate are those who sit on high, who cannot see what pains wash about their feet like scum thundering upon sand. Perhaps it is they we should pity, those empty, lifeless men so alone on their thrones, feeling regal, right, important, the truth all the more pitiful for their delusion. Because they cannot bear happiness, they fear contentment, dread any satisfaction that might steal the fire that drives them on to ever greater heights, dragging with them a belief that they are fuelled by indelible wisdom rather than fear. But fear—" She leaned forward, her gaze piercing his skin. "Fear is all any of you have."

The duchess sat back as suddenly as she had lunged, sinking into her armchair's shadows. There she grabbed her diary from the side table and opened a fresh page, already reaching for the ink and quill that were never far away. All the while, Nic could hardly breathe.

From behind his mother's chair, Silla cleared her throat. "Time to go, Master Nicholas. I warned you this wasn't a good time."

Too dazed to refuse, he was on his feet before he'd even thought to move. Silla's gentle grip on his elbow led him toward the door, leaving the scratch of quill on paper behind.

"What . . . what was that?" he said as Silla opened the door. "I've never heard her talk like that."

"That's because you usually heed my warnings" was Silla's grim reply. A glance back, and she stepped out, gesturing for him to join her in the gallery. "These days are her most lucid and yet her darkest. In these moods she doesn't want to see anyone, even me, and when she speaks it's all—"

"Rage."

Silla nodded. "Sometimes she has a lot of words, is poetic even, like today. Other times she throws things. Like that frog you made. It was no accident that it broke, but she convinced herself it was when exhaustion wore her back into a soft, safe place."

Tears pricked Nic's eyes. "I didn't know. You should have told me—have let me help."

Before he'd finished, Silla shook her head, the streaks of grey in her hair catching the afternoon light. "What help is there, Master Nicholas? The best help is not reminding her of hurts or fuelling her rage."

"That can't be all we can do," he said. "Surely my father—"

"Don't ever bring him here when she is in this mood." Fear flashed in Silla's eyes and she gripped Nic's arm, tight like a tourniquet. "I fear in this mood she would harm him, given the opportunity."

A cold shiver trickled down Nic's spine. "Like she harmed Uncle Francis?"

The question was out before he could think better of it, its words parting Silla's lips in horror.

"Harming him? Who told you that?"

"Master Everel. He told me about the automaton Uncle Francis made her—the one that killed him."

Silla stepped close, but her gaze darted about the empty gallery before coming to rest again on Nic's face.

"Take care with your questions, Master Nicholas," she whispered. "This house doesn't like questions. It likes the past to stay in the past where it belongs. You want to know about your father and Lord Charborough? Then let me tell you that love is not always good, no matter how strong. Sometimes the strongest love is like a poison, and the more you drink the more monstrous you become, until you are standing in a wasteland of your own making. Sometimes the very strongest love is only hate by another name."

Without another word, she slipped back into the duchess's rooms, leaving Nic standing stunned and alone in the bright gallery.

Chapter 14

Nic had never wanted to attend dinner less. Between everything Silla had said and the prospect of facing Dashiell, the urge to send Ambrose with his apologies was great. But he couldn't hide forever, and not wanting to abandon Leaf to keep an eye on Lord Ricard alone, he dressed and went down to the drawing room.

Half the party had already gathered, though to Nic's dismay Leaf wasn't among them. Lady Theresa sat making small talk with Dr. Fanshaw while Lady Lisbeth watched the door, and the duke and Lord Charborough murmured a smiling conversation by the fire. The sight of them couldn't but remind Nic of their abandoned contract and the dozen questions it raised, and of his mother's rage in the dark hollow of her chair.

Sometimes the strongest love is like a poison, and the more you drink the more monstrous you become, until you are standing in a wasteland of your own making.

Had he and Dashiell been allowed to love, might they have ended up the same way?

As though he had been summoned, the door opened to admit the vowsmith. Despite Dashiell being dressed in the height of fashion, with a waistcoat that brought out the bronze of his eyes, all Nic could think of was his bare skin limned in the moonlight, the curve of his naked waist and the heat of his touch.

Their eyes met, and with a faint smile and a disinterested nod,

Dashiell said, "Lord Monterris," as though he hadn't fucked Nic the night before, hadn't groaned and gasped and devoured him.

The coldness was like the living dark all over again, but it was anger that flared in place of panic. To stand there and look at him as though he didn't exist, like he meant nothing—Nic couldn't shake the feeling of being used and discarded, and turned his shoulder.

Things did not improve over dinner. To his left, Leaf was intent on watching Lord Ricard, while to his right, Millie was sombre and answered at random, leaving Nic nothing to do but listen to Lady Lisbeth's flow of Dashiell-related compliments from across the table.

He managed to focus on his meal and let them wash over him, until as the soup was removed the lady said, "Oh, I forgot to ask whether or not we won in the end. At cards."

It was all Nic could do to keep his eyes on his plate.

"Unfortunately, no, my lady," Dashiell said. "In the end, Lord Monterris was just too good."

Nic looked up then and, meeting Dashiell's faint smile across the table, knew the subtle, second meaning had been deliberate.

"Oh well," Lady Lisbeth said. "Perhaps at archery tomorrow you will be able to get your revenge. I myself haven't touched a bow for years."

Nic ought to have looked away, or acknowledged the private compliment with a coy smile, but the easy lightness in the vowsmith's words enraged him. Closure. He'd never thought to ask whether that was what Nic wanted; he'd just sought Nic's permission, his trust, only to once more spit on it and walk away. So for a few long seconds, Nic held Dashiell's gaze unsmiling, and had the pleasure of seeing a concerned notch grow between the man's brows.

"How about you, Master sa Vare?" Lady Lisbeth said. "I can well imagine you are as skilled at archery as at everything else."

"Hardly," Dashiell replied, the word almost a snap. "Though it is often offered as entertainment during lock-ins, so I am perhaps more practiced than some."

"How you must look forward to recreation days during lock-ins. A break from all your hard work."

In the lull that followed, Nic risked a glance across the table only to find Dashiell's stare still fixed upon him—a stare that became a question upon lifted brows, seeming to ask what he had done wrong. Even had the dinner table been an appropriate place for such a conversation, Nic found that every reply that leapt to his tongue was raw and full of hurt, founded on an old, naive dream of love he had once carried. More fool him for having ever been childish enough to want more than Dashiell could, or would even want, to offer.

All too soon the ladies departed, and to avoid a conversation with Dashiell, Nic moved down the table to sit across from Master Everel. The man was nodding as the duke reviewed plans for the following day over his glass of port. "—and luncheon on the terrace if the weather is fine. Then we'll have archery—make sure enough arrows are brought out. Bracers as well, as no one will have their own. And tell the keepers that I want our best hunting birds. A flight display after the archery will make a fine end to the afternoon, but they can't remain once the night air falls, and the fireworks cannot be set up until they are well away."

"I shall inform the staff," Master Everel said, his tone clipped. "Is that all, Your Grace?"

"For now, Everel, yes. All must go perfectly, remember. We are Monterrises. Our reputation is everything."

It seemed an odd time to remind them, the planning of an entertainment hardly what would make or break the family name, yet Master Everel gave a grim nod. "I understand, Your Grace."

Unfortunately, the problem with moving to sit near his father was his father's attention. "I hope you do not intend to embarrass me again, like last night, Nicholas," the duke said, turning Nic's way.

For an instant, Nic could think only of Dashiell having him against the window, recollection of his choice to sing emerging more slowly from memory.

"Your mother might enjoy such performances," his father went on, "but in future you will save them for her rooms rather than our guests. Do you understand?"

"Yes, sir."

Agreement was easy, automatic even, and unable to escape, Nic spent the next ten minutes being lectured on the importance of family pride. He was reminded, once again, that his ancestors had worked hard to get them where they were; reminded, once again, that the first duke had been a favourite of Charles II; and reminded, once again, that he had no greater responsibility in life than to uphold his family name.

He was only saved when Dr. Fanshaw rose from his chair to excuse himself. "I must look in on Her Grace. If you would all excuse me."

"I do hope dear Georgiana will be feeling well enough to join us tomorrow," Lord Charborough said as the doctor departed. "It would be sad for her to miss—"

A crash sounded near the door as the chandelier candles winked out, dropping the room into near darkness. The few on the table went on burning like nothing had happened, providing enough light to make out shocked expressions and the shape of the doctor righting a decorative urn.

A shiver trickled down Nic's spine. He looked around, sure he would find the automaton from the style wing standing right behind him, but there were just shadows suggesting faded wallpaper and rotten wainscotting.

"No need to panic," the duke said, rising from his place. "Likely a window is open upstairs. The air currents in this house can be unpredictable. Let us take it as a sign we have lingered long enough over our wine and ought to join the ladies."

Nic, not sure any of the upstairs windows still opened let alone could produce such a draught, glanced around as the gentlemen pushed back their chairs. The shape of the room remained, yet the details seemed wrong, a hint of mildew hanging in the air like a sour note.

"Nicholas."

His father's imperious tone snapped his attention back and he rose. "Yes, sir. Apologies."

In the others' wake, he made to slide past the duke in the doorway, only for fingers to tighten around his arm. "Nothing," the duke said, voice low, "can go wrong."

He let go as quickly, leaving Nic to walk on with the warning echoing in his head.

Returning to the drawing room with the others, he found Leaf and Lisbeth hunting through a cabinet, a set of checkers and a fox-and-hen board lying on the floor by their knees.

"Oh, now we have extra eyes," Lady Lisbeth said, smiling upon Dashiell's arrival. "We are looking for the missing pieces to these games. Do come and help us, Master sa Vare."

Dashiell did as he was bid, while Nic took a seat at some distance, wondering how long until he could sneak away without his father noticing. The duke hadn't followed them in yet, granting Nic a brief window in which to escape, but he didn't dare. One lecture for the day was quite enough.

After a few minutes of desultory conversation, Lord Charborough said, "Where'd Val get to?"

"By all means, go in search of him, Brother," Lord Ricard sneered.

"No, no, merely curious. It's not as though he can get lost in his own house." The marquess followed this with some hearty laughter, but ill ease spilled through Nic at his father's ongoing absence. He got up and, leaving the rest of the party to their talk, went out into the empty hallway.

"Sir?"

No answer, not even the footsteps or distant murmuring of servants going about their work. No doubt his father was giving orders to Castor or Mrs. Podmarsh and would be annoyed at Nic's concern, but Nic couldn't shake the recollection of the hovering white face and its icy shadows, and so turned his steps along the passage. As he passed the dining room, a hint of smoke and mildew caught his nose, while ahead at the corner candlelight flickered upon the walls.

"The rest must hold," came his father's low tone as Nic approached—a hissed threat with a desperate edge. "*Must* hold."

"Sir?" Nic called. "Is everything all right?"

The duke appeared around the corner, the candle in his hand reflecting bright circles off his dark glasses. "Nicholas. Why are you not entertaining our guests?"

"Lord Charborough asked where you were, and after what happened with Gillingham . . ." Nic left his concern hovering between them. For a moment they just stared at one another, until Nic gathered enough courage to say, "Is there something I ought to know?"

"I appreciate your concern, Nicholas, but matters of household management are not yet your—"

A shriek tore along the hallway and Nic spun. A maid was backing out of the dining room, smoke spilling around her, and Nic's stomach dropped through the floor.

"Fire!" she cried, catching sight of them. "The dining room is on fire!"

A beat of horrified shock held them both stunned, before the duke pushed past Nic, already shouting. "Run downstairs! I want all hands up here at once. Water buckets. Blankets. Everything, now!"

A fearful nod and the woman scurried away as, at the other end of the hallway, the drawing room door burst open, spilling light and guests. The hallway was slowly filling with smoke, shocked cries adding to the rising chaos.

The dining room was ablaze, fire circling the entire space, rising up the walls. Not yet too high, but too big and spread out to be easily smothered with the sacrifice of a coat. Nic pulled his off all the same and hunted in the flickering heat for something—anything—to throw over it. The gentlemen who had so recently left the room hurried back in behind him. Dashiell was already stripping off his coat and Lord Charborough soon followed, shirtsleeves rolled up as a pair of footmen arrived bearing piles of old blankets. Maids with water buckets came next, and out in the passage, Leaf's voice could be heard calling orders to the servants.

"Here, step back!"

Nic wasn't sure who spoke but backed out of the way as water splashed past, hissing onto the flames. Another bucket followed, but the fire seemed determined to rise. With no time to think, only to act, Nic grabbed one of the blankets and smothered a small section to stop it spreading, while his father shouted and water buckets kept arriving.

Bit by bit they fought back the flames, the evening full of smoke that stung at eyes and throat, full of noise and panic—the prospect of the whole Court going up in flames during a lock-in too hideous to consider. By the time the fire was out, the dining room was a charred and sodden mess, and everyone was exhausted. Tea was brought and drunk in silence while the doctor, having returned from looking in on the duchess, checked everyone over, assessing scrapes and minor burns.

When at last Nic pulled himself up the stairs to his rooms, he was grateful to find that Ambrose had warm water waiting, and having scrubbed the worst of the smoke and char from his skin, Nic tumbled into bed.

When the party gathered for archery the following day, it was in a mood of determined cheer. Not once was the fire mentioned during luncheon, yet in its absence it seemed to loom over them, present in every one of the duke's forced smiles. He seemed to think that ensuring a perfect afternoon would somehow erase the previous evening's horror.

As though determined to help in this mission, the weather had turned out fine, sunshine bathing a lawn already dotted with archery targets. Near the pavilion, a large cage of hunting echoes stood waiting for the display that would follow, and for his father's sake, Nic found himself hoping nothing would go wrong.

Everyone had joined them for luncheon, even the duchess, but when it came time to make their way down to the targets, Lord Ricard showed no sign of leaving the table.

"Not coming, Uncle?" Leaf said.

"No, Niece," he said, gesturing to the pile of correspondence sitting at his elbow. "I have no time for such frivolity. I am here only to enjoy the sunshine while it lasts, which is never long in these northern wilds. Mark my words, it will be raining before you get halfway around the course."

He spoke cheerfully enough, but given they suspected his hand in Gillingham's death, Nic wasn't sorry to leave the man behind.

The others were already gathering at the bottom of the terrace stairs, where Master Everel stood handing out bows and bracers to every member of the party. The men all looked slightly odd in their white sporting shirts, as though they had ceased being Brilliants overnight—white linen something they only wore for hunting and hawking. Nic had never understood the tradition and felt strange in his own whites, although the change meant Dr. Fanshaw no longer looked out of place amongst them.

"Lady Leaf," the doctor said, greeting her as he accepted a bracer from Master Everel. "A lovely day for archery."

"It certainly is, Doctor, although now I am worried the fine weather may not last." Leaf glanced up at the white puffs of cloud scudding across the sky.

"It only needs to last long enough."

Leaf smiled upon him. "How very true. Although it would be a shame if rain ruined tonight's fireworks."

Leaning closer, Dr. Fanshaw murmured, "Unless they are like the fireworks in *To Cut a Bargain*."

"Oh no!" Leaf's eyes danced. "Do *not* suggest it, Doctor."

"I assure you, I will be keeping an eye out for shadowy interlopers."

Leaf chuckled and took a bow from Master Everel with a graceful nod of thanks.

"—but I really do enjoy the hustle and bustle of London just as well," Lady Lisbeth was saying as she and Dashiell joined them. "It is just that I have such a fondness for Malvern Hall."

"Are we all ready?" the duke called from the front of the group. "Good. Now as you all know, I am more one for my pistols, but today we are going to—"

"Where do you travel after this negotiation, Master sa Vare?" Lady Lisbeth went on while the duke explained the day's plan.

Dashiell, keeping his voice low so as not to interrupt his host, said, "That depends. Should we finish in good time, there is a contract I can take in Somerset next month or, if I am unavailable for that, it will be back to London."

"You're such a decisive man that you must enjoy being able to choose your work. For me, though, I think I could be happy anywhere so long as I was with my husband."

Nic hoped this play was as obvious to Dashiell as it was to him. But so what if it was? She was an obliging girl, pretty and wellborn, and it wasn't like Nic knew a damn thing about either Dashiell's tastes or his aspirations anymore. Perhaps marriage to her would suit him very well now he had claimed his closure.

Nic stared ahead as the duke and Lady Theresa stepped up to the first target, and tried his best not to think about either Dashiell's marriage or Dashiell's fingers gently tracing down his cheek.

You're beautiful.

"At least the first target is only a short distance," Leaf said, watching Lady Theresa take her shot. "I haven't used a bow for so long that I am sure to miss and land an arrow in someone's leg."

Nic threw her a mocking grin. "Then I shall be sure to stay behind you at all times."

Lord Charborough and the duchess went next, the duchess in high fettle. Her dark mood of the previous day was seemingly forgotten and she proved a fine shot, her arrow neatly pipping the centre of the target to much applause.

"Oh, I am not going to be able to follow that," Leaf said. "Here, you go first, Millie."

Lady Radlay shrugged, and she and Dr. Fanshaw went next, leaving Nic and Leaf to follow.

"Are you all right?" Leaf asked as they took their places. "You look quite worn out and we've barely begun. You haven't been drinking before breakfast again, have you?"

He had seriously considered it, and had been craving drunken oblivion since Dashiell had greeted him with a murmured "Lord Monterris," sending a frisson through his skin he seemed unable to shake off.

"No, not this time, just exhausted from last night."

"It was terrible, wasn't it?" Her lips flattened into a grim line. "Would you rather sit out? I don't mind."

"Not at all. I feel better now we are finally moving."

"And no longer having to listen to Lizzy set her cap at Master sa Vare. Perhaps I ought to tell her that you and he—"

"Don't you dare, baggage. Not a word!"

Leaf giggled. "I suppose he would get in trouble, wouldn't he?"

"A lot of trouble. More trouble than me. I'm just a degenerate earl; he would be in contravention of guild law and could get excommunicated if it was deemed serious enough."

No laugh now, Leaf said, "Would it ruin the contract?"

"I'm not sure. It would probably have to be broken and renegotiated if they thought he had acted in bad faith."

"Quite the risk he took the other night then."

Nic had to agree, and it was all he could do not to glance back at the vowsmith as Master Everel hurried past, handing them arrows before moving on. Deeming it safe to begin now Millie and the doctor were out of range, Leaf stepped up to the line. "Wish me luck!"

"A fortunate garden party to you."

She turned as she loosed, sending the arrow into one of the target's outer rings. "What on earth is that supposed to mean?"

"It's a sigil pun people often make by accident," Nic said, struggling not to laugh. "*Good luck* is *shem la gard enda pi*, but everyone always messes it up and forms it as *shem la gard enpa ti*."

Leaf spun away on the words, calling to Lady Lisbeth still waiting back near the stairs. "Lisbeth, do please lend me Master sa Vare for the rest of the day. I wish to trade partners."

"Cruel, my lady, cruel!" Nic cried, laughing as Lady Lisbeth approached, a question already on her tongue.

"Whatever is the matter, Leaf? I hope you did not distract her, Lord Monterris."

"Worse, he punned in sigils at me and quite put me off."

Dashiell, strolling over in Lady Lisbeth's wake, grinned. "Oh no, did you ask him to wish you good luck?"

"Not you too, Master sa Vare."

The vowsmith bowed. "A fortunate garden party to you."

Leaf threw up her hands. "That's it, I am washing my hands of both of you!"

Nic met Dashiell's laughing gaze and for a moment they could have been twelve years old again, sharing the private joke of two boys smugly thrilled by their knowledge of sigils. But when the smile began to fade, it left Dashiell's piercing stare searing into him.

"Nic, you had better take your shot," Leaf said as Master Everel hurried over, no doubt to see what was keeping them. The rest of the party had already moved on, pair by pair, toward the pavilion. "So long as you promise no more puns."

"No more puns, but only for the rest of the afternoon. After that I make no promises. Apologies, Everel, Lady Leaf was merely upset at her poor shot."

"It is a perfectly respectable shot for your first target, my lady," Master Everel said while Leaf smacked Nic's arm. "Here, some arrows for you to begin, Master sa Vare."

"Thank you." Dashiell took them, only to sigh once the old vowsmith had moved on out of earshot. "He utterly terrified me as a child, but I really hate seeing him run about serving us like a footman."

"It does seem strange," Lisbeth agreed, though she would likely have agreed had Dashiell said the sky was green. "Is he not a good vowsmith?"

"He's amazing actually. Very diligent. Never misses a thing. Which is probably why His Grace has kept him rather than giving him to himself, but—" Nic caught a glance stolen his way as though mindful of his reaction. "If he was Master sa Everel, he could have a much higher guild rank and a successful career of his own."

"Oh, that is sad," Lisbeth said as Nic prepared his shot. "I never really thought about how it must affect non-sasines, not being able to reach high ranks. Perhaps that ought to be changed."

"It's to ensure that vowsmiths taking high-level contracts aren't obligated to specific families," Dashiell explained as Nic aimed and loosed, and a large part of him wished he could fly as his arrow did, away from the conversation. He was no vowsmith, but he shared with Master Everel the fate of one owned—a sasine something he could never and would never be.

As his arrow hit the target near Leaf's, Nic found himself following Master Everel's path across the grass, more in accord with the old vowsmith than ever before.

"Well, we're nowhere near as good as Mama," he said, gesturing to the arrow still protruding from the centre of the target. "But we hit the thing. Shall we move on, Leaf?"

"Yes, by all means, we ought to let Lizzy and Master sa Vare get started."

Offering her his arm, Nic gave only a perfunctory smile to the others before leading her across the grass toward the second target. For a time, she was silent, intent on keeping her skirt lifted and battling with her bonnet, until all at once she said, "You really are very good together, you know. You and Master sa Vare."

"Because we share an old joke about garden parties? That hardly makes up for the fact that he is well travelled, successful, and above all free, while this house is practically my whole world."

She squeezed his arm. "I know, but I think it's true all the same."

When they reached the mark for the next target, Millie and Dr. Fanshaw were already finishing at the third, though the doctor's gaze kept shying in Leaf's direction as she prepared to take her shot. Nic cleared his throat. "I promise no puns this time," he said as she took aim. "But I must tell you that I think you've made a conquest of Dr. Fanshaw."

"What?"

For the second time, she turned the instant before her arrow leapt from its string, sending it wide.

"You, Nicholas Monterris, are a monster. What do you mean I've made a conquest of the doctor?"

"He looks at you all the time."

"Nonsense."

"Nonsense?" He nodded in the man's direction and Leaf looked around, just in time to catch the doctor staring before he turned hastily away.

Leaf sniffed. "He's probably just wondering what's taking us so long."

"I'm sure that explains him staring yesterday too, and the day before."

"You're very silly, Nic. Dr. Fanshaw is merely used to seeing me every other day unless we're in town. Mama has a sickly disposition, you know, and calls him in for every trivial complaint. Now do take your shot."

He did so, but as he was about to loose the arrow, Leaf said, "Dr. Fanshaw may be looking at me, but at least he's not undressing me with his eyes, which is what Master sa Vare does every time he looks at you."

His arrow sailed wide as hers had done, leaving their poor attempts paired at the edge of the target.

"Excellent revenge, my dear."

"It was, yes; however, it is also true. Shall we?"

Together they walked on again, arm in arm across the lawn. Back on the terrace, Lord Ricard remained at the refreshment table, a flicker of white paper all that could be seen of his correspondence. Ahead of them, Lord Charborough and the duchess seemed in fine spirits, and each target they reached had her arrow firmly planted in the centre. Farther on, Lady Theresa and the duke had disappeared behind the pavilion—the same pavilion in which Nic and Dashiell had once kissed, a memory Nic was keen to ignore as they drew closer to its sweeping ironwork.

The weather held out until they were halfway around the course, when dark clouds rolled in over the house. Nic gestured upward. "I think Lord Ricard was right."

"Oh, and just when I was getting the hang of this. Hopefully it will hold off long enough to finish. Where is Master Everel?"

The old vowsmith had been coming by at each target to hand out fresh arrows so they needn't carry them, but a quick hunt of the lawn found no sign of him. "Perhaps I should just steal some from the target. Oh, too late."

The first heavy drops pattered onto the grass around them.

"It's just a few drops," Leaf said. "We can ignore a few drops."

As though this had been a challenge, the sky cracked open, pouring rain in great sheets that turned the world grey.

"I think it's a bit more than a few drops!" Nic called through the sudden downpour, his hair already sticking to his head. Working quickly, he pulled off his coat and handed it to Leaf. "Hold it over your head!"

With Leaf holding Nic's coat awkwardly over her sodden bonnet, she hurried toward the house. Nic followed, rain soaking into his breeches and his white shirt as though he had just jumped into the lake. On the terrace, a small collection of servants raced about bringing in the luncheon table, while the duke stood at the bottom of the stairs directing everyone inside.

"Nicholas!" he called as Nic and Leaf approached. "The birds!"

His father pointed toward the pavilion, and knowing how bad rain was for the echoes, Nic wheeled about without pause and dashed back into it. Behind him, the duke shouted again, and Nic glanced back in time to see his father gesturing after him, Dashiell a rain-smeared figure now following in his wake. The cage would likely have been too awkward for him to lift alone, but of all the people his father could have sent, it had to be Dashiell.

Nic reached the cage out of breath to find the echoes flapping about in agitation. "It's all right, I'm here," he said as Dashiell arrived, a fine sight with his clinging white shirt and sodden dark hair. "Take that side," Nic added, taking hold of his and hauling them up.

The rain had started to ease slightly, but as they headed back with the heavy cage hanging between them, it renewed with fresh vigour. It pelted down so hard Nic was sure it was trying to flay the skin from his face.

Dashiell pointed ahead. "Let's get them to the pavilion!"

It was the last place he wanted to go with Dashiell right now, but he agreed, and the pair of them hauled the cage up the stairs and under cover.

"What ridiculous weather," Nic grumbled as they set the echoes down out of the storm. "My father will be furious that it's ruined his plans. Fireworks and all at this rate."

"Dukes aren't capable of commanding the weather?"

Ignoring this quip, Nic knelt before the cage. Inside, the birds were furiously shaking water from their wings. "You're safe for now. Although it's just a bit of water, you know."

"Quite a lot of water."

Nic got to his feet. "All right, quite a lot of water."

Water that wasn't only being shaken from their feathers. It also dripped from Dashiell, from the tips of his bedraggled hair and the cuffs of his shirt—a shirt that clung to his chest, leaving a hint of skin visible through its fine pale weave. Nic realised too late that he was staring.

"Do you remember the last time we were here?" Dashiell said, staring right back.

Busy hands, the thrill of discovery, hot kisses that went on and on yet were over too quickly—the unfinished moments for which Dashiell had claimed his damnable closure. The flare of anger was back and Nic shook the memories away.

"That was a long time ago."

"Was it?" Dashiell took a step forward, only to stop abruptly like he'd tugged his own leash.

In the path of such restrained tension, Nic caught his breath.

Part of him wanted to slap that beautiful face, yet angry as he was, he couldn't deny he also wanted to slide his fingers into that somehow still perfect neckcloth and pull Dashiell close.

"Nic, I . . ."

Nic braced for yet another apology, but it didn't come, leaving his name suspended alone in the damp air. Voice having failed him, Dashiell advanced another step, close enough now that they shared their next breath, a whisper all that kept their sodden shirts from touching. Once more standing in the shadow of their own ghosts, Dashiell lifted a hand to Nic's brow and brushed back a sodden lock of hair. The soft graze of his knuckles against Nic's skin was both breath and spark, leaving his chest tight and his throat constricted. He needed to move, to escape, to not look at the fond curve of Dashiell's lips.

From Nic's brow, the vowsmith's fingers traced a curving path behind one ear and down, and it was all Nic could do not to lean into his touch, turning like a flower to the sun—all he could do not to hold his breath when Dashiell leaned in, his nose brushing against Nic's in silent question.

His body yearned to mimic the gesture, but Nic knew with certainty now how it would end if he did—with a view of Dashiell's retreating back. And so with their lips all but touching, he murmured, "What are you doing?"

"Trying to kiss you," the vowsmith murmured back, one corner of his lips quirking into a smile. "Is it not obvious?"

"What happened to closure?" Nic didn't move, didn't pull back, lips presented like a challenge. He didn't know if he most wanted Dashiell to take it or realise his error, or how long he could hold himself without caving.

There must have been enough bite in his words, for Dashiell drew back, just enough to search Nic's face, his eyes wide with surprise. And not a little hurt.

Nic could feel the moment slipping away—Dashiell slipping away. What difference would one more kiss make? Dashiell had taken his closure; why could Nic not take his own? Make it even.

Because he's a vowsmith, the sensible part of his mind warned. *Because if he gets caught, his career will be over.*

Beyond the pavilion's iron railings, the rain was beginning to ease. The thunder of it hitting the roof had quieted, and unable to bear Dashiell's proximity a moment longer, Nic pulled away.

"We ought to get the echoes back."

"Yes. Of course." Soft words. Nic dared not look at the man's face, just readied himself to pick up the heavy cage once more. Better not to have needed Dashiell's help, but they could walk back in silence, bearing their sodden cargo, and get on with their lives.

"Uh, Nic?"

The panicked edge in Dashiell's voice cut through Nic's abstraction. The vowsmith stood at the railing, pointing out at something dark lying on the grass beyond. "What is that?"

Nic moved to the stairs, a terrible sense of inevitability growing with every step.

"Oh no." His stomach dropped, and wishing he could close his eyes instead and will the horror away, Nic sped out into the rain. Dashiell followed, the pair of them running the short distance in anxious silence, only to slow as their discovery become unmistakable. A body dressed all in black, its wispy grey hair plastered down by the rain.

Master Everel.

Nic dropped to his knees, breath rushing from his chest. The old vowsmith lay face down in the grass, utterly still. Yet it was not the man's sightless eyes that drew Nic's gaze. It was the arrow protruding from his back.

Chapter 15

At first there was just silence. Master Everel's body had been carried in out of the rain and lay now on the gallery floor, but none of the few there to witness it uttered a word. The horror of Gillingham's death seemed both a long time ago and all too close as Nic stared down at the man who had been a staple of his life for as long as he could remember. An oft-hated staple perhaps, but he could not imagine Monterris Court without Master Everel to stalk its halls.

Eventually, the duke said, "There is, I presume, no doubt he is dead, Doctor?"

"No doubt, Your Grace, no." Dr. Fanshaw rolled up his damp sleeves all the same and, kneeling beside Master Everel, pressed two fingers to the man's pale neck. "No pulse, Your Grace, and he is already growing cold."

Nic found himself staring at his father. Master Everel had been his vowsmith, his secretary, his everything for more years than Nic knew, yet the duke stood as cold as stone while at his feet the doctor performed a cursory check of the body.

He was just a valet, the duke had snarled after Rowerre's death. Too well could Nic now imagine his father saying, *He was just an indentured vowsmith.*

Words started forming on Nic's sluggish tongue, but before he could utter them, hurried footsteps preceded the arrival of the Serral brothers. "Val, my man said—" Lord Charborough halted in the archway, forcing Lord Ricard to step around him. "By God, I was sure it couldn't be true." His gaze darted around the small circle. "What happened?"

"Lord Monterris and Master sa Vare went to fetch the echoes and found him by the pavilion," the duke said, his voice remarkably steady even for him.

Lord Ricard barked a harsh laugh. "Lord Monterris and Master sa Vare seem to have a bad habit of running into dead bodies."

Dashiell drew himself up with a scowl. "This one had an arrow in it."

"An arrow?"

The doctor gestured to the arrow lying on the stones, removed when they'd laid him out in a more dignified manner. "In his back, my lord."

"Killed?" Lord Charborough said. "Surely not. An accident. It must be."

Before anyone could answer, the three young ladies of the Serral party arrived, followed by their harassed chaperone. They had all changed their sodden clothes, though by the look of Leaf's hair, there hadn't been time for her maid to so much as brush it before the news had reached her.

"Leaf," Lady Theresa hissed, trying to shepherd her out. "There is no need for this. It is unbecoming to take such interest."

"What happened?" Leaf demanded, ignoring her. "Dr. Fanshaw?"

"An arrow to the back, my lady," the doctor said. "Quite deep, so unlikely to be a glancing blow. However, as I doubt it would have hit any major organs, the fact that he did not call for help means he probably went into shock and bled out. Not a particularly reliable method of killing someone, but in this case clearly effective."

"Doctor!" Lord Charborough spun a furious glare upon the man. "My daughter does not need to know such sordid details. You will give her nightmares."

Dr. Fanshaw bowed. "My apologies, my lord," he said, though he didn't look at all sorry, nor Leaf at all horrified.

"Theresa, take the girls away; they ought not see such a thing. Refreshments have been served in—"

"I don't want refreshments, Papa," Leaf said. "I want to know what happened. I'm not a child and this lock-in is to negotiate *my* marriage contract. If a man is murdered because of it, surely you must agree it is important to understand why."

"Murdered? Nonsense. An accident. Arrows flying all over the place."

"How can you be so sure, Papa?"

"Because what you are suggesting is ridiculous."

"More or less ridiculous than three people just happening to die quite by chance since we locked ourselves in? Someone," she went on, turning her fierce stare around the gathered group, "doesn't want this contract to go ahead. So who will be next?"

"Nonsense," Lord Charborough blustered again. "Who would—?"

"My uncle, for a start," Leaf said, causing all eyes to turn Lord Ricard's way. "You never wanted Papa to make an offer for Nic, did you, Uncle?"

Lord Ricard's grin grew glassy. "No," he agreed, amicably. "It's a foolish marriage and I don't mind saying so. And I would be well pleased if Vale called it off. But you'll have noticed, dear niece, that I was the only one without a bow in my hand today."

"And the rest of us were in pairs the whole time," Lord Charborough pointed out. "Someone would surely have noticed had anyone slipped away."

A small gasp pulled attention to Lady Theresa, whose hand trembled before her lips. "Oh no, I've just had the most horrible thought."

"Spit it out, my lady," Lord Ricard snapped. "Reticence does not become you now."

Lady Theresa glared at him. "I was only thinking that Her Grace disliked the poor man so much, and she, you know, was very skilled with her bow."

Nic hated that she was right. His mother could have loosed an arrow at the old vowsmith perhaps without even thinking, the way she sometimes sat pulling petals off flowers. And in her darker moods . . .

I fear in this mood she would harm him, given the opportunity.

Nic felt the world stutter to a halt, felt the gazes slide his way as they had on the balcony overlooking Gillingham's body. His mother's reaction had been the true horror that night and now he could only be glad she wasn't present as words defending her lodged in his throat. Beside Nic, his father remained as silent, leaving Lord Charborough to set his hands upon his hips and step forward.

"Georgiana was with me all afternoon, Theresa," he said in a tone of disbelief. "And I can assure you she neither missed a shot nor loosed any extra arrows. This is an extraordinary circumstance, I grant you, but that is no reason to turn such accusations upon our hostess."

"But someone must have done it, Papa," Leaf pointed out as Lady Theresa shrank back. "Where exactly was he found? And which way was he lying? Perhaps if we could map out the ground and consider where everyone—"

"No." Gone was Lord Charborough's usual smile, replaced with a forbidding scowl that could have rivalled even the duke's. "I will have neither the poor man nor our hosts humiliated for your childish desire to play detective, Leaf. Oh, you thought I wouldn't hear you've been poking around the house? Well! This stops now. Unlike in your silly books, there is no murderer here, just a series of unfortunate accidents."

Leaf's eyes widened in the face of her father's fury as he turned to Dr. Fanshaw. "Doctor, perhaps instead of making idle conjecture you could help the servants transport the body to the crypt. The poor man has lain upon the floor being stared at quite long enough."

What could be said in the wake of such words? The duke gave his permission with a nod and Master Everel's body was carried out, hanging heavy between two footmen like an unwieldy roll of carpet. In his wake, Nic found he wanted more than anything to escape, to change his sodden clothes and take a moment just to think, but one pressing question remained unanswered.

"What happens to the contract now?" he said, giving it voice. "Without Master Everel, I mean."

A wary murmur had sprung up, and Lady Theresa had renewed her attempts to get the young ladies out of the room, but Nic's words struck silence back into the gathered party. Most eyes turned to Dashiell, but it was the duke who sighed and said, "There is nothing for it. I will have to take his place."

"No." Lord Ricard shook his head, a flash of fury in his eyes. "That is unacceptable. I will not have you getting your hands on the negotiations."

The duke eyed Lord Ricard with disdain. "You have another suggestion? I am all ears, as I have no desire whatsoever to waste my time sitting in on the negotiations when I have your audit to prepare for. Master sa Vare?"

Appealed to, Dashiell cleared his throat. "The statutes do allow for changes in unusual circumstances and this surely counts as unusual. The rest of the Monterris team can do the actual negotiations, but a pair of vowsmiths are required to manifest the completed contract and His Grace is the only other man here to have attained the required rank."

"This is ridiculous!" Lord Ricard cried. "The man cannot be allowed to negotiate his own contract unless we are allowed—"

"You are welcome to sit in on the proceedings, my lord," Dashiell said coldly, his hauteur only slightly diminished by the damp shirt still sticking to his chest. "However, as it is my job to ensure your interests are maintained whether you are present or not—no matter the identity of the opposing negotiator—I do hope you are not questioning my professional standing? You may, of course, break the contract and withdraw instead if you so choose."

"No." For the second time, Lord Charborough's voice resounded through the gallery, seeming to quiet even the rain outside. He turned a glare on Lord Ricard. "We will not be withdrawing. The negotiations go ahead. I have full confidence in Master sa Vare to ensure our interests are maintained, and I won't hear a word otherwise."

Lord Ricard threw a sneer at the duke. "Killed him yourself so you could get your hands on the negotiations, eh, Val?"

"Ricard!"

"Hardly," the duke said. "The loss of Master Everel to this house will be felt far beyond this moment."

"Good. May you know how it feels."

"Enough," Lord Charborough hissed. "Not another word of this."

With an ugly smirk, Lord Ricard bowed. "As you wish, Brother. But if you'll excuse me, I've had quite enough of you all for the day." He turned to leave, only to pause beside Dashiell. "It seems this contract is cursed. I'd watch my back if I were you, Master sa Vare."

Chapter 16

Nic stood in the middle of his dressing room and failed to dress. His thoughts had been turning endlessly since they'd found Master Everel, though he could hardly have said what he was thinking about. The contents of his mind were just a tangle that occasionally caught on something, only to tear free, leaving a sensation like static under his skin. They'd been so sure it had been Lord Ricard, and now, nothing.

Ambrose cleared his throat. "Is everything all right, my lord?"

"Of course, Ambrose," Nic said, the words more automatic than true. "Something makes you think otherwise?"

"That I had to say your name four times just now to get you to put an arm in your shirtsleeve."

"Oh." Nic looked down at the black shirt hanging around his neck, not entirely sure how it had gotten there. "Apologies." He slid his arm into the other sleeve so Ambrose could do up the buttons. "It's been a strange day."

A hurried knock tapped upon the outer door, then Leaf's breathless voice called, "Nic?"

"I'm in here, Leaf," Nic called back. "Dressing."

"Oh. Are you decent?"

Nic glanced down at his breeches and shirt and shrugged, disturbing Ambrose's work on his neckcloth. "I suppose so?"

Taking that as a yes, Leaf appeared in the open doorway, her expression troubled. "Good evening, Ambrose," she said, keeping out of the valet's way as he fetched Nic's waistcoat.

"Good evening, my lady," the valet replied, doing his best to keep the shock of their familiarity off his face.

Despite her hasty arrival, Leaf just bit at her bottom lip and watched as Nic finished dressing. When at last he was done, Ambrose stepped back to examine his handiwork. "Satisfied, my lord?"

"Yes, but you can't escape since you're our chaperone," Nic said. "So you may as well take a seat. Have a rest."

"I . . . I'm sure I can find something more productive to do, my lord, if you'll excuse me." Ambrose bowed himself out, leaving Nic to stare at himself in the mirror, not sure he recognised the man who stared back.

Moving to stand beside him, Leaf appeared in the reflection, a worried crease between her brows.

"I thought we had it," she said, staring at the pair of them standing side by side in the glass. "It was the only thing that made sense, and now none of it makes sense. If Uncle Ricard wanted to force Papa to invoke the clause, killing *your* head vowsmith wasn't the right choice."

I'd watch my back if I were you, Master sa Vare.

"I suppose it's possible he thought it *would* automatically end the contract, although surely you would want to be sure of that before killing someone." She glanced up at him. "I don't suppose you think much of Aunt Theresa's suggestion? That your mama might have . . ."

"I don't know. I'm sure you've noticed that she isn't always quite . . . with us, but they've lived in the same house all these years, so why do it now?"

Leaf made a face. "That's true. And that being the case, it's far more likely to be someone I brought with me." A pause. "Papa was very insistent this afternoon, wasn't he."

Not a question. Lord Charborough had defended both the duchess and the contract, and had stepped in to protect Nic's father with a ferocity that might have been remarkable had they not already understood why.

"We will have to watch him too, I think," Leaf said. "He's already offered me more money not to kick up a fuss or ask to leave. That school of mine might become a reality after all."

Nic didn't answer, his gaze caught to the sight of them still side by side in the mirror—Lord and Lady Monterris. Before her arrival, he had dreaded the very thought of her. Now the woman staring out of the glass was fast becoming his best friend. He wanted to hold on to her for the rest of his life, but marriage was the wrong shape in his mind.

Leaf looked up at him. "Are you all right, Nic?"

"Yes."

How could he explain the buzz that had taken root in his skin? The anger and the hurt and the desperate need? As well voice the fear that it could have been Dashiell lying there with an arrow in his back.

Leaf squeezed his arm. "I don't suppose you saw anything out of place when you found him?"

"You mean apart from a dead body? No, he was just . . . lying on the grass on the far side of the pavilion."

"Yet your father and Aunt Theresa didn't see him. That means it must have happened after the rain began. Are you sure you're all right?"

Nic finally pulled his gaze from the mirror and spread his arms. "Don't I look all right? I put a lot of effort into looking this good, you know."

"You look . . . I don't know. Angry, but not exactly. I can't explain it. Something in your eyes. Is it Master Everel, or should I blame Master sa Vare?"

His laugh owned no humour. "Neither. Both. Don't worry about me, just . . . take care, won't you?"

"You feel it too?" She turned to face him, one corner of her lips turning down as she pressed them flat. "I'm scared, Nic. This isn't how it's supposed to go. There can be no doubt anymore that Gillingham was murdered too, and to have two members of the negotiation teams targeted . . ."

She trailed off, leaving the obvious conclusion hanging.

"It's about the contract," he said.

"Yes. And if you *really* wanted to ensure a contract didn't go ahead, why not kill one of its principals? Without us, there is no contract."

The truth of her words sank like lead into Nic's stomach. Someone out there had already killed at least twice and failed to get what they wanted. The next time they might make sure of it. And they no longer had a clear suspect to watch.

Nic saw his dread reflected in Leaf's face. Without stopping to think how scandalised Ambrose would be, he wrapped his arms around her and pulled her close. "We're going to get through this," he said. "I promise."

He had sought only to give comfort rather than take it, but his heart swelled as she slid her arms around his waist and rested her cheek against his shoulder. "Good," she said. "I don't want to die. And I don't particularly want you to die either."

"Why thank you."

She tightened her hold around his waist, her grip determined. "You're not going anywhere, Nicholas Monterris."

For a time they stood so, and Nic couldn't but think of how long it had been since anyone had held him without something more being desired, without the charge of lust and expectation. So many of his relationships had been merely physical, transactional, even the ones that had lasted a few months beginning with the knowledge of their end. They'd been enjoyed for what they were and rarely mourned once they were gone, a friend something he'd never found again.

Or not let yourself find, a treacherous part of him suggested. After all, his only experience of friendship had ended in Dashiell's abrupt departure.

Eventually, Leaf stepped back with a sigh. "Thank you, I needed that. I feel far more able to go down to dinner now, though I'm very glad we're just eating and having no entertainments." She turned toward the dressing room door, only to spin back. "Tomorrow we should plan how we're going to get through this lock-in without getting murdered. For now, try not to go anywhere on your own, all right?"

Nic agreed. In the circumstances it was a sensible plan, yet it left him overbalanced like the world had tipped beneath his feet. Monterris Court had never been a comfortable, happy home, but it was all he knew. That such danger now stalked its halls, threatening the people he loved and leaving nowhere safe to hide, added to the angry buzz beneath his skin. And the dread carving hollows in his stomach.

The group that gathered that evening was tense and subdued. With the dining room gutted by fire, dinner was served in one of the parlours, silence predominant. While the others picked at their food, Nic stared across the table at Dashiell. It had always felt dangerous to do so, but tonight he was too angry to care—angry at the murderer for making him fear, at his father for having robbed Master Everel of freedom, and at Dashiell for having sauntered back into his life and captured him utterly, claiming a closure that had been no closure at all.

At first, Dashiell seemed not to notice. When he did, he tried a wan smile, but Nic went on staring like if he stared hard enough, he would be able to see inside the vowsmith's head, be able, at last, to understand him.

Dashiell turned away, but glanced back soon enough, and by the time the second course was laid they were caught in a dance, Nic increasingly determined not to look away, not to let Dashiell decide when they were finished. They had no possible future, but if Nic could take his own closure and prove himself as heartless, perhaps he could walk away as Dashiell had done.

When dinner ended, there was no lingering over the wine, no sitting in the drawing room to chat and laugh and play music, no fireworks or tea or supper, just a desultory series of good nights as the party broke up. Lingering by his chair, Nic watched Dashiell leave, watched him bid the duke good night and head for the open door. There he paused and glanced back, meeting Nic's gaze. One beat. Two. A faint smile and he was gone, turning the wrong direction along the hallway for a man intent on retiring to bed.

"Nic." Leaf was at his elbow, Millie and Lady Lisbeth a step behind. "We're heading upstairs. Would you like to walk with us?"

Safety in numbers was their wise plan, but Nic shook his head. He would be wise tomorrow. "You go. I have some things to do. Don't worry, though, I promise I'll be on my guard."

She gave him a worried grimace, but wished him good night, leaving him to carry his buzzing anger out into the hallway alone. There was no sign of Dashiell. Not that it mattered, for Nic knew where to find him with the same certainty he knew the sun would rise. And sure enough, out in the far reaches of the house, he found weak light spilling beneath the conservatory door. His smile held a grim edge as he pushed it open.

"I thought I might find you here."

Dashiell rose from the window seat, reaching for his discarded coat. At the sight of Nic, he left it where it lay. "Well, it's always been my favourite room," he said, something of a sheepish smile turning his lips. "It feels . . . comforting. Safe."

The words gave Nic pause. "Are you all right?"

"Yes. And no. Did you know there's no statute in the guild charter that allows for a vowsmith to pull out of negotiations when they feel unsafe? Likely because the punishment for harming a working vowsmith is high and strictly enforced, but for the first time I'm not finding that very comforting."

"No, I should imagine not."

Silence stretched, but Nic had no desire to fill it. Dashiell cleared his throat. "The loss of Master Everel must be quite a shock for you. I'm sorry."

The thought of how strange it would be without the old vowsmith had been circling Nic's mind, coming slowly to an unexpected conclusion. "Yes, but also no. I'd seen him more this week than I had for months. Since my father stopped taking apprentices, he's been more like a piece of furniture in my father's study than a member of the family. And you should know we don't *do* family."

Dashiell grimaced and strode to the large aviary to straighten its night cover—perhaps so he didn't have to look at Nic as he said, "I heard about what happened to Louis sa Ellis. He can't have been with you long, before . . ."

"Nine months. And no, I don't know what happened. We had every reason to believe it was an accident."

"Oh, I'm not trying to pry, I just . . . I don't know. I suppose I'm curious about . . . how everything went after I left."

"You mean did I kiss any of my father's other apprentices while sitting on that window seat?"

Dashiell's gaze snapped around. "No, I didn't mean—"

"Well, no." Nic fixed him with an unblinking stare. "Only you."

A flicker of relief? Nic wasn't sure, but the possibility both thrilled and enraged him in equal measure. He stepped forward. "No, after you left, I had to leave the house for such company."

A question seemed to hover unspoken on Dashiell's lips, and well for him it stayed there. One step became a second and soon they stood just as they had in the pavilion, breath hitched, gazes caught, the buzz that had filled Nic since rising to a crescendo like he was holding back a storm. Dashiell took up his whole world, all thick brows and soft, dark lashes. He made no move forward, yet there was something imploring in his gaze, in the way he licked his dry lips.

Nic touched his nose to Dashiell's cheek in an echo of the vow-smith's gesture, receiving it back with the ghost of a laugh. "Old habit," he murmured. "With your Brilliance headaches, I always wanted to be sure before I . . ."

The last of Dashiell's words were but a breath across Nic's lips, the rest swallowed into a soft kiss that troubled the strength of his knees. Moving slowly as though Nic were a nervous animal he feared to frighten, Dashiell slid an arm around his waist and drew him close, and Nic could feel himself losing control of the moment—the moment that needed to be his and his alone.

He pulled away abruptly, quick strides taking him toward the door.

"Nic—"

Nic turned the key and glanced back, catching relief as it crossed Dashiell's face. "I hope you don't mind."

"Not at all," Dashiell murmured as Nic returned to stand before him. "To be honest, I hoped you would come."

"More closure?"

Dashiell's lips parted, but before he could speak, Nic added, "You owe me for that. Why should you be the one to decide what closure looks like? What about what I wanted?"

He gripped the folds of Dashiell's neckcloth and pulled him close—a sharp, hungry movement that elicited a delicious gasp. On its heels, the vowsmith's eyes slid half closed. "Well, by all means, my lord, do whatever you want with me."

"Oh, I will."

He'd had no conscious plan when he'd followed Dashiell, but

still holding him by the neckcloth, Nic now backed him toward the window. There it was Dashiell's turn to drop onto the window seat as Nic had done, the only difference that he was all but fully clothed. Nic stripped off his own coat to match, before sitting on Dashiell's legs, chest to chest, face to face, the vowsmith's bronze eyes shining gold in the candlelight.

"Sit on your hands."

A frown flickered across Dashiell's brow, but he did as he was bid, shifting his weight to pin his hands beneath him.

"That's for your safety," Nic said. "That way you can say you never touched me."

Dashiell huffed a laugh. "Very funny, but if someone sees us, it—"

"If someone sees us, I'll claim it was all me. Don't complain. You got what you wanted, now it's my turn to have you how I want."

Dashiell seemed like he would argue, but as Nic spoke he unbuttoned the front of his own breeches, leaving the vowsmith to swallow any objections and stare. Dashiell's fall front was next, the buttons almost torn away so Nic could slide his hand in, his fingers closing around the man's rapidly hardening cock. He drew it out along with his own, letting them fall heavily against one another in the candlelight.

Dashiell's breath hitched as he stared at the sight between them. "Damn."

"No hands," Nic reminded him. "Or I walk away."

Confusion coloured Dashiell's face, only to be chased away upon a gasp when Nic slid a hand around them both. With his own hands pinned beneath him, Dashiell could only watch Nic's fingers work at each long, lingering stroke, every one of them tight and sure and teasing so much more. Nic tried to focus, to build slowly and draw their moment out, but the sensation was everything he had ever dreamed, leaving the desire to hurry toward an end tearing at his concentration.

While Nic worked upon their joined flesh, Dashiell seemed

unable to drag his gaze away, until all at once he bared his throat and moaned to the uncaring ceiling.

"God, Nic, your hands."

"This is what you can do when you don't get scribe's hand," Nic murmured.

The laugh was almost as beautiful as the moan, and the notch of pleasure between Dashiell's dark brows. "This is not fair," he said, breathless.

"Who said anything about fair?" Nic nipped the point of Dashiell's chin and didn't so much as miss a stroke when the vow-smith tried to bite back. Instead he captured Dashiell's mouth with his own, his kiss a light, teasing thing as he went on building the sensation, every stroke a step toward an ending he both wanted and didn't with all his soul.

"Please let me touch you," Dashiell whispered against Nic's lips.

"No." Nic prefaced his reply with a kiss and followed it with another, each pulling lightly at Dashiell's lips as though he sought to consume him.

"But this is torture!"

Dashiell tried to bite Nic's lip, only for Nic to pull away with a soft laugh. "Torture, huh?"

He shifted the position of his fingers and tightened his grip, the pleasure it sent through his body nothing to the thrill of Dashiell's gasp. The vowsmith's reactions were everything he'd hoped for, from his small moans and whimpers to his requests to be let free. He writhed with every tightening stroke, and when Nic leaned close, pressing their cocks between them, Dashiell let out a cry—a desperate, needing thing, a vulnerable plea more sound than words. And on his lips, Nic's name, repeated like a prayer.

When at last the legs beneath him gave a jerk, Nic pulled back, shifting his hand just in time to save them both from ruined shirts as Dashiell bucked, a hissed expletive caught upon his bitten lip.

Dashiell's reaction was all he needed to let himself go, leaving the heat of their mingled seed covering his hand and the hot huff of their breath upon the air.

For a moment neither of them moved, as though to remain still might keep the clock from ticking on, might keep them caught in that perfect moment. Until Dashiell let out a breath, as much a laugh as a sigh. A light sparkle of sweat beaded his brow, and he leaned forward to touch his forehead to Nic's chest, each breath he pulled heavy and satisfied. And as the first thrill of having Dashiell in his power faded, Nic realised this one closure, this one memory, would never be enough. In truth, all the memories he could gather never could be, because he wanted Dashiell, not once, not twice, but forever.

It was, Nic thought, a terrible time to realise he'd never stopped being in love.

Nic stood abruptly, two steps taking him to his discarded coat and the handkerchief tucked into its pocket. There he stood with his back to Dashiell and cleaned himself and his hands, hoping to still his rising panic.

"Nic—"

"Don't." The word was out before Nic could temper it, and having tidied himself as best he could, he turned, forcing a smile. "It's best if we don't talk, don't you think? I'm done as you were done."

Dashiell had buttoned his fall front and stood to adjust his breeches, but he froze there, beautifully tousled in the candlelight. "You're angry with me."

It wasn't a question, but the slight confusion in the tone lashed Nic to answer all the same.

"Yes!" he cried, and with the truth out he could not stop. "Yes, I am. The other night should have been amazing but you just fucked me and walked out. Small variation on the last time you walked out. As though it meant nothing. As though *I* mean nothing."

"Nic—"

"No, don't trouble yourself. I am quite done."

No sooner had Nic turned than Dashiell gripped his shoulders. "Nic, stop."

"Let go." Nic pulled free and spun away, as angry with himself as with Dashiell and wishing it all unsaid.

Dashiell grabbed his arm. "Nic—"

"Excuse me, Master sa Vare. I'll thank you not to manhandle me."

"Oh no, you can't high-and-mighty lord me into being quiet this time, Nic. You mean everything to me and you always have."

Nic yanked his arm from the vowsmith's tight hold and flung his hands wide, all disbelief, all hurt. "And yet you left without even saying goodbye!"

He spun in search of his coat again, hardly thinking. How foolish to have spoken at all, foolish to have believed he'd wanted only fairness.

"Stop walking away from me," Dashiell growled, and Nic was bitterly satisfied to have communicated something, even if it was just his anger.

"You have no right to demand that now." Nic snatched up his coat, determined to make a proud stride for the door, only to find the vowsmith had dashed ahead of him and pulled the key from the lock.

"You want to know why I left?" Dashiell said, sliding the key into his pocket. "I left because my parents always told me a good vowsmith doesn't have a home, that when you travel a lot, home has to be something you carry with you. So, when I realised that this had become my home—no, that *you* had become my home—I couldn't stay. I feared getting in too deep and still having to go back to my real life when my apprenticeship was over."

You had become my home.

Nic couldn't speak. Couldn't breathe.

"For a while I let myself dream that if I was successful enough, I could earn you," Dashiell went on, a mocking laugh ghosting past his lips. "But I work with marriage contracts enough to know how much I'm worth, and how much less it is than you."

"That's not true," Nic whispered, struggling to swallow the lump building in his throat.

Dashiell pushed away from the door and came to stand before him, to brush a hooked finger down his cheek. "You're sweet, but you know it's true. No amount of success could ever bring the younger son of a baronet near the heir of a duke. I wasn't born a man who could ever hope to love you, so I ran."

Tears dampened Nic's eyes. Dashiell's admission was eating through his anger and flaying him open. Had that been tension he'd felt? The hesitance? Hot and cold blown by the vowsmith's failing attempt to hide his own desires?

Dashiell spread his arms and let them fall, a defeated gesture with a watery smile. "I'm sorry, Nic. I have treated you abominably. I ought to have told you then, ought to have said goodbye, and I didn't. Easier to convince myself you felt nothing for me. That it was only my heart I was breaking."

He gestured toward the rest of the house existing somewhere beyond their golden room. "And I knew the moment the Serrals came to me that I ought to turn this contract down, but I couldn't. I could no more have turned down the chance to see you again than I could have sprouted wings to fly. I hardly slept for days. I bought a whole new wardrobe." He plucked at his now rumpled shirt. "I wanted to be perfect, to impress you, and I walked in and you . . ." Dashiell huffed another mocking laugh and ran a hand through his dark hair. "You looked right through me. And when I followed you into the garden that first night, you made it clear you didn't want me here. What a fool I was for thinking you might care to know me again."

"You broke my heart! I had to protect myself."

"I know. I know, and when you kissed me . . . That you'd done so in anger was all that allowed me to pull away, yet I couldn't help hoping there had been something more. A hope I dared not even acknowledge because I am not brave like you, Nic. I'm not. I'm a coward and I hurt you to save myself. And then I did it again when—fuck, I'm sorry." He gripped Nic's face between his hands and planted tiny kisses over cheeks damp with tears. "You are so perfect and so precious but even now all I want to do is run because we can't do this. I am no more worthy of you now than I was then."

"Dash . . ." Emotion suspended Nic's voice, the urge to scream at the universe almost overwhelming. Because Dashiell was right. Nothing had changed. They had been brought together again for a brief moment, but it was a moment that would end, their lives diverging on separate courses that no power could force together.

Dashiell's smile grew lopsided, seeming to begin in joy and end in misery. "It's been a long time since you called me that. Dash. No one else does, you know."

"I missed you," Nic whispered, determined to swallow the truth that followed, that soon he would miss him again—the best they could hope for a life of meeting every few years, a love spent in snatches, dried and wasted in absence.

"I missed you too. And I am so sorry, Nic, truly. God, even just my behaviour the last few days has been so selfish." He pressed a hand to his brow, his eyes squeezed shut as though in pain. "Utterly unforgivable."

Nic took hold of his face and, drawing him down, kissed his forehead. "Yet you are forgiven. And in truth, mine was not that much better. Just . . . please don't make decisions about . . . about *us* without me. Don't let your back be all the conversation I see."

Us. A word that could encompass so much, yet had to mean so little.

Released, Dashiell nodded and swiped his sleeve across his eyes. "I won't. I promise. Although it hardly matters when all the us there can be has already passed. Even this now is too dangerous, especially after today."

After a third body had been sent to the crypt.

Nic wiped a tear from Dashiell's cheek, somehow holding back his own. "I know," he said, because sixteen-year-old Dashiell had been right. They had no future. They could linger awhile, there in their golden bubble outside of the world, but that would only make it harder to walk away. Better to stop now before they got tangled any further, before they could share and reminisce and bring life to the impossible.

Nic couldn't have said which of them moved first; the space between them simply shrank until Dashiell's nose brushed his, until their lips touched, until Nic clasped Dashiell's face in his hands and sought to express all he couldn't say, to retrieve and hold everything they'd been and everything they could ever be in this one final kiss. A plea that time might cease went unheeded, and when at last they parted to breathe one another's air, Nic felt exhausted, broken, a crazed piece of glasswork that had miraculously failed to shatter. Yet.

Dashiell held out the key. Long seconds it sat in the palm of his hand, a curse neither wanted to touch. Brave, Dashiell had called him, yet knowing what it meant, Nic wished he didn't have to be brave. That perhaps, just this once, he could have chosen instead to be happy. But the world outside would listen to no such pleas.

He took the key. And unable to resist the urge, he then took Dashiell's hand and lifted it to his lips. "Good night, Dash," he said, planting a light kiss upon his knuckles.

Having been released, the vowsmith's hand hovered a moment before he let it fall and swallowed hard. "Good night, Nic."

Chapter 17

Nic woke with the dawn. And having woken, he refused to move, refused to do anything but lie cocooned in his covers and recall Dashiell's words. Dashiell's touch. The taste of his lips, and the joining of their bodies in the candlelight. The way he had gasped and moaned, had made his admissions and spilled his tears. Perhaps if he didn't greet the new day, Nic could hold on to the moment in which it had all been real, despite the guilt that it wasn't Master Everel's death that haunted him most.

Eventually, Ambrose's hovering became so insistent that Nic finally levered himself up and deigned to have a breakfast tray set beside him. There was something terrible about life going on after heartbreak, as terrible as life going on when Rowerre and Gillingham and Master Everel no longer breathed.

When a tap sounded on the outer door, Nic knew it was Leaf even before Ambrose reached it.

"Lady Leaf is here, my lord, and she—"

"And she is horrified that you are still abed!" Leaf swept in, all white muslin and laced flounces. "We have work to do before—" She halted as Ambrose set a chair for her at Nic's bedside. "What is it? What happened?"

When he didn't answer, she turned to the valet. "You may leave us, Ambrose. I am sure my innocence will be maintained just as well if you wait in the sitting room."

"As you wish, my lady." The young man absented himself with a bow, closing the bedchamber door behind him.

Nic tilted his head, achieving a wry smile. "It is quite scandalous for me to have an unmarried young lady alone in my bedchamber, you know."

"And yet you may have any number of unmarried young men in your bedchamber without anyone batting an eye," Leaf said. "Truly men get the best of everything. Now, out with it. It's Master sa Vare, isn't it?"

Nic tried to think of something humorous to say, and failed. "We . . . talked last night."

"Talked? Or . . . *talked*? I feel the pause is significant."

He hesitated, a policy of honesty with Leaf baulking at describing what had actually happened.

"And that pause was also very significant," Leaf said. "It has painted quite the picture for me. Do go on. Although I hope you were more careful this time."

"I locked the door."

"See? You're learning. Congratulations."

She patted his hand and Nic managed a laugh through rising tears. "Do you take anything seriously?"

"Far too much, I'm told, but you're crying." She gripped the hand she'd patted, all humour chased from her features. "What happened?"

So Nic told her, sparing only the details of the tryst. Told her how he'd realised he was in love, how they'd argued, and how Dashiell's admissions now haunted his every thought. By the time he was done, tears dampened Leaf's eyes too.

"Oh, that's all very romantic."

"I thought I'd done something wrong, but he left because he loved me, Leaf. Because he knew we could never be together."

"I'm sorry, Nic. I hope you know that if there was anything I could do to change things, I would."

"Thank you."

"Even though I have to admit that I do not personally understand having such an intense interest in another person."

Grateful to shift the topic into less tear-inducing waters, Nic said, "No? You've never caught your breath because someone walked into a room? Or felt like you couldn't live without them?"

"No, for which I'm quite grateful. It sounds distressing." She shot him a sidelong look. "On which topic, there is something I want to discuss with you. It's about . . . about the provision in our contract to ensure children."

"Oh. Right. Nothing major or awkward."

At any other time, she might have laughed. Instead, she said, "I have been . . . worried. Papa will not talk with me about it since young women are not supposed to discuss indelicate topics, as though what is to happen with my own body is not sufficiently important to set aside such considerations."

She huffed an annoyed breath. Nic didn't interrupt.

"I just wish I knew what they were planning for us. For me, I suppose. Ideally, I would rather not have to . . . you know . . . be intimate, with anyone ever. And to be wholly truthful, I would rather not carry children either. I find the whole idea quite repugnant. Children themselves are fine, just not in . . . Well, and since I assume you know as little about the contract as I do," she went on, picking at the lace on her sleeves and staring at the floor, "I was hoping you could ask Master sa Vare. I know he shouldn't discuss the contract outside the negotiation chamber, and maybe now isn't the best time after—"

"It's all right." Nic clasped her hands and found them shaking. "I'll ask. It's important to you, so it's important to me. And if we don't like the answer, I'll see what can be done about it. Does that satisfy you?"

She pressed out an anxious little smile. "It does. I . . . have no words for how grateful I am that I've ended up in this position with you rather than anyone else."

"I have been thinking the same," he admitted. "It may not be what either of us wanted out of life, but there are many worse fates than to marry one's best friend."

Leaf gave him a tight little hug and wiped tears from the corners of her eyes.

"What a pair we are this morning. One would think people had died!" She laughed a damp chortle, sniffed, and stole a piece of bread off his breakfast tray. "Gosh, it's already ten. I had better go," she added, rising with her prize in hand. "Papa is insisting on spending the morning with me to *brighten my spirits*. I'll escape as soon as I can, though, because we need to figure all this out before someone else dies for this ridiculous contract. If we all end up dead, will they still say it was worth going on with, I wonder?"

On those cheering words, she departed. No doubt she hadn't expected an answer, yet as Nic picked at his breakfast, he found himself mulling it over all the same. That the lock-in had not been ended despite three dead bodies begged a fresh question: Would any price ever be deemed too high?

As negotiations never sat on Sundays, Nic found the duke making his weekly round of the Court's echoes. He stood on the upper landing above the great hall, where the largest aviary in the house was set into the central stairs. Behind their finely wrought golden bars, some two dozen echoes sat on carved branches, pecked at linen leaves, and preened their shimmering feathers.

"If there is any more trouble, move Guinevere back to the conservatory," the duke was saying to the head keeper as Nic joined them. "She may do better in the warmth."

"Yes, Your Grace."

"If you do, move Valour as well. They do well together."

"That they do, Your Grace."

The duke turned. "Something I can do for you, Nicholas?"

"I want to know how many more people need to die before you'll call this contract off."

This earned a long stare, until the duke gestured to his head keeper with a sigh. "Go check the duchess's birds, Hedgeley. I shall be along soon."

"Yes, Your Grace."

Hedgeley hurried off, footsteps fading away down the stairs.

Once they were alone, the duke fixed his intent gaze on Nic. "Your question, Nicholas, suggests you think this contract is the reason people have died."

"Is the possibility so far-fetched? Rowerre died within hours of the doors being locked."

"Indeed, but have you considered that if we didn't want the contract, it needn't have been entered into in the first place? Lord Ricard aside, everyone involved is in favour."

"He hates you."

The duke's brows rose. "We have certainly had our disagreements."

"Is that why you didn't change his contract? When he asked you to save his marriage to Caroline Wivenwood."

The duke stilled. Swallowed. Something wary in the glance he threw around the landing. "How do you know about that?"

"Millie."

"I see."

He let out another sigh and rolled his shoulders, straightening from his ill ease. "I am not so petty as you think, Nicholas. My refusal to assist was purely because vowsmith law is sacrosanct. The net must hold."

"So it had nothing to do with preliminary negotiations between you and Lord Charborough falling through?"

Another long pause. "I cannot but feel you are interrogating me, Nicholas."

Perhaps he was. Nic hadn't sought his father out to demand so many answers, yet having begun to tug on the threads, he couldn't stop.

"No interrogation," he said. "But you talk a lot about our great name and my responsibility to uphold it without telling me anything I ought to know. How will your silence help me when you are gone?"

A smile twitched the corner of his father's lips. "A fine speech. Where has this son of mine been hiding all this time?"

"Right in front of you."

"Is that so? Well, since you have asked—no. My contract with Charles had nothing to do with Ricard's predicament."

"Then why didn't you marry?"

"Because life is complicated, Nicholas," the duke snapped. "Because minds change and hearts change even faster and we cannot alter our futures any more than we can alter our pasts. And I do not see how this particular history's details will help guide you once my honours are yours."

Perhaps they wouldn't, but Nic still wanted to know, wanted to understand, wanted a guiding light to follow in his own darkness. Words he couldn't say. Instead, he recalled why he had come and said, "Is this contract worth the risk that your honours might never be mine?"

His father tilted his head. Silent. Beside them the echoes went on fluttering about, chirping and squawking at one another in their artificial forest. "You fear for your life?" he said eventually, the words quiet.

"My life. Leaf's. Master sa Vare's. If someone would kill Master

Everel, why not one of us? Why not even you or Lord Charborough? I know we need this contract, but is it worth risking further life for?"

The duke stepped close, taking Nic's arm. "These deaths have been unfortunate accidents—yes, even Master Everel's, however it may look. I tell you no one wants to endanger this contract. Do you understand?"

"How can you be so sure?"

"Because I must be. We do not just need this contract, Nicholas—it is *everything*. It must go ahead. We must get through this. It is the only way. Promise me." His grip tightened around Nic's arm, digging in like echo claws. "Promise me you will do what it takes to uphold our name."

Nic hunted his father's face, wishing he could see past those dark glasses, past the facade. The duke tightened his hold, and unsteadied by the hint of vulnerability, of desperation, Nic nodded.

"Yes. Of course. I promise."

His father's lips parted, and for a moment it looked as though he would say more. But something in Nic's tone or his expression must have betrayed his doubts, for the duke stepped back, everything about him, from his face to his stance, closing over like a heavy door. "Good." The word was crisp. Confident. "One day you will understand. The net must hold."

The library door creaked open upon the smell of dust, old parchment, ink, and candle wax. And a hint of the strong tea Dashiell preferred, lingering like a ghost. This room had been the centre of their lives, and in a flood of memories, Nic recalled why he rarely spent longer in there now than the time taken to find a book.

"Nic?"

Nic almost swallowed his tongue as Dashiell rose from one of the chairs, past melding with present in a way that made the world spin. Dashiell, perfectly dressed, perfectly poised, all emotion tucked away behind his professional mask. Nic could almost believe the previous night had been a dream.

He needed to say something, to answer as though the words *I wasn't born a man who could ever hope to love you* hadn't echoed endlessly through his head.

I am no more worthy of you now than I was then.

"Sorry," Nic managed at last, heading for the nearest shelf. "I didn't know you were here. I just need some books."

"Ah, well, I am hiding from Lady Lisbeth. No doubt you've noticed she has taken a liking to me and—"

Nic threw up a hand in unthinking defence. "You don't need to explain."

"Don't I?" Dashiell huffed a small laugh. "If it makes you feel even half as jealous as I feel watching you with Lady Leaf, then I do. Especially after having failed so spectacularly to be honest with you up until now."

"Leaf and I are friends. She has no more interest in me than I have in her." Nic had been about to hide himself in the maze of shelves, but turned back. "Actually, since you're here, I need to talk to you about that."

The vowsmith dropped his book onto the table where a cup of tea sat steaming. "Ominous, but go ahead."

"I need to know what our fathers have agreed upon. She . . . doesn't want to bear children."

"Oh." Dashiell cleared his throat and ran a hand down the front of his beautifully cut coat.

I bought a whole new wardrobe. I wanted to be perfect, to impress you.

"I know you're not meant to talk about the contract," Nic went on. "But I'd appreciate knowing what we're up against."

"Well, no, I really shouldn't tell you, but you've asked, so . . ." Dashiell looked at the floor and scuffed his foot on the boards. "It was contentious in the beginning. Lord Charborough was caught between wanting the, uh, Brilliance of your, uh—" Dashiell cleared his throat. "You have a very high Brilliant ability, and it seemed a waste to squander that by getting Lady Leaf someone else to . . ."

Nic was beginning to wish he hadn't asked, his own cheeks heating like Dashiell's, as much in memory of just what he'd been doing with his supposed Brilliance the night before.

"I hope you can manage these conversations with less stuttering in the negotiation chamber."

"It's easier in a professional setting!" Dashiell cried. "There are formal words, but you don't know them and I hate even having to talk about this with you, so here we are. Long story short, Lord Charborough has had the stud clause struck off and is now quietly confident you and Lady Leaf like each other well enough to do your duty."

For a moment Nic just stared at the vowsmith and his reddened cheeks. "Did he read about me in the preliminary papers?"

"I'm quite sure he did, yes."

Which, Nic realised, meant Dashiell had also read about him in the preliminary papers.

"Right, well, that's a relief."

"A relief?"

"Yes," Nic said, "because if no one else is contracted to be involved, we can disappoint them all at our leisure."

"You wouldn't try to—?"

"No. My feelings on the matter aside, she doesn't want to have sex or carry children, so that's where the conversation ends. And see? It's not so hard to say the words."

Dashiell let out a soft laugh. "Ah, but I already told you that you're far braver than I am."

I am not brave like you, Nic. I'm not. I'm a coward and I hurt you to save myself.

Nic was glad he had asked and could satisfy Leaf's worries, but as Dashiell went on standing there in the aftermath of those words, Nic found he needed to leave as fiercely as he wanted to stay. He turned to the nearest shelf.

By some miracle, he'd ended up in the vowsmithing section, not that it was hard given how much of the library was given over to such texts. While he waited for his heartbeat to slow, Nic trailed a hand along a collection of leather-bound spines, not entirely sure what he was looking for. *A History of Modern Vowsmithing.* Likely that was too broad, but he pulled it out and continued on. *On Contracts for a Stronger Future* seemed more promising, so he took that too.

Dashiell leaned against the shelf. "I thought your interest in vowsmithing was . . . ?"

"So low as to exist in the liminal space between negative and never? Yes."

"Mmm, yes. The same place I store my interest in horse racing and overcooked vegetables."

"And fennel seed cake."

The vowsmith pulled a disgusted face. "Truly foul. I swear Mrs. Beckett only made them so often because she knew I hated them."

"You'll be glad to know she retired a few years ago. I haven't seen a single fennel seed since."

Almost Nic added that while the cook was new, Mrs. Podmarsh was still the housekeeper and as unpleasant as ever, but the ease with which they could fall into conversation only twisted the hurt deeper.

"Perhaps this isn't a good idea," he said instead. "Spending time together like this, I mean. Since you must be a stranger, better you be a stranger."

He wished the words unsaid the moment he spoke them, the thought of watching Dashiell leave unbearable. A flicker of the same hurt crossed the vowsmith's face.

"You're right, of course. And once again, are far braver than me."

"Hardly," Nic said, unable to meet Dashiell's gaze as his dual desires warred within him.

"Well, I'll leave you to it. Whatever you're doing, I'm sure you have it well in hand."

God, Nic, your hands.

Nic swallowed hard. "What does 'The net must hold' really mean?"

Dashiell had pushed off the shelf to leave, but frowned at that. "Only that it's important to remember how even tiny changes in vow law can affect a myriad of other things. Any clause wrongly smithed does not stand alone, but rather ripples out, changing everything to which it is connected. And once done, some mistakes can be difficult to undo. Enough errors in enough places might even threaten the whole, and so we remind ourselves that the net must hold."

An unsurprising answer, yet Nic couldn't quite make it fit with his father's words.

"Did that help?" Dashiell asked when Nic didn't speak.

"I don't know."

"Does this have anything to do with the three dead men lying in your crypt? You think someone wants the contract to fail?"

Abandoning the vowsmithing books, Nic slid his hands into his pockets, closing himself protectively in. "What other reason could there be?"

"I don't know, but I admit I don't see why anyone would want it to fail either. Lord Charborough paid through the nose to make sure this contract went ahead, and I imagine His Grace needs Lady Leaf's dowry too much to want it ruined. I'm . . . not exactly sure how things stand, but matters don't seem to have improved here since I left, and the general talk in most circles is that your grandfather gambled you into serious debt, yes?"

"Something like that."

"You know, I always thought your father would right things. There must be money to be made off the estate, and surely your mother brought in plenty—no, my apologies. It is not my place to speculate."

Dashiell hadn't said anything Nic himself hadn't thought a dozen times, yet he found that of all the things he didn't want to discuss, the ceaseless poverty of his day-to-day life was right at the top.

"The other guests then," Nic said to change the subject. "What motive might Lady Lisbeth have?"

Dashiell laughed. "I think you're safe from her murderous meddling. She seems to have her heart set on me, not you."

Easier to convince myself you felt nothing for me. That it was only my heart I was breaking.

He should have let Dashiell leave.

"My mother?"

All trace of humour faded from Dashiell's face. "Her Grace is ... not always well, but surely there is no sense in ending a contract that would bring in both a new companion and more money?"

"Lady Theresa?"

"Much the same. What does she have to gain? Nothing, surely, since she doesn't stand to lose anything either. She is just here because Lady Leaf needs a chaperone and her mother couldn't spare the time. Though if we're clutching at straws, she has made no secret of her belief that Lord Charborough is throwing Lady Leaf away. She could be trying to save the family money."

"A wise woman. I'm certainly not worth the fortune they must be paying."

The vowsmith didn't answer.

I work with marriage contracts enough to know how much I'm worth, and how much less it is than you.

The length of the shelf stood between them, yet with Dashiell's loving admissions still ringing in Nic's mind, every moment seemed to shrink the space to nothing. So easily could he reach out. A knowing smile. A whispered nothing. A touch, light but familiar. There were so many things Nic wanted to know, so many moments he wanted to experience, so much they could be if only they could breathe life into all that hung suspended between them. Yet it was better not to breathe at all than to be left winded.

"In truth," Dashiell said at last, "I don't think Lady Theresa has any more reason to want this contract ruined than I do."

"All right. You."

For what seemed an age, Dashiell just stared at him. No annoyance, no humour, just an intensity that made something all too like trepidation trickle down Nic's back.

"Oh, I have quite a lot of motives," Dashiell said eventually, his tone light, almost flippant. "Dislike of Rufus Gillingham. A childhood fear of Master Everel. And as for ending the contract, my motive for that is standing right in front of me."

Dashiell was playing along, but though the words were nonsense, his stare wasn't. It stripped Nic bare and tore his breath away, leaving his heart thundering so hard he didn't hear the approaching footsteps until Leaf appeared in the doorway.

"Nic? Oh, there you are, I thought I heard—oh, Master sa Vare, my apologies."

"That is quite all right, my lady. I was about to take my leave." Dashiell's smile was taut. "I have taken up quite enough of Lord Monterris's time. If you will excuse me."

"Of course."

A nod, a bow, and Dashiell strode out into the passage from whence Leaf had come, leaving Nic to the doubtful felicity of watching him go.

"Gosh, what was that about?"

"Nothing," Nic said, determinedly pulling his gaze away. "We were just going over everyone's motives."

Her curious stare lingered on the now empty doorway. "Well, then he could have stayed."

"I think he would feel like he's imposing. You are a marquess's daughter after all."

"And you're a duke's son, but that didn't stop him doing . . . you know . . . *things* with you."

Please let me touch you.

"Well? Did you come up with anything?" she went on when Nic didn't speak. "With the motives, I mean."

"No. Or at least, only to decide that no one has one for wanting to break the contract. Perhaps this isn't about the contract after all. Perhaps it's about something else."

"Like?"

Nic shook his head. "I don't know, but there are enough old hatreds in this house right now that it could be anything."

"You're right. We have no definitive clues, no motives beyond Uncle Ricard wanting to invoke the Requisite Care Clause, and no witnesses. There's a missing page torn from something, a valet pushed down the stairs, an excommunicated vowsmith hung for dramatic effect, and a head negotiator with an arrow in his back. And everyone seems *determined* to believe it all chance."

Determined was the right word, nothing rational about the way the duke had insisted they see the contract through.

"You know what?" Leaf folded her arms. "We should just confront them all. Tonight. At dinner so they cannot escape. Perhaps if we ask the right questions, we'll finally get a good answer."

The prospect of such an evening did not entice, yet neither did the prospect of finding another body. Or becoming one.

Nic went down to dinner with dread locked in his gut. They had spent the afternoon worrying over what questions might help—at least of those they might get away with—and now it was just a matter of asking them.

Despite Master Everel's empty chair, the talk that evening was convivial. At the foot of the table, the duchess listened while Lord Charborough and Millie reminisced about a runaway horse, and Lady Theresa had embarked on a homily about what conduct her father deemed proper for Sunday evenings. Across the table, Lady Lisbeth's dedication to Dashiell continued most of the evening, only to be broken when Lord Ricard leaned in during one of her rare pauses.

"Master sa Vare, I hear the chamber is to be rather empty tomorrow."

The man hadn't lifted his voice, yet the question seemed to cut across conversations, pulling attention his way.

"I believe so, my lord," Dashiell replied, showing no sign he was aware that everyone stared. "Most of the common members of our team left after Gillingham died. Now it seems the same has happened on the Monterris side of the table."

"Gosh, whatever for?" Lady Theresa laughed.

"If I had to guess, Lady Theresa, I should say because they are afraid for their lives."

"But who would want to kill a mere scribe?"

Dashiell swallowed both sneer and reply, returning instead to his plate.

"How right you are, Lady Theresa," Nic said, able to speak where Dashiell could not. "Master Everel, on the other hand, was quite an exceptional man and thus eminently worth murdering."

Lady Theresa tittered. "How you do take my words quite out of context, Lord Monterris."

"Oh, Aunt, you remind me." Leaf set down her fork. "Lord Monterris and I had a disagreement this afternoon and I think perhaps you can help us sort it out. At which archery target did you last see Master Everel alive?"

"Oh. Uh." The lady's gaze darted from her niece to Nic and back. "Well, if I can assist . . ."

"An odd disagreement to have," the duke murmured.

"I think we must have been at the ninth target when he last brought us arrows. Quite near the pavilion. Perhaps you recall more precisely, Your Grace?"

Appealed to, the duke gave a curt nod. "I believe you are correct, Lady Theresa."

Leaf turned her attention along the table to her father. "And you, Papa?"

"Leaf, this is hardly a proper conversation to have over dinner," the man said with a warning stare.

"I am merely trying to resolve an argument by discussing our archery afternoon."

"What exactly is the nature of this argument, Nicholas?" the duke asked.

They had discussed the importance of working out where Master Everel had last been seen alive and by whom, but as Leaf had wholly manufactured the disagreement on the spot, Nic was left to stammer, "Oh, um."

"It was whether or not we completed the fifth target and thus which of us won, Your Grace," Leaf said. "Lord Monterris is quite sure he did and I am equally convinced that he did not."

Chuckles eased some of the tension, but when Leaf shot her questioning look back to her father, Lord Charborough shook his head in warning.

"We saw him at the eighth target," the duchess said, her voice ringing clear. "Just after Lord Charborough saw that ghost in the pavilion."

Lord Charborough coughed, gaze skittering as he became the centre of attention. "Well, no, in hindsight I'm quite sure it wasn't a ghost, just some odd trick of the light that gave me a shock. Everel certainly thought nothing of it when I mentioned it."

"Well, we saw him at the seventh," Millie chimed in. "It wasn't until we reached the sixth that we had to stop and wait, but by then, of course, the clouds were coming over."

Lady Lisbeth took the opportunity to lightly touch Dashiell's arm. "We saw him at the fourth, I believe, Master sa Vare? You suggested that he rest."

It was more information than they had dared hope for, the collective testimony suggesting the old vowsmith had disappeared somewhere between the fifth and seventh targets.

"Well, thank you, everyone, I think that means I won," Leaf said, smiling upon the company. "Perhaps you all also recall where you were between the end of the negotiation session and dinner on the night Gillingham died."

"Leaf!" Lord Charborough's hand balled into a fist on the table. "I told you there was to be no more of this. We have already played your game. Now I want to hear no more about it."

A tense silence bloomed, but before it could take root, Dashiell cleared his throat. "If it satisfies your concerns, Lady Leaf, I am happy to share that I took a walk while there was still light, before retiring to my room to make preparations for the following day."

"Yes, and I was reading in the parlour until it was time to dress for dinner," Lady Lisbeth said.

Lady Theresa sniffed. "Well, I hardly recall. It is so boring here that the days run together."

"Oh yes, dining rooms catching fire and dead bodies turning up all over the place are ever so dull," Millie retorted.

"That is quite enough," Lady Theresa said. "Not all of us have rotted our minds with gothic novels until such things are entertaining. Bodies behind curtains and . . . and mad nuns and such."

At the head of the table, the duke laid down his cutlery. "This conversation is unseemly for the dinner table. Let us not scare off our appetites with such nonsense."

"Hear, hear," Lord Charborough agreed, lifting his wineglass.

Leaf once more fixed her father with a questioning look. "You did not say where you were that evening, Papa."

"Leaf!"

"Leaf, dear." Lady Theresa pressed a hand to her temple. "Do listen to your father. You are making a scene. Poor Gillingham took his own life, and dreadful as it was, there is nothing more to be said about it. Whatever will His Grace think of you?"

"And if he did not take his own life?" Nic asked.

"Nicholas."

"The man killed himself," Lord Charborough interjected over the duke's scowl. "Nothing more to be said, is that not so, Doctor?"

Having been appealed to, Dr. Fanshaw cleared his throat with something of an apologetic inflection. "While it is impossible to be sure, my lord, a later examination of the body provided sufficient reason to doubt that conclusion."

"What? He was hanging from the damn chandelier!"

"And may already have been dead before he got up there."

A beat of silence held while the gathered company grappled with the horrible implications of such words. The duke broke it first, throwing a contemptuous glance at the doctor. "Once again I must object that this is hardly an appropriate conversation for the dinner table."

"Dead before he got up there?" Lady Theresa said, ignoring this. "Oh no, poor, *poor* man."

"Poor man?" Millie scoffed. "What hogwash. It is just like you to point blame at Her Grace for disliking Master Everel when you hated Gillingham just as much."

"Millie! How beastly you are!"

At the head of the table, the duke's chair scraped back. His balled-up napkin dropped onto his unfinished plate and he spun away to stalk for the door. Castor sped to open it for him, and closed it in his wake—the look he threw the gathered company as near deep reproach as the old butler dared.

"Val!"

Lord Charborough rose as, beside him, Millie spat across the table, "*Beastly* is rich. You have your servants flogged if they so much as misplace a handkerchief!"

"Oh, my lord," Lady Theresa wailed at her husband. "Look how dreadfully she uses me. Such nasty ways that she can only have gotten from that mother of hers. If that woman—"

"Enough!" Lord Ricard rose too, throwing his own napkin down onto the table. "I put up with you spitting your poison about Caroline, my lady, but when it comes to my daughter you will hold your damn tongue."

"Oh! *She* is Caroline, but I am just *my lady*!"

"If it were up to me, you would not even be that!"

"Ricard!"

Lord Ricard glared at his brother across the table. "If you have nothing better to do than gasp our names whenever we displease you, do shut up, Charles."

"Ricard!"

With a snort, Lord Ricard took in the sea of shocked faces. "For once, Val had the right idea. If anyone needs me, I'll be—"

Lady Lisbeth shrieked and shrank into her chair, eyes caught to the ceiling. "What is *that*?"

Nic looked up, other cries erupting around him as a familiar darkness oozed through the plasterwork. Descending like mist in heavy swirls, it spread from the chandelier, a dark portent with fingers like cold knives.

Remembering its touch all too well, Nic leapt up from the table as tendrils lashed.

"Magic," Lord Charborough said, and then as though seeking to quell the note of doubt in his own voice, he added, "Some kind of conjuring, surely. Nothing to worry about."

Dashiell looked across the table. "Nic? Do you feel anything?"

Nic shook his head, not daring to mention he had seen such darkness before. "No, nothing. A faint stickiness, but no sigils."

"Oh, but if it is not magic, it must be a ghost!" Lady Theresa cried. "Or that malaise Master Everel warned us about. Don't let it touch you!"

At the foot of the table, Millie had gripped the duchess's hand. "Your Grace? What is that? Your Grace?" But the duchess's eyes had lost focus as she slid away into her own mind, leaving Silla to shake her head in warning, one arm sliding protectively around her mistress's shoulders.

"I can assure you, my lady, that Her Grace has never seen anything like that," the maid said. "Perhaps it would be wise to remove to the drawing room."

"Yes. Yes, everyone out," Lord Charborough said. "No doubt it is nothing, but we cannot be too careful. If you would take—"

A heavy knock sounded on the door.

Lord Charborough visibly relaxed. "Ah, that'll be Val. He will explain what this is."

A second knock. A third. Slow and rhythmic and oddly hollow

as Castor crossed the floor to open it. Dread spilled through Nic at the strangeness of it all, and he started forward even as Castor pulled open the door. Only to halt midstep, sucking a sharp breath. Framed there in the aperture stood the automaton from the style wing, its empty oval face luminescent in the candlelight. From one metal shoulder still hung Nic's ruined waistcoat, its limp cording dragging like so much torn skin.

Amid a chorus of cries, Castor slammed the door.

"What was that thing?"

"Oh, God help us!"

"Castor! What was that? Open the door."

"No! Don't let it in!"

The noise swirled as Nic grabbed for the handle.

"Lord Monterris, no!"

He yanked it open, bracing for the thing to lunge metal fingers toward his throat. But there was nothing. Beyond the door the hallway stood empty, only a hint of automaton oil hanging ghostlike in the air.

"Is it gone?" Leaf said, appearing at his shoulder.

"Gone."

Around him, the parlour lightened, and Nic looked up to find the chandelier candles brightly shining once more. A tableau of guests stared about with frozen expressions of horror, but the darkness had gone, vanishing like it had never been. Yet in its wake Nic thought he felt the faintest sigil, something like a *pa* at the edge of hearing. It seemed to come from a world away and yet hum right beside his ear.

"What is going on here?"

The duke appeared in the open doorway, candlelight gleaming on his dark glasses.

A beat of shocked silence became a babble of panicked voices, but it was Lord Charborough who said, "Castor saw it, didn't you, Castor?"

The duke turned to his butler, brows raised. "Castor?"

"Yes, Your Grace, but as it was not there when Lord Monterris opened the door again, it must have been just a trick of the light."

"A trick of the light?" Lady Theresa cried. "This house is cursed! We are all doomed!"

The duke stepped forward. "It is just a house, Lady Theresa. An old house that has seen much life, I grant you, and one in which there are no doubt a few dormant spells the wrong conditions could set off, but it is still just a house. It cannot harm anyone."

"What about Lord Francis? Why will no one talk about what happened to him?"

Lady Theresa seemed to realise she had stepped into dangerous water as soon as the words were out of her mouth, her lips parting as though in shock at her own daring.

For a long moment the duke just stared at her, before slowly removing his glasses.

Lady Theresa gasped. Nic had seen the scars before, but rarely enough that each occasion was like seeing them for the first time, the shock enough to turn anyone's stomach. They crisscrossed the skin around the underside of his father's eyes like the tangled twigs of an echo nest, turning what ought to be smooth skin into puckered flesh and giving his lower eyelids a ragged edge.

"See ghosts in odd shadows if you must, Lady Theresa," he said, glaring at her with the full force of his frightening eyes. "But I can assure you Lord Francis was not killed by a house. Monterris Court is not alive. It hates no one. And it is not cursed."

He gestured toward the drawing room. "Now, shall we?"

Chapter 18

There was no coming back from such a dinner. No amount of forced joviality could stop Lady Lisbeth from flinching at every sound. No amount of tea could thaw the frosty glares Lady Theresa threw her stepdaughter. And no amount of offered entertainments could ease the feeling they were all holding their breath.

"Well, that did not go according to plan," Leaf said, making a bid for the greatest understatement ever as she drew Nic away from the others. "That was definitely the same automaton, though, wasn't it?"

"Yes, still wearing my waistcoat." Nic dropped into a chair, his whole body feeling like lead. "And that darkness was the same as what it spewed at me in the service passage."

"Do you think it has something to do with the murders? That passage was where the chandelier mechanism was, but I don't know how exactly an automaton commits murder."

Nic realised with a flicker of shock that he'd never told her what he'd found out from Master Everel about Lord Francis's death. He had been too unsure of it, too wary, but he told her now, everything from the old vowsmith's words to his insinuations—the only possible conclusion that, whoever else may or may not have fallen prey since, Lord Francis had been killed by something on an automaton's reel.

"Then we have to find it," Leaf said. "Tomorrow."

"Find the murderous automaton?"

"You have a better plan?"

"No, I just wanted to be clear that was the plan."

"I don't see what else we can do, although if I'm entirely honest, Nic, your house is starting to frighten me."

Monterris Court had never been friendly. The company Nic had snuck into his bed over the years had inevitably found the house dreary and strange. He'd always laughed at them, as he'd always laughed at the ghost stories the servants told and the tales the townsfolk spread, but he didn't feel much like laughing anymore.

"Last time we searched we didn't find anything," he said. "Although . . . we didn't go to the grotto. That's where most of the automata parts are, you know. It's not a light and cheerful space, though, I warn you."

"You shock me. We will just have to take very heavy candelabras for whacking things, because we have to find out what's on that automaton's reel. Did you decipher the tape we found off the negotiation chamber yet?"

"No, there hasn't been a lot of time." Words both true and false, for perhaps there would have been more time had he not been so caught up on Dashiell. "I'll work on it tonight."

"Would it be faster if you asked Master sa Vare for help?"

He glanced across the room to where Dashiell stood staring down into the fire, one foot on the grate and his back to the assembled company. Nic yearned to go to him and offer reassurance, or at least company that might take his mind off the evening's troubles, and that was the problem. He wasn't sure they could be in the same room alone without closing the space, without risking what couldn't be risked.

Leaf's hand closed around his arm. "It's important, Nic. Apart from searching the style wing, we don't have any other leads."

"You're right. I'll ask."

She squeezed and let go.

At the other end of the room, a pair of chessboards had been set up and Lady Lisbeth had been coaxed to play against Lord Charborough. The duke was calling upon his other guests to play as though nothing out of the ordinary had happened. Away from the parlour, the strange darkness did seem less real, like it truly could have been a figment of their collective imaginations. Yet every now and then glances flitted to the ceiling between forced smiles.

"Master sa Vare," the duke said, causing Dashiell to flinch and look around. "Will you play?"

"No, thank you, Your Grace. I think I shall turn in early."

The tea tray had not yet been brought in, but the duke swallowed whatever surprise he might have felt and nodded.

Good nights were exchanged, and pausing only to light a candle at the door, Dashiell let himself out into the darkened house. Nic watched him go, caught by how particular it would look for him to follow now.

"Go," Leaf whispered, and with another brief squeeze of his arm, she got to her feet. "I will play, Your Grace," she said, making her way toward the others. "No doubt you are a far better player than I, but I do so like to learn."

"Ah, don't be taken in by such wiles, Val," Lord Charborough said, grinning at his daughter. "Leaf is by far the best player in the family."

"I find myself unsurprised."

With his father thus distracted, Nic murmured an excuse and escaped as hastily as he dared. He caught up with Dashiell on the second-floor landing.

"Dash." The diminutive leapt so naturally to his lips. Nic tried to swallow it back as the vowsmith turned, his candle burnishing raised brows.

"Nic. Is everything all right?"

"I . . . I need your help with something. Can you meet me in the library?" It had seemed so simple a question, but once out it became the most presumptive thing he'd ever said. "If you're not too tired, of course, Master sa Vare. If you truly intend to turn in early, then by all means do not let me keep you."

"Yes. I mean no, I had no intention of doing so. I . . . Now?"

"As soon as you can—as long as you're sure you can spare the time. I just need to fetch something first."

"All right, good, yes. I'll be there in a few minutes."

It took Nic no time at all to collect the tape from his workbench, yet he reached the library to find Dashiell already waiting.

"There you are." He sounded relieved, his gaze shying to the thin blanket into which Nic had bundled the tape. "I was worried something had happened."

Something like murder or something like getting eaten by darkness? A question Nic swallowed rather than give Dashiell reason to truly worry. He'd already made poor work of Leaf's suggestion that he not go anywhere alone.

Keeping his tone light, Nic said, "Oh, don't worry, I know my way around this house far too well."

"I know you do, but I saw how fast you moved away from that black smoke. Something you've seen before?"

For a moment, Nic wondered how little he could get away with saying, and gave up. "Yes. A few days ago, when I found this."

Unwrapping the blanket, he spilled the slippery bundle of tape onto one of the tables.

"Sigil tape?"

"It had gotten hooked on some wood in one of the service passages."

"Which service passage?"

Nic met Dashiell's troubled look. "The one off the original negotiation chamber. After Gillingham died."

For a long time, Dashiell didn't reply, his gaze seeming to bore into Nic as though seeking answers without having to ask the questions. Then he said, "I only saw it for a moment, but that thing at the door tonight looked a lot like one of those torn-apart automata from the old grotto."

"It did, didn't it."

Dashiell turned away, throwing his arms wide in surrender. "All right, keep your secrets if you don't trust me. I—"

"If I didn't trust you, I wouldn't have asked for your help." Nic caught his hand to stay his retreat, desperate to reassure. "I just don't know all the answers yet."

Having been pulled to a halt, Dashiell stared at their joined hands as though at a problem that needed solving. An easy fix, yet Nic lifted Dashiell's hand instead, turning his own to bring them in line. And there, palm to palm in the candlelight, he imagined interlocking their fingers, imagined kissing Dashiell's palm, imagined never having to let go—each urge growing its own gravity.

At the edge of falling, Nic all but threw himself back. "I'm sorry."

"No. Don't be." Dashiell shook his head as though clearing away a cloud. "I want what you want, and these snatches of time together . . . they hurt, but more and more it's a hurt I cannot help but crave."

"I know what you mean."

They shared a wry smile, all too fond at the edges. Only when it began to grow its own tension did Dashiell finally sigh and look away. "Well, let's look at this tape then, I suppose."

He moved to the table and lifted one end of the snarled tape. "*Miir aht von* . . . Hmm. I was hoping to amaze you by being able to tell from the first few sigils what it was for, but no. If it had started with *bah semit kep*, it might have been a protective charm often built into old houses, and *vivol lu ah baht* is the beginning of a lot of old prayer wheels often used the same way. Sadly, you are not to be amazed."

He'd rattled off the meanings without thinking, all just knowledge he kept stored in his head.

"Not amazed?" Nic scoffed. "When this is why I need your help? You know so much more than I do."

"Ah, but my knowledge is just endless repetition, not talent like yours."

"You're wrong, but I'm honoured you think so highly of my showy nonsense."

"Showy nonsense? Don't sell yourself short, Nic. I can recall sigils, yes, but I can barely make even a globe with my hands." As he spoke, he moved his fingers, achieving a golden disc rough around the edge like a cog. "That," he said as it faded away, "was even worse than expected. How embarrassing."

"Your *taree* wasn't connected properly and you missed *ze* and *petam*."

"Oh."

Nic's heart tightened at the sight of Dashiell silently moving his lips as he ran through the required series, his lined brow adorably confused. "That's a lot of sigils in a short time."

"It is." Nic grinned. "Globes are actually quite hard."

"Ah, but I've made my point." Still he tried again, this time managing something like a half-inflated balloon. "Just lacking speed now, I think."

"No, it's your rhythm. Singing them aloud can help."

Dashiell looked through his lashes, a wicked smile curving his lips, and everything Nic knew about conjuring flew from his mind.

"Are you correcting my rhythm?" Dashiell said, his voice low and vibrant. "I thought you liked my rhythm."

Nic parted his lips upon a reply, only to cough and snap his mouth shut.

With a laugh, Dashiell lifted his hands in surrender. "I'm sorry.

A far better man than I could not have passed up that opportunity. But I've proven my point. Art is not my forte."

"And since half of these sigils aren't for conjuring, translating it isn't mine."

No fire had been lit in the library, yet despite the chill, Dashiell took off his coat and rolled up his sleeves. "Is there any paper and ink? And perhaps a sigil dictionary?"

"At once, Master sa Vare."

"Sorry, I didn't mean that as an order."

"Oh, I assure you I didn't mind."

On that far-too-honest utterance, Nic went to find ink and paper, leaving Dashiell to straighten out the tape as best he could in swollen silence.

Sigil dictionary, ink, paper—a lot of paper, because sigil translation could be a slow, painstaking process. Each individual sigil had a name and a purpose, but that purpose could be changed by the sigils on either side, and two sigils combined could form something wholly new.

It was not a challenge Nic had ever enjoyed, and sitting beside Dashiell made it a thousand times worse. The man was too present, too close, every breath full of his scent.

As though they had slipped back through time to the young boys they had once been, Nic sat unable to concentrate while Dashiell's focus narrowed to nothing but the problem in front of him. Eyes bright, he moved the tape along a few sigils at a time, thumbed through the dictionary, and made notes, his frown deepening. "If *miir* trumps *semitt* . . . then it's not quite a connecting command, but it almost is."

Soon feeling entirely extraneous, Nic sat absently folding a piece of paper, making small slices with some charmwork as he went. Dashiell worked on, not seeming to notice, until Nic had an intricate flower taking shape on the table.

"That's very pretty," he said then, glancing over.

Nic breathed a laugh and brushed the flower away across the tabletop. "Sorry, it's hard to focus. Here, let me be your dictionary assistant." Nic pulled the book close—anything to feel like he was helping.

A small frown marred Dashiell's brow, but he pointed to a sigil partway along the tape. "All right. Can you find this one?"

It wasn't hard, and with Dashiell pointing and Nic searching, they fell into a routine that seemed to eat up both tape and time. The candles burned steadily lower, yet despite the number of pages filling with Dashiell's handwriting, his frown only darkened.

After a while, Dashiell dropped his quill in frustration and ran an ink-stained hand through his hair.

"Perhaps if we can't figure out what it does," Nic said, "we can figure out what it doesn't do."

"No, I'm sure I can work it out; it's just not vow law and it's not conjuring—it's not even charmwork. It's like nothing I've ever seen before. But some sigil will eventually give its purpose away, I'm sure."

Dashiell got to his feet and started to pace slowly back and forth, dragging the tape with him. He was a man with fire in his soul, lit by the challenge, and Nic recognised something of the obsessive way he could himself spend hours working out the exact size of a single gear or practicing a series of sigils until they flowed like music.

"What?" Dashiell said, and Nic realised too late that he'd been staring, smiling like a fool.

"Just you," Nic admitted with a shrug. "You're really good at this."

"Oh."

"Nice to know all your hard work was worth it," he added. "Oh no, don't stop. I was enjoying the show."

As he spoke, Nic made to fold his arms behind his head, but the theatrical gesture was ruined when he hit the ink bottle. It tipped, and although he caught it before it clattered onto the floor, the price was ink spilled over his hands and a pair of heating cheeks.

"That was well done of me," he said, holding his dripping hands over the table.

Dashiell smothered a grin and pulled a handkerchief from his pocket. "It was certainly very dignified. Very graceful."

With a mock bow, Nic rose to take the handkerchief, only for Dashiell to grip his outstretched hand and draw it close. He spread Nic's fingers and brushed the crisp linen over his ink-smeared knuckles.

"I can do it myself," Nic said, his voice a little hoarse.

"This is easier," came the low reply. "Besides, you might somehow manage to spill more if *you* try to clean it."

A nonsensical excuse, yet Nic let Dashiell keep his hand, let him go on wiping the mess with the handkerchief balled in his palm. There was no getting rid of what had already dried, but the vowsmith diligently cleaned all that could drip or smear, working from the base of each finger to its tip, first one side and then the other, front and back. By the time he finished the middle finger, Nic's entire world had shrunk to nothing but the space where their hands met.

When he reached the little finger, Dashiell first slid off Nic's signet ring to wipe it clean. Yet having polished the ink from its face, he went on staring at it. The Monterris family crest stared back. This the name, the history, the immutable fact that chained Nic to a different life—a thought that must surely have been in Dashiell's mind when, slowly, he slid the ring back into place.

"This hurt is like a knife in my heart but I cannot stop," he said, lifting Nic's hand. The kiss pressed to his knuckles was soft. Slow. Dashiell's lips seeming to stick a moment as though unwilling to part from his skin. "But if I don't," the vowsmith added, drawing

Nic's hand closer to plant another kiss to the back of his wrist, "I don't know what will happen."

Turning Nic's arm, Dashiell pushed back the rolled edge of his shirtsleeve to reveal soft skin, before lowering his lips to the inside of Nic's wrist. "Although at some point, I might stop caring."

Dashiell looked up, his expression half question, half promise, and all need. Nic knew they had no future. He knew the dangers, knew the risk to Dashiell's career and his own contract. Being caught would leave both their lives in ruins, and yet he did not move. Could not. What was one more kiss when his heart already ached? What was one more moment pressed against each other and gasping? No one would know. No one would see. No one—

The door creaked open.

Dashiell dropped Nic's hand as though it had been a hot coal and Nic stepped back, cheeks heating as the duke strode in.

"Ah, Nicholas. Master sa Vare."

"Father."

They had moved quickly enough, Nic was sure, but the duke's brows rose all the same.

"Your Grace," Dashiell said, somehow managing an easy bow. "I have been assisting Lord Monterris with some sigilwork."

The duke's gaze swung from Dashiell to Nic, seeming to take in everything and nothing. "Well then, do not let me keep you. I merely saw the light and, given the late hour, wished to be sure one of the servants had not left a fire burning."

"Oh, I did not realise it had gotten so late." Dashiell glanced at the clock over the cold fireplace. "I ought to sleep since we are meeting in the morning."

"Do not hurry to bed on my account. I don't doubt your ability to negotiate under any conditions." His gaze swept to Nic, but he merely added, "And now I am assured the house is not going to try to burn down again, I will bid you both good night."

Dashiell tucked his ink-stained handkerchief away as the duke departed. "I must go. The tape is yours, but if I may keep the notes, I could let you know if I have an epiphany."

"Please do," Nic said, his mouth dry.

Dashiell gathered the papers he'd covered in scrawled notes, yet did not make immediately for the door. "I . . . shall bid you good night, Lord Monterris."

"You don't have to call me that."

"No, but I think it will be safer if I do." The vowsmith pressed a thin, wan smile between his lips. "Good night, my lord."

Nic nodded, the gesture leaving him hollowed by the complete impossibility of everything he wanted, even when that everything was only one man.

"Good night, Master sa Vare."

It wasn't until Nic collected the tape that he realised what else Dashiell had taken—Nic's charmworked paper flower. It had been just a silly little thing he'd made with restless hands, and it hurt to realise it might be all of him that Dashiell would ever have to treasure.

Chapter 19

The grotto of Monterris Court was located on the ground floor. Grand doors led in off the old style-wing entry hall, the front doors of which had long ago been bricked up to keep out the worst of the weather. Moss tumbled in over the bricks and leaked across the flagstones, and the only light in the hall came from cracks high in the outer wall.

"These became the front doors when the central rooms were thought too old-fashioned," Nic said as they entered the hall armed with a lantern and heavy candlestick. "Until one of my ancestors switched back to using the current entry when the hook wing was added, abandoning this side of the house because *it* had become old-fashioned."

"I think that's the story of every old house in the country, although usually with less decay and no automata." Leaf crossed the floor toward the closed grotto doors—two normal-sized doors set within a faux door large enough to fit a giant. "Will these be locked?"

Nic adjusted his grip on the candelabra he'd liberated from the ceremonial dining room. "Not usually, but my father might have locked them before your arrival to be sure no one would see it. He hates the place."

He'd been in the grotto any number of times, spending hours digging through the piles of automata pieces. He and Dashiell had explored the place often as boys too, pretending its obsidian walls were portals to other worlds. Now, for the first time, fear trickled down his back as they approached its doors.

"I don't like this," he said. "If that thing is in there, we have no idea what it's going to do."

"And if it's not in there, we're going to have to make a search of the whole house until we find it. But just think, if we can get its reel, we should be able to solve at least one mystery, if not stop all this awfulness before it goes any further."

She was right, yet still Nic's steps slowed, his reluctance a visceral tension against which his legs pulled.

Somewhere in the distance, a door slammed. Leaf lifted her candelabra. "What was that?"

"A door, but—"

Another banged shut and Leaf spun, the sound seeming to come from everywhere and nowhere all at once. A third slammed with the finality of a crypt cover, yet its very hollowness sounded all wrong.

"I'm not sure where that's coming from," Nic said, staring at the closed grotto doors, their heavy rings like round eyes. Old spells that lay dormant, his father had said, but Nic knew the house like he knew his own palm and he'd never seen anything stranger than the piles of automata themselves.

He strode toward the doors with renewed determination. "Come on. Let's get that reel."

"Nic, wait. Look!" Leaf had grasped his arm and gestured toward the base of the grotto doors with her candelabra. "Does that mean it's in there?"

Darkness leaked from beneath the wood like heavy smoke, billowing slowly.

"It must be." Nic stepped back, the memory of the service passage all too close.

"What do you think it is?"

He shook his head, retreating another step as it began oozing across the floor. "I don't know, but it swallowed me entirely, like I ceased to exist. It even went down my throat. I hate to think what might have happened if you hadn't been there that day."

A new, even more horrifying thought followed. Would he have been its next victim?

A similar thought must have occurred to Leaf, for her hold on his arm tightened. "Do you think that's how it gets people? Some . . . magic that incapacitates?"

Except it wasn't magic, at least not sigil magic, the air once again tainted with only stickiness and a whisper so faint he had surely imagined it. Something smothered. Old. Dead.

"I think maybe," Leaf said, swallowing hard, "it doesn't want us to take its reel."

As though in response to the suggestion, the darkness lashed at them, whipping like a velvet hand. With a fearful cry, Leaf flinched back, still gripping Nic's arm as though she feared to let go. "We need to get out of here," she said, tugging him away. "Come on!"

Terror had lodged in Nic's throat like it owned spikes, and it took a fierce yank from Leaf to get his feet moving. Together they fled across the stones toward the stairs, where he thrust her on ahead and glanced back. Before, the darkness had been like swirling clouds, but now night rose from the floor like a boiling sea, faces forming on its shifting surface.

Nicholas.

The name shivered through his skin more feeling than sound. It came again, seeming to call to him, and Nic lingered on the bottom step staring out at the rising darkness.

"What are you doing, Nic! Come on!" Leaf pulled him up the stairs in her wake, not slowing even when she reached the upper landing. Sprinting as though her life depended on it, she sped along the passage, her soft shoes skidding as she turned the corner, floorboards protesting. Together they ran on through the style wing's abandoned rooms, not stopping until they reached the front antechamber, where Leaf tore open the door. She darted through into the main house without looking back, leaving Nic to close and lock it behind them.

For a long minute they stood catching their breath, both staring at the gap beneath the door.

"Are you all right?" Nic asked when no darkness materialised.

"All right?" she repeated, the words possessing a manic edge. "There's an automaton down there that probably wants to kill us, and we can't even reach it. So much for your house not being like that castle in *The Mysteries of Udolpho*. What happened to no black veils?"

"At least I was right about there being no Italian counts?"

Leaf threw up her hands, amusement tugging at the tense line of her mouth. "Oh, well, that's all right then."

Nic grinned, needing to ease the tension ratcheted in his chest before it unravelled him. "There aren't any ghosts in *The Mysteries of Udolpho* either. Although, thankfully, we're not in a book."

"It might be better if we were. At least in a book you can usually be sure of a happy ending." She sighed, looking along the hall to where weak winter sunlight bathed the worn carpet. "We need a new plan. Whatever is going on, that thing is dangerous and we have to figure out a way to stop it. You"—she jabbed his chest with the tip of her finger—"need to decipher that sigil tape we found because it might be related. I am going to warn Lisbeth and Millie not to go anywhere on their own no matter what. If I was able to save you from . . . whatever that darkness is, then so long as we all keep together, we'll be safe, right?"

"Right," Nic said, and wished he couldn't hear the doubt in his own voice.

Having promised not to go anywhere alone, Nic spent the afternoon in his rooms trying to read the sigil tape and failing. Dashiell had been right: it read like neither vow law nor conjuring work nor even automata instructions, the mixture of sigils wholly bizarre.

When it came time to make the daily trek down to the drawing room for dinner, Nic enlisted Ambrose's company, yet even his new valet's imperturbable calm couldn't keep Nic from glancing at every shifting shadow. He arrived to find Lord Ricard the only guest present, the man sitting at one end of the room while the duchess sat at the other, Silla hovering nearby.

"Good evening, Mama," Nic said, receiving a distant smile as he sat beside her.

"Oh, Nicholas," she said. "Are you well? It feels like an age since I saw you last. At the Seftons' ball, was it not?"

He couldn't decide whether he was glad or sorry she had once again found the safety of her daydreams: glad for her smiles, sorry for their lie.

"I am very well, Mama. And yourself? After last night's strange dinner."

Silla didn't speak, but the intensity with which she stared at him from behind the duchess's chair caught Nic's attention like a hook, her warning no less forceful for being silent.

"Strange dinner?" the duchess said, a notch of confusion cutting between her brows. "I . . . don't remember that. Why don't I remember that?"

Nic glanced around to be sure Lord Ricard could not hear and found Leaf arriving with her father. "You probably don't remember because it wasn't so remarkable. Shall I come sit with you tomorrow? We could read; it's been a while since we did that. I think we were partway through Bougainville's *Voyage around the World*."

"Ah yes! He was going to Patagonia!"

At the second opening of the door, Nic turned again and his gaze lingered on the welcome sight of Dashiell's arrival. He had changed from his plain black smithing attire into evening dress, his coat the one with the cinched waist he had worn the first night—the night he had hauled Nic out of the pond. They had shouted at each other then, but now when their gazes met, it was a soft, fond smile they shared across the distance. Nic held it longer than he ought, only to turn back and find his mother watching him.

She leaned forward, taking his hand. "I'm trying, my love. The only thing I ever wanted was for you not to end up like me."

"What do you mean, Mama?"

"We aren't all prisoners for life, but we are all still prisoners." Her grip tightened, fingers digging into the back of his hand. "When you own me, will you set me free?"

Her words tugged upon his heart, the bright hopeful light in her eyes pricking tears into the corners of his own. "Yes. Yes, Mama, I will."

She let go and sat back with a sigh, leaving Nic to blink away tears he dared not let fall.

By the time the dinner bell rang, Nic had composed himself enough to rise and offer the duchess his arm without his smile trembling. With Silla in their wake, they fell in behind Dashiell and Lady Theresa, the lady leading the way to the parlour with an unceasing flow of chatter. "Lizzy really is such an obliging girl, quite a second daughter to me. Sadly, as Withington's youngest, I fear she is little thought of at home—you must know how that is, as a younger sibling yourself."

Dashiell murmured an unnecessary assent, Lady Theresa already rolling on without him. "Withington is a very good man, but he lost his wife some years ago and men, you know, just don't know how to manage daughters."

As they reached the parlour door, Castor bowed and pushed it open.

"It is always the way when—"

The lady broke off with a shriek, backing away from the door with a hand pressed to her mouth. In the corner of his vision, Nic caught a glimpse of shadows and the slivered edge of a white face, there and gone like a blink of imagination.

"The Faceless Man!" Lady Theresa cried, her hands trembling. "He was there, sitting in Lizzy's chair."

A murmur of mixed concern and confusion passed through the gathered group. Until Lord Ricard sneered. "Do keep moving, my lady, or you'll have Vale taking off his glasses again to assure you there is no such thing as ghosts."

"He was there! Tell them, Master sa Vare—you must have seen him too."

Everyone in the hallway fixed their eyes on Dashiell, but the vowsmith went on staring at the unoccupied table. "I admit there did seem to be something in Lady Lisbeth's chair for a moment."

"See! It was a warning. This house is haunted and monstrous."

"It suits you well then," Millie said with a triumphant sniff.

"You are a snake, Millie Radlay," Lady Theresa hissed, turning on her stepdaughter. "No wonder Lord Radlay died. Driven into an early grave!"

Gasps rippled back along the passage, even Lady Theresa pressing her hands to her mouth in shock as though she could force her own words back in.

"Aunt, that is too much!"

"Theresa!"

Near the back of the group, the duke let out a long-suffering sigh. "If we could at least reach the dining table before we are at each other's throats tonight."

Between so ill a beginning and the previous night's dinner still hanging over them, it was no cheerful meal—relief the paramount emotion when the party finally escaped back to the relative safety of the drawing room.

As had become their custom, Leaf immediately drew Nic away from the others. "Did you have any luck with that sigil tape? I am dreading what might happen next if we don't work this out."

"No," he admitted. "I got a little further; the combinations just don't make much sense. A lot of connecting commands and shapes, more like someone was just practicing sigils than trying to make something specific."

"That is not very helpful."

"I will ask Dashiell later if he's had any thoughts." He looked around. While the rest of the company had divided into chattering groups, Dashiell had taken up a periodical. This might have been unremarkable, but sitting with one leg balancing on the knee of the other, the strong, shapely length of his thigh was fully on show. Nic groaned. "Although not while he's sitting like that."

"What? Really, Nicholas Monterris? He's just sitting."

"No, he's sitting like *that*."

"What's . . . erotic about it?"

"What's *not* erotic about it? I'm only fortunate he's not sitting with his knees apart, leaning his elbows on them."

Leaf turned a horrified gaze on him. "That would be enough to make you . . . ? No, do not answer; I will never understand. It all just sounds so . . . messy and uncomfortable."

"I suppose in a lot of ways it is, but I see that"—Nic gestured at Dashiell—"and it's like my whole body is on fire and I *want* to be messy and uncomfortable with him as much as I can."

"That," she said, "is one of the most sensible explanations I've ever heard."

He had to laugh. "I'm not sure there was anything sensible

about what I just said. Especially given how getting messy and uncomfortable with him is an extremely bad idea."

"Yes, but Millie always makes it sound rational to want such things, and so I feel wrong for not having the same desires. You make it sound entirely irrational. And you haven't told me I will change my mind once I experience it. Or fall in love."

In looking around, Nic had found Dr. Fanshaw watching them from across the room, or more accurately watching Leaf. Before, he might have pointed this out and encouraged her as she encouraged him, but instead he just smiled.

"You are who you are, my dear. Shall we rejoin the rest of the party?"

She didn't rise, just looked around at the company with a frown collecting between her brows.

Near the fire, Lord Charborough was in full voice about one of the translations he was working on, Lady Theresa had silently taken up her stitchery, and Lord Ricard had brought his glass of wine and was drinking it with a determination Nic knew well. Millie and Lady Lisbeth had settled at a small table for a game of cards, while Dashiell went on reading, the position of his leg unchanged. Even the duchess was in fine spirits. Usually, she left the drawing room soon after dinner, but this evening she was bustling the servants about as they brought in the tea tray.

"I suppose we should join them for tea," Leaf said after a time. "At least nothing can happen when we are all together like this."

"If you prefer, I can fetch you a cup instead?"

He gestured to where his mother had started serving the tea, handing cups to Lady Theresa, who passed them on to waiting hands.

"No, that's all right." Leaf rose and shook out her skirts. "I will fetch my own and sit with your mama. I want to be sure she gets used to me so it's not a shock when suddenly I'm around all the time."

Dashiell had fetched himself a cup and returned to his chair, but had not yet taken up the periodical again. Nic met his gaze as he walked past and held it as long as he dared, rather than risk his eyes sinking back to admiration of the vowsmith's legs.

A cup clattered at the gaming table and Lady Lisbeth hastily rose. "Oh no, Millie, what a mess! Let me fetch a napkin."

Cards abandoned, Millie sat blinking, tea staining the front of her dress.

"Oh, poor thing," Lady Theresa said, seeming determined to make up for her earlier words. "Run upstairs and change, Millie dear; that dress is done for."

Leaf had been crossing the floor in search of her own tea, but halted abruptly. "Millie?" Her voice emerged tight. "Millie, are you all right?"

Heads turned. Lord Charborough craned his neck to see what was amiss. Millie was trying to rise from her chair only for her hand to keep slipping off the back. She blinked bleary eyes, seemingly exhausted.

"Millie?" Having returned with a napkin, Lady Lisbeth gripped her friend's elbow to hold her steady. "Millie, what is the matter? Millie!"

Lord Ricard surged up, his chair crashing back. "Out of the way! Millie, what is it, are you sick? Are you hurt?" He took his daughter from Lady Lisbeth's hold and gave her a little shake. "Millie? Millie!"

Millie's eyes rolled and her knees gave out, all but dropping her from her father's arms. He half caught her as she collapsed, the pair becoming a tangle of limbs and rose chiffon upon the floor.

"Millie!"

Panic quivered in his voice as he patted her hands, her face— a man trying to wake her, repeating her name over and over. Yet she seemed not to see him, not to hear him, convulsions twitching through her body faster and faster.

Lord Ricard gripped her shoulders hard as though to stop her. "Please, Millie!"

Her name choked in his throat as her head fell back, as she stilled, as all the tension released from her body upon a long-awaited sigh. Glassy-eyed, she stared at nothing and drew no more breath, and for what seemed like an eternity the whole room stilled with her. Until Lady Lisbeth screamed, stealing away all hope that Nic had imagined the whole.

Chapter 20

Panic gripped the room as Lady Lisbeth's scream cascaded into gasping sobs. "I don't—I don't understand," she cried, tears streaming down her cheeks. "What happened? We were just playing cards and then—and—but—" Her gaze met the still body of her friend and she turned away, retching.

"What could have happened?" Lady Theresa cried, while beside her Lord Charborough stared numbly. "Doctor? Doctor! Do something!"

Dr. Fanshaw had already knelt at Lord Ricard's side, the man still clutching his daughter as though if he kept holding her, she couldn't slip away.

"If I may, my lord," the doctor murmured.

"The tea." The duke's voice was quiet, yet it carried, cutting through every other sound with its sharp warning. "No one touch the tea!"

Nic looked at his own hand, though he knew it to be empty. Leaf, too, had no cup, but Dashiell's sat balanced on his knee. Hardly thinking, or perhaps thinking too much, Nic grabbed it—hoping it looked full because it was—and poured the contents onto a nearby plant. Dashiell's gaze snapped up.

"Did you drink any?" Nic asked.

At the gentle shake of Dashiell's head, some of the tension binding Nic's chest loosened. Other cups were poured out, but just as many had been abandoned as the Serral family gathered around

Millie. Nic didn't want to think of it as her body, the word too final an acceptance that the lifeless flesh owning her face was no longer her at all.

Tears were pouring down Leaf's cheeks as she knelt within the circle of her father's arm. Lord Ricard had bent his head to Millie's, his shoulders shaking. And Lady Lisbeth sat trembling on her chair with her face buried in her hands. Only Lady Theresa stood a little apart, furiously blinking.

Nic had only known Millie since her arrival, yet the lump in his throat was too painful to swallow—a lump that swelled when he thought of how different the scene was to the discovery of Master Everel's body. How heartlessly they had all stood and stared and argued, not even the duke having shed a single tear.

The shame of it burned, and without thinking Nic reached for Dashiell's shoulder—a steady support upon which he could lean as he let himself feel his own failings. In death as in life, he'd treated Master Everel as nothing.

Dashiell lifted his hand to Nic's in a fleeting touch of acknowledgement, the way it lingered seeming to yearn toward providing more reassurance than so slight a gesture allowed. It ached Nic's heart, and suddenly conscious of watching eyes, he pulled his hand away.

The duke had risen from his chair to give orders to a staring footman, and for a moment his dark glasses seemed to look Nic's way, but if he'd seen anything amiss, it didn't show on his face.

"Did anyone else drink the tea?" he asked the company at large as the footman sped out.

"I had a sip," Lady Theresa whispered. "Oh."

"I did too," Lord Charborough admitted, his voice rough. He still had an arm around a sobbing Leaf, who had threaded her hand into Lady Lisbeth's.

As pale as his shirt, Dr. Fanshaw rose from the group at Millie's side. "As did I. And I'm afraid Lady Radlay is beyond any assistance I can render."

It was a mere statement of fact no one could have doubted, yet the words still seemed to strike the company anew, sending out a ripple of silence.

The door opened, bringing Mrs. Podmarsh hesitantly into the room. There could be no doubt the footman sent to fetch her had described the scene in detail, for she looked immediately to Millie's body, her eyes widening as she dropped into her customary curtsy. "Your Grace sent for me?"

"That I did, Mrs. Podmarsh," the duke said. "Tell me, who makes the tea?"

"The tea, Your Grace?" The old housekeeper's gaze darted about the room as she spoke, from the tea tray to the abandoned cups spread upon tables throughout the room. "The tea," she repeated, voice constricted. "I believe the cook sometimes does so. Else it would be one of the maids."

"Gather anyone who had access to the tea things. There has been an incident and no servant may leave the house until we have answers."

"Yes, Your Grace. At once, Your Grace." The housekeeper bobbed another curtsy, followed by a second. "Would Your Grace like the servants brought here, or . . . ?"

"No. Gather them in the blue saloon and I will be along when I am able."

"Yes, Your Grace."

With a lingering, horrified look at the weeping Serrals, Mrs. Podmarsh hurried out.

"You cannot think one of the servants responsible," Leaf said, her tone one of deep disgust despite the sniff she gave as she wiped her eyes on her shawl. "What reason could they possibly have?"

"Are you suggesting that someone here had greater reason, Lady

Leaf?" the duke said, as lightly as if he had been asking her the time of day.

"Certainly greater reason than someone who did not know her!"

"And at whom do you intend to point your finger?"

Having withdrawn his arm from about Leaf's shoulders, Lord Charborough dropped his head into his hands. "Leaf, hold your tongue for once in your life, I beg of you," he hissed, a man goaded beyond endurance.

"But, Papa—"

"No, enough! Have those ridiculous books of yours taught you nothing but to suspect your own family of such horrors?"

Leaf's teeth gave an audible snap as she shut her mouth, anger flaring in her red-rimmed eyes. If Lord Charborough noticed, he ignored these signs of fury and pulled himself to his feet with a weary sigh. Having risen, he swayed a moment, forced to steady himself on the back of Lady Lisbeth's chair.

The duke took a hasty step toward him only to halt like he'd pulled himself up short. "We will find out what happened, I can assure you," he said, though whether he spoke to Lord Charborough or Leaf was impossible to say.

"What happened." The murmur came from the floor, and every occupant of the room drew a sharp breath at the first sound, first movement, first sign of life Lord Ricard had shown. The man looked up, his face a hideous mask, swollen around the eyes yet hollow-cheeked. "What happened," he repeated, slowly getting to his feet, "is that you have taken *everything* from me."

He advanced on the duke, hands balled. Someone shouted. Another screamed. And in that instant, Nic thought of the story Millie had told them. He had felt the young Ricard's pain in every word, but that hurt was a fierce, ugly rage now as he threw a fist toward the duke's face. To Nic's shock, the usually so stoic Duke of Vale flinched back with a visceral cry, raising his hands. "Ric, no!"

The unexpected nickname acted like a pail of icy water thrown over the threatening lord, and for a pair of straining seconds he froze. The duke, too, had stilled, chest heaving as he seemed to fight back both fresh panic and the old horrors that had produced it, until the tide of Lord Ricard's anger surged twice as hot and he charged.

Dashiell leapt from his chair. Lord Charborough lunged for his brother's arm, while Leaf cried out and threw herself in front of Millie's body as trampling feet came all too close.

Nic dashed into the furore, grabbing for Lord Ricard's other arm as Dashiell stepped between the two men. The duke flinched back again as Dashiell shoved in front of him, dodging Lord Ricard's fist to press his palms flat against his employer's chest and shove.

"Ricard!" Lord Charborough growled. "Stop this!"

Finally getting a good grip on the man's arm, Nic hauled, and with a combined effort, space was forced between them. Eventually the arm Nic held went slack, and with something like a mocking laugh, the fight went out of Ricard and he slumped back against the sideboard with an angry clatter of wineglasses.

"I'm done," he said. "You can let go."

Nic did so, retreating a few steps to brush his hands down his coat, as desirous of avoiding his father eye as of not glancing at Millie's body.

"If you wish to leave, then we will leave," Lord Charborough said, eyeing his younger brother as he stepped into the aftermath. "Be damned to the forfeit funds, but such behaviour—"

"No. I am not paying a fortune in forfeit to the family that killed my Millie."

"Ricard! You can't say that when—"

"Can't I? I may not be able to prove it was by their hands, but by God it was in their interest and that is enough for me."

"Oh, my lord," Lady Theresa sobbed, dashing forward to clutch her husband's sleeve. "Please let us go home. I do not know how it is possible to go on."

He shook her off. "Be quiet, my lady. This is not your concern."

"Not my concern?" She threw up her arms. "As nothing is allowed to be my concern be it never so important! Poor Millie is dead!"

"And you cannot lie that you are not happy for it, my lady, so *be quiet.*" Having cowed his wife, Lord Ricard spun back to his brother. "No, I will not forfeit. Invoke the Requisite Care Clause. This is far beyond anything and you cannot deny me now."

All air was sucked from the room upon a chorus of indrawn breaths. Lord Charborough's jaw slackened, his gaze shying toward the duke. "But, Ricard, think what you are asking."

"I know what I am asking! Complete the contract in the days you'll have left if you must, Charles, but let the king's men crawl over this damned rotten pile in its aftermath."

Nic felt like a spectator, forced to watch as events that had been set in motion before he'd been born burned toward a conclusion he could neither see nor understand. The sense of being caught in an inevitable tide was overwhelming, yet so deeply familiar it held a terrible sort of comfort. He knew nothing of control, his life having always belonged to another.

Yet now even the certainty he'd thought he had was being torn away. Triggering the Requisite Care Clause would bring a contingent of royal guards and vowsmiths from London, leaving only the time it took them to arrive in which to complete the contract. That meant five days, six at most. Completion might be possible in that time, but the circumstances of the clause being triggered would have to be investigated, filling the house with the king's men only for the requested audit to bring still more.

Lord Charborough swallowed hard. "Ricard . . ."

"Don't you dare *Ricard* me," he hissed, stepping close to grip his brother's chin. "I am your family, Charles. If you wanted him to be your family, you should have married him when you had the chance and left me the damned title."

For long, aching seconds they stared at one another, until Lord Charborough looked away. "All right." His voice sounded hoarse and he yanked free of Ricard's grip with a bitter glare. "Master sa Vare. Invoke the Requisite Care Clause in my name."

"As you wish, my lord."

Hateful in triumph, Lord Ricard spun upon the duke. "Question your servants if you wish, Val, but you are done. Done, you hear me?"

When Nic's father made neither sound nor movement, Ricard snorted. "Coward." He turned back to Millie then, some of the anger sliding from his face. For a moment he closed his eyes, as though being unable to see her would make her loss untrue. He drew a deep breath. "I will carry Millie back to her room now."

"If I might suggest the crypt, my lord," Dr. Fanshaw said from his retreat by the door. "The cold—"

"Shut up."

The doctor's jaw snapped shut, and as one they all watched as Lord Ricard bent to gather the still form of his daughter into his arms, exactly as he might once have done when she'd been a child suddenly made bereft of her mother.

When he reached the door, Lord Charborough opened it for him in silence, and equally without sound stood aside to let him pass. Dr. Fanshaw followed.

"We shall see her comfortably settled," Lord Charborough said to no one in particular, and himself stepped out in their wake.

The door closed with a resolute click.

With the three men gone, bearing their precious burden, air slowly returned to the room—tense and bitter though it was.

"I shall certainly question the servants," the duke murmured, dropping onto the sofa beside his wife with a display of exhausted ease that attempted to elide his earlier terror. "We ought to be thankful that no one else appears unwell."

Beside him, the duchess sat glassy-eyed, staring at nothing, her hands caught tightly together in her lap. That she was still present despite the noise and horror shocked Nic, a glance around the room discovering no sign of Silla.

"Yes, but we ought to tip out our cups all the same," Leaf said, wrapping her arm around Lady Lisbeth's sagging shoulders. "And the tea tray should be removed."

Whether or not it had been her intention, Leaf's words drew all eyes to the tray still sitting in front of the duchess, and from there to the silent duchess herself.

With a sniff, Lady Theresa said, "Does anyone recall whether dear Millie picked up her own cup or had one handed to her?"

When no one answered, Lady Theresa turned her gaze to the duchess. "Your Grace, perhaps you recall. Since you poured the tea."

The duchess's hands tightened in her lap but she didn't look up. Nic's heartbeat sped as fresh worries churned his stomach, yet at her side, the duke said nothing.

"Your Grace?" Lady Theresa repeated, regaining some of her hauteur.

When his mother flinched, Nic stepped forward. "As you were yourself the one handing out the cups my mother poured, Lady Theresa, we could as well ask you the same question."

"Are you suggesting that I had something to do with this, Lord Monterris?"

"Not at all. Merely pointing out that you had as much opportunity and far greater motive."

"How dare you say such a thing to me, you impoverished—"

"Aunt!" Leaf stormed across the room. "You will not abuse Lord Monterris in my hearing, especially when he is right. You have been ghastly to Millie since we arrived, and now this!" Her voice broke on a sob and she turned her face away, features screwed up as she sought to keep tears from flowing. "Before anything else happens, Lizzy and I are going upstairs. Good night, Aunt. Your Grace."

Having gathered Lady Lisbeth within the circle of her arm, Leaf paused only to grip Nic's hand in farewell before sweeping out upon swallowed sobs.

Thus abandoned, Lady Theresa lifted her chin and looked about the scattered remains of the scene, at the empty space where the members of her family had stood. "I will also bid you good night, gentlemen. *Your Grace.*"

In the wake of her departure, only Nic and Dashiell remained with the duke and duchess. Still seated on the sofa, the duchess's hands clenched and unclenched in her lap, while her angry gaze darted about the room as though at shadows.

The vowsmith rose, clearing his throat. "I ought to depart too, as I must attend to that clause. It is, of course, my duty to do as my employer requests, but I would like you to know that it is a duty I will perform with great regret, Your Grace."

A small, wry smile twitched the duke's lips. "You were the best apprentice I ever had, Master sa Vare. I would expect nothing less from you than precision and diligence. Perhaps you could do me a small favour, however. You may feel it is overcautious of me, but I would be grateful if you would first walk with Nicholas to ensure he makes it safely back to his rooms."

"Of course, Your Grace." Dashiell bowed. "And in the circumstances, I cannot deem anything overcautious."

Caught between the desire to escape and to remain with his mother in Silla's absence, Nic awaited some explanation, some sense that his father understood the duchess was in a dark place.

None came. The duke just met his questioning stare with raised brows.

Dashiell touched Nic's elbow. "Shall we?"

Nic couldn't outstare those dark glasses. That impassive face. He glanced at his mother, at her visceral anger, and looked away.

I am but a prisoner. When you own me, will you set me free?

Nic nodded. "Indeed, Master sa Vare, I shall not keep you longer."

Skin prickling under his father's watchful gaze, Nic walked with Dashiell to the door, but escaping into the hallway beyond did nothing to ease the tension in his every muscle.

"Are you all right?" Dashiell whispered as they started along the passage, Nic hardly heeding his surroundings for the haze in which he walked.

"Fine," came the automatic reply, an instant before a scream roared in their wake. A scream of fury, of hate, of pain like Nic had never known, followed by a crash of glass. They both froze, yet it seemed Dashiell understood more than Nic had thought, for he didn't sprint back, just stood watching him. The silent question in his gaze dug deep as the next primal scream cut into Nic's soul.

"Wait here."

Nic hurried back to find the drawing room door firmly shut, the shouts that were emanating through the inlaid wood all his mother's. Another crash of glass or ceramic or crystal, but no sound of a second voice, no gentle hush or murmur the way Silla would have spoken to her.

Nic knocked, more from habit than necessity, before turning the handle. Hardly had the door begun to open than it stopped, hitting a foot. The duke's foot. His father stared out through the crack, scarred eyes appearing over the top of his dark glasses.

"I can help," Nic said.

For a long moment the duke looked at him while taut screams of rage whirled. "Go to bed, Nicholas. I will take care of this."

"No. Mama?" Nic shoved the door so hard that the duke flinched back, letting Nic push through into the room. "Mama."

The duchess stood seething, shards of broken teacups and vases littering the floor around her. She had pulled the pins from her hair and let it tumble loose in a wild nest, and tore at the tresses as she let out another scream that seemed to be wrenched from her very soul.

"Mama." Nic gripped her shoulders. "Mama, it's me."

She tensed. Silent. He tightened his hold and held her troubled gaze. "Mama, I'm here for you."

"Here for me?" She raised her hand as though she would hit him, would claw at his face, but Nic refused to flinch and she froze, fingers flexing. "Nicholas?"

"Yes, I'm here. I can stay with you. Or I can take you to Silla. Just tell me what you need."

The hand that almost struck him slid down his cheek, not a soft caress but the hard rub of her palm as though she'd forgotten how to touch. "Will you set me free?"

"I will, Mama, I will. You have my word."

Some of her fury dissolved upon a sob and she threw her arms around him, not a hug, rather the desperate clutch of a woman clinging on for survival. He held her there, letting her cry upon his shoulder, increasingly aware of the silence behind him. Nic didn't turn, didn't so much as glance back, keeping his attention for his mother alone.

After a few long minutes, she whispered, "Silla. I want Silla."

"All right. I'll take you."

He slid his arm around her and she dropped her head onto his shoulder as they turned toward the door. There the duke stood stiff, watching them approach.

"You do not know what you are promising, Nicholas," he said. "To be a duke takes sacrifice and duty."

"And cruelty?"

His father looked away. "You have no idea what it means to lead a family."

"Well, if this is what it looks like, I hope I never do."

Awaiting no reply, Nic strode past him, helping his mother out into the shadowy hallway. A little way along, Dashiell remained where he'd been left, holding a candle like a beacon. Wordlessly, the vowsmith waited for them to join him, before he led the way through the house toward the duchess's rooms.

They found Silla waiting in the gallery, her hands white at the knuckles. "Oh, Your Grace. Master Nicholas. I heard what happened."

"Silla—"

The duchess pulled from Nic to fall upon her maid, clinging to her as she had clung to Nic in the drawing room. Silla wrapped her arms around the shaking woman and patted her back. "Hush now, you're safe with me. Let's get you comfortable."

Over the duchess's shoulder, Silla mouthed "Thank you" before turning to take her the rest of the way to her rooms. Nic watched them go, Dashiell standing beside him.

Once the duchess and her maid had disappeared, Nic let go a long, heavy sigh. "You may now walk me to my door, Master sa Vare."

"It would be an honour."

Nic tried to laugh but the sound wouldn't come, so together they left the gallery in silence, returning back along the hallway. "You're a good son," Dashiell said as they reached the stairs.

"I'm not sure that's true, but perhaps I will be from now on."

For a moment it seemed like Dashiell would argue, but he swallowed his words and instead turned to mount the stairs.

"I hope you don't mind that I am walking you to your door," he said as they neared the top.

"No." Nic flicked him a smile as they walked the last distance to his rooms, their shoulders brushing close. "I was just very angry the last time you offered to."

"I know."

Upon reaching Nic's door, they stopped, sharing an awkward smile.

"Thank you for making sure I didn't get murdered," Nic said.

"And thank you for letting me ensure you didn't get murdered. It was the most enjoyable part of the evening. Especially since tedious forms now await me."

"Will there be time? To finish the contract, I mean, before the king's men arrive?"

"Assuming there are no great arguments, yes. Though I may get rather less sleep than I generally like."

Nic nodded. He needed to say good night, needed to step inside and close his door so there would be something more between them than air, but he'd never wanted to escape Dashiell less, never wanted to protect himself less than in that moment. He wanted to throw caution to the wind and pull Dashiell close, to say that although they couldn't have forever, they could at least have now, but if they were caught, the risk was all Dashiell's. And so, from some deep core of self-control, Nic dredged up the words: "I should let you go. Before we both get murdered standing in the hallway."

"Wouldn't that be a thing," Dashiell agreed with a forced laugh. "I suppose you'd better get inside then, while I run for the safety of my room."

"Make sure you're quick. Or I'll have to risk my life to check on you."

"After which I would have to risk mine to check on you."

The answer that they could avoid all that by spending the night together was on the tip of Nic's tongue, but he bit down hard and smiled instead. "Let's not have that happen. Well. Good night."

"Good night."

Before he completely lost the ability to move, Nic pushed open the door and stepped inside. And having closed it, he leaned against it, every part of him feeling tight and fragile, his skin prickling.

Just as the world had gone resolutely on after Rowerre's death and would again now, so it would when Dashiell once again walked out the doors of Monterris Court, breaking Nic's heart.

He sighed and rubbed his eyes and, letting go a long, slow breath, pushed away from the door.

Despite a lamp left burning and the low glow of the fire, Nic's rooms were full of shadows. They were familiar, comforting shadows, however, one even pooling around the base of a half-filled wine decanter.

Thank God.

As he made his way toward it, a gentle knock sounded on the door. Nic dashed back and yanked it open to find Leaf standing on the threshold, a candle trembling in one hand, the other clutching a fistful of her fine dressing gown. "May I come in?"

"Of course, but . . . Ambrose isn't here to chaperone us. I could call for—"

"No. There is nothing I care about less than my honour right now." She slipped in beneath his arm as she spoke, leaving him to close the door in her wake.

"Were you just . . . sitting around in the dark?" she asked, pausing in the middle of the floor.

"I just got in. I'll light some more candles."

Leaf reached out to stop him. "No, don't. There's something comforting about sitting by a glowing fire in the dark."

"Well, I have a glowing fire, but other than wine I have nothing else to offer, I'm afraid."

"Bring the wine down here," she said, settling on the carpet before the fire, her dark hair tumbling loose. "I'm here for your company, but given the circumstances, wine is an excellent addition."

Having paused only to kick off his shoes, Nic joined her sitting cross-legged on the carpet with the wine tray set before them. For a time, they sat in silence, each staring into the flames, deep in thoughts that had a sticky quality.

"I can't believe she's gone," Leaf said eventually. "Millie has just . . . always been there. The older cousin I looked up to. She even played with me when I was little, though I must have been very annoying. How many better things could she have been doing than entertaining a childish cousin? We grew apart once she married, but after Lord Radlay died last year, we saw a lot more of her and it was nice. Not nice that he died, of course, just . . ."

"I know. I'm sorry. I wish none of this had happened, especially under my roof and in the process of negotiating our marriage."

"It does feel very inauspicious, doesn't it? Although perhaps people will say it's lucky in a perverse way, like how they say it's actually lucky when a bird does its business on you."

"I can confirm that there is nothing lucky about getting covered in bird droppings, and I should know, given how many birds we have. I've never understood why people say that."

Leaf took a large mouthful of wine and turned from contemplation of the fire. "I think people say it because they're uncomfortable dealing with another's distress, so would rather pretend the cause doesn't exist and tell everyone they should actually be grateful for suffering."

"That feels disturbingly accurate."

"Doesn't it, though."

"On that note, perhaps this would be a good time to ask your father to break the contract again," Nic said. "He might even sasine you if you ask for the twenty-fourth time."

She rolled a wry smile his way. "I just tried. He has very stubbornly refused, but I think I will soon have another five thousand pounds for my school fund."

Nic couldn't think of anything to say that didn't sound awful, so instead he stared into the fire and let long minutes pass in companionable silence.

"I just don't know what to do," Leaf said eventually, putting her glass down. "First, we were sure it was Uncle Ricard, then a murderous automaton, and now I cannot but wonder if it is someone else, and that automaton is merely an oddity. Or worse, perhaps it is all three at once. Gosh, I wish she'd never come with us. I wish I could do something, could turn back time just long enough to take that cup out of her hand."

She sniffed and set her head on Nic's shoulder. He slid an arm around her, and there, side by side before the dying fire, they sat for a long time. Leaf let tears trickle down her cheeks, and Nic didn't let her go until she pulled away, wiping her eyes.

"Do you want to talk through it?" he said when she managed a tremulous smile and a thank-you. "See if there's anything we might have missed?"

Leaf shrugged. "Where's the point? We've failed to figure anything out so far and I don't imagine that will change."

"Excuse me, what have you done with Lady Leaf Serral?"

"What do you mean?" She gave a watery laugh. "I'm right here."

"No, you can't be. You're suggesting we give up."

"I'm being realistic."

"Would Mary Mallowan give up?" Nic asked.

"Mary Mallowan is the author, Nic, not the detective."

"All right, fine, would Mary Mallowan's fictional detective character whose name I don't know give up?"

That earned him a faint smile. "No, she wouldn't. I suppose

you're right. We may as well keep trying to find the answer even just as something to do until we get murdered."

Nic blinked and reached for his wine. "Morbid. Where do we start?"

"I don't know. I think I'm too empty for ideas right now." She shifted some cushions as she spoke and lay down, curling up like a cat.

"You are more than welcome to stay as long as you like," he said. "But I feel required to ask whether your maid at least knows where you are."

"Yes, I told her. She was scandalised and insisted on coming with me, but I managed to talk her out of it. And yes, I know it's not the done thing, but since they're making us marry anyway, what more can they expect?"

It was an indisputable argument, and satisfied that no one would set up a screech because Lady Leaf had gone missing, Nic rested his back against the chair and downed the last of his wine. He wanted more, but for now the warmth of the dying fire alone would have to provide all the much-needed comfort. Although in truth, even a blazing fire and an endless supply of wine could not have quelled the new fear Millie's death had seeded. An hour ago, they had thought themselves safe so long as they were never alone. And then Millie had died in a room full of people.

Nowhere was safe anymore.

Chapter 21

When Nic woke, the recollection that Millie was dead trickled back like a slowly settling fear. It chilled him more completely than the room had chilled overnight, such that pulling the blanket tighter didn't help.

Partway through the night, Leaf had woken enough to scurry back to her own rooms, but Nic hadn't bothered to move from his sofa. At some point, he'd gotten cold and dragged a blanket over himself, but the idea that a bed could provide comfort and safety seemed ridiculous now.

Ambrose arrived with the sun and gave a start upon finding Nic on the sofa, yet with nothing but a murmured good morning, he'd set about the task of stoking the fire and tidying the wineglasses, bringing up a breakfast tray, and setting out Nic's clothes. He seemed to be at a loose end too, and wondering whether the mood downstairs was half as tense as upstairs, Nic finally pulled himself upright.

"Good morning, Ambrose," he said, rubbing sleep from his eyes. "How is everything downstairs after last night?"

"*Awful* is the most appropriate word, if I'm honest, my lord," Ambrose said, shifting dishes around on the breakfast tray. "The kitchen staff were thoroughly questioned by His Grace, and almost all the extra hands hired for the lock-in haven't come in this morning. Neither have some of the staff who come daily from Charlton."

It took Nic a moment to recollect that of course the staff were still coming and going, the lock-in magic only affecting Brilliants.

"Do you think someone downstairs might have done it?" Nic asked, accepting the tray.

When Ambrose didn't immediately answer, Nic looked up and found consternation twisting the young man's features.

"You can speak freely with me, Ambrose. I would rather you always did."

"Well, my lord, to be perfectly honest, it seems a foolish notion."

"I thought you might say that."

"But His Grace seemed to think so," the valet added quickly. "So perhaps it is the case after all. I don't know the new staff well, but they seem like decent, hardworking people the same as everyone else. And the young lady who . . . who . . . the young lady, she wasn't known to any of us, and her maid kept herself apart with the other Serral staff."

Serral staff who would have far more reason to harm Millie than any at the Court.

"It could have been an accident perhaps," Ambrose said when Nic didn't answer, his tone buoyed with determined hope.

Nic picked up a slice of bread, hardly heeding it. "Perhaps."

"I must admit, up until last night, most of us had written the deaths off as an upstairs problem."

A sharp laugh burst from Nic's chest at that. "I cannot blame you," he said. "I think it's extremely an upstairs problem, and for your sake, I hope it remains so."

"Oh, well, thank you, my lord. I hope it isn't too forward of me to wish for your safety too."

"Not at all, Ambrose, I appreciate it."

With that said, Ambrose returned to pottering about, while Nic's thoughts slid away to the tangle in which the previous night had left them. It had been one thing to believe Lord Ricard capable of killing Gillingham to invoke the clause, another entirely to think he would harm his own daughter. He'd had no reason or opportunity to kill Master Everel either, and poison seemed an odd choice for a ghost or an automaton. The possibility that someone had just taken advantage of the mood in the house to kill Millie couldn't but occur to him, but if it was about the contract after all, then their killer had only five days left to see it broken—less if Dashiell worked fast enough.

Dashiell, the most obvious next target, along with Leaf and Nic himself.

The thought spurred Nic to his feet—an urge to move made impotent by not knowing what to do next. After all, how could he protect the people he loved most without knowing what he was protecting them from?

Conversations carried well up the stairs and Nic paused a moment on the landing to listen. Behind him, the echoes of the central aviary chirped and fluttered, wholly uncaring of the mood floating up from the great hall.

"And my clothes were strewn everywhere!" came Lady Theresa's voice. "My maid was very distressed and is still trying to salvage what she can. Silk should not be crumpled so."

"I will speak to the staff at once, my lady," Mrs. Podmarsh returned.

"Lizzy's room too. All her books thrown about."

"Some of the pages were torn." Lady Lisbeth's voice had a quiet, hollow quality.

Drawing a deep breath, Nic continued down the stairs.

"Ah, Lord Monterris, perhaps you can shed some light on our misfortune," Lady Theresa said in greeting, turning stiff hauteur his way.

"I will certainly do whatever I can, Lady Theresa. Something is amiss?"

The lady parted her lips to speak, but it was Lord Charborough who said, "It is nothing so great, Monterris, just an unfortunate mess no doubt made by some of the servants."

"Unfortunate mess?" Lady Theresa turned on him. "Charles, my room was *ransacked*. Things thrown everywhere. In the middle of the night too! Especially after what happened to dear Millie, the thought of someone being in my room while I slept makes me shudder."

Lady Lisbeth did shudder, and glanced toward the entry hall where the Court's giant old doors stood locked.

"Your room too, Lady Lisbeth?" Nic asked, fresh dread settling in his stomach.

"Yes." A quiet whisper. "Although nothing seems to be missing. Not even the pearl necklet Mama left me."

"And you, Lord Charborough?"

The man gave a defeated little gesture. "Well, yes, my room was certainly tidier when I went to sleep than when I woke."

Nic turned his gaze toward Dr. Fanshaw, who had so far remained silent at the edge of the group. "Doctor?"

"Unfortunately so, my lord. As with Lady Lisbeth, many of my books have been torn and everything strewn around, but nothing appears to actually be missing."

When Nic turned next to Mrs. Podmarsh, he had the questionable joy of seeing the usually haughty housekeeper shy away from him. "I'm afraid I have no answers, my lord," she said, not meeting his gaze. "I will, of course, question all the servants. To be out of bed and—although many have not come in today, for—" She stopped. Drew herself up. "I will find out at once, my lord."

She departed upon the words, leaving Nic to deal with the distressed guests. A job that would fall to him now, he realised, with his father having taken Master Everel's place in the hasty rush to finish up negotiations.

"You have my apologies," he said. "I have the greatest faith in Mrs. Podmarsh to find out what happened and ensure it doesn't happen again. In the meantime, do not hesitate to ask if there is anything I can do to assist in making the remainder of your stay as pleasant as possible under the circumstances. I would not wish you to feel neglected while my father is busy ensuring the negotiations are completed in time."

Lady Theresa gave one of her little sniffs. "We thank you, Lord Monterris, but other than getting out of here as soon as possible, we have all we need. I do wish you had just called the whole thing off, Charles."

For the second time, Lady Lisbeth glanced toward the locked doors. "At least Master sa Vare invoked the clause last night," she said. "I saw him post it on the door this morning."

"Did he have his rooms ransacked?" Nic asked, disliking the way fear was starting to colour his every thought. "Did he mention?"

"Oh, he did not say so, though he was very kind and said he was so sorry I had been made distressed."

"Such an excellent young man he is," Lady Theresa said. "It is a shame he isn't better born, of course, but he is respectable and has such fine manners that I am sure your father will be very much in agreement."

Lady Lisbeth reddened. "Master sa Vare has made no such indication, ma'am. I do not expect—"

"Just you wait, dear." Lady Theresa patted her hand.

"In truth, all I can think about is Millie," Lisbeth whispered, the glance she threw Nic fearful. "I keep thinking I will turn and find her beside me, keep expecting her to appear with an amusing story. And when I close my eyes, I can see her sitting there, frowning at her cards, her last words a complaint that I had dealt her such a poor hand."

Tears stood in her eyes and she turned her head. "I'm sorry. It is all just such a shock."

Nic pressed his lips together hard to keep emotion from spilling onto his face. He hadn't known Millie Radlay that well, but he still sometimes walked into his rooms expecting to find Rowerre tending the fire, still turned to speak to him only to find him absent. How much he would have liked someone to confide in about Dashiell, someone to advise him whose love he had never doubted.

"It is indeed all very affecting," Lady Theresa said. "Poor dear Ricard is naturally so overset that I fear we will not see him for the rest of the lock-in, and I myself could not sleep a wink last night. Especially after that dreadful . . . thing came to the parlour door the other night and seeing that ghost at the table. What if some malicious spirit is picking us off one by one? We could any of us be next."

"Theresa, please," Lord Charborough said with a weak laugh. "It is difficult enough to have lost Millie without making it into a spectacle."

"The cup Millie had . . . ," Lisbeth said, swallowing hard. "That was the one you first handed me, Lady Theresa. I passed it on and came back for another. What if . . . what if I was the target? After all, you said you saw the Faceless Man in my chair and—"

Lady Theresa slid an arm around the young woman's shaking shoulders. "See, Charles, you should have just called the whole thing off at once and let us go home."

"If I genuinely believed there to be foul play afoot, then I should have done so," Lord Charborough said. "But a series of unfortunate accidents is—"

"Accidents." Lady Theresa clicked her tongue at him. "Being hunted one by one by ghosts is no accident. And if it is not malicious ghosts, then I have no doubt at all that it was Her Grace. Not," she added, reaching a placating hand Nic's way, "that I think she meant to harm anyone, I assure you. One has only to spend a few minutes with the poor thing to realise she's quite touched in the head."

"Words I will thank you not to repeat, Lady Theresa," Nic snapped. "She is not always entirely with us, I grant, but she has never, and would never, harm a soul."

"Then what of Lord Francis? Or Lord Ellis's boy? If no one will explain what happened to them, what are we supposed to think?"

Her words recalled Master Everel's admission that the duchess had been involved in Lord Francis's death, but refusing to let doubt show on his face, Nic drew himself up. "You are supposed to think nothing. Truly it is surprising that in my lifetime only two people have died within these walls. That is, until your arrival, Lady Theresa."

"Lord Monterris! I was willing to forgive your accusative observation last night, as we had all had quite the shock, but repeating it now is rather too much."

"You did hand me the cup," Lady Lisbeth whispered.

"Now, now." Lord Charborough stepped in. "We are all bereft by the loss of poor Millie, but such bickering will not help. We don't even know if it was due to the tea, when something else entirely could have been ailing her."

Dr. Fanshaw agreed with a low murmur. "And as it is, unfortunately, difficult to tell after the fact whether poison was involved, I can only recommend that everyone be vigilant."

"That is all very well for you to say, Doctor, since you can leave any time you like," Lady Theresa snapped. "Never before have I wished so much not to be a Brilliant! Come, Lizzy, perhaps we should keep to the second-floor sitting room for the remainder of the lock-in. If we stay together and do not wander, then we shall not make such easy targets."

Nic couldn't like Lady Theresa, but he was thankful that she at least was taking the threat seriously, and hoped she would keep Lady Lisbeth firmly under her wing for the final days.

"Doctor," Lord Charborough said once the ladies had departed. "If you would look in on Leaf this morning, I would appreciate it. Poor thing said she got hardly any sleep last night and is lying abed."

"Of course, my lord."

"And I do hope you will have an eye to her these last few days, Lord Monterris," the man went on. "There will of course be no further entertainments given the circumstances, but your company may keep her from worrying unduly."

"I will do whatever I can to ensure she feels comfortable," Nic said. "Especially since this will soon be her home too."

It was a strange truth, one that had been slowly creeping upon him, that while the lock-in would soon end, Leaf would not long after become a permanent fixture of his day-to-day life. They got along well, but it was ultimately a future in which neither of them got what they wanted, where the best they could hope for was company in their disappointments.

The oddness of Nic's pronouncement seemed to strike the marquess too, for he looked momentarily taken aback, as though somewhere along the way he had forgotten he was negotiating the departure of his daughter. There would still be a wedding ceremony, of course, and likely a grand party to celebrate it, but in a contracted marriage the signing of the papers superseded the speaking of any wedding vows. Which meant within a few days Nic and Leaf would officially be married, at least in the only way that truly mattered under vow law.

The marquess soon excused himself, followed by the doctor, leaving Nic standing alone beneath the great hall's shining chandeliers. Despite what he had said, he had no confidence that Mrs. Podmarsh would return with any answers about the ransacked rooms, and was far more concerned about them than he had dared let on. It suggested that if some*one* rather than some*thing* had been behind Millie's death, they hadn't gotten what they wanted.

Of course, Lord Charborough had made light of it, waving off the possibility of foul play. His own contract to marry a Monterris having fallen through, he seemed determined to ensure this one didn't. He'd put an enormous fee and his eldest daughter on the table to make it happen, and now ignored every risk. There had been something between him and the duke, of course, but even a longstanding love seemed no reason for such foolhardiness.

The beginnings of a headache prickled over his scalp, threatening later suffering, yet Nic found himself chewing over the question of Lord Charborough's motives all the same. And knowing it was a question he could not answer alone, he spun on his heel and made for the brightly lit rooms of his mother's sanctuary.

Nic's knock sounded overloud in the gallery, even his mama's flock of misfit echoes quiet. From beyond the door came no sound, no voices or footsteps, like the house itself was pressing silence upon him to stop the questions rising in his throat. When no answer came, he knocked again and turned the handle.

"Mama? Silla?"

No doubt the duchess was just out getting some air, yet after the previous night, the emptiness resounded. It had been a long time since he'd been in his mother's rooms alone, and the space was eerie in her absence. No humming, no gentle rustle as Silla moved about, ever present—not even the scratch of quill on paper as the duchess filled yet another page of her diary. It sat open upon the side table, however, and Nic made his way toward it with unanswered questions burning on the tip of his tongue.

Without picking it up, he looked down at the double spread

of his mother's hasty scrawl. At the top of one page, a date stared back. Not today's, not yesterday's. The second of August, 1790.

"Twenty-six years ago?" He turned back a page and the date changed from August to July, then into the beginning of 1789.

Nic looked around, wondering what had become of the diary she had been writing in only the other day. Quick steps took him to the writing desk, where he pulled open the drawer and froze. There, piled on top of one another, were several diaries. They all looked the same, differentiated only by the amount of ink splotched on their leather covers.

He pulled the topmost book from the drawer and let it fall open. The first date was from 1788, and flipping to the end, he found the final entry dated the fifteenth of May 1791. *Time is a perplexing thing,* it began. *Hours able to go missing at a blink if one does not keep track of them.*

Leaving the book open to that last page, he picked up another and turned to the end. There the same date, the same entry: *Time is a perplexing thing, hours able to go missing at a blink if one does not keep track of them.*

He reached into the drawer and all but snatched out another book, but even before he found the final entry he knew what it would say.

Time is a perplexing thing, it began. *Hours able to go missing at a blink if one does not keep track of them.*

"All the same book," he whispered to the empty room. "She's writing the same diary over and over."

Having trapped the old diaries back in their drawer, he returned to the side table. And opening the book to a random page near the beginning, he started to read.

She first sees Monterris Court in the spring. Large blossoming trees line the drive. Their roots are thick, buckling and cracking the stones, leaving carriages to bump the final stretch to the door, but the discomfort is almost worth it, she thinks, for the sweet scent and the bright colours, and for the chirrup of cheerful birdsong. She has been too well bred to stick her head out the window, but not so much that she cannot admit she wants to.

Nic looked away to ease the hollowing sensation in his gut. His mother had written as though telling someone else's story rather than her own, yet the scene she painted was all too real, the moment one she would have experienced herself. He flicked over some dozen pages.

Everel bows to the duke, bows to her, and strides out, closing the door behind him. He isn't a cheerful companion, not even a friendly one, yet without him the room chills. The duke is sitting at his desk surrounded by his papers. Correspondence and trade sheets, scribbled notes and tallies, and the occasional line of smithed sigils—all the company he ever seems to need or want.

Nic knew that feeling and turned still more pages.

Francis sips from his glass, chair creaking as he leans back. "I'm not very forgetful, I'm afraid, but fortunately I'm good at reading people. You wish your late brother had contracted you to a different family. Honestly, I'd think there was something wrong with you if you didn't. I've wished all my life I'd been born with a different name, so cheers."

She knows it must seem desperate, pathetic, that so small a moment of kindness has reached inside her, but there in that quiet, airy room full of gears and reels and the scent of oil, she doesn't care.

His lips are soft and warm and taste of wine, the illicit act

*nothing to the sheer joy of feeling, for even the briefest moment,
like she is alive again.*

Nic stared at the page, heart thumping hard. And as though to
stop the certainty growing in his mind, he flipped on.

*She runs her hand over the mound of it beneath the new coat.
Children are a woman's joy, her mother used to say, but she's still
waiting for that joy. Perhaps it will arrive with the child. Or perhaps there is something wrong with her.*

No.

*Lord Charborough strides into view. She gasps, but neither
hears her. They are too focused on one another and the tirade
that has reddened the marquess's face. She only catches every
second word, so low is his voice, but it's about money and pride
and names and glory, and he's spitting the words now, their existence mere vehicles for the purging of his rage.*

"You should have given it up, Val. Instead of us."

*For the first time she sees something like real pain flit across
her husband's face, but before she can make sense of this sign of
humanity, he's taken a step forward. Is speaking. "I know," he
says. "But we don't live in a world where choices can be unmade.
I've signed. You've signed. This is what we have now."*

*Lord Charborough closes the space. He grips her husband's
chin, fingers digging into his cheeks with anger and hatred
and yet something far more primal. Still holding him there, he
presses a kiss to his lips—a fierce, hard thing that pushes him
back against the door with a thud, and her duke doesn't fight.
Or he does but it's a battle for supremacy, and while the goal is
each other's destruction, they are fighting with their hands and*

their tongues and their weight and the lean musculature of their increasingly naked bodies.

She watches longer than she ought, her body aflame. She has enjoyed Francis's company many times, yet it has never been like this, never a battle of wills as much as of bodies. Never full of a hunger she can feel as though it's her own but can give no name. She has hidden her tryst well. But here, in Charborough House, within hours of the marquess's wedding, they live only for each other.

"Master Nicholas?"

Nic dropped the diary onto the table as though it had burned his fingers, and looked up to find Silla standing by the door, her surprise slowly turning into a disapproving scowl.

"Silla, I—"

"That is not yours to read, Master Nicholas."

"I know, but . . . she isn't writing as herself, and it's just the same dates over and over like she's trapped in her own past. Tell me you've read it too."

For a moment, Silla just stared back, then she carefully closed the door. "They are the years she cannot let go. For a while, I hoped she would work through them and emerge out the other side, but no. The time we live in is only a dream to her. *That*"—she pointed at the diary—"is her reality."

"She wishes she never married my father."

"Every day." It was a whisper, yet it cut deep. "It was just the two of them by then, Miss Georgiana and her brother. Her father had left her a fortune, and marriage to a duke ought to have been such a boon for the family. But then, you know, or perhaps you don't, that Mr. Cardwell—her brother—died not long after, leaving her no one she could reach out to for help. And with his death there was also no one to benefit from what she increasingly saw as her sacrifice."

"She was alone."

Silla drew herself up. "She had me. It just wasn't enough. You were born into this lonely prison, Master Nicholas, but she came here from a rich life full of parties and gaiety and flattering suitors, a world where she had her whole life ahead of her. A shock to find, upon arriving, that her money had disappeared and her whole life was already behind her."

And so she lived in a dream world, because the desert the duke had made of their existence was too much. For a full minute, Nic found he couldn't speak, could only stand there as anger boiled through him—not just anger at the duke for what he had wrought, but at the society that had made it possible. But what shocked him most was the flare of anger he felt toward his mother, for abandoning him to protect herself—unfair, he knew, yet it burned hot all the same.

"Did she do it, Silla?"

The maid's brows contracted into a harsh line. "Are you asking me if Her Grace poisoned that poor girl?"

"I need to know."

"Of all the people I thought would ask that," Silla whispered, a whisper that cut its disappointment deep into Nic's heart.

"I ask because the Serrals have suggested it and will no doubt suggest it again to the king's men when they come. I have told them it is not true, but—"

"But you doubt."

Nic looked away. "You told me yourself that in certain moods you feared she would harm my father. One teacup is very much like another, after all."

Silla folded her arms, glaring at him, the reticent servant vanishing in the flames of stubborn loyalty.

"I'm not telling you anything, Master Nicholas."

"Why? What is there to hide that won't just make her look guilty?"

"Why?" Silla hissed. "Because I know what you're doing. It's what everyone does. Ask only the questions that will prove her guilt and nothing else."

Nic stepped forward, shocked that Silla flinched back. "Silla, look at me. I love my mother. I wish I could go back in time and tell her to run. I don't want to believe she could harm anyone—"

"No one, Master Nicholas." Silla shook her head, tears sparkling in her eyes. "She couldn't hurt anyone. Yes, I know I said I worried that in her dark moods she could harm His Grace, and I meant it, but that is in a fit of rage, not a calculated attack. I've known her longer than anyone and I can promise you she would never knowingly hurt a soul."

Knowingly. The word had weight. Doubt. Was a crack in her assurance and Silla seemed to recognise it, grimacing when Nic asked again, "Then tell me what you know. About last night. About all of this. About Lord Francis. Anything that could help."

The maid looked to the ceiling, blinking away tears. "If I do, Master Nicholas, you have to promise me you will be her ally, because without you she has none. Only me, and no one ever listens to me."

Tears sprang to Nic's own eyes and he nodded. "You have my word, Silla. I promise I will do everything I can to make sure she is safe, but I can't without knowing what I'm keeping her safe from."

Silla sighed, letting go not only a breath but a sliver of fear.

"Her Grace has said nothing about last night, but she also took nothing with her, unless you think she can manifest poison out of the air? And since she never leaves the house, I'm not sure where she is even supposed to have gotten it from. As for Lord Francis. Yes, he did make her an automaton—something she could have of him when he wasn't around." Her little laugh was bitter. "It conjured his face and spoke to her. And to you. Awful thing, it was." Staring into the past, Silla's eyes burned bright. "Turned it on him she did, yes, but not like that. She might have hated him by the end, but it was his own *experiments* that did for him."

Might have hated him by the end. Nic's thoughts slid back to the snatches of diary he'd read, and he found that his budding suspicion had grown solid.

"Lord Francis was my father."

Even as he spoke, Nic realised it wasn't a question. And when Silla went silent, he knew the answer all the same. The headache that had begun threatening earlier was growing more insistent now.

Pressing a wry smile flat between his lips, Nic nodded. "Thank you, Silla. I should go."

He made for the door, only for Silla's fingers to close around his arm. "Wait." The word was a panicked hiss that shivered through his skin. "Be careful, Master Nicholas. I know you think finding out all the answers will end this, but knowing is more dangerous than you can imagine. Please, take care. It would destroy your mother utterly if anything happened to you."

She let go on the words, yet Nic could still feel the tight band of her fingers around his arm. "What do you mean?"

She threw open the door. "Go, quickly. I should not have said anything. Forget I spoke. I'm just a foolish old woman." For a moment it seemed she would say more, her jaw working, but she shook her head and resolutely held the door for him to leave. "Please, Master Nicholas. Your mother will be back from her meeting with His Grace any minute, and it will best if you are not here. Go."

"With His Grace?"

She shoved him out into the gallery, and before he could ask again what she had meant, the door slammed closed.

Knowing is more dangerous than you can imagine.

The words echoed inside Nic's aching head as he made his way back across the gallery. What had happened with Lord Francis to make her say so? Or with the duke and Lord Charborough? Something during the negotiation process of his mother's contract? Or to do with the money that had disappeared? In truth, any number of secrets might still be lurking, but after more than twenty-five years, what had made them matter now?

It would destroy your mother utterly if anything happened to you.

Nic paused at the end of the gallery. He needed the answers, but perhaps there was a way to get them without having to ask the questions. The archive hall would have a copy of his mother's marriage contract, other documents, too, because ensuring the net held required keeping assiduous records.

A shrill cry cut through Nic's thoughts, and as though he'd been waiting for something to happen, he was moving before he fully registered the sound. He ran toward it, panic lodged in his throat. Another body? It could be Leaf, or Dashiell, could even be his father—every individual fear had become an image upon translucent paper, their outlines merging to create something far more terrible than the sum of its parts.

As he sped back toward the great hall, the panicked scream came again, high-pitched and frantic over an undercurrent of fluttering wings. With the Brilliance headache threatening, the flurry of wingbeats buffeted his mind like a discordant gale, adding to the already fast-growing maelstrom.

Out of breath and with a hand pressed to his head, Nic slid to a halt in the archway to find echoes filling the hall, the air thick with hundreds of wings. Diving and wheeling, they flew about, all black and deep blue and shimmers of gold. On the floor, Lady Lisbeth knelt screaming, her hands over her head as the birds brushed by, each flail that attempted to shoo them only increasing their interest.

For a shocked instant Nic stood frozen while wings battered around him, until laughter drew his gaze upward. Upon the railing of the upper landing stood the duchess. She was dressed only in her nightgown, her hair hanging in loose golden tresses, arms spread as the birds flew around her. "Fly free!" she cried, laughing as they swirled, no care for the distance down to the hard floor below. "Be free! Free!"

"Mama!"

Nic sprinted up the stairs, through the storm of echoes. Feathers and claws brushed past his face but he had eyes only for her, thought only for the woman standing so precariously as though her life meant nothing. At the landing he did not slow. He stepped onto the travel cage she'd used to climb up and lunged for her. His arm slid around her waist and he pulled her back with more desperate fear than care. Her laughter cut into a cry and they fell, footing lost, to land heavily on the boards in a tangle of golden hair. There Nic lay winded, his head a throbbing wreck, but he held on to her, not yet willing to risk letting go. And in his arms, the duchess's laughter became sobs.

A sharp whistle sounded overhead, a two-beat command that sent every echo in the hall diving for the floor. The duke descended the stairs as noise became silence, became stillness. One of the birds settled on the floor by Nic's head, tucking in its wings with a flutter and a coo.

"Your Grace!" Silla appeared, out of breath as though she'd chased Nic all the way, and finally he let his mother go.

Silla helped her up, leaving Nic to pull himself slowly to his feet, shoulder aching where he had hit the floor. Settled echoes scattered the hall, gently trilling "Free, free," while from the stairs above the duke only watched.

Chapter 22

Nic's headache got worse. It was, he knew, the natural trajectory of headaches, yet despite having had quite a few he still hoped every time that it would go the other way.

After helping Hedgeley gather the echoes and get them back to their cages, Nic had spent the rest of the day lying on the settee in the old den. It had always been his retreat when beset by Brilliance headaches, for even with the curtains drawn his own rooms were too bright and too loud with old sigilwork. His grandfather's old den, on the other hand, had no windows and was entirely full of soft chairs, card tables, and hunting trophies. And a faint scent of old pipe smoke.

Sometime in the afternoon, Ambrose had fetched Dr. Fanshaw, who had come bearing his medical bag and a collection of elixirs. With the way his head had been thumping—every single ghostly trail of magic in the house becoming a scream—Nic had not been optimistic. Yet the doctor had offered him a draught of buckthorn and another of karan myrrh and somehow, miraculously, the pressure and pain had begun to subside.

It took time, however, time in which he had nothing to do but lie in the dark and breathe ancient air, trying and failing not to wish Dashiell were sitting with him as he had sometimes done when they'd been boys. Instead only his father had come by, trailing in complaints rather than sympathy. First he complained about the number of staff who had given their notice, then about guests who blamed their own untidy habits on ransacking ghosts, before returning to the ever-fruitful topic of his son's inequities.

"I had hoped you had grown out of these childish headaches, Nicholas," the duke said, slowly pacing the room with a rhythm that seemed to hammer against Nic's skull. "It is hardly commensurate with your dignity to be hiding away in the dark."

Nic's head ached too much to argue or attempt explanation, especially when not a single word of his remonstration was new. It seemed to have a fresh bite, however, and Nic couldn't but wonder if he was being deliberately punished for his recent offences.

"Well," the duke said, scuffing to a stop beside the settee with a dissatisfied air. "At least since the Serral party are refusing to come down to dinner until the contract is complete, I will be spared the need to explain your absence at the dinner table. Now would not be a good time to have them begin questioning the soundness of your mind."

Thankfully, his father had departed after that, leaving Nic with a new thought to occupy his mind—a fierce desire to inflict his next headache upon the duke instead.

Whether thanks to such malicious imaginings or the doctor's elixirs, the pain had subsided into mere fragility by the time Ambrose brought his food. "Dinner, my lord," the young man whispered, the sound rasping across Nic's senses. "Would you like it here, or . . . ?"

"Here is fine," Nic said, pulling into a sitting position with a wince. "Thank you, Ambrose."

"And Master sa Vare is asking if you are well enough for him to step in, my lord."

"Oh."

Before Nic could think of a more eloquent reply, Dashiell appeared in the doorway. "Only if you can stomach my presence," he said, voice low.

"When you put it like that, it sounds as though I find you disgusting," Nic said, managing a faint smile.

"Not what I meant."

"I know. But yes, I think I can stomach your presence for a little while."

Dashiell stepped in and took the nearby armchair while Ambrose fussed with the dinner tray, the small clinks of glass and ceramic like flicks upon raw nerves. The worst of the headache had subsided, but it would still take a few hours—and likely another of the doctor's draughts—before Nic could face the world without cringing.

"I heard from the doctor that you had one of your headaches," Dashiell said. "I am glad to find it hasn't laid you out as completely as they used to."

"I think that is more due to the doctor's elixirs than any sudden fortitude on my part, however much my father continues to insist I should be able to determinedly Monterris my way out of having them, like I choose to suffer merely to be interesting."

Dashiell grimaced. "Ah, he's still at that, is he?"

"Always."

Having finally finished arranging Nic's dinner to his satisfaction, Ambrose stepped back. "Is there anything else you need, my lord?" he whispered, the extra sibilant whistle making Nic wince.

"Please don't do that," Nic said, causing consternation to twist the young man's face.

"Do what, my lord?"

Nic tried to swallow his annoyance—an annoyance that had more to do with a lingering grief that he would never have had to remind Rowerre.

When Nic didn't immediately answer, the valet looked wide-eyed to Dashiell in a silent plea for assistance.

"It's the whispering," Dashiell said, his voice a low murmur. "It makes a whistling that is worse than just speaking normally, even when you try not to. Just pitch your voice down and keep it as monotonous as you can."

Because of course Dashiell had remembered.

Nic waved something of an apology at Ambrose. "Not your fault I'm a finicky bastard to take care of. I will be all right in a few hours, but I shall have to find out what the doctor puts in his elixirs, because they were far more effective than the ones old Dr. Palmerston mixes up."

"He is certainly a handy man to have around," Dashiell agreed. "Though he gave me strict instructions not to trouble you for long, so now that I have assured myself you are well, I should probably leave you to an evening of much deserved rest."

"Ah, but you should know there is no rest for the wicked," Nic said, because he didn't want Dashiell to go but couldn't ask him to stay. "When I head back to my rooms it will be to work on that sigil tape. That is once I'm sure that touching it won't feel like getting hit repeatedly over the head with a harp."

Dashiell's laugh owned an edge of grimace. "I would say just leave it to me, but I'm afraid I've had no epiphany about it. The more I look at my notes, the more I fear it's just gibberish. All those half-complete *ba met* commands and repeated conjurings of firelight."

"*Ba met* commands don't work when they're only half-complete."

"I know, that's why I said it was gibberish. And more likely to induce a headache than help one."

Nic gave him a piercing look. "Are you just telling me its gibberish so that I'll rest instead of working on it? If it mollifies you at all, I was only going to work on it for a short time anyway, since I need to go down to the archives tonight."

"The archives? Dare I ask why?"

"Truthfully? Because I want to find my mother's marriage contract."

"Her marriage contract?" Dashiell glanced around the den as though he expected one of the stuffed stag's heads to solve his confusion. "But why? What do you hope to find?"

"I don't know exactly," Nic said, because he couldn't say "because maybe these murders aren't about *this* contract," or "because Uncle Francis was my father," or "because I don't understand what happened to her money" or any of the other thoughts that tangled in his mind.

Dashiell's brow furrowed. "Given the circumstances, wandering around at night on your own for an 'I don't know exactly' seems unwise. Would you like company?"

Nic examined his face and found it devastatingly earnest. The answer was yes, but Nic shook his head. "No one knows I mean to go, and I'll go late enough that everyone is asleep anyway. So, you see, you needn't worry about me."

"Not worry about you when four people are already dead?"

A deep boom like a distant gong filled the room with the scratch of sigils, their accent familiar and unmistakable. Nic pressed a hand to his head, turning an accusatory look Dashiell's way. But the vowsmith had not moved his fingers and had no quill in hand, the magic his and yet lacking the stickiness of fresh work. Dashiell's gaze snapped toward the door.

"That's the alarm."

"The what?

"The alarm on the doors." Dashiell leapt to his feet. "A Brilliant is trying to get out of the house."

The vowsmith was gone on the words, dashing out into the hallway, his warning shout swallowed by yet another resonant boom. Nic pushed away his dinner tray and got to his feet, hating the feeling his head was shaking loose. He followed anyway, hurrying out in Dashiell's wake.

Nic arrived in the entrance hall to find Lady Lisbeth dressed in a warm pelisse with a small bandbox on the floor by her feet. Fingers curved to desperate claws, she scratched at the sigils covering the doors of Monterris Court, sending sparks of fracturing magic spitting into the air.

"Stop!" Dashiell shouted as he sped in, only to pull up short when she seemed not to hear him.

Footsteps sped along the hallway like a storm, and in a breath of soft muslin and rose oil Leaf brushed passed Nic in the doorway. "Lizzy!"

Where Dashiell's voice had not registered, Leaf's collapsed Lady Lisbeth's knees beneath her. The young woman dropped in a billow of green velvet, and pressed shimmering ink-smeared hands to her face.

"I want to go home, Leaf. I want to go home," she cried. "I don't want to die. Please let me go home!"

As Leaf knelt on the floor beside her sobbing friend, Nic slowed his approach, uncomfortable with having come to stare at the lady's distress—a distress he felt in his soul, as he felt the powerlessness of her desperate bid for freedom.

"I'm sorry, Lisbeth, you know I cannot," Leaf said, the look she threw her father as he appeared all glare.

Lisbeth, hunting the slowly arriving company, fixed her gaze on Dashiell then. "Oh, Master sa Vare, please! Please let me go. You can do it, can't you? Please?"

A flicker of pain crossed Dashiell's face as he shook his head. "I cannot, my lady. To open the doors for any Brilliant would void the contract, and so is something only His Grace and Lord Charborough can do."

Though she had surely known the answer, Lady Lisbeth gasped a sob and seemed for a moment like she would grip his hand and beg, only to ball her fingers into tight fists. She glanced up at Lord Charborough, and bowed her head. "I don't want to die," she whispered.

A long, taut silence dragged in which no one spoke. Dashiell flexed his hands and looked up at the entry hall's vaulted roof, daring no further words.

With a disgusted sniff, Leaf rose. "Come Lizzy," she said, holding down her hands to her friend. "Let us go back upstairs together. We needn't see anyone else for the rest of the night, or tomorrow either."

For a moment it seemed as though Lady Lisbeth would turn back to the door, would tear at the sigils, but shrinking in upon herself, she took Leaf's hands. And slowly, without a word to anyone, Leaf led her trembling companion out of the hall.

The archives of Monterris Court took up half of the vaulted crypt beneath the house. Part cellar and part library, it was a strange, cluttered space by day, but without any light spilling down its light wells, the vast hall was oppressively dark. Even Nic's lantern seemed barely to illuminate an arm's length in front of him as he made his way down the stairs.

Halfway down, his foot landed on what felt distinctly like an arm rather than a step, sending the memory of Rowerre's unmoving body lancing through him at the speed of panic. Nic swung the lantern down, revealing first a dark sleeve, then Dashiell's bronze eyes hastily blinking beneath sleep-tousled hair.

The vowsmith winced, shielding his gaze from the light with one elegant hand. "Nic? I must have fallen asleep. Please get that out of my face."

He did so, but folding his arms over the panicked racing of his heart, Nic went on glaring at him. "What are you doing here?" he said. "Were you sleeping on the *stairs*?"

"Not because I thought 'Hey, you know what would be comfortable—stairs!' I was waiting for you, you idiot."

"What?"

Dashiell hauled himself to his feet, still blinking away sleep or the ghosts of bright light swimming in his vision. "What what? You said you were going to the archive tonight, and since you refused to take my concerns for your safety seriously, I waited here for you instead."

"Thus putting *yourself* at risk?"

"I was keeping watch."

"Until you fell asleep."

"That part," Dashiell admitted with a wry smile, "was unplanned. Did you bring anything to eat?"

Nic found himself staring at his old friend, unable to keep a smile from creeping upon him, so completely was Dashiell the young man he remembered in that moment.

"Ah, no. Sorry. No food."

"Oh. Well, I'm still coming with you, but I want you to know, Nicholas Monterris, that I am very disappointed. We used to always take food on our late-night adventures."

Nic grinned, unable to resist the pull of Dashiell's smile, of how easily they could fall into their old camaraderie. "Duly noted, Master sa Vare. Duly noted." He gestured to the door at the bottom of the stairs. "You're likely to get in a lot of trouble if you're caught in here, though, so—"

"You know, I've been thinking about that. Entering your archives doesn't actually contravene any specific guild laws, so to get into trouble for it, either your father would have to lodge a complaint and risk losing the contract—"

"Which we know he won't do."

"Or Lord Charborough would have to lodge a complaint claiming that it diminished my ability to negotiate on his behalf. But since these are *your* archives, not his, that's hardly a persuasive case."

"Even so," Nic said, descending the rest of the stairs. "You don't have to be here."

"I know."

Nic huffed a small laugh, unable to argue with that and finding he didn't want to. "Well, thank you for coming," he said as he paused in the entry arch to get his bearings. "And not just because it's safest to stick together. I . . . didn't actually want to do this alone, but I didn't want to ask Leaf either. These worries about Mama feel too personal to share with her just yet."

Belatedly realising the obvious conclusion Dashiell could draw from such a statement, Nic cleared his throat and added, "Besides, your knowledge of contracts might come in handy. I think the family ones are over here."

It took some time to find the right shelves, but once they did, Dashiell dug around in the boxes until he found a heavy document laced down one side like a coverless book. He handed it over, and Nic tilted its front page toward the lantern he'd perched on one of the shelves.

> Contained herein is the vowed and signed
> marriage contract between
> Valentine Nicholas Edmund Monterris,
> His Grace the Duke of Vale,
> and
> Georgiana Elizabeth Cardwell

Georgiana Elizabeth Cardwell. How different a life she'd had with that name. Nic passed a hand over his eyes and heaved a sigh.

"Are you all right?" Dashiell asked. "If your headache is—"

"No, it's fine, I just . . . don't know if I'm ready to read this, even though I need to know what it says."

Having let go another sigh that didn't help, Nic forced himself to turn the cover page and read the opening paragraphs. Barely had he made it halfway through before a dreadful exhaustion crept over him.

"It's all lists and numbers and clauses written in deliberately obtuse contract language," he groaned. "I'm not sure what else I expected, really, but it's so hard to read."

With a dramatic flourish, Dashiell held out his hand. "Then allow me to offer you my services, my lord. Deliberately obtuse contract language and random collections of numbers are, in fact, my forte."

Nic handed over the sheaf of papers, ashamed by how relieved he felt not to have to dig through it. "I don't know what it is," he said, leaning back against the opposite shelf. "I can read actual books for hours and forget to eat, but give me pages like that and my gaze slides off before the end of the first line."

"A lot of people have that problem with different things," Dashiell said, flicking over a page. "You'd be surprised. My eyes hate musical notation. Or, rather, my brain does. I couldn't tell you how many times our music teacher smacked my wrist because my thoughts wandered."

"Huh, I didn't know that. I always just assumed you were amazing at everything."

Dashiell glanced back over his shoulder. "Oh, like you? Yes, *and* that damn smile of yours. When you're being mischievous you only have one dimple, did you know that?"

Nic hadn't and found he couldn't say so, found he couldn't say anything at all when Dashiell's gaze lingered, a knowing warmth in his smile. It took every ounce of Nic's strength to keep his feet firmly planted, to look away and save them both from another indiscretion.

"So, what do you want to know?" Dashiell asked, returning to the contract.

"I don't know. Everything, really."

"We could be here for a long time if you want every detail. Ducal papers are, as a rule, about twice as long as everyone else's due to all the additional responsibilities to the crown."

"All right, well, how about whether anything to do with her money was unusual, like whether she brought in more or less than you'd expect. And . . . whether there was a stud clause."

Dashiell had started flicking through the pages but he paused at that, looking up. Their eyes met, but when Nic didn't explain, the vowsmith went back to turning pages. "All right. I'll start there."

Unable to stand still while Dashiell scoured the old marriage contract in search of Nic's much needed truths, he started to pace.

"No stud clause."

The words halted Nic in his tracks and he spun back. "Not at all?"

"None. You . . . were expecting one?"

A nod. To say more would mean exposing his mother's personal words, and those words hadn't been meant for Nic's eyes let alone another's ears.

A frown creased Dashiell's brow, but he said no more, returning instead to the contract. Pages were turned, and having been turned they were turned right back—the method of reading a contract not so much start to finish as a dance from clause to clause, tracing the net of sigils that bound it to the wider world.

"I can't see anything particularly unusual in here either," Dashiell said after a time, his quiet words all but swallowed by the cavernous space. "No caveats of note, no rules governing the use of her fortune or its return. Twenty thousand pounds is the dowry sum."

"Twenty thousand pounds," Nic repeated. "That should have been enough to invest in the estate and make it profitable again, don't you think?"

"That might depend on what has been mortgaged and whether debts needed servicing, but I admit I don't know much about estates as such. My older brother learned estate management while I was apprenticing."

A hint of bitterness lay hidden in the admission, and Nic realised it was something they'd never talked about. The reminder that there were still so many things they had yet to discover about each other, and now never would, caused unexpected pain.

"Well," Nic said to say something. "I guess we know about the same amount then, since my father has not yet deigned to teach me anything, though I have asked numerous times."

"Nothing?"

"Nothing. Not about the estate, anyway. Echoes, yes. But that's not very helpful when it comes to knowing how poor we are and why."

Dashiell let the contract fall closed with a papery thud and handed it over, before setting off along the shadowy shelves. Nic hastily tucked the contract back into its box and hurried after him, lantern swinging.

"What are you looking for now?"

"Estate documents. I don't know anything about estate management, but I do know how to read boring papers, which should help."

Nic trailed after Dashiell in silence, carrying their lantern while the vowsmith strode from shelf to shelf, muttering to himself and scanning dates. It took him some time to gather the various papers he apparently needed, before he stopped and sank cross-legged onto the stones in the middle of the floor. Piles were made, important pages were lined up for easy reference, and short stacks were sorted and laid out with the cover papers perpendicular underneath—the whole such an organised affair that Nic felt like an intruder in a private space. All he could do was stand at the edge and hold the lantern aloft, watching the movement of Dashiell's hands, the shifting of his expression, and the way he tapped his fingers on the papers as he read. It was excruciatingly slow with the night chill seeping in, yet Nic could have stayed all night in that comfortable closeness—an intimate scene in which there was no charge of passion, just the delight of watching Dashiell work with no hint of his professional mask. Too easily could Nic imagine long nights spent sitting so by a warm fire, just the two of them.

"Oh," Dashiell said eventually, breaking the companionable silence.

Nic switched hands on the lantern, causing the light to swing over Dashiell's workspace. "Oh?"

Dashiell didn't elaborate, just flipped more pages and checked more dates, his expression darkening.

Nic's patience fractured. "Oh what? What is it?" And when the vowsmith seemed not to hear, he added, "Dash?"

Dashiell looked up, and his lips started moving silently as though trying out words only to find them all insufficient. At last, he sighed and dropped a short stack of papers to run a hand over his eyes.

"I, uh, can't be entirely sure of course. I could be missing something, because while I understand business papers, I don't understand estates. Also your father's system is pretty complicated and dense. And—"

"Yes, I understand that all your pronouncements come with caveats—you're a vowsmith. Now spit it out!"

The vowsmith huffed a little laugh, but it was soon swallowed by something all too like dread, and Nic's heart slammed into his ribs as he waited. Eventually, Dashiell said, "It's gone."

"What is?"

"The money."

"My mother's money?"

"No, all the money."

Nic stared at him. "I don't understand."

"The principal, the estate, almost all the original investments," Dashiell said, shifting some papers around as he spoke. "They're almost all gone."

"I still don't understand. What do you mean the *estate* is gone?"

"I mean that the Monterris family owns very little land, having sold it off in pieces to satisfy the demands of very large debts."

"My grandfather's and great-grandfather's gambling debts?"

Dashiell held some papers up for him to see, though they may as well have been in a foreign language for how little Nic understood them. "Yes, but see here? There are more, in the time since your father became duke. Although not recently. During your lifetime it's been all shifting money around and desperately trying to stay afloat."

"Are you telling me my father gambles too?"

"No, that seems unlikely, but perhaps Lord Francis did."

For a moment Nic could only stare at him, stomach hollowing. "How big were these debts?"

"As best I can tell, about a hundred thousand pounds, give or take."

"A hundred thou—" Nic clamped a hand across his own mouth, as though by forcing the words back in, he could change their meaning.

Dashiell reached out a hand—an instinctive offer of comfort he soon let fall. "I'm sorry, Nic. I think the reason your father doesn't teach you anything about the estate is because there's nothing to teach, and because if you had access to . . . all this, you would know what he doesn't want anyone to know."

No land. No money. His inheritance nothing but a name and a history and a mortgaged and mouldering old house filled with hatred and ghosts. He'd always thought distantly of what he would do when he inherited the estate—the knowledge that it would one day be his a constant that underpinned his life. Now even that poor surety dropped away, leaving him standing on nothing.

On the floor, Dashiell gathered up the papers and began carefully reorganising them into their respective piles and boxes. As he worked, his gaze flitted back to Nic over and over—a man wary lest Nic fall. But Nic did not fall, not yet.

"Thank you," he said, managing a smile once Dashiell had finished putting everything away. "I wouldn't have found out any of that without your help."

Dashiell grimaced. "I do not feel worthy of thanks, having been the bearer of such news. Remember, I could be wrong, I might have missed something entirely, but . . ."

"But you're confident enough that even your doubt sounds doubtful. And don't blame yourself. Better I know the truth."

"Are you all right?"

"Honestly, I don't know," Nic said as they started back toward the archive door. "That wasn't what I was expecting. I think it will take some time to sink in."

So as not to draw attention to themselves, they walked in silence back through the dark house. It was no short journey, so widely did Monterris Court sprawl, yet in Dashiell's company the time passed as though it were nothing. All too soon they were making their way up the stairs to their respective rooms.

Dashiell had accompanied him because it wasn't safe for anyone to walk around the house alone, but Nic stopped when they reached the second-floor landing where their paths diverged. He held out the lantern. "You take this. I don't need the light. I could reach my door from here with my eyes closed."

"You want to part here?"

"We have to somewhere," Nic said, hating how perfectly those words mirrored their future—a future down to mere days now the king's men were already on their way.

Dashiell hesitated, but he took the lantern. "All right."

"Thank you, again," Nic said, hyperaware of the way light fell across Dashiell's face, touching him in ways Nic could only dream of. "Good night."

"Good night."

Like a man fighting the force of gravity, Nic continued up the stairs. No sound of Dashiell's retreating steps joined the chorus of his own, but he dared not turn and risk seeing him just standing there, because then he might never turn back.

The corridors of Monterris Court felt colder in Dashiell's absence, and Nic took the last flight of stairs two at a time, thinking of his warm bed. At the top, he paused a moment and glanced back to be sure the vowsmith hadn't followed, only for a nearby creak to rip terror down his spine.

"Who's there?" Nic spun about, gripping tight to the banister. When nothing struck him from out of the darkness, he peered into the shadows, his heart slamming into his ribs. "Hello?"

No movement. No sound. Until a little farther away along the passage, a step scuffed. "Who is that?" Nic demanded, starting after the retreating sound. Foolish to shout at a ghost and even more foolish to follow one, yet the need to know trumped self-preservation and he gave chase along the dark passage. That it could be the automaton only occurred to him an instant before the figure froze and turned, betraying the smooth curve of a pale face like a crescent moon against the night. Nic drew a sharp breath but didn't slow.

"Wait!"

He lunged, snatching at the thing's arm, only for his fingers to slide right through and close upon air, a spark teasing his skin like the flick of flint and steel. The lack of solidity overbalanced him and he stumbled forward, through a ghost and into the darkness beyond—an empty darkness that stretched away to where the passage ended in a small pool of moonlight.

Breath catching, Nic spun, the space around him feeling suddenly too open, too vulnerable—hands ready to reach from every direction. Nothing but cold darkness limned with moonlight stared back, its emptiness as frightening.

Quick steps took Nic to his rooms, though he glanced back a dozen times. Nothing seemed to follow, yet still his heart thundered in his throat as he pushed the door open to be met with the cheerful glow of a banked fire.

"Nic?"

Nic spun, panic spiking, but it was just Dashiell approaching in his small sphere of lantern light. "It's just me," he said, raising a hand. "Sorry, I didn't mean to scare you."

"That's all right." Nic leaned back against the doorframe and pressed a hand over his thundering heart. "I saw that ghost again, and idiot that I am, I thought chasing it was both wise and possible." He forced out a slightly manic laugh. "Did you come because you heard me shouting at it?"

"Yes. No. I mean yes, but I had already turned back to come after you."

In the wake of such an admission, Nic's heartbeat went on racing for a whole different reason.

"Can I come in?" Dashiell added when Nic just stared. "I . . . I was hoping we could talk."

"Talk. Right. Of course." Nic pushed his door wide and led the way inside, the disappearing figure of mere moments before all but forgotten as Dashiell followed.

"Sorry," Nic added when the vowsmith closed the door behind them. "I haven't had a chance to light any candles yet."

"Good thing I still have the lantern then." He set it on the side table and fixed Nic with a long intent stare.

Nic swallowed. "What . . . what was it you wanted to talk about?"

"It's . . . I've been thinking. About us. A lot, really, and since I promised to make no decisions about us without—God, why is this so difficult?" Dashiell ran his hand back to front through his hair, making a beautiful mess. "Look, Nic, I know we don't have a future, but with our days together running out, I find I would rather have something now than nothing ever."

Nic stared, his breath suspended as Dashiell hurried on, all nerves. "I know your father—and you!—desperately need this contract to go ahead, so I understand if you dare not risk anything for fear of it foundering on our indiscretion . . . God knows I have tried to tell myself this is madness, but I cannot stop thinking about you. I cannot stop thinking about how much I will regret my silence when it is too late, because this is the only time in my life I will ever be able to call you mine."

The words hung between them—beautiful words Nic wanted to fold up and tuck into his heart, wanted to shred and consume over and over. He had been thinking the same thing for days, and now here Dashiell stood, asking permission like the risk was Nic's alone.

"Dash." His name came out a whisper. "If anyone finds out, you could lose your job. You could be excommunicated from the guild. Are a few days with me really worth that risk?"

"Yes."

He answered quickly, and when Nic hunted Dashiell's face he found no sign of disquiet, only a fierce gaze that went on meeting his and stealing his breath. And Nic could no more have turned him away than have flown.

"Then perhaps you should lock the door."

A smile flickered across Dashiell's face, owning a mischievous twinkle.

"Shall I take that as a yes?"

"Yes, but . . ." Nic stepped close in the lantern light, the very sight of Dashiell standing there wanting him filling his heart to bursting. Leaving the words hanging, Nic brushed back a stray lock of the vowsmith's hair, before sliding his hand gently down to cup his cheek. Eyes half closed, Dashiell turned against his hand, leaving his breath to dance over Nic's wrist—quick, sharp breaths full of tense anticipation. For days they had been holding themselves apart, clinging to their armour, but this was a chance for something else, something more. Something they both knew would add extra hurt to their parting.

"Stay with me tonight," Nic whispered, shifting his hand to nuzzle against Dashiell's cheek. "No fuck and done this time. Let's just pretend that everything we want is possible."

"I like the sound of that," Dashiell murmured back, a rough edge to his voice. "That everything we want is possible. I can do that."

He sounded sure, but the gaze that met Nic's held a hint of shyness, of wariness, as though some part of him was afraid of all he wanted. Yet he leaned in and brushed his nose to Nic's. Granting permission or seeking it, Nic wasn't sure, but that caring little gesture was so very Dashiell that his heart swelled, love overflowing.

Nic kissed him then. And having kissed him once, kissed him again, pushing him gently back against the door and earning a groan that vibrated down his throat. Nic pressed against him, wanting every part of his body to touch and be touched, to fit perfectly against Dashiell like they were made to be.

Like a key to a lock, some final hesitance Dashiell had been carrying seemed to shatter then and he gripped Nic's face, kissing him like it was the last time they would see one another, like one of them wouldn't survive the night. Under the force of it, Nic felt drunk. Reckless. Alive. But although they could pretend what they wanted was possible, could steal what time they could, one way or another it would soon run out.

Chapter 23

Nic didn't wake when Ambrose brought his breakfast tray, nor when he brought his shaving water, but eventually his young valet's insistent pottering gnawed through the exhaustion.

"Good morning, my lord."

With a weary groan, Nic blinked into the sunlight, only for a smile to spread his lips as memories of the previous night returned in exquisite detail. Once Dashiell had locked the door upon the world, they had existed outside of it. There they had needed fiercely at first, before the realisation they had time crept upon them and they'd taken it, the night filling with lingering kisses and the kind of slow undressing where every piece of skin became a new, delightful discovery. They had gotten to know one another again, but while every new familiarity was shadowed by past or future heartache, that knowledge had invigorated rather than diminished them, like a pair of flames determined to burn bright and furious before the end.

An hour before dawn, Dashiell had dragged himself back to his own bed, leaving Nic to a deep if short sleep he would happily have given up entirely.

"Good morning, Ambrose," Nic replied with a yawn. "I hope that breakfast tray has very strong coffee on it."

"I'm afraid not, my lord, but I can go ask the kitchens for some?"

Nic waved a hand. "Don't trouble yourself. There will be some in the breakfast parlour once I drag myself out of bed."

"I'm afraid the breakfast parlour is locked this morning," Ambrose said, laying out Nic's clothes. "It seems there was something of an accident in there yesterday and the carpet is being cleaned. Although with how few staff we have, I don't know when that will get done."

"Oh, another accident. We're having poor luck losing so many rooms."

A knock sounded on the door. Ambrose made no move, no doubt expecting Leaf to let herself in, but when she didn't, he set down Nic's waistcoat and headed out. He returned a few moments later, his face an expressionless mask.

"Master sa Vare is here to see you, my lord."

"Oh. Right. Show him in."

Nic suddenly wished he was already up and dressed, but when Dashiell strode in—neatly attired in his black vowsmith's garb and perfect in every way—the vowsmith's eyes brightened.

"Well, hello, darling," he said, the words almost a purr. "Look at you still lazing in bed."

A quick glance found that Ambrose had thankfully remained out in the sitting room, and Nic could only hope he would stay there feigning a complete inability to hear. Dashiell didn't seem troubled by the valet's existence, and sat on the edge of the bed, his lips curving as he pressed them to Nic's in a lingering kiss.

"I wish very much I could join you," he murmured.

"Well, I wish I had gotten up and didn't look such a mess."

"You look delightful."

"Haystack and all, I suppose."

"If someone ever succeeds in taming your hair, I will have very strong words to say in their disparagement."

Pulling back, Dashiell set one knee on the bed and threw the other over Nic, his breeches pulling tight around his thighs as he straddled Nic's hips. The sight of Dashiell sitting there atop him—

all crisp black coat and perfect neckcloth, his beautiful features alight with an impulsive grin—was enough to make Nic sure he was dreaming.

"How do you look this good on so little sleep?" he asked.

"If this job teaches one anything, it's the ability to go without sleep. Now, I only have a few minutes until I have to run and you cannot mess me up," Dashiell added while pressing a series of kisses to Nic's lips, each a little deeper than the last. "But I refuse to go down to the chamber without—" The words vanished into a kiss, through which Dashiell drew a deep breath as though to inhale every shred of Nic's being and carry it away with him.

What started as playful kisses took on heat, and it was all Nic could do not to grip that fine coat, not to tear at Dashiell's neckcloth or run hands through his oiled hair.

"This is unfair," he said, the words ending in a moan as Dashiell ground against his stiffening cock. "Extremely unfair."

"Is it any satisfaction that I am torturing myself too?" came Dashiell's breathless reply. "God, I just want to eat you!"

He nipped at Nic's lip and, pressing his hands to Nic's chest, sat back with a growl. The movement rocked them against one another and Nic couldn't help but slide his hands up Dashiell's breeches, over tight muscles and smooth fabric to his hips. There he dug his fingers in, half in lust, half in a desperate desire never to let him go.

For a few glorious seconds, Dashiell sat there like a manifest god. Then with an indignant roar of frustration, he threw himself off the bed to stand staring down at Nic like he really did want to eat him whole.

"Damn." He winced, adjusting himself and his breeches to hide his arousal as best he could. "I have to go, but you had better be here when I get back."

Nic groaned, rock hard now beneath the covers. "Where exactly do you think I'm going to go?"

"That had better be a promise."

The vowsmith lingered, his gaze locked on Nic with an intensity that seared, before he turned away with a final, frustrated growl.

"All right, I'm going. But I want you to know that I don't want to."

"Duly noted, Master sa Vare."

With a snap of his jaw, Dashiell strode out, leaving Nic buzzing head to toe. As the main door closed behind the vowsmith, he buried his face in the pillow, smothering a laugh that was half groan as he sought to commit every detail to memory.

Ambrose cleared his throat. "Are you ready to dress, my lord?"

Nic rolled over. "Oh, I probably should, shouldn't I?" He looked up into his valet's troubled countenance. "Please don't tell anyone Master sa Vare was here this morning."

"Oh no, not a word, my lord. That's one of the first things Rowerre taught me—that a good valet is both discreet and loyal."

A simple declaration, yet it twinged Nic's heart with both sadness and gratitude. Rowerre was gone and yet still, in his way, was looking out for Nic all the same.

"Thank you, Ambrose, that means a lot to me."

"You're very welcome, my lord. I believe the shaving water might still be warm."

With Ambrose's increasingly skilful assistance, Nic was soon neatly attired, though his hair remained as unmanageable as ever. Glancing in the mirror, he assessed his appearance based on Dashiell's imagined reaction when he returned, and couldn't contain an amused smile—a smile that dimpled one of his cheeks and not the other.

When you're mischievous you only have one dimple, did you know that?

For the second time that morning, a knock sounded on the door, but this time it opened almost immediately.

"Nic?"

He stepped out into his sitting room to find Leaf hovering just inside the door, her maid a wary shape behind her.

"Ah, you are up," Leaf said. "I was going to leave you be in case you were still suffering with that dreadful headache, but I needed a few minutes away from Lizzy, so here I am."

She looked more exhausted than Nic felt, with dark circles under her eyes and a grim set to her mouth. Guilt at having stolen so much joy for himself while she went on suffering couldn't but weigh him down.

He went to her, taking her hands in a reassuring grip. "I am perfectly well this morning, but you look dreadful. Is Lady Lisbeth still overset after last night?"

A flicker of amusement crossed Leaf's face at his unflattering observation on her appearance, but it vanished just as quickly. "She is a little calmer this morning, and Dr. Fanshaw has given her something to help her rest, but I fear between her distress and my own I barely slept last night. And all I can think about is how good Millie always was at cheering us up."

Determined to keep his own evening activities to himself, Nic wrapped his arms around her, earning a glare from the maid still standing in the open doorway. "I'm sorry," he said into the soft curls of Leaf's hair, all other words seeming insufficient and trite. "I hope you know if there's anything you need of me you only have to ask."

"I know," came her muffled voice from the breast of his coat. "But in truth I don't know what I need. I want to be alone and yet I hate the silence. I want to find out who did this, yet I know it won't bring her back. Right now, I think I just need a few minutes not having to worry about someone else." She looked up. "I left Lizzy with Aunt Theresa so I could escape. I hope you don't think that's heartless of me."

"Not at all. I imagine it's hard enough to grieve such a loss without having to care for someone else's grief at the same time."

Leaf stepped out of his hold with a sigh. "You do understand. I knew you would. I will go back soon, but for now I just need a few minutes without having to hear about how close she came to her own death." Confusion must have shown on Nic's face, for Leaf added, "That ghost, you know. The one Aunt Theresa saw in her chair, she is determined it was a portent."

"I saw one last night," Nic said. "A ghost."

"Was it the Faceless Man too? Where?"

"Just the other side of the landing, after I came up the stairs. Scared all hell out of me because I thought it was someone lying in wait, but then it ran."

"Ran?"

"That might not be the best word," Nic admitted, and explained how he had heard it, had followed it, had called after it. How he had put his hand right through it.

Leaf shivered at his description. "You think it was running away from you?"

"It felt like it, but I suppose it could have just been going that direction along the passage."

"What else is even up here except for your rooms?"

"All the family rooms used to be up here. The ducal suite and the duchess's official rooms are down that way; my parents just don't use them. I'm not sure whether they ever did before I was born, but Uncle Francis definitely used the rooms at the other end."

The urge to tell her what he'd learned about his uncle burned the tip of Nic's tongue, but like his mother's secrets, they were truths he wasn't sure he was ready to share.

Leaf chewed on her lip. "Perhaps the Faceless Man really is your uncle's ghost. I didn't think much of the idea when my aunt suggested it, but it makes a frightening sort of sense, doesn't it. Especially with that automaton roaming the house too. Just think—the thing that murdered him turned on others in revenge."

He wished he could tell her it was ridiculous, wished he could tell her the possibility hadn't occurred to him. Instead, he said, "But why now? He's been dead for twenty-four years."

"You heard what my aunt said about our fathers, how they disagreed on who would give up their title. I am sure that's no small part of my uncle's bitterness. Perhaps the event of another Serral and Monterris contract has awakened his rancour from beyond the grave?"

The house hates us all.

It was on the tip of his tongue to tell her she sounded like the gothic novels she so disliked, but what rational explanation could there be for Nic's hand having closed on air? Or for the living darkness that had chased them from the grotto doors? And while Leaf had something else to set her mind to, her melancholy expression had lightened just a touch.

"Perhaps we should look in Lord Francis's rooms," she suggested. "In case that's where his ghost was going."

Nic had no desire to visit his uncle's rooms with the newfound knowledge the man had not been his uncle at all, but he agreed, wanting more than anything to keep the hopeless light from returning to Leaf's eyes.

Having dismissed her maid, Leaf waited in the sitting room while Nic grabbed a few bites from his breakfast tray. It had been so long since he'd had a good meal that he ended up finishing every crumb, but soon Nic was leading the way along the upper hallway toward Lord Francis's distant door. The possibility he had been following the man's ghost the night before made Nic uneasy, distressed at the thought of reaching for his arm only to miss it by twenty-four years.

With the lingering feeling he was walking with ghosts, Nic pushed open the door. They were met with dim light and faded old carpet, moth-eaten cushion covers, and dirty windows. Lord

Francis's rooms were much like Nic's own, comprising a large sitting room with its own dining table, and an adjoining bedchamber and dressing room. Although where Nic's rooms got cleaned regularly and use alone was enough to keep the worst of the dust at bay, these had a feeling of long neglect.

"I was expecting this to be more interesting," Leaf said, turning slowly to take in the sitting room.

"You see if this really was like *The Mysteries of Udolpho*, this room would have been locked," Nic said. "And everything would be draped in holland covers and cobwebs. And there would be a portrait somewhere hidden behind black curtains."

"There's still the bedchamber."

Leaf walked on toward the open door. Nic made to follow but halted as a lingering hint of magic brushed past his attention. He turned a circle in search of it, gaze raking the dusty old bookshelf, the dusty old mantelpiece, and the dusty old sofa with splits in its silk upholstery.

"Oh, this is a little better," Leaf said from the bedchamber. "No black curtains or cobwebs, but the room is a mess. Come see."

Abandoning his search for the spent magic, Nic joined her in the open doorway. The room beyond looked much like Nic's own in layout, but that was where the resemblance ended. Books and cushions and old trinkets lay strewn about the floor, the layers of dust having been disturbed as the room was upended from its long hibernation.

"It looks like it got ransacked the other day too," Leaf said. "Although it seems odd to ransack an unused room, unless someone was searching for something. Either that or you have an untidy ghost and it has looked like this for a while. When were you last in here?"

"Not for years. There never seemed any reason to visit."

Because he hadn't known who the man truly was. Nic passed a hand over his eyes and found himself wishing they hadn't come.

"Are you all right?" Leaf touched his arm. "You look as exhausted as I do. Not more morning wine, I hope."

He was tempted to lie so he needn't admit to having had even a moment of joy while she mourned, but he knew it for a foolish impulse. "No, I . . . just didn't get much sleep," he said. "Dashiell and I went to the archives last night. To get a copy of Mama's marriage contract."

Leaf's brows rose, and Nic realised he couldn't explain without going all the way back to his mother's diary, to the duke's failure as a husband the night Millie had died, to the way life had always been at Monterris Court and the secrets Silla had spilled. And so there in Lord Francis's bedchamber, he sat on a faded old chair and told her it all. All the way to the moment he had discovered his inheritance was gone.

A parade of expressions crossed Leaf's face but she didn't interrupt, waiting until the end to say, "I'm sorry, Nic, that's all so awful for her. What a mess our parents seem to have made of everything. Do you think I should tell my father about your estate? He might finally call the contract off before something even more awful happens."

"I think he already knows."

"Oh? What makes you say that?"

"Just think. Four people are dead, one of whom is his niece, yet still your father resolutely refuses to break this contract. You cannot tell me that is just because I have a high Brilliance affinity."

"He knows you need the money. No, stop." She gripped his arm. "Remember what Millie said? That Uncle Ricard had even tried to ruin your father's business dealings? Perhaps Papa finally found out and is trying to make amends. It is exactly the sort of thing he would do. He wouldn't admit fault or apologise, he would just write a bank draft." She gasped. "This was an apology proposal! Of all the ridiculous, stubborn men. And now with the Requisite Care

Clause invoked he's even less likely to pull out, because he would be leaving your father with the devil of a mess and no money to show for it."

She threw up her arms and let them fall in a defeated gesture. "You know, I've never had the urge to drink away my miseries before, but I think I'm starting to see the appeal. Oh let's get out of here. I've already stayed away from Lizzy far longer than I meant."

Glad to escape, Nic followed her back into the sitting room, unable to shake the feeling that if he turned his head just so he might catch sight of Lord Francis in one of the chairs. How different life at the Court might have been had he lived. How much less lonely.

"So is your lack of sleep merely to do with searching through archives, or does it have something to do with—?"

"Stop." Nic lifted a hand to both silence and still her as he turned his head, hunting the trace of magic that scratched at his mind once more.

"I was only asking—"

"Shh, there's something here." He stepped toward to the door, letting his eyes slide out of focus as he sought the sense caught somewhere between touch and sound.

"What do you mean—*oh*. Are you doing your magic feely thing?"

"Can we not call it that?"

"We can *not* call it a lot of things, but that doesn't answer my question."

Closing his eyes, Nic took a few more steps, trying to tell if it was getting stronger or weaker—hard when it was but a scratching whisper at the edge of hearing. "It's not very strong. Maybe a week old or so. Here, warn me if I'm about to walk into something."

He stepped slowly forward, hands outstretched, letting his extra sense guide the way.

"There's a bookshelf in front of you."

Waving a hand in front of him found Nic the edge of a shelf, and the feeling grew as he traced his fingers along the wood. The Brilliance sang as he patted around, pressing his fingertips to each papery spine until magic pulsed through his palm, too faint to form an accent but palpable all the same. "Here."

Nic opened his eyes to find Leaf already leaning into his vision. "Oh, it's a wooden box. I didn't see it there until you touched it."

She pulled it from the shelf—a simple wooden box, unpainted and unmarked, owning a thin brass hinge but no opening latch. As Leaf tilted the lid, sigils appeared, etched in a border around its edge.

"It's just one of those magical trick boxes," Leaf said, handing it over. "Perhaps something Lord Francis left behind."

"It wouldn't feel that strong after a year let alone more than twenty. No, someone left it here recently."

"But why?"

"I don't know. That depends on what's inside."

Leaf shook her head. "Trick boxes are next to impossible to open without the right code, Nic. And some of them are made to explode if you hit them with a hammer."

Nic smiled and tucked the box into his coat. "Ah, but you see, I know an excellent vowsmith."

They headed for the door, and as Nic pulled it closed behind them, he could imagine the ghost of Lord Francis smiled.

Chapter 24

With hours to wait until negotiations finished for the day, Nic made a start on the box. He'd sent Ambrose for paper and quills and ink, then pushed him into a chair at the sitting room table, a sigil dictionary in hand. The young man didn't have the Brilliance but he could read, and Nic needed all the help he could get.

It hadn't taken long for Ambrose to get the hang of looking up each sigil, and for a time, the only sound in the room was the flip of pages and the scratch of quill on paper. It wasn't until the clock struck four in the afternoon that Ambrose cleared his throat.

"Excuse me, my lord, but . . . what is this for?"

"So we can open the box," Nic said absently, mulling over the possible meanings of a pair of sigils.

"But why? What is inside?"

"No idea."

"Oh."

A few minutes went by, then Ambrose added, "Is this one of those things I shouldn't tell anyone about, my lord?"

"Not a word, Ambrose. Not a word."

The clock was just creeping past five when a quiet knock fell upon the door. Nic's gaze snapped up, fixing to the woodwork before Ambrose even moved to open it. When he did, the door swung open to reveal Dashiell, still attired in his formal work coat and breeches.

"It's Master sa Vare to see you, my lord," Ambrose said.

"Yes, I can see that, Ambrose. Um, you can go. No, don't worry about this," Nic added when the valet glanced at their unfinished work. "I'll ring for you when I need you."

"Yes, my lord. As you wish."

A bow and the valet hurried out, leaving the vowsmith to close the door behind him. With his heart beating fast and a smile fluttering on his lips, Nic rose from the table.

"You're rather earlier than I expected given the time limit you're working under."

"That's because your father is far more concerned about getting it done than arguing the details." Dashiell said. "He doesn't even join us most of the time, since he's not allowed to actually negotiate, which means as long as we don't fall behind, I can choose not to sit longer than I must." He came to sit on the edge of the table and flicked Nic's cheek. "And why would I with you waiting for me? Although—" The vowsmith glanced down at the strewn papers. "You seem to be in the middle of something." He picked up the box and turned it over. "Oh, a trick box. It's smithed shut?"

"So it seems. Leaf and I found it today and I want to know what's inside."

"Found it where?"

Nic met Dashiell's questioning stare, ready to lie, but no lie would come. "On a bookshelf in Lord Francis's rooms. Leaf thinks the Faceless Man might be his ghost come back to ruin us."

"You know, before coming here I would have said I didn't believe in ghosts, but this house feels alive now in a way it didn't when we were young. And we had better imaginations back then too."

As he spoke, Dashiell turned the box over, examining each of the sides. "How did you find it?"

"I . . . felt it. Not fresh, but not old either."

"I thought you might say that, because see these two lines of smithing on either side? They're visual binders. A less potent version is commonly used inverted to find important files, while this is technically illegal. *Ven ek amor zef lejorn si*," Dashiell read. "Not easy to pull off, but when done right it's like a command that refuses to be seen, a slippery space for your eyes. Looking at it, you would see the book beside it, say, then the one on the other side, with the space between made up of both like they stretch to fill it."

As Dashiell explained, Nic found himself staring at the box. Not just any trick box then, rather a very expensive and illegal one.

A wry smile twitched Dashiell's lips. "You really want to open it. What do you think you'll find inside?"

"I don't know, but I'm sick of secrets, Dash. The estate. The money. The debts. And now people are dying for my marriage contract. Somewhere there's a clue that will help untangle this riddle and maybe this is it."

The vowsmith gave a sharp nod. "All right. It shouldn't take too long with both of us working. At the very least I promise to be more useful than Ambrose." As he spoke, he drew off his coat and laid it over the arm of the sofa, before pulling out the chair Ambrose had recently vacated. "You even have the dictionaries ready to go," he added, rolling up his shirtsleeves and laying bare lithe arms.

When Nic didn't immediately join him at the table, Dashiell looked up, an eyebrow cocked in question. "Everything all right?"

"Yes. Just distracted by your arms."

Dashiell tried not to grin and failed, his lips twitching. "The sooner we get this done, the sooner we can get properly distracted," he said, drawing the box close.

"Yes, but really it was rude of you to roll up your sleeves like that. Casual, getting-down-to-business Dashiell really does it for me."

"I'll have to remember that."

Nic groaned and Dashiell tossed him a quill. "Here, make yourself useful. Let's see how fast we can do this." Lifting the box to peer at the tiny sigils, Dashiell went on, "Ready? I think this is where you were up to. Next is *am. Lelos. Ves.*"

Quill to page, Nic hastily scrawled as Dashiell read, pausing only when Dashiell needed to consult one of the books laid out on the table. For the most part he was reading bare sigils, but occasionally he would interrupt his stream to add translations he already knew, like "That's darkness" and "That means to prioritise; note that underneath."

Nic did, enjoying the commanding ease with which Dashiell made his way around the box—all vowsmithing sigils unlike the tape had been. While he thumbed through one of the dictionaries, Nic said as much, causing the vowsmith to look up.

"Oh, are you trying to tell me that I'm being overbearing?"

"Let's call it assertively competent," Nic returned.

Dashiell's eyes twinkled. "And you like that, do you?" In a breath, he'd leaned close, lips pressed to Nic's without pause for permission. Dashiell's lips were soft, the kiss gentle yet needing, the fierce desire it owned barely contained like his self-control was fracturing. Without thinking, Nic groaned against his mouth. He wanted everything Dashiell was holding back, but no sooner was the sound out than the vowsmith pulled away, leaving him hungry. "God I love that little groan of yours," Dashiell said, and looked resolutely back at the book.

"That," Nic said, "was very cruel."

"Don't worry, love, I always pay my debts."

Love. Like *darling.* Single, beautiful names that thrilled him on Dashiell's tongue.

"Ah, *teth.*" Dashiell snapped the book closed. "That's an unusual one."

Nic wrote the sigil down, but before the ink was dry, a knock fell upon the door for what felt like the dozenth time that day.

"Nicholas?"

The duke.

Nic sucked a sharp breath. They were just working on sigils, but between the existence of the box and Dashiell sitting there in his shirtsleeves, it was all trouble. Hissing swear words between his teeth, Nic grabbed the box and thrust it at Dashiell, while lifting the tablecloth with his other hand.

"Are you serious?" Dashiell whispered.

"Just do it! He can't see you here."

The knock came again. "Nicholas?"

Dashiell slid beneath the table with the box, and though he was still rustling about getting comfortable, Nic couldn't keep his father waiting.

"You can come in, sir. The door is unlocked."

He opened a book to a random page and pretended to read, his heart thumping so hard the duke was sure to hear it. The handle turned, and with a creak of old hinges, the door swung in. Nic got to his feet in the required show of respect.

"Sir," he said. "My apologies. I forgot Ambrose wasn't in. Will you sit?"

The duke closed the door behind him, but shook his head.

"My errand is of no great length," he said, eyeing the papers strewn over the table. "Although I am glad to see that you appear to be feeling better. And that you seem to be reapplying yourself to your vowsmithing studies. Something for which I have Master sa Vare to thank, I think."

"Oh. Yes." Nic had to swallow annoyance at the satisfaction in his father's tone. "He has been helping me with a few things when he has the time, but I doubt I am proving a capable student."

The duke hummed a note of disapproval. "Perhaps if you applied yourself, you might. But I did not come to argue this point, merely to enquire how Lady Leaf Serral is faring. What with the loss of her cousin."

Displays of empathy had never been the duke's forte, but before Nic could digest his surprise, his father added, "The finalisation of the contract may rest on her willingness to remain, after all."

That at least was in character, but Nic couldn't shake the feeling his father was looking around, that he had come for something else entirely. He couldn't know about the box, couldn't know Dashiell sat huddled beneath the table, yet Nic felt laid bare as he said, "She is very upset, naturally. Although if you want to know whether I think she will ask Lord Charborough to break the contract, then no. I don't think so."

The duke nodded, ever expressionless. "Good. It has been a trying time for us all, but we must, and will, get through it."

"Yes, sir."

With nothing but a lingering stare at the papers, as though he could force Nic to study through sheer determination, the duke stepped back into the hallway and closed the door behind him. Muffled footsteps retreated.

Letting out a relieved sigh, Nic dropped onto his chair. "You can come out now. He's gone."

Dashiell slid the box out onto his own vacated chair, but did not follow. Unseen beneath the tablecloth, he touched Nic's knee, then slid his hand up the inside of one thigh.

"What are you doing?" Nic said as Dashiell's other hand made the same journey up his other leg. "Dash?"

The vowsmith's head emerged from beneath the tablecloth, his smile demure as his fingers edged toward the fall front of Nic's breeches.

"I'm paying my debts. I told you I would."

He unbuttoned the fall as he spoke and Nic groaned as questing fingers found his rapidly hardening cock. "What debts?" he asked, his groan becoming a laugh, which turned as abruptly back into a groan when Dashiell's breath tickled his bare skin. "You know you don't have any."

"I know. I'm just making excuses to touch you."

Nic meant to reply, but Dashiell ran his tongue slowly up his length and what even was rational thought anymore? The only man he had ever loved was kneeling between his legs, a tablecloth draped over his head and his fingers around Nic's cock.

"You don't have to do this," Nic said.

Dashiell sat back, enough to look up at Nic through his lashes in a way that really didn't help. "You don't want me to?"

"Not what I said."

"Then just sit there and put up with me doing something I've wanted to for a very long time."

"Put up—" The rest of his words were swallowed into another groan as Dashiell lowered his head, taking Nic wholly inside his mouth. "Oh, *fuck*."

A sensible man would have told him to stop. A sensible man would have pointed out that the door wasn't locked and they'd already come so close to being caught, but one look at the man kneeling between his legs and Nic could not speak. The world out there no longer mattered—there was just him and Dashiell, and the vowsmith's wet mouth making quick work of his straining arousal.

Adding a hand, Dashiell soon had Nic unable to do anything but lean back in his chair and bite back moans. It wasn't just the warmth of his mouth, wasn't just his tight grip or his playful tongue, it was the knowledge it was *him*—the sight of Dashiell working hungrily almost enough to end him on the spot.

"Dash," Nic said, his name a gasp, but if Dashiell cared for the warning, he didn't heed it. Didn't slow. Just kept drawing Nic inexorably on toward his conclusion until his hips jerked, the movement uncontrollable as he smothered a cry. Pleasure rolled over him, and on a final shudder the cry became a groan that sought to express the full extent of his appreciation.

As the sensation faded, Nic set his hand tenderly on Dashiell's hair. And slowly, deliberately, the vowsmith swallowed and looked up.

At the impish expression on his face, Nic let out a breathy laugh. "You rotten, monstrous—"

"You're welcome." Dashiell grinned, nothing about his messy hair and his damp, reddened lips like the serious, proper vow-smith everyone else saw. He licked those lips—slightly swollen in the aftermath—in a way that made Nic want to own him utterly. "That was fun," Dashiell added, his eyes half-lidded and his cheeks flushed. "Although it would have been more fun had we risked it in the library."

"In the—you are *monstrous*."

"You said that already."

"Well, excuse me if my brain isn't functioning at the highest level right now."

Dashiell slid out from beneath the table, but rather than take his own seat, he sat on Nic. Chest to chest and with his own cock hard against Nic's abdomen, Dashiell snatched up the box they'd been translating.

"Now, where were we." He cleared his throat. "Ah, we were at *teth*. After that is *ek*. Then *woq*."

"How am I supposed to write anything down with you sitting on me?"

"You pick up the quill, dip it in the ink, then press it to the paper."

Nic feigned taking an angry bite from Dashiell's chest. "I thought being the smart-arse was my job and you're meant to be the serious, studious one."

"I thought so too, but being with you makes me feel giddy and slightly drunk, so you'll have to put up with it. Now are you going to write this down or not? *Ek. Woq.*"

A fuzzy warmth spread through Nic that had nothing to do with what Dashiell had just done and everything to do with his words. It had always been so easy spending time with him. From their first days together as boys through to every moment they'd stolen since he'd returned—Dashiell the sun to which Nic turned without even thinking.

"*Ven. Ek* again. *Amor*," Dashiell went on, turning the box to peer at the next line. "That's an interesting one. I've only ever seen that used on old maps. Anyway, it's followed by *zef*—"

"Slow down! I can't write as fast with you crushing my legs to jelly."

"Oh? Do you write with your legs?" Dashiell said, shifting his weight until Nic could feel his hardness pressed even more firmly against his stomach. The urge to scream at the world, to hold Dashiell tight and never let him go no matter the consequences, was difficult to subdue, and tears stung Nic's eyes. "*Zef. Lejorn. Si* and—oh." Dashiell sat back, and turned to look at the page Nic had been writing. "*Ven ek*," he said, before reading back along the line. "Wow."

"What is it?"

"This box," Dashiell said, bringing it between them, "would, in a public space, defy at least three laws. It's not only smithed shut and semi-invisible, but those last sigils are for undisclosed reporting, and there's an old curse added in for good measure. It has been proven to be nonsense, but it's illegal for guild smiths to use it all the same."

Nic stared at the box. "Perhaps . . . perhaps you ought to go and let me finish. You have your oath to consider."

"As I sit here on top of the opposing principal of my current contract, having just joyfully sucked him off?"

Nic huffed a laugh. "When you put it like that . . ."

"It sounds ridiculous, yes." Dashiell swung his leg over Nic and stood up. "Although I *am* worried. This seems less 'fun trick box' and more horrifying trap. I'd want to be sure—really sure—I knew the purpose of every sigil before opening it."

On the mantelpiece, the large clock started chiming the hour, only for a collection of Nic's automata to join the chorus.

Dashiell sighed. "I love all your creations, but I do wish you could make one capable of pausing time. There is nothing I want to do less right now than go dress for dinner."

His voice held a hint of derision, such an everyday thing made absurd.

"Although if it comes to that, there is nothing I want to do less than be negotiating your marriage contract. Especially knowing that as soon as it's done I have to walk out that door and not know when I will see you again. I—" He spun away, running his hand through his hair, gripping a handful for a desperate moment. "I can't even be here for you when the royal vowsmiths descend en masse. And I can't lie—between a slew of dead bodies and a non-existent estate, sorting out both the Requisite Care Clause and the audit is going to be hell."

"Those aren't your messes to clean."

Dashiell turned back, his smile crooked. "No, but is it so terrible that I want to take care of you? Want to protect you from all that? And no, don't remind me that you can take care of yourself; I know you can. I just don't want you to have to do it alone."

The words were like a fist squeezing Nic's heart. What could he say? To voice his frustration with the world would achieve nothing. That within days Dashiell would walk out of his life was an incontrovertible truth Nic had just been ignoring for his own sanity.

"I don't want to do this," Dashiell went on, frustration flaring.

"I don't. I cannot leave this house without knowing when I will see you again, but whenever I think about how next we can meet . . ."

He trailed off, leaving the problems to hang silent between them—Nic's lack of freedom while his father lived, that he could not leave his mother, that Northumberland was a very long way from London. And that was before they even considered the future risk to both the contract and Dashiell's career should it ever become known that he and Dashiell were lovers. Someone with a grudge, someone like Lord Ricard, could challenge it and force repayment of the dowry sum. All things they both knew, all things neither could say.

Dashiell had said he hadn't been born a man who could ever hope to love Nic, but Nic hadn't been born a man who could love at all.

"I shouldn't have been born a Monterris, huh?" he said, desperate for a moment of levity. "Quite the mistake on my part."

Dashiell gripped his shoulders. "We will find a way. We must. I cannot bear a future in which there is no us."

Us.

The word landed in Nic's chest like a lead weight, stealing his breath. What he wouldn't give for a future that contained such a word.

A knock sounded on the door and Nic pulled from Dashiell's hold, glad of the moment to breathe. "Yes?"

"His Grace wants to see you, my lord. In his study."

Nic had started toward the door, only to pause at the unfamiliar voice. Normally, summoning him was a task Master Everel would perform—the voice of an unknown servant further evidence of just how much had gone wrong since the lock-in began.

"Right, thank you," Nic replied through the woodwork rather than risk anyone catching sight of Dashiell. "Tell him I'll be there in a few minutes."

Footsteps retreated as Nic reached for the door handle, not sorry for the excuse to step away and loosen the grief tightening his chest. "I had better go so he doesn't get suspicious."

"Wait."

Half a dozen long strides brought Dashiell to stand before him. Leaning in, he brushed his nose against Nic's, and when Nic returned the gesture with more instinct than sense, Dashiell kissed him. It was a soft kiss, almost tentative, fearing a spark that could set them both alight. Yet still Dashiell stepped closer, threading his hands into Nic's hair with a gentleness that cracked Nic's heart open. Dashiell kissed him like he was the most precious thing in the world, like nothing else mattered, like the moment never had to end. Like *they* never had to end.

When Dashiell slowly drew away, their lips seemed almost to stick, pulling Nic briefly with him. Before he rocked back into cold reality.

"I love you, Nic," Dashiell said. "I just . . . wanted to tell you that."

Nic was quite sure his heart stopped. That his mind froze. That he ceased to exist in any way beyond the body that stood there staring. The truth was that he knew. Knew Dashiell loved him as he loved Dashiell, but had needed it to remain unspoken to save himself from breaking.

Words stuck on Nic's tongue. More than anything he wanted to tell Dashiell he felt the same, that he loved him with every tiny piece of his heart, but if he spoke, there would be no more hiding, no shield, just a bare truth he wasn't sure he could hold. And so he just stared, lips gummed together while his heart lurched and tore, the door behind him the only escape. He parted his lips to say something, to at least explain his silence, but nothing came out. And unable to face Dashiell's troubled expression a moment longer, Nic fled.

He wrenched the door open and stepped out into the hallway, before pulling it closed as rapidly behind him. But closing the door and hurrying away along the passage didn't change anything. Dashiell had still stood there, had still spoken, and Nic still wanted to scream.

"Shit," he hissed, hardly seeing where he was going. "Shit! I can't do this. I can't. I—" He gripped a handful of his own hair, fighting back tears that would change nothing. He ought to have avoided Dashiell completely. Have refused his company and his conversation. Yet had he been able to go back and start the lock-in again, Nic knew he wouldn't. Because even if pain would soon be all he had left, that pain held the truth that he had been loved, and no one could take that from him.

He wiped his eyes. He couldn't go to see his father in such a state, and the need for self-possession in the duke's presence calmed some of the turmoil roiling through him.

Belatedly, Nic realised he'd missed the stairs to his father's rooms and scuffed to a halt. Only the locked doors of the old ducal suite stood ahead, their delicate brass and enamel inlay shining in the last of the evening light.

A shadow flickered in the corner of Nic's vision. Thoughts leaping to ghosts, he made to turn, only for a sharp pain to bite into his side. A blade flashed as it spun away, red with blood, hitting the floor with a heavy thunk. But before Nic could move or shout or even think, darkness closed over his head. Fabric fluttered against his face and tightened around his throat, and a kick to the back of one knee dropped him to the floor, leaving him spluttering musty velvet. Shock was all he had time to register before he couldn't breathe. Weight on his chest. Fingers tightening around his throat.

Realisation of what had happened rushed in upon rising panic, but he couldn't scream. Couldn't move. Could only feel death creeping close as he tried to buck his assailant off, tried to pull their hands away, scratching at skin in a desperate attempt not to die.

Death was the only way to escape being a Monterris, and a small part of him yearned for the peace beyond the hated name and its pointless responsibilities, but Nic could still smell Dashiell. Still taste him. Still see him standing there bearing his heart.

Nic clawed and bucked and tried to roll, yet still death closed its determined fingers tighter. Darkness sparked at the edges of his vision. He was going to die. He was going to die without having told Dashiell he loved him too. If only he could have one last moment to scream the truth, but with no breath and no voice, he had only his hands—hands that, as a conjuror, he was used to working with in silence.

The idea was less an idea than a flash of desperation. No time to think. No time to practice. Time only to let go of his assailant's hands and shape final, desperate sigils with shaking fingers.

A strangled stutter of sound rent the air, followed by a sustained wail so loud Nic felt his assailant flinch. Their grip loosened a touch, but not enough.

Darkness crowded in.

Chapter 25

Every inch of Nic hurt. His side ached and his throat burned and he wanted to be sick, but the thought of moving enough to vomit was too exhausting. Voices murmured around him. Candlelight flickered like golden ghosts through his eyelids. Steps scuffed. Eventually, it occurred to Nic to wonder where he was and why, the softness of what felt like his bed not fitting with the sense he was surrounded by people. When memory at last hit him, he flinched and cried out, dry, tired eyes opening upon a collection of concerned faces.

Fear coursed through him like a visceral liquid that reached his gut and sent him lunging for the side of the bed. Bile burned his already burning throat and splattered upon the floor, leaving him shaking.

"You're all right, Nicholas," came his father's low, commanding tone. "You're safe now."

"Nic!" Leaf cried, her voice cracking on a sob. "Thank God. I was so worried."

Her tearstained face came into focus. Her eyes were red and her hair was a messy nest formed by agitated fingers, yet she forced a tremulous smile and gripped his hand. He tried to squeeze back, but his muscles ached, managing only a weak twitch.

"What . . . happened?" he asked, voice a croak as he hunted the gathered group for the person he most needed to see. Dashiell, there, standing off to the side behind the Serral brothers, his face pale and his expression unreadable.

Lord Ricard snorted a harsh laugh. "You don't remember?"

"You were set upon and strangled," the duke said, the words catching a little, his voice thick. To anyone else it might have sounded calm enough to be heartless, but the subtle, restrained vibrance made tears prickle Nic's eyes. "You have Master sa Vare to thank that you're still with us. He heard you scream."

"Awful business," Lord Charborough said, his tone faint. "Damned good thing Master sa Vare was on hand."

"There was almost a dead body. Of course he was on hand," Lord Ricard muttered with a sour look Dashiell's way.

The vowsmith's jaw set, but he said nothing.

Lord Charborough passed an exhausted hand over his eyes. "Please do not stand there and pick a fight with our vowsmith in the last days of this negotiation, Ricard. Come, we ought to leave Lord Monterris to the doctor's ministrations. Give him some privacy."

"As though I wished to linger," Lord Ricard said and turned for the door, but Leaf showed no sign of moving from Nic's bedside.

"Leaf." Lord Charborough set a hand upon her shoulder. "Come. Lord Monterris needs to rest and I need to keep you close where you are safe."

"Just a moment, Papa. Nic, you don't remember who it was that attacked you?" Leaf asked, still holding his hand.

Nic frowned, trying to think through the details, only to wince away. Away from the musty dark velvet, away from the weight on his chest and the fingers around his throat and the knowledge he would die without telling Dashiell the truth.

"No."

"Well," the duke said, bending to ruffle Nic's hair with a tight smile, "since you are now awake, I must go reassure your mother.

I understand she has been inconsolable since you were taken up for dead."

He turned to depart, leaving Nic's stunned gaze following him to the door.

Leaf, no doubt seeing nothing remarkable in such a display, tightened her hold on his hand. "I hope you will remember more when you're feeling better. We need to know who it was if we are to stop this from happening again, because there is no way this could have been just an accident. Even small details could help, like what their hands looked like or their smell or—"

"If you please, Lady Leaf," Dr. Fanshaw said, stepping forward with his most concerned expression firmly on his features. "Lord Monterris needs rest."

"Oh, yes. Of course, Doctor."

She let Nic go and rose, giving in to the insistence of her father's hand.

With the Serrals having departed, only Ambrose and the doctor remained. And Dashiell. The vowsmith lingered just a moment—a moment in which their eyes met and held and Nic hardly knew if he most wanted him to stay or go, his throat too sore and his mind too muddled for the conversation Dashiell deserved. It was for the best perhaps that he turned away, leaving Nic surrounded by flickering candlelight and silence.

With Ambrose's assistance, the doctor checked Nic's wound. It seemed he had already patched it while Nic was unconscious, but he clicked his tongue over it all the same.

"Someone was going for your kidney, if I had to guess," Dr. Fanshaw said with the blandness of one discussing fashion. "You're lucky they missed and only gouged some flesh. This will hurt for a while, but it will heal."

After that, the doctor left too, saying he would return later and could be summoned any time if needed. Nic must have dozed after that, because when he next looked about, a tray of food sat on the side table.

"Ah, you're awake, my lord," Ambrose said, his words lacking the confidence of even that conviction. "You ... uh ... have a visitor, if you would like. He wouldn't come in without seeking your permission. Master sa Vare. He's in the sitting room."

"He's allowed," Nic croaked and cleared his throat, though it didn't seem to help. "So long as no one knows he's here."

The young valet's nod was solemn as he went back out. It seemed an age before he returned, Nic's heart thumping like a drum the whole time only to thud all the harder when Dashiell appeared in the doorway. He leaned against the frame, sleeves rolled up, box in hand and a soft smile on his lips.

"You don't have to let me in; I would as happily sit out here and work on this. I just . ... I would rather stay close and be sure you're safe."

Nic tried to pull himself up into a sitting position, but everything hurt too much and he gave up halfway, propped on pillows. "You can stay," he whispered as loudly as he could. "As long as *you're* safe."

"As long as *I'm* safe?" Dashiell's laugh held no humour. "You mean is my job safe? As though I care. But no one will come looking for me tonight. And Ambrose has the door locked like a sensible man."

Dashiell brought his quill and ink and sat down at Nic's dressing table with the box—a man intent on busily not disturbing him. While he worked, Nic lay unmoving, not quite asleep yet not quite awake, letting the comfortable sounds lull him into rest. Occasionally Ambrose would come and go or Dashiell would glance over to see if he was still awake, but neither of them spoke, expecting nothing.

Time passed in blinks and stretches, counted only by the slow burning down of the candles. Eventually Ambrose asked if Nic would eat, and as much to ease the worry from the young man's face as because he knew he ought, Nic agreed. With one strong arm, Ambrose helped him to sit upright, propping more pillows behind him, before bringing over a small tray served from the larger one on the sideboard. Orange soufflé with a side of vanilla custard, a plate of buttered asparagus, and a poached pear drenched in sweet, sticky wine.

"All my favourites," Nic said, his voice still a whisper, though he managed a smile.

"I'm glad I remembered rightly," Dashiell said from the dressing table. "They brought up so much food that Ambrose was flustered. Though of course, had I been wrong, I would have blamed him."

Dashiell didn't seem to expect a reply and went on working, leaving Nic caught between gratitude for the silence and a growing desire to say everything that needed to be said. That Dashiell could sit there at all, caring about him so fiercely despite how they'd parted, was astounding. Nic was sure he wouldn't have had the strength to hold his tongue had their positions been reversed.

"Dash . . ."

The vowsmith glanced up but shook his head. "Don't trouble yourself tonight, Nic. Just eat and rest."

"And if I want to trouble myself?"

Dashiell pressed out a flat smile. "Then at least eat first. I refuse to be the cause of your collapse."

"I am not such a weak creature as you think."

"Weak?" Dashiell's brows flew up. "Nic, you had the presence of mind to use conjuring to save yourself. I don't think you weak and never have."

"Oh, so it worked. I wasn't sure when my father said you heard a scream."

"I did. It just didn't carry like one leaving a throat." His expression became grim. "God, Nic, I was sure I was going to lose you. I've never been so scared as I was sprinting down that hallway." He wiped his eyes and looked away. "Don't mind me, it's been a long day."

Nic closed his eyes, no longer sure which path was brave and which cowardly. He found he didn't much care.

"I love you too," he whispered. "Telling you that was all I thought of when . . ."

"Nic, you don't have to—"

"But I do," Nic said as a tear trickled down Dashiell's cheek to be caught at his jaw by the swipe of his sleeve. "In a perfect world, it wouldn't be Lady Leaf Serral I was marrying."

Despite everything, Nic's heart thudded with foolish fears that Dashiell would laugh, would say he had never thought of marriage, that he had other plans, that—

"I would love that." Dashiell leaned back in his chair, watching Nic with deep affection. "Unless you're not talking about me, in which case forget I said so while I sink through the floor in embarrassment."

"Of course I meant you," Nic said, the sound painfully croaky. "You would make an excellent duchess."

"It's my hair, isn't it? It would look good with a coronet."

Nic laughed until he coughed, hating the feeling that his neck was bruised.

"I'm sorry." Dashiell sighed. "I shouldn't make you laugh."

"Better to laugh than to think."

"That's true. God, what I wouldn't give for your perfect world. The life we could have." A hint of his earlier frustration flared, but he swallowed it with a forced, brittle smile. "At least you are safe. That is more important."

No wild sentiment, yet the knowledge that he almost hadn't been safe sent Nic back into the darkness, back to his desperate gasps and those merciless hands closing tighter and tighter. Not mechanical hands. Not the grip of a ghost. Strong hands of flesh and blood. Someone had tried to kill him—someone with whom he was still locked in—and there was nothing to stop them from trying again.

"I'm scared, Dash," he whispered. "What if they come back?"

Dashiell was out of his chair in an instant, half a dozen strides bringing him to Nic's side. "I've been trying not to think about it. Finding you like that once was already—"

His voice broke on the last words and Nic could only imagine what it must have been like, sprinting along the hallway in panic. Dashiell must have found him with whatever had been covering his head and a bloody gash in his side. Had blood spilled onto the carpet? How many seconds from death had he really been? He didn't want to think about it, yet thought about it all the same.

For a long while they didn't speak, just stared at one another while trapped in their own troubled thoughts, until abruptly Dashiell kicked off his shoes. That done, he climbed over Nic to settle on the other half of the bed. "Well, I'm not going anywhere," he said. "That way you don't have to worry about me and I don't have to worry about you. No, no complaints, no worries someone will find me. This is where I'm meant to be."

"And you keep saying you're not brave," Nic murmured, too tired to fight.

"This feels like more of the same cowardice to me. I'm too scared to leave you in case something else happens and I'm too late."

Nic traced a finger along Dashiell's jawline. "What else is bravery but to risk everything for another's safety? To risk everything to spend time with me though we will still have to part? Telling me that you love me even though it changes nothing? I call that bravery."

For a time, Dashiell just met his gaze, a slight notch cut between his brows. "I suppose you're right," he said eventually, yet the words sounded almost dismissive—a truth he didn't want to examine. He gestured to the tray of food. "You should eat, and if you can't, you should sleep. Dr. Fanshaw will be very angry with me if I keep you awake."

Part of Nic wanted to argue, but exhaustion had long been tugging at his thoughts, and at least with Dashiell beside him, he wasn't afraid of what might be waiting outside his door. As though determined not to talk anymore, Dashiell grabbed the box off the dressing table and settled back against the headboard, leaving Nic nothing to do but curl up beside him and fall asleep, his every breath full of Dashiell's scent.

Nic woke to the first hints of predawn light etching shapes from the darkness. The grey light had crawled a little way across the bedcovers and come to rest upon Dashiell's face, there on the pillow beside him. Asleep, his features were relaxed, perfectly at ease in a way Nic had rarely seen. No smile, no frown, just the smooth curve of his lips, the line of his brow, and dark eyelashes like slashes of ink upon his skin. Nic wanted to run his fingers over it all, committing the contours and curves to memory, but instead he drank it all in with his eyes so as not to wake him.

As he lay staring, a final certainty slowly sank into Nic's soul. He wanted this. He wanted to wake up beside Dashiell every day. Wanted to fall asleep beside him every night. Wanted to be part of his life, not just now but always. The wild idea that they could just run flittered into his mind, but the only way to put himself out of his father's reach would be out of England. Dashiell would have to disappear too, and stop working for the guild, or else the duke would always know exactly how to find them. And that was without even considering the mother Nic could never leave behind.

The impossibility mounted the more Nic thought about it, yet he must have dozed off, for he next woke to the bed moving and the murmur of low voices. The pale caress of winter sun had crept further across the bed and Dashiell had just climbed over him. Ambrose stood waiting alongside a man Nic guessed was Dashiell's valet. There was still so much of Dashiell's life he knew nothing about—a painful reminder upon which to wake.

"I have everything laid out ready, sir," the man was saying. "But you may have to take your breakfast in the chamber."

"Slipping away?" Nic murmured.

Dashiell spun back. "Oh, I'm sorry, love, I didn't mean to wake you." Despite his valet's worried look, the vowsmith sat on the edge of the bed. "How are you feeling?"

"Fine," Nic lied, his voice still croaky. "But you have to go."

"I do, or your father will be searching the house for me. Promise me you'll take care while I'm gone. Ambrose, you are not to let Lord Monterris out of your sight, you understand?"

"Yes, sir."

"Good." Dashiell cupped Nic's face in his hands and pressed a gentle kiss to his forehead. "I cannot bear a world in which you are not mine, but even less can I bear one which does not have you in it at all."

Behind him, his valet cleared his throat. "The time, sir."

"I know, Martin. I'm coming."

The vowsmith pulled to his feet, yet he did not immediately move toward the door. A hint of that frustration was back in his face, as though he was just barely keeping himself from shouting at the world.

The two valets shared a worried glance, but with a final nod, Dashiell headed for the door. Martin hurried after him. "Let me step out first, sir, to be sure the hallway is empty."

In Dashiell's absence the room was colder, yet without the

vowsmith's grief pressing upon his own, Nic breathed a sigh all the same. He had thought choosing to spend these days together would hurt, not that the desire to have them never end would tear them to pieces. Such impotence in their rage, with every possible solution no solution at all as the clock ticked away their final days.

Despite the trouble filling his mind, his body seemed determined to sleep, drifting off upon fears. Partway through the morning the doctor checked in, yet the draught he gave Nic only made him drowsier and he was hardly aware at all when Leaf arrived, her maid in tow.

She was still sitting with him when Dr. Fanshaw returned.

"Is he all right, Doctor?" she asked. "He doesn't seem to know I am here."

"I gave him a light opiate elixir earlier," the doctor said. "It seems to have a stronger effect on him than most. I should think he can hear you, though; he's just caught somewhere between sleeping and waking."

"He is a very sensitive Brilliant, so perhaps that's why." She sat for a moment looking down at Nic, a deep exhaustion drawing her features. "Have you learned anything that could help us find out who did this to him?"

Dr. Fanshaw sighed. "Unfortunately not, my lady. I am a very poor detective's aide, I'm afraid. Given the wound is on his right side, either his attacker is right-handed and came from behind, or was left-handed and came from in front."

"I don't think we have anyone left-handed in the lock-in party, do we?"

"Not that I have noticed, my lady."

"You know, you don't need to 'my lady' me, Doctor. At least when we're alone. I feel like examining a dead body together is an acceptable threshold for a closer acquaintance."

His smile was wry. "Perhaps if I was a Brilliant I would agree, but unfortunately I was born without that gift and so you must always be 'my lady.'"

"And if I told you I think it's stupid that we put Brilliance on such a pedestal? You are far more useful and knowledgeable than I am, you know."

"That is not for me to decide, my lady."

Leaf sighed. "I should go, although I admit I'm terrified of stepping out that door, even with my maid. Having failed to kill Lord Monterris, anyone wanting to break this contract for good would surely look at me next, no?"

"My lady . . ."

Leaf rose. "Take good care of him, Doctor."

As the afternoon progressed, Nic slowly found himself again, like his body was coming back into focus around his thoughts. Leaf did not return, but the doctor visited twice more, noting Nic's progress with a satisfied nod and a soft grunt.

"While I recommend you don't leave your bed this evening, my lord," he said, "I would not object to you getting up tomorrow so long as you are careful dressing."

Nic's body agreed, yet his mind rebelled at the thought of remaining another moment in bed while he and Dashiell were running out of time. While outside his door someone wanted Nic dead. The realisation that this couldn't go on had been slowly sinking through Nic's fear all day until it had at last hit his iron core.

"I'm sorry to disappoint you, Doctor," he said, sitting up to test his aches with a few careful prods, "but as soon as Ambrose returns, I'm going to see my father."

He had sent Ambrose to check whether the duke was sitting in the chamber that afternoon. With not being allowed to negotiate, his movements were far more varied than Dashiell's, his presence at the table dependent on whether he was needed for smithing work.

Dr. Fanshaw heaved the sigh of one used to not having his strictures followed. "You are of course your own master, my lord, but I strongly recommend you at least lean upon Ambrose's arm for the journey. Tearing the wound back open would be unwise at this point."

"Oh, don't worry, I'm not planning on going anywhere alone ever again."

The afternoon was fast advancing when Ambrose returned. He'd been gone long enough for Nic to start worrying, but had come back bearing the intelligence that His Grace had just left the chamber. "He was in there when I arrived, so I waited a while," the young valet said, determined to be helpful. "And now he's gone to his study, my lord."

"Thank you, Ambrose. Just fetch my dressing gown and we can go."

It took many long minutes to make it down the stairs even with Ambrose's assistance, but Nic soon stood outside his father's study as he had done so many times before, his heart thudding in his still-aching throat. His knock sounded hollow and overloud, and in the silence before his father answered, Nic fought the urge to be sick.

"Come in."

The duke sat at his desk in his shirtsleeves, cleaning his prized pistols.

"Nicholas." He paused, brush in hand. "Are you sure you feel well enough to be out of your bed? I hope you did not venture out alone."

The hint of concern reminded Nic of the previous night's gesture, as though the ghost of his hand remained in Nic's hair.

"I am well enough, sir," Nic said, glad the croak in his voice was less pronounced now. "Enough to no longer be served by lying in bed. And no, Ambrose is waiting outside."

"Very well. Your errand must be very important to have brought you here in your dressing gown, so do enlighten me."

He had come on a mission, yet as his father sat waiting to hear it, Nic's courage flagged. "You sent for me," he said, to buy himself some time. "Yesterday evening. When—" He broke off as the pressure of those hands around his throat returned in a flash.

A frown marred the duke's brow and he set down the half-dismantled pistol. "I did not. Recall that I came to see you. To ask about Lady Leaf's . . . mood."

He had, and Dashiell had hidden under the table—the whole a lifetime ago. Almost it had been. "But . . . someone knocked on the door and said you wished to see me."

"As I was testing these in the long gallery when you were found, I assure you I did not. It is, however, an unpleasant thought that anyone could have knocked on your door and lain in wait for you." The man's frown crinkled into something like fear as he glanced to the door. "I hope you mean to keep Ambrose with you at all times from now on."

His father's fear was unsettling, yet it was the opening Nic needed for the real reason he had come. "I am, sir, but what is to stop someone poisoning me instead? Or Leaf? You have to call this off—or ask Lord Charborough to do so. In the circumstances, he would surely oblige."

"Nicholas, we have had this conversation already. We need this to go ahead. You assured me you understood."

"I hadn't almost just died!"

The duke pushed his pistols aside and gestured to the chair. "Sit down, Nicholas."

It was an order, yet there was a note of fatigue he had never heard in his father's voice, and for a moment it held him frozen, feeling as though he had somehow stumbled through a mirror into an alternate world where his father was a living being.

The duke didn't press his invitation, just waited, his glasses reflecting Nic's indecision back at him. At length Nic sat, wincing at the pain in his side.

"This is about Master sa Vare, I take it," the duke said. "I had thought that somewhere in your endless string of male company over the last few years you would have forgotten about him."

Nic caught a breath, as shocked by the words as the gentle manner in which they were spoken. Having stared, open-mouthed, he eventually managed to splutter out, "You knew."

"Of course I knew. I am not imperceptive, nor are young boys as clever as they think they are. And as much as I did not wish to lose my best pupil, it was as well he left us when he did."

"I love him."

"I don't doubt it. Nor do I doubt that he loves you. You represent every shred of wildness and creative spirit he admires and wishes for himself but does not have. You are, indeed, extremely well suited. But you are a Monterris and your duty is to your family and your name—that the burden we must all bear. You could not marry a mere vowsmith, the youngest son of a baronet, no matter what his career prospects were even then. So when he asked to leave, I let him go. Before either of you could embark on idealistic dreams. Breaking this contract now will, however, change nothing. You are still a Monterris and he is still unworthy of you."

It was on the tip of Nic's tongue to argue, to rage at so pathetic a notion of worth, but his father hadn't said anything he didn't already know. It wasn't his future with Dashiell he had come to fight for, rather to ensure they had futures at all.

"Very well, sir, but this is not about Dashiell. This is about the four people who have died under our roof. I was almost a fifth and we cannot—*cannot*—keep doing this. Nothing is worth so many lives; nothing is worth the risk that as the contract nears completion my attacker may become desperate enough to try again, whether I have Ambrose with me or not. If I die, the contract will be broken anyway. Is seeing it through truly worth the risk of having no heir?"

Across the desk, the duke sighed and drew his dark glasses from his nose, bearing his scarred eyes. "Everything that can be done will be done to ensure your safety, Nicholas. I understand you are upset at what happened, but—"

"Upset? Someone in this house tried to kill me. Someone who is still here. Someone who might look at every protection you put around me and kill Leaf instead. The only thing I am upset by is your determination to ignore the fact that someone wants this contract broken and will go to any ends to see it happen."

"I assure you that no one wants this contract broken except you."

"Me?"

For a moment the duke just met his gaze, his eyes, so rarely uncovered, now bright and fierce and furious. "You gave me your word you would do whatever it took to uphold the Monterris name."

"Dying for it seems counterproductive at this point!"

The duke clicked his tongue. "Such dramatics are beneath you, Nicholas."

"Dramatics?" Nic pushed to his feet, pain twinging in his side. "If you do not have the courage to put life before money, then I will."

Anger coursing through him, Nic turned for the door.

"Don't you dare." The duke had risen from his desk but remained leaning upon it, scowling. "If you do anything that so much as risks this contract, I will make sure you never see your mother again."

"What?"

His father's dismissive gesture was almost a shrug. "She has shown herself completely incapable of existing in society these last few days. No one would think it strange if she were sent to an asylum. Truly it is only forbearing of me not to have done it sooner."

"You wouldn't."

"Wouldn't I? You are a Monterris, Nicholas. I own you and I

own her and I will damn well do whatever I must to keep this family going!"

The duke's fist slammed onto the desk, and for the first time Nic truly realised that when his father said the word *family*, it was only ever the name he meant, never the people who carried it. Numerous times throughout his life he had wished not to be a Monterris, but never had he felt such complete disgust at the very sound of the name.

"Of course," the duke went on, smoothing his tone, "if the king's men find her guilty of killing Lady Radlay and Master Everel, I may have no choice."

"She didn't do it."

"Didn't she? You will certainly find it difficult to convince them otherwise without my support."

Those uncovered eyes bored right into Nic's, the nests of scars around them etched deep and dark like slowly opening fissures. "I hope I have made myself quite clear, Nicholas. You are a Monterris. And while you continue to disappoint me with your lack of duty, I am quite sure your love for your mother is genuine. The contract *must* be signed, do you understand?"

Nic wasn't sure what he had expected, only what he had hoped, yet the outcome was so far beyond anything he had thought possible that anger roared in his ears.

His father might have been chiselled from stone for all the sign of life he gave—stone against which Nic knew he could lash himself like waves against a cliff to no avail. There was no argument that could change the truth that his father owned him as he owned Nic's mother, that death was the only way to escape being a Monterris.

"Yes, sir," he bit out. "I understand."

"Good."

With care, the duke slid his dark glasses back into place, becoming once again the impassive statue Nic knew so well.

"Now, if you are done. I have things to be getting on with."

Nic spun for the door, tore it open, and was halfway to the stairs before Ambrose could react.

"My lord!"

Fury powered Nic partway up the first flight before pain and fatigue took over, and it was as well that Ambrose was there to save him from falling. The young man's arm closed around his waist and Nic had to steady himself with a hand upon the wall, waiting for faintness to subside. Once it did, they continued the rest of the way at a far more sedate pace, with Ambrose thankfully holding his tongue.

By the time they reached the third floor again, some of Nic's fury had burned itself out upon a familiar resignation. Foolish to have hoped for better. Foolish to have hoped for anything at all.

When Ambrose pushed open Nic's door he stepped in, only to kick a piece of paper left sitting on the floor. As he bent to pick it up, a bolt of shock crackled up Nic's spine.

"Give it to me," he demanded, holding out his hand. Ambrose did so, dropping into Nic's palm the cut and folded paper flower he had made that night in the library. The flower Dashiell had taken with him as a poor memento. It hadn't been on the floor when they'd left—no, someone must have slid it beneath the door in his absence. But not Dashiell, who was still down in the chamber.

Unsure what to make of it, Nic turned the flower over and almost bit through his own tongue. On the other side, someone had penned a message along its folded stem.

You have been seen. End it, or he will be next.

Chapter 26

Nic paced, panic catching at the edge of every thought. He'd shoved the flower into his pocket, leaving its threat to Dashiell's life burning against his leg.

End it, or he will be next.

Awful words, but that someone had stolen the flower from the vowsmith's room made them all the more frightening.

Dashiell was in danger. He needed to get out of the house while he still could, contract be damned, yet the duke's words still rang loud in Nic's ears. He could not risk his mother being sent away or being sacrificed to the king's men when they came asking questions. She had been alone in this wretched house since her marriage, more prisoner than wife, and he could not let her down when she needed him most.

A tap sounded on the door. "Nic?"

Dashiell. Nic wasn't ready to face him, but fear that someone might attack the vowsmith if he stood out there alone sent Nic scrambling for the lock. With the flower still heavy in his pocket, he pulled the door open upon Dashiell's relieved expression.

"Oh thank God." The vowsmith stepped inside and closed the door firmly behind him. "Even though I knew you would likely sleep all day, I've still been beside myself with worry. How are you? Should you be up?"

He gripped Nic's hands as he spoke, and it was all Nic could do not to pull away, needing to calm his own panic. "I . . . I just needed to move," he said. "The doctor gave me something for the pain that knocked me out for a few hours."

"He's not worried about the wound, is he?"

"No. It's fine."

Nic needed to tell him about the threat that had been waiting, needed to tell him that he could not be in Nic's rooms, that they couldn't be together even for now, but under Dashiell's intent stare, the words twisted up on his tongue.

Nic extricated his hands, needing not to be so close. "Are you staying?" he asked as lightly as he could. "Or did you just drop by to check on me?"

"I don't know."

There was something heavy in the words that set Nic's heart thumping hard against his ribs. "What do you mean?"

"I mean," Dashiell said, stepping closer, "that I don't want to stay at all. I want to go. I want to break the lock-in and leave. With you."

"What?"

Another step. "I cannot bear to lose you, Nic, cannot bear to sprint down that hallway again and be too late. But even without that danger, I . . . I can't keep doing this. I know that all sense says we have no future, but I cannot accept that. I won't. Not when we could just walk away and never look back."

For a moment Nic could only stare, a rush of joy at those words hastily souring, for no amount of determination or love could change the cold facts. To run away would shame Leaf in the eyes of society. Would shame Dashiell's family and utterly destroy his career. It would ruin the Monterris name for good, and worst of all would mean leaving Nic's mother behind.

"We can't do that."

Dashiell closed the rest of the space between them with a few quick steps and took Nic's face in gentle hands. "Yes, we can, Nic, listen to me. I don't care about my career—no, I mean it," he added when Nic scoffed. "There have been times since I arrived when even I could not fathom the risks I took to be with you, until I realised I didn't care if I was caught, not really, because if I ruined the contract, then perhaps somehow we could be together after all." He huffed a laugh at that and looked away, cheeks heating. "Shameful, I know," he admitted, striding to the window as though to avoid Nic's gaze. "Not that that was my plan, just that some part of me always knew I would never be able to give you up once I had found you again. That I might have to decide between my career and you and that you would win every time."

They were the sort of words Nic had always thought he wanted to hear, yet they were all wrong, because Dashiell had thought only of his own sacrifices.

When Nic didn't answer, Dashiell turned back from the window, the afternoon light limning his dark hair. "I said there might come a time when I stopped caring about the consequences. It seems now we've reached it. I want you, Nic, and I don't care what it takes to have you."

Words that filled Nic's heart as utterly as they chilled it, Dashiell not caring how many others were left in ruins for his love. In Nic's head, Silla's warning rang loud.

Sometimes the strongest love is like a poison, and the more you drink the more monstrous you become, until you are standing in a wasteland of your own making.

He stared at the vowsmith, at the fire in his eyes and the stubborn set of his jaw, and the fear that no explanation would ever be enough shivered through him. Even the smallest possibility that Dashiell might still break the contract no matter what Nic said was too great a risk when it was his mother's life that hung in the balance. He couldn't even show Dashiell the threat penned on the flower, because with his life and his heart in danger, the vowsmith would have only greater reason to break the contract himself.

The realisation of what Nic had to do sickened him to his soul. *End it, or he will be next.*

"That's a lot to sacrifice for some good fucks." Nic heard his own voice, dismissive and cruel, and though he could see no other path but to push Dashiell away, he hated himself for such words.

Dashiell's brows contracted, all confusion. "What? What are you talking about? I love you. I've always loved you and I will always love you." He stepped closer, sending Nic's heart fluttering in his chest. "Nic, I know I am not worthy of you. I have always known that, but I would break a thousand contracts if it meant having the chance to prove myself, to one day hope to deserve you."

The tug toward Dashiell was visceral, the urge to throw everything and everyone away for this man so strong it was frightening. Nic swallowed it all down.

"You are more than worthy, Dash, but my future is here and it always has been."

For a moment Dashiell just stared at him and Nic forced himself to stare back, to hold his ground and not break, to grip tight to the knowledge that this was the only way and just. Not. Break.

"What?" Dashiell's eyes darted about Nic's face, hunting for understanding. "What is this about?"

"What this?"

"This *you*!" Dashiell cried. "Last night you wanted to marry me. Today it's just goodbye?"

Nic made himself shrug. "Last night I'd almost been murdered."

The hurt that crossed Dashiell's face was like a punch to the gut. "Nic." He lifted his hand as though to touch Nic's cheek, only to pull it away. "No." Such a short, curt word, snapped as though at the universe. "No. That is not how this ends. I want you in my life, Nic, and I don't care what I have to sacrifice for it to happen. If I break the contract, it falls on me, not you. It isn't neat, but if this is the way it goes, then let's take it. Let's take it and run and never look back."

Nic wanted to scream, to throw all the reasons they couldn't into Dashiell's face, but Dashiell was no fool—he knew them all, he just didn't care.

"Run?" Despite his frustration, the slight sneer Nic achieved around the word made him sick. "If I wanted to run from my life, don't you think I would have done so already?"

"Nic." Dashiell lightly clasped his face in his hands and Nic wanted to pull away as much as he wanted to lean in. "Listen to me, please. We have but one life, and rare are the moments we get to choose what it can look like."

"Choose?" Nic pulled free so sharply he almost lost his balance. "You say that like I've ever been able to choose anything."

Nic tried to move past him, but Dashiell stepped in the way. "Then choose now."

"Choose now?" A flare of anger tore through him and Nic threw up his arms in mock defeat. "Then I choose to do my duty and stop torturing myself with vain hopes. Choose to stop living in snatches of what might have been. Choose to stop pretending the world is anything but what it is!"

Silence choked the room and Nic's every breath came sharp and fast, his throat aching with the effort of holding back tears. This was it. This was really it. The end. And in a few days, they would never see each other again.

A step scuffed nearer, and Dashiell's low rumble spoke all too close. "I don't know why you're doing this. Tell me you don't think we could be happy. That you think we're not worth sacrificing for— that I'm not worth sacrificing for. Tell me to leave. Tell me never to come back. Tell me that's what you want and I will go."

A tear ran its trail down Nic's cheek, followed by another. He didn't look up. Couldn't. Dashiell was standing there, *right there*, so close he could reach out and press a hand to his chest, could feel that fierce heart beating and beating for him, but Nic could only close his hands into tight fists.

"Don't make me do this." His words were barely a whisper.

"Tell me you will be happy. Tell me you will not live with regret."

"Please, don't."

"Tell me!" Dashiell gripped his shoulders. "Look at me, Nic. Look me in the eye and tell me you don't want to be together. That you don't want to fight for us."

Nic looked up. It was easier to meet Dashiell's gaze than he thought it would be, as though something inside him had already died and could no longer grieve.

"I don't want to fight for us," he said, the dead monotone coming out steady. "I don't want this."

Inside he was screaming, but Nic held his ground as Dashiell's gaze hunted his face, his grip tightening upon Nic's shoulders. For a moment it seemed he would keep arguing, that he would break down Nic's defences, and almost Nic wished he would no matter how impossible it would be to bear the wasteland they left behind. But after a few long moments, Dashiell let him go. Nodded curtly.

"All right. Then I guess this is goodbye."

Nic couldn't speak, could only nod while his internal scream grew all the louder, shattering through his body.

Dashiell ran a hand through his hair. Licked his lips. Lingered.

"All right," he repeated. "Goodbye, Nic."

And having spun on his heel, Dashiell strode toward the door. It was wrenched open, and in a swish of vowsmith's black, he was gone.

Nic broke. He dropped to his knees, and lifting his face to the ceiling, let out a cracked, almost soundless wail, tears pouring unchecked down his cheeks.

Nic drank.

With the door locked against the world, he sat in his rooms and emptied glass after glass. It didn't help. He could still remember every word Dashiell had said, could still remember the gentle way he'd taken Nic's face in his hands, could still remember how the words *I don't want this* had tasted on his own tongue. And so he drank some more.

The next morning he woke feeling wretched, yet could hardly have said how much was due to the wine and how much was the broken heart. Or the still-healing wound cut into his side.

Yet as though it were any normal day, Ambrose brought his breakfast tray and his shaving water. At least no ill news came with them—a small mercy. The chance that ending things might not have been enough to save Dashiell's life had haunted Nic's thoughts. He would breathe a little easier once negotiations began for the day—a glance at the mantelpiece clock telling him that wouldn't be for another half hour.

A lifetime ago, Dashiell had snuck in on his way to the session and sat atop Nic, covering him in kisses. Now there was just silence while Ambrose helped him dress, as though such a mundane thing even mattered.

Nursing an aching head, Nic took his time, and was halfway through shaving when a sharp knock sounded on the door. Now that Ambrose was keeping it locked, he couldn't just wait for Leaf to let herself in, so the valet put down Nic's razor and went to open it.

The door lock clicked and the hinges squealed their faint protest, before a familiar voice said, "Ambrose. If you would give this to Lord Monterris."

Nic moved before any rational thought could stop him, stepping out into his sitting room as Dashiell made to leave.

"Dash."

The vowsmith turned, his expression one of furious hauteur. Yet a tiny hint of hope shone in his eyes, filling Nic with guilt for having spoken at all when there was nothing more he could say— nothing he should say. Better this way. Better for Dashiell to go in hate than in love.

And he needed to go—needed not to be seen in Nic's company at all. Instead, Dashiell gestured to the box in Ambrose's hand, its lid sitting open a crack.

"I finished it," he said, the words hard. "And no, I did not look inside. It not being my place to do so." A bow. "Good day to you, my lord."

As the vowsmith walked out, the urge to call him back, to change his mind, to throw everything away, was almost overwhelming. Nic balled his fingers into fists, and went to take the box from Ambrose's hand.

It looked much the same as it had when he'd found it, but here and there Dashiell had scratched out sigils and added new ones, leaving it covered in the lingering feel of the vowsmith's magic. It was almost as cruel as the smell of him that lingered on Nic's pillows.

Despite his confidence in Dashiell's work, Nic tensed as he flipped open the lid. Nothing happened, just the faint creak of a stiff hinge leaving Nic staring down at a single crumpled piece of paper torn along one edge.

"Oh shit," Nic breathed. "Ambrose? Quick, go fetch Lady Leaf. Now!"

"Yes, my lord."

As Ambrose departed, Nic pulled the page from the box and set it on the table, smoothing the crumples as best he could. A page from a ledger. The Serral crest was faintly inked at the top like a watermark, followed by neat lines of accounts and expenses. *Two books for Charles £8 6s. Greasing coin, paid to Gillingham £20. My lady's shawl £60.*

At the next line, Nic drew a sharp breath.

Lord Francis Monterris—services rendered £10,000.

Hurried steps heralded Ambrose's return, but even when Leaf swept in saying, "Ambrose said you found something," Nic didn't look up from the page, just slid it across the table toward her.

"Oh! Is that the page your valet was holding?"

"Read it."

A moment of silence hung while she read, then, "Oh! But . . . my aunt got that shawl just before we came. Yes, see, the date at the top of the page is from last month. That cannot be right."

At last, Nic looked up, meeting her frown. He'd had the very same thought, but it was slowly giving way to another, to the possibility that the Faceless Man hadn't been the ghost of Lord Francis at all.

Nic thought of his father's hand on his arm as he hissed in Nic's ear. *We don't need another useless conjuror in this family.*

"Oh," he breathed, before his voice failed entirely.

"Oh?"

The faint hints he'd caught of the ghost's magic had always seemed to come from a great distance as though from beyond the grave, but perhaps it had just been the feeble whisper of an accent even more closely related to Nic's own than the duke's.

"Nic, what is it?" Leaf said when he didn't answer. "You think he's still alive?"

He looked into Leaf's confused face, his own surely twisting like his stomach. "'We don't need another useless conjuror in this family.' That's what he said to me, Leaf, the night you asked me to sing. *Another* conjuror. I think you were right. Lord Francis *is* our ghost."

The grotto hall sat empty and silent, no sign of the dark sea that had once swirled after them, filling the floor. Pinpricks of light pierced through the bricked-up doorway to the front courtyard, while the large edifice containing the grotto doors loomed ominously.

"Are you sure he'll be here?" Leaf said as they reached the bottom of the stairs and began across the old flagstones.

"There's nowhere else he could be."

"All right, better question. Are you sure this is a good idea?"

The truth was that he didn't know. If Lord Francis was his ghost, then the man had already passed up numerous opportunities to end Nic's life, yet Silla's warning that knowledge was dangerous kept pricking at his thoughts.

And so, before they'd come, Nic had fetched one of the duke's many pistols from the drawer in his study. Loaded and ready, it was tucked into the lining of his coat.

"I think it'll be all right," Nic said eventually. "I've seen him enough times now that I'm sure if he wanted me dead, he would have already done it, but . . . if anything happens, run."

"Nic—"

"I don't think it will; just promise you'll run."

Cheeks paling, Leaf nodded. "All right. I promise."

They made it halfway across the flagstones before the first door slammed. As it had the last time they'd tried to reach the grotto, another followed, sending off a distant crescendo.

"Just like before," Leaf said, and Nic turned, hunting for any movement in the hall. It was still, yet the dusty air began to take on the thick, sticky feel of spent magic. It began as the faintest hint, before it oozed beneath the doors upon a tide of familiar darkness.

Leaf tensed, crushing Nic's hand as the inky cloud spread across the cracked flagstones, reaching lashing tendrils toward their feet. "What do we do?"

"Pretend it isn't there."

"That's a lot easier said than done, Nicholas Monterris."

"Close your eyes."

"What?"

"Close your eyes," he repeated, squeezing her hand as the thick shadows stretched toward them. "It might feel cold and strange but we'll walk through it together. Trust me."

Leaf shut her eyes, and pulling her with him, Nic stepped into the black sludge. At first it felt like nothing, before a harsh cold crept across his skin like a thousand tiny pinpricks. From somewhere nearby, a scream reverberated, yet like the slamming doors it seemed to have no one source. Nic took another step. The darkness rose, clawing up his legs and catching upon Leaf's skirt like wisps of charred cloth.

"Where is that scream coming from?" Leaf's voice sounded as far away as the scream sounded close, echoing through the darkness as Nic edged forward.

"Ignore it!" he called back. "It's not real."

The door was gone, obscured by whipping dark clouds—clouds that swelled up over them on a rising tide. Just like back in the service passage, the darkness slid up Nic's chin and poured into his mouth like cold knives. Leaf's hand twitched, but he just tightened his hold and stepped forward, his attempt to call out to her swallowed by the night. The floor, the walls, the door—all had vanished into the smothering black fog that seemed to live both within and without.

Nic reached out. One step. Two. Pushing through the heavy night until his fingertips brushed wood. Another step and his palm flattened against it. Eyes closed, Nic hunted the handle and bolt, his hand all that assured him they were there.

There was no sound of grating metal as Nic pulled the bolt, yet surely it moved, and he reached for one round handle and pushed.

The door swung open, tearing at the darkness. Like so much shredded paper it dropped away, leaving only real darkness in its place beyond the door.

"That was awful," Leaf whispered, jerking her lantern up. It illuminated a short stone passage blackened with age.

And the pale face of an automaton.

It floated toward them atop a dark cloak, and Nic fought the urge to reach for the pistol. "Stop!"

The figure halted, and from a little over an arm's length away, it stared at them as they stared at it. Then the tendrils of darkness hanging off its frame fell away like so much mist, revealing the black of a Brilliant's shirt and the shimmering threads of a fine waistcoat. The mask was next, swept off by a slim-fingered hand. The face beneath belonged to a stranger, yet those dark eyes and that mess of faded golden hair were all too familiar.

"Hello, Nicholas," the man said, his lopsided smile producing only one dimple. "I've been wondering whether you would find me."

Chapter 27

For a long moment Nic stared at the man before him, seeing himself reflected back. "Lord Francis Monterris," he said, eventually finding his voice. "Back from the dead."

The older man's smile slipped a little. "I think you should both come in. Don't worry, I have no intention of harming you."

"Your word as a gentleman?" Nic said, surprised at the bite in his words.

"My word as a gentleman." Turning to Leaf, Lord Francis added, "Lady Leaf Serral, we haven't been properly introduced. I am Lord Francis Monterris and it is an honour to meet you."

He held out his arm, and with a glance at Nic, Leaf took it. "A pleasure to meet you too, Lord Francis," she said as he led them along the short passage into the grotto. "I've never met someone who has come back from the dead before."

Lord Francis laughed at that, everything about him polished and charming.

"I assure you the story is far from exciting. I am merely the hairless sheep of the family, eating all the grass and providing no wool, as Val always says."

Despite the assurance of safety, Nic was glad of the weighty pistol in his pocket as he followed them into the cavernous grotto. He had been there often in his time, but never had it been so brightly lit, the light from the old chandeliers glinting off a shimmering stone ceiling like a sea of stars. The slick obsidian walls once used as conjuring screens had always looked like dark portals, but now the round tables dotting the space were shabby anchors to reality, each covered in books and gears and oil tins, and coiled-up lengths of shimmering sigil tape. At one, a tray of scones sat with a coffee-pot sentry, and Lord Francis pushed his tools into a messy pile to make space before offering them chairs at the hastily cleared table.

"Now, why don't you tell me what brings you?" Lord Francis said, as though they were merely paying a morning call.

A mountain of questions pressed against Nic's tongue, yet he knew they needed to tread carefully. Start small. He gestured at the pieces of automata scattered on the tabletop. "We ran into your automaton upstairs."

"Impressive thing, isn't it? I didn't expect any of them to still work. The reel inside that one was badly corrupted, but that's hardly surprising after so many years."

"You mean all that 'I am here for you, Nicholas' stuff is meant to be on there?" Leaf asked.

"Yes, although I assure you it didn't used to sound quite so frightening. And at least it did a good job of scaring you away before you found me."

"Was that why you left it there?"

Lord Francis gave an easy laugh. "Oh no, winding it up to scare you off was just a very desperate plan on my part. Like the darkness. That is just a particularly thick variant of conjurer's black, used to make a canvas. It was the first thing that came to mind when I panicked and needed to stop you seeing me, but then when it worked so well, I started having more fun with it."

"Fun?" Nic repeated. "It isn't so fun when you're on the receiving end."

"I'm sure it's not," the man said affably, and poured out a cup of coffee. "Coffee, Lady Leaf? I only have the one cup, I'm afraid, but I'm quite sure Nicholas isn't a coffee drinker."

"Oh, thank you, no," Leaf said.

"All the more for me then." And with the cup in hand, Lord Francis leaned back in his chair, gaze fixed on Nic. "I don't think you came to find me just because of my automaton, did you, Nicholas."

The nonchalance piqued Nic, and he had to swallow a snap of annoyance and the urge to punch the older man in the face. "No. You've been following me around. It was you I saw in the first night. And in the service passage. And in the hallway outside my room. Twice. You're the ghost that disappeared beneath my fingers."

Lord Francis smiled at that, a handsome smile beneath the hints of dissipation. "Mere illusory trickery."

"But why?"

For the first time since they'd sat down, the smile on Lord Francis's face slipped into something wry and solemn. "If I'm honest? Curiosity. You were but a wrinkled, screaming little bundle in your nurse's arms when I left, and Val has never brought you to town. I wanted to see how you'd turned out."

"Because you're my father."

Nic hadn't thought to say it, yet the words were out and could not be unsaid, and he found he wasn't sorry. Especially not when chagrin eclipsed the man's easy smile.

"Resemblances can be—"

"You don't need to deny it," Nic said. "Silla told me."

"Ah." Lord Francis set his cup on the table. "I don't imagine she's all that complimentary about me, but . . . yes. It was never officially in the contract, but Val made it clear an heir would be my duty. Not that it was an onerous task. Georgie and I loved each other in a way, though perhaps more as havens from the life Val built for us. She didn't want me to leave at all, but Val and I . . . came to an agreement."

"Kick you out, did he?" Nic sneered. It was exactly the sort of thing the duke would do, preferring to pretend his brother was dead than deal with the consequences of having a profligate on his hands. "I know about the debts."

"I see." Some of Lord Francis's suavity vanished beneath a bite. "You are rather better informed about me than I expected." With something of a shrug, he spread his arms in defeat. "Behold, then, the family wastrel. That explains why you've been shooting daggers at me at least. Though you cannot pin the whole of the Monterris ill fortune on me, however convenient a scapegoat I am."

"I know about your father's and grandfather's debts."

"Ah, but did you know Val lost a substantial amount of Georgie's fortune in bad business debacles? No? Well, you can thank Lord Ricard Serral for that." He gave a mock little bow in Leaf's direction.

If he had hoped for surprise, he was to be disappointed. "Millie told us that," Leaf said. "She said he did it after his marriage fell through."

"Ah, he may have started then, he's just never stopped."

"Is that something you help him with too?" Nic asked.

"Too?"

Unable to hold on to the question any longer, Nic pulled the crumpled sheet of paper out of his pocket. Keeping his hand on it, he slid it a little way across the table. "Ten thousand pounds to Lord Francis Monterris for services rendered. You're not here because you were curious about me. You're here because you were paid to be here—paid to ruin this contract with your ghosts and automata. Ransacking people's rooms? Making darkness leak through the dining room ceiling? What was he hoping to achieve? Scaring everyone into calling it off?"

A hint of wariness entered the man's face as he glanced from Nic to Leaf. "Something like that, yes."

"And Rowerre stole this from Lord Ricard."

It wasn't a question, but as Lord Francis nodded, a collection of disparate thoughts coalesced around a single memory. The slicing charm that had ruined Nic's awful waistcoat the afternoon the Serrals arrived—something no one in the house ought to have been able to do. Something that had not just been an act of sabotage, but a statement to catch someone's attention. That someone just hadn't been Nic.

"Rowerre was your valet before he was mine," Nic said. "You sliced that waistcoat to get his attention and then asked him to steal this. Why?"

Lord Francis's look became sardonic. "You might have noticed the date on this page. That it proves I'm alive makes it particularly useful for blackmail, don't you think?"

"Lord Ricard is blackmailing you as well as paying you?"

"Handy that the one allowed him to undertake the other, isn't it?" Lord Francis's hand twitched as though to reach for the page, only to stay the impulse. "I assure you that if I had known Rowerre would get caught, I wouldn't have asked him."

Rowerre, more father to Nic than any Monterris had been, because he had stayed.

Nic withdrew the page and tucked it back into his coat pocket, Lord Francis watching all the way. "Perhaps you've noticed Ricard hates Val with the heat of a thousand suns," the man said. "Some of that has always blown onto me, you see."

"Because His Grace refused to change the contract he smithed between Uncle Ricard and Caroline Wivenwood." This time it was Leaf's unexpected knowledge that earned her a long stare from the prodigal Monterris. "Millie told us that too."

Lord Francis's brows rose, and a smile flickered back onto his features. "There's more to it, you know. Would you believe Ricard and Val used to be friends? No? Inseparable, they were. Our father spent more time in town than here—not many gambling hells in the Northumberland wilds, you know—and we always went with him. Val and Ricard were both studying vowsmithing at the time under Lord Kettering, while Charles went to Harrow and then Oxford, studying his classics—the pretentious older brother they both sneered at. Until one day Val didn't."

Both studying, like Nic and Dashiell, side by side with their work every day. How easy it had been to become the best of friends. How easy to become more.

"Val totally ignored Ricard after he discovered Charles," Lord Francis went on, his lips curving as though he enjoyed the taste of his tale. "He loves hard, does Val, the sort of love that forgets other people exist. I was used to it, to being out in the cold, but Ricard was used to being in the sunshine, to being Val's whole world. He didn't take the change well. That contract with Caroline Wivenwood—Ricard didn't want Val to be involved, but Charles insisted. He was Lord Charborough by then and had that power. It ended up the last contract Val ever smithed, too, because our father died not long after and Val had to give up his work. No doubt that's why Ricard thought it would be nothing to him to make the changes he needed."

"So why didn't he, do you think?" Nic asked. "Was it just because it went against his oath?"

"Perhaps. Although Val had paid Ricard the singular attention of warning him against marrying her in the first place, so maybe he thought he was saving him in his own way." Lord Francis threw a look Leaf's way. "Thought she might take after her father and be a dangerous mess."

"People say—*said* that to Millie all the time."

"No doubt. But that was when Ricard started trying to ruin Val in earnest, to stop him righting the family fortune. Our father had left us deeply in debt—even more deeply in debt, I should say. I can't throw all the blame Ricard's way, but he's the one who introduced me to my first gaming hell too. Val didn't notice, of course. Everything was always about Charles."

"But they didn't marry," Leaf said. "Why not?"

Lord Francis spread his arms in something of a shrug. "Ah! The one part of the story I don't know and so cannot tell you. Ricard was sure Val would give up his debt-ridden inheritance and become a Serral—did everything he could to persuade Charles against it. I could have told him it wouldn't happen, but we weren't the best of friends by then. You see, Val promised our father to always uphold the family name, and to save us if he could, so he couldn't leave a wastrel like me to take the reins, could he? Instead Charles agreed to become a Monterris and Ricard might finally have forgiven Val then, but it all fell through and they never spoke of it again. Ricard blamed Val. He'd lost his wife and the promise of the title, and still had to deal with Charles."

Nic stared at Lord Francis as the pieces of the story fell into the missing places in Nic's mind. It was so . . . banal—four young men who had become tangled in one another's lives, only to drag the snarl of hurts behind them thereafter, destroying all that lay in their paths.

Lord Francis had spoken with ease, yet as silence met the end of his story, he added, "I recommend not mentioning to any of them that I told you their secrets."

"I hope that isn't a threat, Lord Francis," Leaf said.

"Oh, not at all," the man laughed, relaxing back into his chair, his coffee untouched on the table. "I have no reason to take sides in this fight. I got away from all that when I left."

"When you died," Nic said.

Lord Francis gave an ironic half bow. "Death *is* the only way to escape being a Monterris."

Nic flinched, hating the sound of those words on the lips of a man who had escaped where he could not. A man who had escaped leaving the family deeper in debt than ever, while giving no thought to Georgiana, left behind with a baby and a man less emotionally available than stone.

"So you've just been, what? Doing whatever you like all these years?" Leaf asked. "Pretending to be dead?"

"More or less. Val was the only one who knew at first. I had thought Georgie did, but it turns out Val lied to her too."

"I was told an automaton killed you," Nic said, reluctantly realising that he'd already learned more truths from Lord Francis than from his parents combined. "That's why they were all pulled apart and shut in the style wing. So they couldn't harm anyone else."

The skin crinkled around Lord Francis's eyes in a way that made him look younger. "That's Val through and through, telling you a fib about automata so he had reason to smash them up. Bet he ripped up at you when he found out you'd taken an interest in making more of them."

"He hates everything I do," Nic admitted. "Although I'm starting to wonder if that's because everything I do reminds him of you."

"Most likely," came the grim reply.

"How did you even get away with being dead for so long?" Nic asked, hating how petulant the words sounded to his ears. "Surely someone would have recognised you."

"I don't exactly hobnob with the ton these days, but yes, I have to be careful. The conditions on which Val let me escape was that no one should ever know. It hasn't always been easy without death papers, but it's worth it."

"No death papers were written up?"

"No." He gave a small, wan smile that entirely lacked any warmth. "Another of Val's stipulations. He couldn't accept a situation that robbed him entirely of his spare heir."

"So really you could have come back at any time. You just didn't."

"I'm here, aren't I?"

Nic set his hands on the table, leaning forward. "Yes. But only because you were paid to come and ruin this contract, not because you wanted to."

Lord Francis held his hard gaze with his own steady stare, but it was the older man who blinked first.

"You know, Nicholas, I meant it when I said I wanted to see you, to see who you'd become, but you're right, I could have come earlier. I left because I couldn't stay. I convinced myself it was best to remove a cause of friction from the house, but really it was only for me. Because I couldn't face having to watch the collapse I had helped cause, or the fading of Georgie's sanity." He ran a hand through his golden hair and Nic fought the urge to touch his own. "I don't think staying would have helped her, or made a difference to Val, but it might have made a difference to you. It must have been difficult growing up caught between madness and ice."

Angry tears pricked Nic's eyes. "You don't get to come back here now and pretend to understand what my life has been like."

"Nic," Leaf said, his name a gentle warning.

Lord Francis lifted his hand. "No, my lady, there's no need to defend my honour; I assure you I deserve his wrath. Nicholas, you aren't wrong, I have earned nothing in life, but I want you to know, if I could do anything to make up for it, I would."

"There is nothing I want from you." Nic rose from the table, fuelled by a sudden desire to be somewhere else, where he needn't see himself reflected back. "I used to think there was nothing worse than having an absent father, but it turns out there is. Having two."

"Nic!" Leaf cried, the sound muffled by a hand pressed to her lips. But Nic had spun away, having no plan but to put space between himself and the man he couldn't bear to look at. Not, he realised, because he wished him gone, but because Nic wished bitterly he'd been there all along.

As Nic made for the door, he heard Leaf say, "My apologies, Lord Francis," as though they were already husband and wife— his behaviour somehow her responsibility. "I'm sure he will come around. It's been quite a stressful lock-in, what with . . . everything."

"I understand, Lady Leaf," Lord Francis said, all proud solemnity. "And may I just say I'm very sorry for the loss of your cousin. While I am quite sure Georgiana had no intention of poisoning *her*, it is little comfort when you have suffered the loss all the same."

Nic halted in the entry arch and spun back. "You think Mama did it?"

Still sitting at his ease with his coffee cooling before him, Lord Francis raised his brows. "Surely two people who are as well-informed about what is going on as you ought to have worked that out by now." With a small grunt of effort, the man levered himself onto his feet, once again running his hands through golden hair. "Perhaps you didn't want to see it, but I did, with my own eyes. I've been your ghost, remember? Lord Charborough saw me in the pavilion that day, and I saw Georgie loose that arrow at Everel."

The flat, emotionless words stunned Nic. "You saw but didn't do anything to save him? Or warn anyone?"

"No." That sardonic look was back. "Ten thousand pounds is a lot of money I'm being paid not to be seen. Money I can't afford to pay back. Besides, there was little I could have done. The man went into shock and I can't say I was all that sorry to see him go. Nor would I have been particularly sorry if she had succeeded in poisoning Val—there's no love lost between us. Oh, don't give me that look, Nicholas. I've seen enough of you these last few days to know you'd have shed no tears. That she got the wrong person I am sorry for, and I have no doubt that will be the end of it."

His words were cold but they weren't wrong, lashing at Nic's guilt for the lack of grief he had felt since Master Everel's death.

"That is quite an awful thing to say about anyone, Lord Francis,"

Leaf said, something stiff and furious held beneath her polite tone. "What about Nic? Would you have been sorry to see him die the other night? No doubt since you see everything, you'll be able to tell us who did that too."

"What?" Lord Francis sat forward, the word almost a growl.

"Oh, you didn't know?" Leaf's brows shot up. "Someone tried to stab him, and when that failed, strangle him."

To have it stated in her matter-of-fact tone shed the memory of some of its power, but the smothering darkness and the struggle for breath was still too close, and Nic looked away from Lord Francis's patent horror.

"When?"

"The night before last," Leaf said.

"And you have no idea who did it?"

This he directed at Nic, who shook his head. "Not Mama."

"No. I'm sorry. Are you all right?"

That Lord Francis's concern was genuine was the worst part. Nic wanted nothing from the man, not even his sympathy. "Oh, I'm excellent, Uncle. Come on, Leaf. I think we should leave Lord Francis to his coffee."

Nic spun away, furious steps taking him out along the passage.

"Nicholas, wait!"

But he didn't wait, didn't turn or even slow. He'd heard all he wanted of Lord Francis's explanations and excuses, and seen enough of his mocking smiles—that Nic could see so much of himself in the man's face making it a thousand times worse.

"Well!" Leaf said as she caught up partway across the old entry hall. "That didn't go very well."

"It went as well as it had any right to. Did you hear how he talked about Master Everel?"

"And your father, yes. I wonder how Uncle Ricard found out he was still alive."

Nic snorted. "Likely he needed money and went to tell Lord Ricard himself in the hope of selling family secrets."

They slowed as they reached the stairs up to the style wing proper, Leaf chewing on her lip. "Though I guess we have some answers now at least. It sounds like Uncle Ricard probably pushed your valet down the stairs, and perhaps he really did kill Gillingham, too, in his first attempt to get Papa to invoke the clause. Then I suppose because the opportunity was there, your mama killed Master Everel and tried to kill His Grace."

Lord Francis had sounded sure, had seen her do it, yet Nic found himself shaking his head. "I cannot believe it. Your aunt had as much reason to kill Millie. And Everel was last seen alive by Millie and the doctor, not Mama and Lord Charborough."

Leaf squeezed his arm. "I know you don't want to believe it's possible, Nic. I'm sure Lord Francis didn't either, but it *is* the most sensible of all explanations." When Nic didn't answer, she added, "I can't say I much like the idea of it being true either, given that once we're married, I'll be living here with her. But who else could it have been?"

"But then who tried to kill me?" he said, needing to shift the topic—his refusal to believe his mother a murderer based all too much upon a feeling. "How many murderers do we have?"

"I don't know. There is a Mary Mallowan book where everyone was the murderer."

The idea that every member of their lock-in party had blood on their hands was not comforting, nor did it feel right. It was the contract that had brought them all together, and whoever might have dirtied their hands since, the contract was surely the reason why.

Nic and Leaf spent the afternoon together in his rooms, alternately pacing and sitting in gloomy abstraction as they tried and failed to make sense of all the pieces. Meeting Lord Francis had answered a lot of questions, yet somehow there seemed just as many left. Lord Ricard had paid the man to sneak in and run amok while he sought to get the Requisite Care Clause invoked, which explained why the hauntings had stopped with Millie's death. That the duchess had killed Master Everel and accidentally killed Millie made an awful sort of sense, yet then why had anyone attacked Nic? The longer they tried to fit the pieces together the more questions they had, and again and again they'd fallen back on the same old problem—no one but Lord Ricard had reason to want the contract broken.

Nic had planned on another evening of lonesome inebriation, but partway through the afternoon Ambrose brought the news that the contract was all but complete. It would be signed the following afternoon, and to mark the occasion, the duke had suggested they all gather one last time for dinner—a suggestion that, in Nic's case, he took to be the order that it was.

And so, both tense and heartbroken, Nic gathered the shattered shards of his armour and dressed for one final dinner.

When Ambrose delivered him to the drawing room that evening, Nic found neither Leaf nor Dashiell already present, the only occupants of the room the three men of Lord Francis's story. The duke and Lord Charborough stood ensconced together by the fire, while as far away as it was possible to get, Lord Ricard sat idly moving pieces at the chess table. Nic couldn't but think of Ricard's part of that story, about a friendship lost. How long and how utterly the man had held on to that hurt.

Nic made his way across the room to the chess table's second chair. "May I join you?"

Lord Ricard looked up, a flash of surprise hastily crushed with a sneer. "If you must, Monterris."

"I think I must." Nic sat, unable to swallow a wince as the movement tweaked his still-healing wound. "You see, I found something of yours today."

Nic took hold of a black rook and moved it forward.

"Something of mine?" Lord Ricard asked, countering with a move of his own like they'd picked up halfway through an already-begun game.

"Yes. A piece of paper, to be precise." Nic moved his rook again, paying the game little heed. "It seems to have been torn from one of your ledgers."

Holding Nic's gaze without a flicker of expression, Lord Ricard made another move—a pawn pushed forward with a small shove. At the other end of the room, the door opened and Leaf and Lady Lisbeth walked in arm in arm. Leaf's brows rose at sight of him sitting with her uncle, and to be sure she did not approach, Nic gave an infinitesimal shake of his head.

Returning to the game, he pushed forward one of his own pawns, mirroring his opponent's move. "You do not appear interested in the loss of one of your papers, Lord Ricard," he said as he did so. "But it bears a striking resemblance to the one I saw in Rowerre's hand the night he died. Something you want to tell me, perhaps?"

"That your valet shouldn't have been rummaging around in my room?"

"A crime worth murdering for?" Nic asked, trying to hide his surprise at so easy an admission.

Lord Ricard gave a dismissive shrug, shifting his bishop. "He wasn't meant to die. My man spied him hunting around and came to find me at the party, but when I went to confront him, he ran. I caught up with him at the top of the stairs and we fought over the page . . . the rest you can imagine. I didn't push him, though, if that's what you think."

Rowerre's last moments presented with little more than a shrug, like he had hardly been a person at all. Lord Francis had spoken in the same callous tone and Nic found himself swallowing anger for the second time that day.

Once again, the drawing room door opened, this time spilling Lady Theresa and Dr. Fanshaw into the room. That left only Dashiell unaccounted for. Nic tried to swallow his worry to chase the anger down.

He pushed forward another pawn. "Ten thousand pounds to Lord Francis Monterris," he said. "How long have you known he was still alive?"

Lord Ricard's smile was all too amused, like the smile of the not-so-dead man himself as he sat nursing his coffee. He took the pawn Nic had moved, sweeping it off the board. "How long have you?"

"You really didn't want this contract to go ahead, did you. Ten thousand pounds is a lot of money to pay someone to play ghost and frighten everyone off."

For a long time, Lord Ricard stared at the pieces before him, a faint smile turning his lips. Eventually, he jumped a knight—an unexpected move that brought it close to Nic's king. "Ah, but you see, no amount is ever too much where Val is concerned."

How strong the friendship must have been to have soured so viciously. Unbidden, Nic found his gaze shying toward his father and Lord Charborough, who had been joined now by others yet still stood side by side as though no one else existed.

The drawing room door opened once more, and Nic's heart leapt at the sight of Dashiell. The vowsmith's gaze made a quick circuit of the room and came to rest on Nic, reflecting back his relief for a beautiful moment—a moment soon eclipsed when hurt and anger turned Dashiell away.

Trying to ease the pained flutter of his heart, Nic drew a deep breath and moved his king out of danger. "And the blackmail?"

"No amount is too much," Lord Ricard repeated, countering by once more putting Nic's king in check. "But why keep paying when you can get what you want for free?"

Nic moved his king again. "And what is it that you want? Enough information to ruin my father? Or is this all just about the contract?"

"Cute of you to think I have any interest in confiding in you or anyone," Lord Ricard said, malice sparkling in his eyes. "I don't owe you anything."

He reached across the board, carrying his queen to once again threaten Nic's king, the movement enough of a stretch that it pulled back the man's sleeve, exposing his wrist. A wrist upon which the tips of scratches were just visible, where fingernails had dug into his flesh. And for a sickening moment Nic was back lying on the floor, trying to suck air through dark velvet while he clawed at the hands squeezing his throat.

Nic's breath caught, panic searing through him as he stared at the cuts, at Lord Ricard, at the slowly dawning smile on the man's face.

As though from somewhere very far away, the dinner bell rang.

"It was you." Nic's words were a whisper. "You tried to kill me."

The smile broadened as Lord Ricard tugged his sleeve back into place. "And I was so close too. But what are you going to do about it now, break your precious contract?" He gestured to Nic's checked king, his expression a hateful grin. "Your move, Monterris."

Chapter 28

They went into dinner. It seemed, in the circumstances, a ridiculous thing to do, yet caught in the routine, Nic's body made the walk from the drawing room to the parlour without any conscious input from his mind—a mind still reeling. Unable to stop seeing that grin and those scratches, he was trapped back in that moment beneath Lord Ricard's squeezing hands, knowing he was about to die.

Somehow, familiar etiquette took him through the motions. He sat, moved his napkin, nodded to the footman who served his soup, and took up his spoon. Around him no one was speaking. All the sounds were the clink of cutlery and the rustle of small movements, the clearing of a throat and the pouring of wine.

A glance down the table revealed Lord Ricard in his usual place, a faint smile curving his lips as he ate. He didn't look up, but a frisson of panic shivered through Nic all the same.

And I was so close too.

"Nic?" He flinched as Leaf leaned close, earning him a surprised look. "What's wrong?"

Almost he said "Your uncle just admitted he tried to kill me" loud enough for the whole table to hear, but as Nic watched Lord Ricard go on calmly eating, he realised the man was right. What was he going to do about it? What difference did it even make? They were still locked in, still going to sign the contract tomorrow, and Nic was still stuck in his hated life.

Nic found his gaze pulled to where Dashiell sat silently focused on his meal. Perhaps feeling the attention, the vowsmith looked up. Their eyes met, and as though Nic had been a total stranger, Dashiell smiled a faint acknowledgement and looked right through him.

"Nic?"

"Oh, sorry." He forced a smile for Leaf. "I'm perfectly well, I assure you."

He hoped he'd spoken loud enough for both Dashiell and Lord Ricard to hear, determined to show one that he had no regrets and the other that he could not be intimidated no matter how much nausea swirled in his stomach.

"I trust we are not expected to take tea in the drawing room this evening, Your Grace?" Lady Theresa said, breaking the silence.

"Not at all, Lady Theresa," the duke said, something of a sigh on the edge of the words, like he had been waiting for just such an attack. "It merely seemed fitting that we should mark the end of the lock-in with dinner, after which you may of course return to your rooms if you so wish."

"Is every dish going to be poisoned then?" Lord Ricard asked far too cheerfully, before ladling another spoonful of soup into his mouth.

Lady Lisbeth dropped her spoon with a clatter, her face pale.

"Ricard, please," Lord Charborough said, his sigh as long-suffering as the duke's. "That is quite unnecessary."

"Just wait until someone else drops dead and tell me so again." Lord Ricard gestured across the table at Leaf. "I'm only surprised my dear niece has not suggested we catch our murderer by all swapping soup bowls and watching to see who refuses to eat."

Irritation reddened Lord Charborough's cheeks, but before he could snap at his brother, Lady Theresa said, "Oh no, do not suggest it, my lord. Though I do agree it is frightful to eat anything here now. The only reason I feel safe tonight is because Her Grace has not joined us. How very much I look forward to telling His

Majesty's men all about this." Leaving no time for Nic to come to his mother's defence, the lady turned toward Dashiell. "I do hope there will be nothing to hold up the contract's signing tomorrow, Master sa Vare?"

Dashiell bestowed one of his professional smiles upon her. "It is all but done now, my lady. There are just a few things His Grace needs to check before we can proceed."

Given the speed with which the contract had suddenly been finalised, Nic couldn't but wonder whether Dashiell had been dragging out its completion before Nic had broken his heart.

"Oh, well, that is good news." The lady sniffed. "Although if it is so close, I don't see why we cannot just sign now rather than spend another night in this wretched place."

"This *wretched place* will soon be my home, Aunt," Leaf pointed out.

"Oh, Leaf, of course, I just—"

"Don't try to dig yourself out of that one, my lady," Lord Ricard said with a laugh. "And you can't hurry good vowsmithing. These things have to be ever so perfect."

A sidelong look was thrown along the table to the duke, Lord Ricard's smile turning smug and unpleasant before flicking Nic's way like a whip. It was gone as quickly, attention retracted to his meal as though nothing had happened.

Nic found his heart hammering and had to focus on breathing, on not returning to that moment in the hallway when Lord Ricard's hands had closed and closed around his throat.

Instinctively he touched his neck, only to pull his hand sharply away. Dashiell looked over, a hint of something that could have been concern vanishing on a hope as he turned away with a dismissive sniff. This the man who filled Nic's entire heart, all the more now for the extra space pain seemed to have carved. The pain of knowing how soon he would leave, of knowing that once he stepped out that door they might never see each other again. Dashiell would go back to his life angry. Determined to forget Nic's very existence, he would marry and move on, and all Nic would have left were these memories.

At least his father and Lord Charborough could have kept meeting, because unlike Nic they answered to no one else. Why, then, they hadn't married still made no sense. Lord Francis had said the duke hadn't been able to give up his title because he'd made a promise to their father, but surely nothing had stood in the way of Lord Charborough becoming a Monterris.

Nic pulled his gaze from the examination of Dashiell's beloved features to glance at his father. He'd made a promise too, a hasty, careless thing he no more wanted to keep than he wanted to lose the man he loved. The Monterris name ought to be consigned to the gutter where it belonged. Perhaps it had meant something once, to the Monterrises who had built the Court and their fortunes, who had fought battles alongside kings, but all it had now was debt and misery, torturing those unlucky enough to bear the name.

Death was the only way to escape being a Monterris.

A death he'd come so close to. Lord Francis had needed to pretend for his half freedom, but seconds were all that had kept Dr. Fanshaw from having to write Nic's death certificate.

Nic sucked in a breath.

"Something amiss?" Leaf whispered, leaning close again.

Nic thought to nod but wasn't sure he did, everything seeming to freeze around him. The idea forming around that long-hated phrase was big and important yet slippery, the sort of idea that made normal breathing insufficient. He stared at Dashiell. It had never been Nic himself who was dangerous to him, only ever his name. But if he was no longer a Monterris . . .

Across the table, Dashiell flicked a quick scowl at Nic's ongoing stare, as though he knew the line of Nic's thoughts, as though to tell him it was already too late. Even if it was, the idea went on growing inside Nic's mind, unravelling a path to freedom not only for himself but for his mother too, if he was careful. He just needed to die.

Dinner could not end fast enough after that. Lord Ricard all but forgotten, Nic's whole body thrummed with sudden purpose, with plans where he'd never been able to plan before. Not yet for a future—he dared not think so far when so much could go wrong—but for the *possibility* of a future.

At the end of the meal, the guests parted in pairs or waited for servants to walk them safely back to their rooms. With only relief at parting for the final time before the next day's signing, it ought to have been oppressive, but it was all Nic could do to suppress a grin as he offered his arm to Leaf.

"Allow me to walk you to your room, Lady Leaf."

No sooner had she set her hand on his than he whisked her away, leaving her good night to her aunt trailing behind them.

"Nic? What is going on?" Leaf said, having to lengthen her stride to keep from being dragged. "I could barely get a word out of you at dinner and now you're trying to pull my arm out."

He turned a grin upon her as they made their way to the stairs. "Death is the only way to escape being a Monterris."

"So you've said."

"No, you don't understand." He glanced back at the last members of the party lingering in the drawing room door and lowered his voice. "My father owns me because I am a Monterris. The only thing about me that is dangerous to Dashiell is my name. The only reason I have no freedom is my name. The only reason you're being made to marry me is my name. But if I died, I would no longer have that name."

Leaf blinked. "Yes, but you would also be dead."

"No!" They'd reached the stairs, and Nic let go of her arm to grip the banister and spin back, barely suppressing a grin. "Because it's all just paper, Leaf. It's all just smithed contracts connected around us like chains, controlling the way we live. No one cares about what's real; it's what's on the piece of paper that counts. *The net must hold.*"

"I think I understand what you're saying," she said, following him up the stairs two at a time. "But . . . does that mean our contract would be broken?"

"Yes, because Nicholas Monterris would be dead. Just imagine how much pressure you could bring against your father to sasine you if it were true."

As they reached the second landing, Leaf parted her lips as though to argue, only to snap her mouth shut. Her eyes widened.

"Oh."

If Ambrose was shocked by the arrival of Leaf alongside his master, he didn't show it, accepting an order to fetch the doctor without a flicker of concern. It took only five minutes for the doctor to arrive, yet it felt like five years. Leaf was as tense, the pair of them pacing about, holding the possibilities close lest they start to feel too real.

Standing by the door, Nic unlocked it the moment Ambrose tapped, and pulled it wide to invite the doctor in.

"Lord Monterris, is your wound troubling you? I can make up another draught of—"

"No, thank you, Doctor," Nic said. "It is as well as can be expected. I have a far more important reason for asking you to come."

The man's brows rose as he looked from Nic to Leaf and back. "More serious than near strangulation and a gash in the side makes it quite a serious matter." He glanced around as Ambrose locked the door in their wake. "Especially when it seems you still fear it happening again."

"Something we should all fear. If someone wants this contract broken and is willing to kill to achieve it, then we're all in danger until the ink is dry tomorrow."

For a moment he thought to admit he knew who had attacked him, but Lord Ricard seemed to belong to a whole other time.

"In truth, Doctor," Nic went on instead, "I don't wish to risk any more lives for a contract I do not want. This house is a prison, the Monterris family a long-desiccated wasteland of old hatreds, and I no more wish to bring Leaf into it than I want to remain part of it myself. But when I planned to break the lock-in to ensure no one else died, my father threatened to send Mama to an asylum if I did."

Dr. Fanshaw had been steadily regarding him, but he winced at that.

"Ah." Nic nodded. "I see I don't need to explain to you why that stayed my hand."

"No, my lord, I . . . have enough experience that I can heartily endorse never sending anyone to such a place, and certainly not someone as fragile as Her Grace. I am yet, however, to understand why I am here."

"I asked you to come because there are other ways to break a contract. One way, specifically, that would also allow me to escape my life. Allow me to save my mother. And to love someone Lord Nicholas Monterris is not allowed to love. You see, all my life I have been told that death is the only way to escape being a Monterris. So I ask you, Doctor, how close did I come to dying the other night? And was it close enough?"

For many long seconds, Dr. Fanshaw stared at him and Nic stared back, not yet daring to hope as the light of realisation slowly dawned across the man's face.

"You want me to write you a death certificate."

It was exactly what Nic wanted, yet his heart pounded sickeningly at the truth of it. "Yes."

"No doubt you are well aware that such a thing, given you are living and breathing, would be an unethical and illegal use of my position under medical jurisprudence."

"Yes. Though I would argue that while it might be illegal, it is not unethical. What is unethical is a society that robs me of all autonomy and puts my life solely in the hands of another. A society that values me only for the Brilliance in my blood and tells us it makes me better than you. A society where we've turned magic into a cage and love into an impossibility, such that murder is an easier resort than words. A society that I, frankly, do not want to live in. My father will not sasine me, but you can kill me."

Once again, Dr. Fanshaw met his gaze with a silent, considering stare and Nic found his chest tightening. This was his one hope, a hope that couldn't but swell for every moment the doctor did not refuse.

"You make a compelling argument, Lord Monterris," the doctor said after a time, the words soft, apologetic. "But you will not be surprised to learn there are some impediments to your request. The first is that in order to be binding, a death certificate requires not only my signature, but the signature and workings of a vowsmith."

A small smile twitched Nic's lips. "I don't think that will be a problem."

He might have destroyed any hope of a future with Dashiell, but he had no doubt the vowsmith would at least grant him one final request.

Dr. Fanshaw's brows rose. "I see, but it is, sadly, the lesser issue. The risk to my reputation, you know, is no small thing, and the likelihood of two peers challenging my signature in the royal court is a frankly terrifying proposition. And yet you're right. That is not a society in which I wish to live either. I understand your wish to be free, and your wish to save your mother from what would be little better than a slow and painful death. And I, too, understand what it feels like to love someone Dr. Edwin Fanshaw is not allowed to love. So while I am not saying yes, I am equally not saying no. If we can find a way to mitigate the dangers . . ."

Nic gripped the chance of a yes with both hands and heart. "In order to challenge the certificate, would an alive Nicholas Monterris have to be presented to the court?"

"That would generally be the way, yes."

"And if I was nowhere to be found? Living in secret would not be my first choice, but I would have as little desire to be found and challenged."

"As for the reputational risk," Leaf said, speaking up for the first time, "there is only so much hearsay either my father or His Grace would spread given how closely such a tale concerns them. A good many questions would be asked if His Grace made it known his son and heir preferred a false death and obscurity over becoming duke."

Now that Leaf had drawn attention to herself, Dr. Fanshaw turned her way. "Is this what you want, my lady? I cannot but consider that there are two of you standing here, two of you involved in this contract. However much I can dismiss the harm to your fathers after such a lock-in, I cannot dismiss the harm the contract's loss might do you."

Leaf drew a deep breath, knitting her hands together in front of her. "Dr. Fanshaw. Edwin, if I may. I am not a romantic young woman. Whatever might generally be assumed from the closeness of our relationship, Nic is not my lover and never could be. What I want is for him to be happy with the man he was made for, away from here where he can be free. That I will be considered something in the nature of cursed goods after the gruesome death of my contracted fiancé will also not hinder my attempts to convince my father to sasine me."

A notch of confusion appeared between the doctor's brows. "That is what you want?"

"It is what I have always wanted. I hope one day I will achieve it and open a school for magical young women. Until then, not being married to Nic is a good first step."

The doctor nodded slowly, adjusting his glasses. "You continue to amaze me, Lady Leaf. If that is truly what you wish, then timing is our greatest impediment. While I remain in this house, I fear they could force me to retract any certificate. Although"—a rueful smile crossed his face—"I suppose as a non-Brilliant, I can leave at any time. I think your mother will have to find herself a new physician in future, my lady. I have been thinking for a while I ought to move on from Harwick, and now it would seem that time has come. There is nothing . . . wise . . . keeping me there."

They shared a long look, fraught with understanding, before Dr. Fanshaw nodded. "All right. I'll do it. As a doctor I took an oath to save lives, which means that ending this contract before it can claim another is not so far outside my remit. Besides, how could I forgive myself for refusing?"

Nic gripped the man's hands, his heart soaring. "Thank you, Doctor, you have no idea how much this means to me. I will do everything in my power to ensure you suffer no ills from it."

"Then I think, my lord, we have a plan. Allow me to find some ink and paper."

"Allow me, sir," Ambrose said, hurrying off to Nic's writing desk while the doctor settled at the sitting room table. As the things were gathered, Nic couldn't keep from grinning. Leaf, however, looked troubled.

"Nic." She touched his arm, her voice low. "Are you sure about this? I mean really sure. I know we've just argued very successfully, but think . . . you would be giving up everything."

Of course she was right. He would be giving up his name, his family, his inheritance—almost everything he had ever known. Yet he would be gaining freedom. Gaining the chance to make his own choices. The chance to once more see Dashiell's face lying on his pillow, to forever have the Dashiell who had sat on the floor of the archives working in the lantern light, and the Dashiell who had stood there willing to give up the world for him.

"No. Not everything."

Leaf squeezed his arm. "He really means that much."

"He means the world to me, but . . . I know being sasined isn't so complete a break with your family, but would you change your mind about freedom if it was?"

"No. You're right. I wouldn't."

At the sitting room table, Ambrose had gathered everything the doctor needed—a crisp sheet of paper, ink, and a mended quill— and as though they all stood at a death vigil, no one spoke while Dr. Fanshaw very carefully wrote out a full death certificate. At the top the document's name and date, and it could have been for anyone until his pen wrote *Nicholas Francis Monterris, Earl Monterris*. Nic stared at it, chest tightening as the doctor went on writing. *Born fourth of April, 1791. Died thirteenth of November, 1816.* Died. It was exactly what the man would have written had a few seconds not made the difference that night, and for a moment Nic felt like he was standing beside himself. *Cause of death*— The doctor hesitated, before writing *Strangulation*, and a chill fell over Nic that he could not shake no matter how much he needed this death.

From there, the doctor left lines for a vowsmith, wrote in his name, position, address, and, at the bottom, the hasty scrawl of his signature.

"Well," Leaf said as the doctor picked up the sheet to wave it gently, waiting for the ink to dry. "It seems our lock-in could soon be over. Are you . . . planning to speak to Master sa Vare tonight?"

The question of what was to happen next sped Nic's thoughts upon possibilities. To pull this off before the duke found out, to save his mother, he would have to move fast. It wouldn't be safe for her to leave until dawn, but the more time Silla had to prepare, the better.

"Yes," Nic said. "But I think morning is the earliest he can smith it. Ambrose?"

"My lord?" The young valet all but stood to attention, his eagerness warming Nic's heart.

"I'm going to need your help. Dashiell—Master sa Vare, he . . ." Nic sighed. "He will refuse to see me if I ask; he's too wonderfully stubborn. Can you speak to his valet? Tell him I need to see his master alone and see if he will let me in. Explain as best you can. Tell him . . ."

Nic trailed off, unsure what to say. Tell him that he could make his master smile again? That he would be doing what Dashiell really wanted beneath that stubborn exterior? They were things Nic hoped were still true, but the vowsmith's last chilly stare had looked right through him.

"It's all right, my lord," Ambrose said. "I . . . think Martin will understand."

The knowing note in his valet's voice heated Nic's cheeks. "Oh. Good. Thank you, Ambrose. If you go now, I will get ready to see Mama. I need to see her first."

The doctor rose from the table, folding the signed certificate. "Is there anything else I can do for you, Lord Monterris?"

"Apart from not call me Lord Monterris ever again?" A smile flickered on Nic's lips, the words yet too good to be true. "No, thank you, Doctor. You have given me everything. Please take care of yourself."

"That I can do." Dr. Fanshaw held out the folded paper. "One death. May you spend it well."

Nic took it, all but holding his breath. The power contained upon the page was enormous—a true freedom, and one that would not force Dashiell to give up everything. Yet it was nothing until Dashiell smithed it. Nothing until Dashiell agreed. Until there was once more a *them* to fight for.

Chapter 29

Silla opened the duchess's door just a crack, peering out amid a glow from within.

"Master Nicholas?"

She didn't open the door wider, but didn't shut it in his face either. Her gaze flicked to Ambrose standing at his side, something of a brief gesture of recognition.

"I need to speak to you," Nic said, voice low in the silent gallery.

"No, I have already said too much. And now His Grace is threatening—"

"I know, but I . . . I have a plan. Please. Let us in."

Again, her gaze flicked to Ambrose, seeming to ask the question she could not voice, and at last the woman stepped back just enough to let them slip through the door.

The duchess's sitting room was lit only by a dying fire and the branch of candles Silla carried with her, leaving the rest of the room a collection of shadows. A brighter glow came from the bedchamber, along with a faint hum, always out of tune, that reminded Nic of what he was trying to save. Whether or not she had really loosed an arrow at Master Everel or accidentally poisoned Millie Radlay, Nic found he didn't care. She deserved a better life than the one to which the duke had consigned her.

In the half-light, Silla raised her brows. "Well, Master Nicholas. What is this plan? Because if you think pleading with His Grace or trying to make a deal with him will work, I can assure you—"

"No. We're getting out of here, Silla. All of us. Here." Nic pressed an envelope into Silla's hand. "This is all the money I've made selling my automata this last year. It's no fortune, but it will get you and Mama safely away. There's enough here to hire a chaise from Charlton and take—"

She pushed the envelope away like it had burned her. "No. I cannot do that to her. His Grace will come after us. He's never let her get far and if she fails this time . . ."

The admission that this wouldn't be the first time the duchess had tried to flee was only shocking for how unsurprising it was.

"I think this time he will have his hands full." Nic held the envelope back out, hovering in the air between them. "I'm going to break the contract, Silla. I'm . . . the doctor has written me a death certificate. Nicholas Monterris is going to die and I am going to be free, and my father is going to hate that far more."

Silla's hand flew to her lips. "Oh, Master Nicholas, are you sure? That is no small step. And no matter what you do, you may still never escape him. Your mother hasn't."

"I have never been more sure of anything, so that is a risk I must take. Please, Silla, take the money. I cannot leave here without her."

The maid took the envelope, something hesitant in the movement despite the light now burning in her eyes. "So long as you mean it."

"I mean it. Pack lightly, only what you can carry on foot, and be ready to leave first thing in the morning. I'll ask Master sa Vare to smith my certificate just before dawn. That will break the lock-in so there are no alarms on the doors, and if you go early enough, no one will see you. Hopefully you'll have at least an hour before my father notices anything amiss with the contract papers—enough time to walk to Charlton and hire a chaise. He'll expect you to go to London or to the border, so go west instead. To Carlisle. If you don't feel safe enough there, leave a message for me at one of the inns so I can follow."

"Yes, Master Nicholas. I will. I will, thank you."

From the dressing room, the sound of the duchess's discordant humming continued unabated, a haunting call. "Should I talk to her?"

"No, I think it is best that she stays calm while I ready everything. You should go. In case . . . in case His Grace begins to suspect."

"All right. Remember, just before dawn. Chaise from Charlton. Get to Carlisle and wait there. And if you can't—"

"I know."

"And if we become separated . . . I hope a letter addressed to Master sa Vare courtesy of the vowsmith's guild will find me."

Silla pressed out a wry smile. "I hope so too, Master Nicholas. Now go. Quick. I have much to do."

She reached for the door to let them back out into the gallery, yet Nic paused on the threshold. "Did you know that Lord Francis is here? That he's still alive?"

No flicker of surprise, only a grimace. "Not until a few days ago. He . . . he came to see Her Grace and I refused him." A glance at Ambrose again, but she seemed to decide he was worth trusting. "He wanted her to know he was alive, in case she felt responsible for his death. As though he hadn't already chosen to abandon her long before— No. She needs him in her life no more than she needs His Grace."

Silla pressed a hand to her lips. "And now I have said too much. Go, Master Nicholas." With a wave of troubled hands, she urged them out. "And please take care," she added in a whisper as she began closing the door behind them. "His Grace is not lightly crossed."

With a fearful grimace, she closed the door, leaving Nic to

worry just how much trouble he was courting. But he could not let such worries pull him off course now, could only return back along the gallery with Ambrose at his side. Despite everything the young valet had been a party to so far that evening, he remained silent.

"I ought to ask no more of you than I already have, Ambrose," Nic said as they made their way through the Court's dark hallways, their single candle holding back the night. "But I hope you will keep my secrets. At least long enough for us to get away."

"If what you need is for me to feign ignorance, then I will do so, my lord." The young man cleared his throat and flicked a sidelong glance Nic's way. "I would, however, also come with you if . . . if you wished."

Nic halted. "Ambrose . . ."

"Even if you do not wish for me, I think I will be moving on from here after . . . all of this."

"If you mean it, then yes. I would be most grateful for the company. I don't know whether Master sa Vare means to forgive me, nor how we will manage to get out of my father's orbit, and I haven't exactly travelled very widely, but—"

Ambrose set his hand on Nic's shoulder. "One step at a time, my lord. I'd warrant Martin is already wondering what's keeping us."

Grateful for the steadying hand, Nic nodded. "Yes. Of course. Thank you."

They kept walking, but despite Ambrose's sensible advice, Nic's nerves fluttered all the more sickeningly with every step. Until then he'd been flying on the thrill of freedom and possibility, not daring to think how terribly it could all go wrong, or how bittersweet a freedom it would be without Dashiell.

As they made their way up the stairs, Nic tapped his pockets, a nervous check that he had everything he needed. "All right, what's the plan?"

"It's very simple, my lord," Ambrose said. "I am to knock while

Martin will be waiting to open the door. When he does, I will push you in, he will step out, and we're done. You can then talk to Master sa Vare while we keep watch from the empty room across the hall."

Nic grinned, half amusement, half nerves. "The look on his face is going to be priceless. God, I hope he doesn't shred me for this."

"I am . . . quietly confident."

"Oh, you are, are you? I wish I was."

They turned in to the second-floor hallway, and as Ambrose led the way, Nic realised he had no idea which room Dashiell had even been given. Dashiell had always come to him, and the idea of bursting into the vowsmith's private space for the first time at such a moment made Nic's stomach knot.

All too soon, Ambrose halted outside a door near the end of the guest room suites. The hallway was empty, yet Nic couldn't but be aware that behind some of those doors, Serrals were finishing up their evenings or preparing for an early night.

"Are you ready?" Ambrose whispered, raising his hand to knock.

The answer was no, but Nic nodded. "Yes. Just do it."

The valet knocked. A murmur sounded within. Followed by a step, and the door pulled open upon Martin's familiar features. Nic caught the flash of an amused smile, before Ambrose shoved him in the back, sending Nic stumbling past the vowsmith's valet and into the room.

Dashiell had been sitting at the writing desk, only to rise, quill still in hand, shock turning to fury as his valet stepped past Nic and out into the hallway.

"Martin!" Dashiell snapped at the already closing door. "You—" He dropped the quill, his glare slicing toward Nic. "Lord Monterris. I know this is your house and you may go wherever you like, but I would request you allow me the privacy of my room."

"Dash . . ."

The nickname was like fuel thrown upon a fire and Dashiell's features twisted. "You no longer have the right to use that name. I have done all you wished yet still you torture me. Please leave."

Each step a hard snap of fury, the vowsmith strode for the door, and desperate not to lose his only chance so quickly, Nic stepped in front of it.

"I know I have no right to your name and even less right to beg that you listen," Nic said, the door handle digging into his back as he stared down Dashiell's ferocious glare. "But I am begging anyway. Please."

Dashiell didn't speak, but neither did he try to push Nic out of the way, and knowing it was the best he could hope for, Nic flew. He pulled the charmspun paper flower from his pocket and held it out.

"I lied to you," he said, pressing it into Dashiell's hand. "I found this waiting under my door that day."

Dashiell's eyes darted along the stem, his lips moving as he read the neatly penned threat. Between his brows, the knot of fury loosened a touch, softening into confusion. Into horror.

"'End it, or he will be next.' Nic . . ." He looked up. "You should have told me."

"I couldn't!" Nic cried, throwing his arms wide in defeat. "I was too afraid. I know you, Dash—you're a stubborn bastard when you make a decision, and you were so angry at the world that you would gladly have abandoned everything for me, caring nothing for the consequences. But I could not be the man who ruined Leaf, could not be the man who ruined you, could not abandon my mother."

Dashiell's jaw set, his fierce gaze searing into Nic and speeding his heartbeat to a sickening gallop. He had earned no forgiveness yet, but Dashiell was listening and for now that was enough.

Nic drew a deep breath. "I went to see my father that afternoon. I told him we needed to end the contract before someone else died for it, but . . . he refused. And threatened that if I did *anything* to endanger it, he would send Mama to an asylum."

"Nic . . ."

"I was out of options. I couldn't break the contract to save you and could not be the man you were asking me to be. I was frightened and desperate and so . . . I lied. Better you left here hating me but alive than never left here at all."

Tears rolled down Dashiell's cheeks. "God, I wish you had told me, Nic. Because your father made me an offer today. He said he would let us live together after the contract was signed, so long as it was kept secret. He said he would look the other way and ensure the Serrals did too . . . if I took the audit clause out of the contract."

"What?" Nic stared at him, unable to fit this new knowledge into his head. His father had never so much as hinted at such a possibility.

"It's a huge risk," Dashiell went on, brushing tears away with his sleeve. "And I already refused, but I can go back to him, can tell him I'll do it and then—"

"No."

Dashiell froze, fear flickering across his face. "No? Please, don't do this to me again, Nic."

"No, because I have a better idea. One that doesn't risk you getting in trouble. Which allows me to save my mother. And which means my name and my rank will never get in your way."

The vowsmith shook his head slowly. "I told you, I don't care about my job. I was willing to flee the country entirely to be with you."

"Yes, but I don't care about my name and rank either. We may still need to do that—flee the country, I mean, at least for a time— but this way we can live our lives on no one else's terms. I would be free."

"I don't understand."

Nic withdrew the doctor's folded certificate from his coat pocket. "I've always been told that death is the only way to escape being a Monterris. And now Dr. Fanshaw has kindly granted me my freedom." Dashiell all but snatched the paper from Nic's hand and unfolded it. "It needs only your work to make it true," Nic went on. "And to break this contract before someone else dies for it."

The vowsmith lifted a hand to his mouth. "Nic," he gasped through fingers that trembled. "This . . ."

"Would make me no longer a Monterris," Nic finished for him. "Would make me no longer an earl. No longer the heir of a duke. No longer constrained by any contract or any tradition, and no longer owned. With this I could, for once, truly, choose."

He gripped Dashiell's hand and lifted it to his lips. "I love you, Dashiell sa Vare. Loving you is who I am. Loving you is who I've always been and who I will always be. And as someone who can finally choose something for themselves . . ." Still holding that hand, Nic sank onto one knee. "Will you marry me?"

Dashiell swallowed hard, a shy edge to his amazement. "Do you mean it?"

"I've never meant anything more. Although I totally understand if you don't want to marry a worthless nobody without even a name to his name."

With a shaky smile, Dashiell pulled Nic to his feet and clasped his face in his hands. "You ridiculous, glorious man, you could never be a worthless nobody. I never loved you for your name."

"That doesn't answer my question."

"Yes! Of course, yes, I will marry you. It's going to take some effort and artifice to make that certificate stick, but . . . a hundred times yes. I love you, Nic. You broke my heart when you said you didn't want to fight for us. I kept telling myself there had to be something I was missing, that you couldn't mean it, but knowing how much less I am worth than you made it all too believable."

Nic leaned close, touching his forehead to Dashiell's. "I'm so sorry. I didn't know what else to do. I couldn't—"

"I know."

"You wouldn't have—"

"I know."

Together they laughed, brushing away tears, and when they kissed, it was a gentle kiss that could go on forever—this a kiss that knew it wouldn't be the last.

"Right, well, you had better tell me the plan," Dashiell said when at last he pulled away enough to speak, warm breath dancing across Nic's damp lips. "Do I smith it now? Or do we wait?"

"I would say now, to be sure no one else gets attacked for this contract, but it's not safe for Mama to leave until daylight. Silla is packing. I told her just before dawn."

"Just before dawn." Dashiell nodded. "I can do that. It will immediately void the contract. Are you planning to leave with her?"

Nic shook his head. "No, as his heir I'm more important, so I have to make sure if my father finds me, he doesn't also find her."

"He isn't going to like this."

"No. But quite frankly I don't care what he likes."

Dashiell turned and paced to his writing desk and back. "Even so, we can't linger. If he finds out before we leave . . ."

"Could he force you to undo it?"

"No. He won't be able to correct the certificate. Once your death is registered throughout the net, erasing you from contracts, it would take a full challenge and a lot of work to have it amended. But I don't doubt he would strive to do it, so long as he could produce you as proof that you're still alive."

"You mean if I don't get out before he knows, he will lock me up until he can drag me before a court."

The vowsmith grimaced, fear crowding his features. "Something like that, yes. We're going to have to be quick and quiet. Take almost nothing. Say no goodbyes. If we're lucky, he'll hear nothing about it until he checks the contract at the beginning of the day's session. You had better think of the best way out of the house, where none of the servants are likely to see us."

"I can do that, but we'll have to give Mama at least half an hour's head start—enough to be sure she's reached Charlton."

"Of course."

Dashiell went back to pacing, a frantic sort of energy building as he murmured plans. As neither a Brilliant nor house staff, Martin could be sent out ahead. They could have a chaise waiting. For the duchess too. The man knew how to be discreet.

Such plans kept spilling from his lips until, abruptly, the vowsmith turned. "Does Lady Leaf know about this?"

"Yes. She was with me when the doctor wrote it. She's looking forward to being less marriageable, having had an affianced husband die gruesomely on her."

A grin flickered across Dashiell's face, only to be swallowed by a fretful nod. "At least Lord Charborough will want nothing but to hush this up as fast as possible. We just need to get through the first few weeks. So long as the duke doesn't find you in that time, I think we can brazen through without having to leave the country. It's not like anyone in town knows what Lord Nicholas Monterris looks like after all, and soon you will be a sa Vare. At least . . . if that's what you want."

The question hovered, doubt shadowing Dashiell's expression.

"Of course, I—"

"No, don't say *of course*." The words were a snap and he let out a shaky breath as though to steady himself. "I woke up this morning knowing after today I would never see you again. That you didn't want me anymore. There is no of course."

"God, Dash, I'm so sorry." Nic wrapped his arms around him and pressed kisses along his brow. "I wish I could take it all back. I want to be a sa Vare. I want to be yours."

"And I want to be yours." The vowsmith pressed close. "But

the look on your face when you said you didn't want this . . ." He grasped Nic's hips. "I can hardly believe you're really here, that this is really happening." His fingers dug in hard, his voice rough with the lingering hurt. "I'm afraid you are a dream, here to torture me. Please, Nic, tell me this is what you really want."

"Dash . . ."

"Tell me! This whole plan could be thwarted come morning. I need to know. I *need* to know."

Nic gripped his face between his hands. "Dash, you are my everything. I want you. I need you. I want to be your husband—to be a sa Vare and never leave your side."

For all the fine words, the vowsmith didn't yet meet his gaze, but some of the tension dropped from his shoulders. "You mean it?"

"I mean it."

A small laugh huffed between Dashiell's lips. "I guess we're even now, huh?" He looked up then, as much apology as relief in his eyes. "Having a conversation with your retreating back wasn't much fun."

"I'm sorry."

"So am I."

With a shuddering breath, Dashiell let the last of the tension out of his body, his shoulders slumping. "You know, I was so angry I almost threw your father's damn trick box in the fire. Until I realised it would be far meaner to open it and make you feel bad. Gloriously petty, I know. What was in it?"

"Oh, it—" Nic froze. "Wait, my *father's* trick box?"

Dashiell's brows rose. "No one else could have made it. I almost missed some of the sigils, they were so tiny, and some of the clauses—I could never have made anything like it. It really is a shame for the profession that His Grace had to leave it so young."

Nic stared at him. Lord Ricard had chased Rowerre to get the page back. A page with which he could blackmail Lord Francis into helping sink the Monterris family even further. It had made sense that Lord Ricard, thinking it very amusing, would hide the page right there in the man's room where he could walk past it daily and never see it. But if it hadn't been him . . .

"That means it was my father who took the page from Rowerre's hand," Nic said, gaze sliding out of focus. "That's what was in the box. The crumpled page Rowerre had the night he died, torn from one of Lord Ricard's ledgers. Showing he'd paid Lord Francis Monterris ten thousand pounds for services rendered."

"What? Why did Rowerre need an old ledger page?"

Nic heard the question, yet his thoughts had spun away. If his father had taken the page from Rowerre, then he knew Lord Ricard had paid the prodigal Monterris to ply his mischief. Unless the duke hadn't known what Lord Francis had been paid for at first— perhaps until that night he'd scared them with the darkness coming through the ceiling.

"Nic?"

More questions spilled on the heels of such thoughts. He'd thought it likely his father knew Lord Francis was in the house, but for how long? And why allow him to stay unless it had just been too late to kick him out? Had he arrived with the Serrals? Surely Leaf would have noticed.

"Nic? Are you . . . ? Is he still alive? Is that what's going on?"

Dashiell's question got through Nic's whirl of thoughts. "Yes. He's down in the grotto, when he's not playing ghost. He made the darkness. And that automaton. He is our Faceless Man. He—"

Nic's gaze fixed on the notes covering Dashiell's writing desk— all their attempts at translating the sigil tape he'd found in the service passage. Just after Lord Francis had sent his heavy darkness pouring down Nic's throat.

"The tape. The answer is something to do with the tape. Lord Francis must have put it there."

He glanced at the mantelpiece clock. It was not yet ten, but with all the guests staying in their rooms, the servants would likely have finished their work already, leaving the house empty.

"Where is *there* exactly?" Dashiell said, confusion knotting his brow as he tried to follow. "The service passages go everywhere."

"It was . . ." Nic paused. He'd walked in from the negotiation chamber, along to a corner, and it had been on the right-hand wall. "It was near the main drawing room."

"The one that was locked up?"

Nic stared at him, thoughts slowly coalescing around an answer he couldn't quite grasp. "Yes. That one." He made for the door.

"Wait." Dashiell grabbed his arm. "Are you sure this is wise? We need to be preparing to get out of here."

"I won't be long. If I can prove Mama innocent, I must."

Dashiell hunted Nic's face a moment. Then nodded. "All right, but I'm coming with you."

Chapter 30

The drawing room door unlocked with a heavy click. Dashiell pushed it open, its slow yawn pulling Nic's chest taut as the vow-smith halted on the threshold, candelabra held high. "But . . . this isn't the right room," he said. "Is it?"

Standing at his shoulder, Nic took in the space, and something of both thrill and dismay tingled down his spine. It wasn't the same room, at least not as they had last seen it with its freshly polished wood and new paint, its shiny charmspun metal and its glittering chandelier. Now it had the faded old grandeur Nic knew well, all cracking paint and tarnished fittings, its curtains faded and its fireplace blackened.

"Surely some coals falling out of the fireplace couldn't do this," Dashiell said.

"No, this is what it used to look like. Before—" With a terrible suspicion creeping upon him, Nic pulled the bundle of tape into the candlelight, sliding fingers along it. There would be one sigil that gave away what it did, Dashiell had said, and halfway along, Nic found it.

"Oh, that is clever. There, look. *Itbri*. A block, so it doesn't work unless it's connected to the other half."

Using his fingernail, Nic scratched out the sigil.

The room brightened, the chandelier flaring into life above a space once again fully restored—all gleaming wood and plush sofas, shimmering brocade curtains and no hint of decay.

Dashiell spun slowly, jaw dropped. "It's just an illusion."

"Just an illusion. That's what the damn tape is for." Nic said the words, yet he could hardly believe them, hardly believe the depth of desperation required to undertake such a risky ruse. But how else to make the house look impressive for guests when they had no money to fix it?

"It's really good." Dashiell touched the wall. "He didn't have to build illusory walls or curtains, just . . . paint illusions onto the ones that existed using law commands. It would have taken ages to get it just right, so it looked like it was really stuck."

"Three weeks, I should say." Anger flared. "He didn't come because Lord Ricard paid him to. He's here because my father needed him. I got it wrong and he just never corrected me."

Taking the candle, Nic went back along the hall to the parlour in which they'd dined earlier that night. There the chandelier was still lit, the room gleaming and warm despite the late hour.

It took only minutes to find the tape, tucked into a recess near the chandelier mechanism. Nic pulled it out like he was spilling the Court's guts onto the floor. The chandeliers died and the warmth faded, the light of Dashiell's candle showing only cracked floorboards and corners of lingering mould.

"Every room?" Dashiell said, but Nic had already gone back out. His skin was aflame now, anger driving him along to the smaller drawing room, the sitting room, the gallery. Each one alight with illusory candles, each one reverting to its faded, rotten grandeur upon a tug of silvery tape.

"Every room," Nic said, striding toward the negotiation chamber. "Every damn room. Everything a farce like this entire family."

Like all the other rooms, the negotiation chamber's chandeliers burned bright. One hung over the head of the long table, one over the foot, while to the side of the room the two letters patent remained upon their easels. On the sideboard sat the stack that was the all-but-finished contract, but Nic spared it only a glance as he searched for the door-shaped crack in the wall that would lead into yet another service passage.

With Dashiell holding the candle behind him, Nic hunted for the tape in the dusty space, yanking it from its home with a gleeful crow. It had stopped mattering why the tape was there, stopped mattering what questions he had sought to solve. Gripped by fury, Nic dragged the tape out of the passage, preparing to dump it in the middle of the table for all to see.

"Nicholas?"

The voice brought Nic up short as he stepped out of the passage, the bundle of tape in his hands. The duke was approaching slowly down the room toward them, his attention flitting from Nic to Dashiell behind those dark glasses. "What are you doing?"

Too angry even for dread, Nic brandished the tape in his face.

"You asked him to come. Lord Francis. Because as the house of higher standing, we had to host the lock-in, but you couldn't bear for anyone to see how far we had fallen." He gestured about the room, tape rattling in his hand. "*You* brought him here to cover the rooms in illusions. *You* locked the drawing room when I took its tape without realising what it did. *You* locked the breakfast parlour when it stopped working. And the dining room fire? That was you too, wasn't it?"

"What else would you have had me do?" the duke hissed. "This was a chance to put all the talk to rest. No more snide comments about our house being like our fortunes, no more prying questions about why no one is ever invited here—the Serrals could have returned home with only praise."

Nic sneered. "You say that like it matters what people think. Like their opinions can change the fact that there is no fortune." He tore the tape in two. Half the room sparked back into life, fixtures polished and glowing as though cut down the centre by time. "What is this even for when there's nothing left?" Nic raged on. "You demanded a promise that I uphold our name, but what is there to uphold?" He tore the tape again and again, dropping sections of the illusion off-kilter, colours shifting. "I know there is no estate left. No principal. There is nothing and there hasn't been for years. You have kept Mama and me locked up here for a lie!"

With a final tear, Nic threw the pieces of tape in the air. One corner of the room flickered a lurid shade before darkening into its far more familiar, decayed state.

Like falling snow, the shreds of tape settled gently around them. "Are you quite done?" the duke said.

"I don't know. Are you?"

The duke lashed out to slap him, but knowing it was coming Nic stepped back, letting the hand graze past his face. "Always easier to just hit me, isn't it? Like that will make me a better son." He lifted his hands in surrender. "I am done."

The urge to tell the man that he was not only done tearing apart the rooms but done being his son was almost too much, but Nic swallowed it down. "I will bid you good night, sir."

Nic started for the door, but the duke stepped into his path. "You think this is easy?" he demanded. "You think I wanted to inherit such a wretched pittance? You think I wanted to sacrifice *everything* for this house? For our name?" He stepped closer. Gripped Nic's chin hard with his long fingers. "Duty is all there is, Nicholas. Duty is all we are given." Without letting go, he turned to Dashiell. "Master sa Vare, if you would kindly ring for Castor."

Dashiell hesitated, before moving to the bellpull by the fireplace, where only half a fire now burned its illusory flames. "As you wish, sir."

While the vowsmith did as he was bid, dread started trickling through Nic's anger. They needed to get away. Needed to save the duchess. Yet Nic remained caught as his father's shaded eyes bored into his.

"I thought you might prove me wrong, Nicholas," the man said, his fingers digging harder into Nic's cheeks. "I thought you might prove yourself, might allow me to pass on the responsibility safe in the knowledge you would honour the burden as I had done. But no. I was right all along. You are too much your mother's son."

"Or too much my father's?"

The duke flinched, hand twitching.

"I know," Nic went on, gripping his father's wrist and prising the man's hand from his face. "I know. That's why you hate that I conjure. Hate that I make automata. Hate even my messy hair. You look at me and see only the wastrel who put the final nails in this family's coffin."

"And am I so wrong?"

From the doorway, Castor cleared his throat. "Your Grace?"

"Castor. Have candles brought in, and send for Lord Charborough and Lady Leaf. We are signing the contract."

"Now, Your Grace?" the old butler hazarded. "At such a late—"

"Yes. Now. Go."

"Yes, Your Grace."

The man scurried out, leaving the dread that had been creeping over Nic to settle like a lump in his gut. This wasn't how it had been meant to go. They ought to have had time, to have been able to escape before the contract was signed, and now . . .

The duke pulled out the chair at the head of the table. "The head of the table is yours for the signing, Nicholas. Sit. Such a simple command; perhaps you can do this one thing without disobeying me."

Nic stared at the chair. Dared not glance Dashiell's way as their plans collapsed around them.

"Sit!"

At the other end of the room, the door sat open like a cruel invitation to run, but it was too late. Swallowing hard, Nic moved to the table. Took the chair the duke held out for him.

"See? Not so difficult," the man said, tucking his rage back behind his impassive facade. "Now, Master sa Vare." He turned to the vowsmith. "I suggest you get everything ready to sign."

Without awaiting a reply, the duke strode out, taking the air in the room with him.

On the tabletop, Nic's hands trembled.

"Do you want me to smith your certificate now?" Dashiell asked, voice low. "And end this before he comes back?"

"No. There's no time to get away, and I told Mama dawn."

Dashiell appeared beside him, expression troubled. "You're going to sign it?"

"There's no other way, but even if I do, the death certificate will still void the contract afterwards, yes?"

"Yes, because Lord Nicholas Monterris will cease to exist."

"Then we sign the damn thing," Nic said. "And tomorrow when he thinks it's all settled, we can make new plans. It might even be better this way. Without worrying about the lock-in, I can get Mama away, then you can smith it once we're safe."

They shared a look, fresh plans turning behind Dashiell's eyes. "You're right. I don't like the idea of leaving without you tomorrow, but it may be easier if your father thinks he's won." A curt nod, and he squeezed Nic's shoulder. "All right. We just need to get through this."

Dashiell moved to the sideboard and began shuffling through the contract's many pages. With no other task but to be present, Nic clasped his shaking hands on the table. Overhead the dark chandelier hung like a collection of dusty old shadows, while the other end of the table emerged into the light of a whole different room.

Time seemed to slow and yet speed all at once, untethered from any sense of normality as Nic sat waiting. At the sideboard, Dashiell went on working through what needed to be done to prepare, while over the mantelpiece a grand clock ticked slowly toward the bottom of the hour.

Both sooner than expected and yet terribly late, footsteps heralded arrivals and Leaf walked in, her hair hastily put up and with Lady Theresa scowling at her side. "Well, if this isn't a ridic—" The lady gasped, flinching back into the doorway. "What has happened to the room?"

"It's merely an illusion, Lady Theresa," Nic said, impressed at how calm his voice sounded. "At least, half of it is."

Leaf gazed around, the same awe in her face as when they'd first explored the style wing. "Which half?"

Lightly spoken words, yet her eyes fixed on him, intent with a different question. Ending up signing the contract late that night hadn't been part of the plan, but he couldn't explain, could only seek to reassure her—and himself—with a smile.

Slowly, Lady Theresa made her way around the strange room, touching the cracked tiles and tarnished metalwork. "It looks very real," she said. "Some of your work, Lord Monterris?"

"No, Lady Theresa. Not mine."

Before he could be tempted to explain, Lord Charborough and Lord Ricard arrived, trailing similar questions. Nic flinched as Lord Ricard threw a menacing smile his way before dropping into a chair near the other end of the table, quite at ease.

"They're illusions, Charles," Lady Theresa was saying. "My lord, do come and see."

"I have no interest in anything except getting out of here, my lady," Lord Ricard said. He pushed Leaf's designated chair out with his foot. "Here, Leaf, you had best sit so we can get this over with as fast as possible."

"I am quite willing to do so, Uncle," she said, moving to the chair. "Though I would like to know what has changed that we are suddenly signing tonight. It is almost eleven." She threw another questioning look Nic's way, but he was no more able to answer than before.

Lord Charborough moved to lean on the back of his chair, the gathering Serrals leaving Nic feeling alone and exposed at the opposite end of the table. "Yes, and where's Val? We can't exactly get started without him."

"We'd better hope he doesn't get murdered then," Lady Theresa tittered.

It was a poor jest and Lord Charborough turned to berate her, only for his words to stall upon the sound of running steps. They grew louder, approaching along the hallway, the footfalls so heavy they set the chandelier tinkling over Nic's head.

Lord Charborough unfroze. "What on earth—?"

The door burst open, smashing back upon its hinges as Lord Francis sped in, his eyes wild.

"Nicholas! Move!"

Cries met his arrival. Lady Theresa recoiled in shock, but it was anger that flared first in Nic's chest. "Lord Francis, you—"

"Move! The chandelier!"

The man's panic hit Nic like a stone and he looked up. Up to where the chandelier trembled, its chain rattling.

Time slowed, every breath a thousand and yet not enough. Never enough. As the rattle of the chain became a roar, Nic tried to throw himself out of the way, and all was glass and dust and the great vacuum of nothingness that came before the loudest sound he had ever heard. It crashed over him in a torrent, and Dashiell screaming his name was the last thing he heard.

Chapter 31

Existing as nothing but a whole-body ache, Nic cracked open stinging eyes. One felt crusted, but he was too dazed to do more than note it and groan.

"Nicholas?" A hand rested on his shoulder, shaking him gently.

"But why is he here?" Lady Theresa shrieked. "He's meant to be dead!"

"Please be calm, Aunt. Nic, are you all right?"

Hazy shapes hovered overhead, his sluggish brain sure this was something he ought to focus on.

"Nic? Can you hear me? Love, please say something."

Dashiell's voice was a siren song calling him through the mist. "I like it when you call me that," Nic rasped, his throat raw.

"Oh, thank God, you're all right. You had me so scared."

Other voices babbled around him, as impossible to focus on as their faces or why he was lying on the floor in a pool of pain. He concentrated on Dashiell, his face the one lifeline. "I wish you would call me that again," Nic said, wondering vaguely if he was drunk.

"Unwise in the circumstances, perhaps," came Lord Francis's murmur through the mire, and a tugging sense of wrongness made Nic blink, trying to bring the room into focus. Leaf knelt to one side of him, Dashiell the other, with Lord Francis hovering overhead. The wrongness deepened.

"What happened?"

"The chandelier fell on you," Leaf said. "You're lucky you weren't killed. Do you think you can sit up? Or shall I send for Dr. Fanshaw?"

"What he needs," Lord Francis said, "is to be helped into a chair and fetched some port rather than have everyone cluster around him. Here." He held out his hands. Port and less crowding sounded excellent, so Nic allowed himself to be helped up. Every movement seemed to engender hisses at unexpected pains and the swimming of his head, but Lord Francis's grip was firm as he guided him toward a nearby chair. One end of the room was full of scattered glass lustres, the chandelier's curled frame lying at a drunken angle where it had smashed off the end of the table.

"Lord Francis, you have a hell of a lot of explaining to do," Lord Charborough said as the man poured Nic a glass of port from the miraculously unscathed sideboard.

"I'm not sure I owe you anything, Charles," Lord Francis threw back and, returning across the debris-strewn floor, he held out the glass to Nic. "Oh, don't eat me, Master sa Vare," he said when Dashiell gripped Nic's hand to stop him from taking it. "I'm not trying to poison him. See?" The man took a theatrical sip from the glass and held it out again. "Satisfied?"

Dashiell took the glass. "If it's all the same to you, I'll wait a few minutes and see if you die first."

"Damn it, Francis," Lord Charborough snapped. "What have you done with Val?"

A movement in the doorway caught Nic's attention a moment before the duke's low voice said, "I'm here, Charles. But all this ends now." Standing in the open door, the duke held one of his prize pistols, its barrel flashing silver in the candlelight as he swung it from guest to guest around the room. "We are signing the contract *now*."

Lady Theresa gasped, shrinking back, but Lord Charborough just set his hands on his hips.

"Come now, Val, that's not necessary."

"Isn't it, Charles?" His gaze seemed to take in the room, from an injured Nic to the shattered glass and wood spread across the floor. "Master sa Vare. The contract."

For a moment it seemed like Dashiell would refuse—loath to leave Nic's side—but with a lingering glare at Lord Francis he crunched his way across the debris to the sideboard. He returned with the large but unassuming stack of paper, smithed with magic so fresh it still shimmered and sang. He placed it on the unbroken end of the table, beneath the chandelier that still flared bright with its illusory light.

"Well, we're ready to sign," Lord Charborough said as Dashiell spread out the pages that required signatures. "You can put that damn pistol away now, Val."

Every gaze turned to the duke standing between them all and the door. Behind his dark glasses his expression was ever unreadable, though there was a hard set to his mouth. And the hand holding the gun was remarkably steady as he swung it toward Dashiell. "Take out the audit clause."

Nic's heart leapt into his throat, his lunge up off the chair halted only by Lord Francis's hand closing around his arm. "Careful," the man whispered with a small shake of his head. "Calm."

Nic swallowed. The audit clause. The audit clause Lord Ricard had forced on them the first night, the audit clause the duke had offered Dashiell a life with Nic to remove, the audit clause that would prove to the world just how poor they were—no money, no land, nothing.

"Pathetic, Val." Lord Ricard laughed. "You think we don't already know that you've been scraping the bottom of the barrel for years."

"No small thanks to you," Lord Francis said, letting Nic go to scowl across the room.

"And with no small thanks to *you*," Ricard retorted, bowing back. "So desperate for money you would sell out your own family. Ridiculous, the lot of you."

"More or less ridiculous than being willing to pay through the nose for a decades old grudge?"

Lord Charborough stared from his brother to Lord Francis and back. "What are you both talking about?"

"I think you already know, Papa," Leaf said, looking almost sadly up at her father. "That's why we're here, isn't it? You found out Uncle Ricard has been ruining His Grace for years, so you offered a ridiculous sum of money for this contract in reparation. What you might not have known was that Uncle Ricard paid Lord Francis for help to do it. Lord Monterris's valet stole the ledger page that proved it."

While they spoke, the gun didn't so much as tremble in the duke's hand, its barrel still aimed right at Dashiell's head.

"And then Lord Ricard pushed Rowerre down the stairs to get it back," Nic said, not taking his eyes off the pistol. "Before trying to murder me."

"What?" Lord Charborough cried. "Ricard, did—?"

"Don't waste time being shocked," Nic snapped. "Just order Master sa Vare to take out the damn audit clause. Now."

There was a horrible pause while all attention dragged back to the vowsmith standing tense and motionless in the face of the duke's silent threat.

"Yes, by God, just take the clause out, Master sa Vare," Lord Charborough said. "Damn stupid thing was never needed in the first place."

At the table, Dashiell turned over the first few pages of the contract, his hands shaking. And still standing in the wreckage of the chandelier, Nic felt the racing of the vowsmith's pulse as though they shared one heart. The urge to step forward and put himself between his father and Dashiell was almost overwhelming, but

Lord Francis was right. The situation needed calm. So Nic held his breath while Dashiell found the clause, held his breath while he took up a quill and crossed it out. Sigils followed—*ankh, tep, dor, et,* each a whisper, though Dashiell's hands were tense, leaving the command emerging stuttered. Even so, the words so recently smithed into the paper were disconnected from the whole and, eventually, Dashiell stepped back. He swallowed hard. "It has been removed, Your Grace."

"Now you can put that damn thing down," Lord Charborough growled at the duke. "And we can sign it."

"Indeed."

The duke lowered the pistol, and at last Nic drew breath.

Trying to look merely like a stiffly outraged professional and almost succeeding, Dashiell invited them to the table. "If you please, Lord Charborough. Make yourself known, then your signature is needed here."

Rolling back his shoulders, Lord Charborough approached the table to hold his hand over the presented page. And while Dashiell formed sigils, the man said, "I make myself known as Charles William Algernon Serral, the Most Honourable Marquess of Charborough."

Within seconds he was signing and it was Leaf's turn. The duke followed, and while Nic stared at the shimmering air and felt the scratch of magic against his mind, he couldn't stop thinking about the gun that had pointed at Dashiell's head. And the duke's unquavering demand that he remove the audit—an audit which had been in the contract since the very first night. An audit that would have brought down the attention of the royal accountants had it been signed. And like the gears of a long dormant automaton, Nic's mind ground into action, that single spark soon sending his thoughts whirring. From that very first night all the way to the chandelier that had been destined for his head.

At the table, the duke put down the quill, and all eyes turned to Nic.

"Lord Monterris?" Dashiell's tense tone cut through Nic's thoughts. "It awaits only your signature."

Their eyes met across the room. Nic had thought this moment would be easy, simply signing in the knowledge that it would soon be undone by the death he still carried in his pocket, but he made no move toward the table. Instead Nic turned to stare at his father.

"You hid that ledger page in Lord Francis's room because you were holding it over him, didn't you?" he said. "Because you were making him help you—not just with the illusions. What better killer than a man everyone thinks is dead?"

"Sign the contract, Nicholas," the duke said, the words quiet and hard.

"No." Nic shook his head as horrors went on spilling into it. He turned to Lord Francis still standing at his side, the man's expression a grim rictus. "Mama was just your scapegoat. You killed them, didn't you? Gillingham. Everel. Millie. You weren't here because Lord Ricard paid you. You came to make the illusions, and then my father blackmailed you with that damn page." He turned back to the duke, his certainty a heavy burden. "Each murder was just an increasingly desperate attempt to make the Serrals cry off. We couldn't afford to break the contract, but you needed them to, didn't you? Because while it had an audit clause, you couldn't sign it."

Nic gestured to the broken remains of the chandelier. "Even just now, you chose to kill me rather than sign it with that audit clause still in. Would a falling chandelier killing one of the principals trigger the accident clause, do you think, Master sa Vare?"

"I . . . should think so," came Dashiell's quiet reply. "He wouldn't get paid any forfeit, but neither would he have to pay any."

"Finally found a use for me, sir?" Nic's lips twisted into a mocking smile. "As a corpse."

The deadly click of a pistol's hammer being cocked cut through the room as the duke lifted the gun. Nic stared down the barrel, his father's face a blur beyond the shining silver circle. He sucked a shocked breath, only for the barrel to swing away, its aim coming to rest once again upon Dashiell.

"Sign it, Nicholas."

The first time he had not believed his father would truly put a bullet through the vowsmith, but this time the gun aimed at Dashiell's head had promise. And a hair trigger.

Mouth dry and hands shaking, Nic made his way to the table. He dared not look at Dashiell, just silently stepped in front of him to reach the contract. The hand he held over the page trembled, every finger covered in tiny cuts.

"I make myself known as Lord Nicholas Francis Monterris, Earl Monterris," he said. The words were rough in his throat, but it was almost over, almost done, and with a feeling of quiet triumph Nic took up the quill and signed—the last thing he would ever sign with that name.

"Now give me that," Lord Charborough said, striding up to the duke. "Unless you're going to shoot me, Val." He held out his hand, and for a moment the two men stared at one another over the loaded pistol, before with a soft laugh the duke let it go. The weapon dropped into Lord Charborough's hand, and with a practiced thumb, the marquess uncocked it. As one, the whole room drew breath.

Lord Charborough did not immediately step back. Instead his hand ghosted down the duke's cheek. "Tell me you didn't do this," came his hoarse whisper. "Tell me we didn't drive you to this. That we haven't so lost our way."

Nic waited for the lie. His father was so good at them, but the longer the silence stretched the more he realised he just wanted to be wrong. The duke said nothing, and second by second Lord

Charborough's grip on the uncocked pistol tightened until at last he looked away.

"Lord Francis?" Leaf spoke into the silence. "Have you more lies for us? Or finally some truths? Was it easy to take a spare bow and kill Master Everel from the pavilion? Easy to kill Gillingham and hang him from the chandelier? And Millie. Was that you, or did you let His Grace do that one himself?"

All eyes turned to the profligate Monterris. The man had folded his arms, but his gaze flicked to Nic as he said, "I rather think in the circumstances, Lady Leaf, that I will hold my silence."

"Ha! It's too late for that," Lord Ricard spat. "I will make sure you both hang for his. Having the thing signed won't save you."

The duke laughed, a long peal manic at the edges. "That doesn't matter," he said, pushing the words through his dreadful amusement. "Since I have already given up everything for this family, what is one more sacrifice to keep it alive?"

"You killed my Millie!"

"It wasn't meant to be her!" the duke cried, something almost pleading in the words. "I wouldn't have done that. A shock to realise that you had no such qualms when it came to my son."

Lord Ricard advanced on a snarl. "You rotten piece of—"

"Ricard." Lord Charborough stepped in front of him, the word quiet and brittle on his lips. "You have not been blameless in all this. You ought to have left well alone instead of doing everything you could to ruin him. Instead of trying to kill Lord Monterris into the bargain, and for what? Still more revenge?"

Lord Ricard flung a hand in the duke's direction. "He took my wife from me!"

"It would have been against the guild charter to change that," the duke said, a hint of his laughter returning upon exasperation. "You were asking me to break the law. And—"

"And then you couldn't even stay the course with your own

damn contract so I could have my title. Yes, I did everything I could to ruin your fortunes, I don't deny it. And yes, I tried to kill Monterris. But that is nothing to what you have done. Hitting closer and closer to me since I arrived in the hope that I would blink, but fuck you, Val, I will never blink!"

"As you have been hitting at me for years," the duke hissed back. "Undermining business deals. Taking Francis to gaming hells. Ruining *everything* I tried to build."

Lord Ricard gave a disgusted snort. "I'm only impressed you noticed, since I'm always invisible to you."

Stepping close, the duke tore off his dark glasses. "You think I don't remember you every time I look in my mirror? You think I have ever forgotten? Even if I wished to, you would never let me."

The two of them stood close for a heartbeat, holding their years of unspoken anger in bloodied hands. In another time, another place, it could have been a different moment, one made of tears and memories and the sorrowful smiles of old friends. Here they could only hold their hurts and look away—this the wasteland they had made of their lives.

A wasteland Nic refused to inherit.

He reached into his coat pocket for the folded sheet of paper that was his entire future. "Death is the only way to escape being a Monterris," he said, pulling it out. "You've told me so since I was a child, but I refuse to accept your fate, and I refuse to inherit your pain." He laid it on the table, looking to Dashiell. "If you please, Master sa Vare, my death requires only a moment of your time."

"Death?" The duke's gaze whipped his way. "Nicholas. You cannot—"

Lunging, Nic snatched the pistol from Lord Charborough's slackened grip and lifted it, sighting right into the duke's scarred eyes.

"Don't you dare tell me what I can and cannot do," he hissed, while the song of Dashiell's working sigils whispered against his mind. "I am done listening."

It was not the first time Nic had held a pistol, but never before had he stood before his father and held all the power. The realisation that he could just pull the trigger and change the world was intoxicating, and in that moment, he understood some part of Lord Ricard's desire for revenge. But as he stared into his father's uncovered eyes, Nic realised there was nothing he needed. No amount of the man's fury would have mattered, no acceptance would have been enough, and if he pulled the trigger now, he would live with ghosts forever.

With a huff, Nic lowered the gun and handed it to the marquess. "Take it. I am done."

"Nic." Dashiell had his quill poised over his death certificate, his signature all it now required. "Last chance to change your mind."

Nic didn't so much as glance at his father. "Never."

And so, with a nod, Dashiell set his quill to the paper and signed the death of Lord Nicholas Monterris.

The moment he finished, the faint shimmer still emanating from the freshly signed contract died like a snuffed candle, only traces left to fade like so much stretching smoke. From a few paces away, the duke stared at it—a man watching all he had worked for become nothing.

"A fine end to your sacrifice, Val," Ricard said, and spat on the floor. "To your precious name."

"But I don't understand," Lady Theresa said, finding her voice as she took an abortive step toward the table. "A death certificate? But he is not dead. Ought we challenge it?"

"And be stuck contracted to a family of murderers?" Leaf asked. "A foolish idea in the circumstances, I feel, Aunt. Truly, we should all be grateful to Nic for saving us that embarrassment."

With a pained groan that seemed to be wrenched the length of his body, Lord Charborough said, "I wish you had just told me, Val. I would have had the audit clause removed if you had explained."

"Explained what?" Lord Ricard sneered. "What is there to explain? He just didn't want his pride smarting."

At those words, the duke's exhausted gaze flicked to the pair of letters patent still hanging on their easels beside the table, and a final realisation dropped into Nic's gut like a lead weight.

"No," he said. "No. That's not it." Shaking his head, he turned to Dashiell. "What did you say about the estate? No land. No money. Nothing." He pointed at the Monterris letters patent, from which the imperious portrait of King Charles II stared back. "There are requisite ducal thresholds built into the king's law."

Quick steps took Nic to the easel, where he lifted a hand to skim over the old vellum. Vellum held magic well, but it had been smithed over a hundred years before, leaving even such powerful magic dead to Nic's touch. It might have been just blank paper beneath his hand, until about halfway down the tiniest of whispers hummed against his fingertips. Bending close, he found a line of sigils that was little more than suggestion, so small it would need a magnifying glass to read.

His stomach lurched and he could hardly tell if he was glad or sorry to be right.

"This is why," Nic said. "Because it's already too late, because it's been too late for a long time. Pulling off this contract would have allowed us to keep treading water, but an audit would prove we'd already sunk below the threshold. And that you'd defied the king's law. Did Master Everel find out? Is that why you killed him? And Louis sa Ellis, too? No wonder you stopped taking on apprentices after that."

"I gave my father my word that I would uphold our name, just as you gave me yours," the duke said, advancing toward him. "Only you chose to be selfish and think only of your heart, while I gave up *everything* I loved."

A final realisation bloomed sour in Nic's mouth. "This is why you broke off your contract with Lord Charborough."

"Val?" The marquess's voice trembled. "Is that true?"

"Of course it's true," the duke bit back. "I could not leave my life to be with you, but nor could I bring you into my world. Make you take on *this.*"

Lord Charborough said nothing, a lump in his throat seeming to have grown too large for words. Lord Ricard was not similarly afflicted.

"You lying shit, Val," he said with a hollow laugh. "I wondered time and again how you kept floating, but I never would have suspected you of this." Drawing close, he added, "*It would have been against the guild charter to change that, huh? And I was only asking to keep my wife.*"

"And I only wanted to have my husband!" the duke cried. "But you stole that future from me when you ruined me, as you stole your own chance at the title you wanted so very much."

No laugh now, Lord Ricard's hand clenched into a fist. It was more threat than intent, but the duke flinched away from him as he had after Millie's death, his own hands reaching protectively to his eyes.

You think I don't remember you every time I look in my mirror.

Had that very fist once swung for the duke's face, shattering his glasses into the soft skin around his eyes? Scars left by the man he had once called friend.

The memory must have been in Lord Ricard's mind even as he shook out his fist and turned away. "Castor? Castor!" he called, striding for the door. "I know you're still hovering around somewhere. Now that this bloody lock-in is over, get the magistrate over here at once."

His sudden movement left a void in which the question of what would happen next hung heavy. Leaf stepped into it. "Before we have to deal with magistrates or His Majesty's men, I have something that needs signing too, Papa. And no, it cannot wait. I present you my certificate of sasinage, for the twenty-fifth time."

Lord Charborough stared at the paper she withdrew from her reticule, its edges worn and dog-eared. "No." He shook his head. "Absolutely not."

"Papa." Her words were measured. "You used me. You knew in what bad shape the Monterris family was and chose to gift me and my dowry to them as an apology, and now if you wish me to remain silent about your hand in all of this, you will sign."

"I will not. It was bad enough that you would have let Monterris choose a mere vowsmith over you. You cannot now—"

"It was you!" Dashiell's jaw dropped. "I'd been wondering what His Grace could have had to gain, but it wasn't him. You threatened to kill me if Nic didn't break things off."

Lord Charborough's eyes widened, and for a few guilty seconds he said nothing, before barking out a laugh. "What foolishness is this? I—"

"Papa! That is enough." Leaf dipped a quill into the ink and held it out, her hand steady. "Sign it. Now. Whatever you may have hoped to achieve with your threats, I am not going to marry Nic. He is dead now after all, and no one else will want me when I am plagued by such ill luck. This is the best way, even if you don't see it yet."

He stared at the quill. "People will talk."

"Most likely," she agreed. "But of all that will come out after this, you signing my sasinage will be the least of it."

A shattered man, Lord Charborough took the quill and closed his eyes in a moment of silent agony. Then he at last bent over the certificate she'd carried with her since her eighth birthday, and signed. Task done, he slid it away as though he could not bear to look at it.

"What a mess we have made," he said, the bitter words spoken as though at the universe. "What a mess I have made." He passed a hand over his eyes and paused there while the world spun on heedless of his grief.

"Yes, and it's a mess we must stay a few days to help clear up," Leaf said, a commanding note in her voice as she tucked the folded certificate back into her reticule. "Although for now, I think while we wait for the magistrate, someone should send for Dr. Fanshaw. Nic had a chandelier almost fall on him after all."

Nic hadn't forgotten, and with the first inklings of hope that it might finally all be over, the cuts and bruises he had been ignoring were making themselves known. He knew he ought to stay and be present when the magistrate arrived, but he shied away from the responsibility, knowing all too well who the man would be coming for. Perhaps there was something worse than having two absent fathers. Both of them being murderers.

Seeming to understand without him needing to speak, Leaf squeezed his hand. "Go. You do not need to be here." She looked to Dashiell. "Master sa Vare, do help Nic up to his rooms. And . . . take good care of him, won't you?"

"On that, you have my word, Miss sa Serral."

Her smile stretched, real and warm and content. "Hearing that name is never going to get old. Now go, both of you. There will be time enough to deal with the repercussions of all this tomorrow."

Nic found he had no stomach to argue, and nodded. "All right. Thank you."

Dashiell's arm slid around Nic's waist, and though at first he thought he needed no such support, his legs soon proved him wrong, weakening beneath him as they started their escape. Despite the bruises it would leave, the falling chandelier felt like it belonged to a whole other life. And in the most important way, it did.

Lord Charborough had moved to the foot of the table, something of a final sentinel watching over the destruction they had all wrought. Dashiell brought them to a halt before him. "If I am no longer required here, sir," he said. "I will help Lord—" The vow- smith stopped, smiled, and went on, "I will help Nic up to his rooms to be tended by the doctor."

Lord Charborough's forced smile was all sorrow. "Yes, yes, you may go. And I'm sorry, for what it's worth. That threat was me, or rather it was my valet. He overheard yours talking about the pair of you and after everything that had happened, I couldn't let—" He bit off the words and heaved a heavy sigh, shaking his head. "It doesn't matter now. I will stay here with Val. Until the magistrate comes."

Nic glanced at the loaded pistol still held tightly in the man's hand. Beside the table, the duke stood stone-faced, like something inside him had broken, so completely had everything torn apart around him. Perhaps for the first time, Lord Charborough would give him the kindness of choice. Nic found he hoped so, and as Dashiell helped him on toward the door, his gaze lingered a mo- ment on the man he'd always called Father—a silent farewell more grim than sorrowful.

Before they reached the door, Lord Francis stepped into their path, forcing Dashiell to halt once more, Nic supported within the circle of his arm.

"I'm sorry, Nicholas," the man said, his lips pressed into a thin line. "Truly, I am. I ought to have told you the truth when you came to see me."

"Yes, you should have," Nic agreed. "Goodbye, Lord Francis."

Coldly polite, Dashiell nodded to the man, before he and Nic continued toward the door.

"I hope you won't live to regret this night's work," Lord Francis called after them, but for all the retorts that leapt to Nic's lips, he would not give the man the satisfaction of a reply.

With Dashiell holding much of his weight, Nic half walked and was half carried up the seemingly endless stairs to his rooms. The door opened upon a strange familiarity, everything exactly as he had left it despite how much had changed. They found Ambrose wringing his hands and soon put the fretting valet to work fetching the doctor and taking word to Silla.

Later, once Nic's fresh cuts had been tended, he climbed into his bed. Within a few minutes, Dashiell slipped in beside him, pressing his bare chest to Nic's back and holding him close. There they lay in the darkness, safe and together and but unable to find sleep. Nic was exhausted, yet for a long time his mind would not rest. He kept hearing the chandelier crash, seeing the gun point at Dashiell's head, and feeling the magic caught on the king's vellum. He wanted none of it.

Dashiell breathed evenly, but Nic was sure he was awake, the pair of them lying in silence at the beginning of their new lives. Everything had changed and yet nothing had and there was comfort in that. Comfort, too, that no matter how awful the days to come might be, Dashiell would be with him. That whatever uncertainties lay ahead, Dashiell wasn't one of them. They had time now, not just moments snatched from a future that could never be, but forever in which to build a life.

Epilogue

Nic woke to the distant clatter of hooves and carriage wheels on the cobbles outside. He had gotten used to the noise of London after a lifetime upon the Northumberland moors, but it still had the ability to shake him abruptly out of sleep once morning came. And it was morning, warm spring sunlight creeping across the floor to the bed, where it reached faint fingers over a sleeping figure. There on the pillow beside him lay the face of his husband—a sight he would never tire of in all his days. All beautiful features and dark brows, he was the most perfect thing in Nic's entire world.

"Are you staring at me again?" Dashiell murmured, eyes still closed.

"How can you tell?"

Dashiell cracked open one eye, a small, sleepy smile turning his lips. "You hold your breath."

"Well, that's embarrassing."

"Says you. I think it's cute. And besides," Dashiell added, sliding an arm under Nic's shoulder to draw him close in the tangle of bedsheets, "I like that I take your breath away."

Nic groaned. "Oh very funny," he said as Dashiell planted sleepy kisses along his jaw.

Another arm wrapped around Nic, and a hand slid up into his hair. "I am, aren't I?" Dashiell said. "I guess that's why you love me, Nicholas sa Vare."

Dashiell's trail of kisses ended on Nic's lips and Nic pressed against his husband's naked body in the warm morning light. What started as playful teasing soon became something deeper, hotter, and more needing. The memory of days when they had thought this impossible were still too close, able to fan even the lightest of touches to a blaze, and that morning was no different. Soon they were gasping against one another's parted lips and making no effort to stifle moans and cries as they shared one another's existence— the knowledge of just how close they had come to losing each other never far away.

"Perhaps I should send my excuses to Lord Tilburn," Dashiell murmured when once again they lay side by side, warm and sweaty but very sated. "He can find another vowsmith for this afternoon, as this one needs to spend the day in bed with his husband."

"And what if I cannot spare you the time?" Nic returned with faux hauteur.

"Oh, is your meeting with the conjuror's guild today?"

"No, tomorrow, but automata don't just make themselves, you know."

Dashiell sighed. "Fine, I can send my excuses and then follow you around the house like a lapdog begging for pats."

A tentative knock sounded on the door, and Nic couldn't but wonder how long the servant had been waiting before deeming it safe to interrupt. "Yes?" Dashiell called.

Nic drew the covers up but made no effort to shift from the circle of his husband's arm. "It's going to be Lord Elton's man here again," he said. "With yet more things that will only take a moment of your time."

"Things that will only take a moment of my time are the bane of a vowsmith's life."

But when their butler poked his head into the room, it was to say, "Miss sa Serral is waiting downstairs for Mr. sa Vare. I . . . uh . . . told her you were not yet up and about—"

"Oh, we have absolutely been up and about," Dashiell murmured against Nic's shoulder.

"—but she insisted on waiting."

"Thank you, Fairly," Nic said. "Tell her I'll be down soon."

"As you wish, sir."

Fairly backed out and closed the door, leaving Nic to pull himself out of bed and head for their dressing room.

"Nic."

Nic turned, and caught his breath at the beautiful sight of his husband lying propped on an elbow in the mess of their bed. "Yes?" The word came out slightly strangled.

"You don't have any regrets, do you? About . . . being just *Mr. sa Vare*? I can't help but think that if you hadn't killed off Nicholas Monterris, you would still have been your own master now. And still an earl. I know there wasn't much land left, but there was some, and, well . . ."

I hope you won't live to regret this night's work. Lord Francis's words had often haunted Nic's thoughts, but he hadn't until that moment realised they'd been haunting Dashiell's too.

"No," Nic said, and though he'd wondered over the same possibilities, he meant it. "My name and my title never gave me anything but pain. I don't need them. I don't want them. Besides, it's better we be equals, so you'll always know you were a man born with every hope of loving me."

Dashiell looked away, touching the corner of his eye. "You remember that, huh?"

"I remember everything you said to me that night. My name and my rank are the reasons you left me, and I don't ever want you to have those reasons again."

Nic knelt on the edge of the bed and pressed a soft kiss to Dashiell's lips, breathing deeply of his scent and his very existence, before pulling back to smile fondly upon him. "I love you, Dash.

And I promise you I have no regrets. I have everything I need right here."

The vowsmith reached up, lifting himself off the pillow to take hold of Nic's face and kiss him in return, lips lingering there as though loath ever to part. But part they had to, and once he had drunk his fill, Dashiell let himself fall back onto the pillows. There he lay smiling up at Nic, with the faintly dazed look of a man who still could not believe his good fortune. It was a feeling Nic shared wholeheartedly, and the urge to jump back into bed all day was very strong indeed.

When he didn't move, Dashiell lifted an eyebrow at him. "Something amiss, darling?"

"Only that you are still lying there and I could be lying with you instead of standing here."

Dashiell's smile took on a wicked glint and he threw the bedcovers back in invitation, bearing the length of his naked body.

"You . . . are excessively cruel," Nic said with a groan. "But I fear if I do not go now, Leaf will soon be up here just letting herself in, demanding to know what's keeping me."

Dashiell grinned. "And no doubt she would find the sight that met her eyes very instructive."

"*Never* suggest such a thing, because you are absolutely right," Nic said, turning hastily away toward their dressing room. "Argh, what a hideous thought. Ambrose? Ambrose! Quick, my clothes, before Leaf does something indecorous."

Twenty minutes later, Nic, fully attired in the latest town fashions, made his way downstairs. Their London house was nothing to the enormity of Monterris Court, but it still had an abundance of rooms over three floors—rooms they didn't put to the same uses as most members of the ton. Master and Mr. sa Vare had no need of a ballroom or numerous saloons, but in addition to Dashiell's study, they did need a library, a workshop for Nic's creations, and a space for Nic's echoes.

"Where is Miss sa Serral, Fairly?" Nic said, reaching the bottom of the stairs.

"She's in the parlour, sir."

Leaf had visited often enough since they'd moved in that Fairly had given up his disapproval of unmarried ladies paying social calls on gentlemen, though as Nic entered the parlour he found a second reason why the old butler had saved even his frown—Leaf wasn't unaccompanied.

"Mama." Nic's heart leapt at the sight of his mother sitting at Leaf's side, the pair of them neatly attired in grey half-mourning dresses. "Fairly did not say you were here as well."

"Oh, is that why you took so long," Leaf said, rising to take his hands. "How monstrous you are, Nic."

Lady Georgiana smiled up at him. "Good morning, my love," she said softly. "You look very well."

"I am very well, Mama. You look well too."

"I am, dear one. I am." She squeezed his hand, but there was a wry, fragile edge to her smile, and Nic nodded to Silla sitting in the corner of the room. The loyal maid nodded back.

No longer being a duchess seemed to suit Lady Georgiana very well, but the transition back into the real world hadn't been easy. With Nic unable to risk people realising who he was, it had been impossible for her to live with them—fortunate, then, that Leaf had needed a companion to set up her own establishment. The two got along well, but while Leaf was charging ahead into her new life, Nic's mother took tiny steps like the floor was strewn with glass.

"So what brings you here before breakfast?" Nic said, striding over to the gilded cage in the corner.

"Before breakfast?" Leaf cried. "It is well past ten. Just because you have a beautiful husband to lie abed with, the rest of the world doesn't cease turning."

Nic's cheeks reddened, but he smiled. "He *is* beautiful. Good morning, Avery."

In her grand cage, Avery flapped her wings and preened. "Love Nicholas. Love Nicholas," she sang, and the two hatchlings tucked into the breeding box cheeped and chirruped and fluffed about, seeking attention.

"Love you too, Avery. Yes, and you, Nalendes. Agata. You aren't forgotten, you fluffy little fluffets."

He turned back to find both women watching him, sharing an amused smile. "Yes?" he said. "I have to tend to my children, you know. Are you just paying a social call?"

"Yes, dear one," the duchess said. "You need not fear that something is always amiss. Sit down. Tell us how you are."

Letting go a tense breath, Nic sank onto one of the chairs and told them about his meeting the following day with the conjuror's guild and how his work on the new automata was going, carefully avoiding all mention of what had brought them to this moment.

While they talked, Fairly brought in tea, and with cup in hand Nic settled into the blissful mundanity of life. Lady Georgiana spoke of the book Silla had been reading to her, Leaf was full of excitement over having at last found the right location for her school, which she hoped to open in the autumn, and Nic told them of their plans to travel to the Continent come summer.

"And how is Master sa Vare?" Leaf asked. "I hope he has not been called away to any more lock-ins recently."

"Oh no, most of his work keeps him in town during the season," Nic said. "No one wants a lock-in when they could be at a ball. Although I'm amazed how many people think they need a vowsmith at all hours of the day and night, and guild messengers are never far away."

As he finished, he found both Leaf and his mother smiling at him fondly. "What? What did I say?"

"Nothing," Leaf said. "You just make a very good husband. Only thankfully not mine."

As though summoned, Dashiell walked in. Neatly attired in his vowsmith coat, its buttons polished to a golden shine, he smiled his beautiful smile upon their guests before making his way to Nic's side.

"I'm heading out, love," he said, bending to kiss Nic's cheek. "But I'll be back this afternoon. You know, if you can spare me any time." An amused smile at a shared joke. "I thought we might go riding. Or take a drive out to Richmond. Think about it. I intend to be entirely at your disposal no matter how many people might need merely a moment of my time."

"That sounds wonderful. I'll see what I can do to clear my schedule for you."

They shared a warm smile before Dashiell stepped back. "Until later then. And many apologies that I must run," he added to Leaf and Lady Georgiana. "I am due at Lord Tilburn's."

Having wished their guests farewell, Dashiell headed for the door. And though the urge to call him back might always be present, Nic just watched him go. Because now he knew the man he loved would always return, and that there would always be a later, a tomorrow, a future.

Acknowledgments

I began the book that eventually became *The Gentleman and His Vowsmith* quite some years before its publication, and for a long time it seemed genuinely to be cursed. But despite all the hiccups along the way, sheer determination and love for this project and its characters prevailed. That it has made it now into your hands requires me to thank a few people.

Firstly, the book's earliest readers, especially Sara, Belle and Christine. These are the poor friends who suffered through reading it chapter by chapter when I first started writing it as a fun side project amid my contracted work. Their enthusiasm fed mine, and somehow we ended up with a finished draft much faster than should have been possible in the circumstances.

Secondly, I must thank my agent, Julie Crisp. This book had to be shelved for a time while I dealt with getting PMDD and no longer being able to work properly, but when it was finally revived, she not only provided excellent editorial feedback but also patted and soothed my intense stress levels as she sold it.

Thirdly, Nivia Evans and Sophie Robinson for believing in it, and for helping to shape it into the book it is today. When Nivia left Orbit (where she published me as Devin Madson) to join Saga, I thought it was goodbye, yet here we are once again working on a book like we never stopped. And Sophie has been a very welcome new addition to our team, bringing sharp insights and ideas.

Of course, a book is only words without the people who work

so hard to make them into actual books, so enormous thanks goes out to the production teams at both Saga and Tor UK—especially the editorial team at Saga who had to put up with me making far too many changes to the prose at the copy editing stage (I'm so sorry!). Also, to the cover artists and designers who gave this book a face, the marketing teams and the audio producers. Truly it takes a village to make a book.

Outside of book land, I want to give special thanks to six very important people.

The first is Sara, to whom this book is dedicated. Our conversations and friendship formed the initial inspiration for the character of Leaf, and she has always believed in me, inspired me, made me laugh, and been there when I needed her. And almost every book that has touched me as an author over the years was recommended to me by her.

The second is my eldest daughter, Maddie, who read the original version of this book when we were selling it and championed it all the way—even to the point of doing English assignments on my as-yet-unpublished manuscript. The joy of having a child old enough now to read my stories and shout at me about them is impossible to describe. I look forward to sharing many more.

Thirdly I must, as always, thank my husband, Chris, for his tireless support and endless patience as I put in ridiculous hours and wail whenever the words just aren't working. He always has my back and reads anything and everything I need him to, including doing a final cold read of this book in search of errors. Best husband ever.

The fourth is Belle, my own personal cheer squad. It is Belle who helps me through the day-to-day grind of writing and editing and sitting alone at my desk, cheering me on and believing in me even when I do not. We talk of everything and nothing, and even when I'm just counting down how many pages I have left to edit, she always has kind words and all too much sense.

And lastly, my mum and dad, for never telling me that being an author was a terrible goal in life, and always being there for me whenever I need them. Especially mum for the early introduction to Georgette Heyer, Jane Austen and lots and lots of murder mysteries. Really, this book is entirely her fault.

Author Interview

What was the first book that made you fall in love with the SFF genre?

That's quite a difficult question, because my journey into SFF started really young. As child I was obsessed with the Redwall series by Brian Jacques, and then every sci-fi book written by Ken Catran. That developed into love of Terry Pratchett, who taught me that humour and depth are not mutually exclusive. After a side quest into Regency romances, I returned to SFF as an adult when I read the Belgariad by David Eddings. So I wouldn't say that any one of those authors or books made me fall in love with SFF, rather that together they kept me in love with it all the way.

Where did the initial idea for *The Gentleman and His Vowsmith* come from and how did the story begin to take shape?

The original idea for this book came from (1) the desire to write a book that was extremely just for me, combining everything I love most, and (2) a wish to explore family structures and their power dynamics. What would happen if a family was treated like a business, family members like property? Just like in our world, families would vary in the way they approached it, but such a system would encourage autocratic tendencies and cause some interesting chaos. And interesting interpersonal chaos is my favourite place to find stories. Right from the beginning of the very first draft, I knew I wanted to write about how this family structure made for an impossible love, and it just flowed from there.

What was the most challenging moment of writing *The Gentleman and His Vowsmith*?

I think the most challenging thing was the balancing act required to structure a book that, while primarily a romance, was also a mystery, also a gothic novel, and also a Regency novel full of dinner parties and tea in the drawing room. One where the friendship developed between Nic and Leaf is almost as important as the driving romance between Nic and Dashiell, and where so much past needed to be brought into the present. In hindsight, it was quite an ambitious idea, but I didn't think about that until I was deep in the editing weeds and it was too late to run.

The Gentleman and His Vowsmith is set in Regency England but is infused with magic. What was your approach to bringing magic to "our" world? Is there a world-building element that you're particularly proud of?

Originally, back in the wilds of time when I wrote the first draft of this book, it was set in a secondary world with very strong Regency vibes, so I wasn't so much bringing magic into our world as I was bringing the whole story into our world. Much of the story hinges on the idea of familial ownership, so that was where I had to start when considering how magic would change the power dynamics already at play within a Regency setting. To maintain the restraint and etiquette-focused vibe of the Regency, the magic also had to be restrained and rule bound. Therefore art and flare and energy are suspect, while vowsmithing—which is essentially magical lawyering—is highly prized.

The world-building element I'm most proud of was actually a complete accident. In the original, secondary-world version,

Dashiell had been named Dashiell sa Vare, and I had grown so used to his last name that I didn't want to change it even though it made little sense in a Regency setting. Then while working through the idea of how self-ownership would function in the new setting, I came across the term *sasine*, a historical word meaning the conferring of possession of feudal property. This worked perfectly for the idea I was trying to convey and incidentally also provided an excellent excuse for why he had a *sa* in his name.

The characters in *The Gentleman and His Vowsmith* are fascinating and realistic in how they approach love and life. If you had to pick, who would you say is your favourite? Who did you find the most difficult to write?

While I love Nic and Dashiell's relationship and cannot get enough of them, Leaf is my favourite individual character. She is just so much fun to write, and always easy. She began as an homage to a very good friend of mine and the conversations we have, and soon took on a life of her own. Just as my friend is one I couldn't live without, I wanted Nic to have the same, and they ended up wonderful together.

Interestingly, I would say Nic was probably the hardest. Perhaps that is just because as the point of view character, he needs to be the most known and understood by the reader, but sometimes I can't help but think he was also a little . . . shy? I find that occasionally I come across a character who it takes time to extract the truth from, like they aren't ready to tell you exactly how it happened and how they felt about it until you get to know them a bit better. So while he didn't change enormously from first draft to final, more of his personality came out with each draft, and he became both angrier and more determined, and more vulnerable—quite a balancing act!

Who are some of your favourite authors and how have they influenced your writing?

Terry Pratchett I already mentioned, but his influence on the humour of my work cannot be overstated. He has always been my go-to author for looking at how depth and humour can coexist within a story, even within one scene. The other most notable longtime influence is Georgette Heyer, whose books I have been obsessed with since I was a teenager. She taught me the art of the Regency romance, and also that romance and mystery could go so very well together. More recently, Cat Sebastian has become my absolute favourite author of queer romances. Every one of her books has so much heart and joy. Even when she's writing about times when queerness wasn't accepted, she carves a realistic and hopeful space for happy endings in a way I greatly admire.

Without giving too much away, what can readers expect from you next?

Readers can expect more gothic-infused queer Regency romance with murders! The next book will focus on new characters within the same world, though I would absolutely love (and have already secretly planned) some stories I want to write one day telling the extended adventures of Nic and Dashiell and Leaf, solving more mysteries, and navigating the strange world of magical London together.

And, finally, if you could take one literary detective on a quest with you, who would you choose?

It's probably a terrible choice for completing a quest without anxiety, but honestly, I would take Dirk Gently, Douglas Adams's rather weird and unorthodox detective. Things would certainly never be boring with him around. If I included TV detectives, I would consider adding Jonathan Creek to the quest party as well.

He has the twisty sort of mind required to invent magic tricks and solve locked-room mysteries, but combines it with introversion, living in a windmill, and being the kind of man who always has a thermos and a sensible coat appropriate to the English weather. Dirk Gently's chaos and Jonathan Creek's determined dullness would make for a hilarious team.